Praise for *Fragile*

"[A] simmering, tragic tale. Fans of authors like Jodi Picoult will want to read this one in a nice comfortable chair. . . . Unger's fans won't be disappointed."
—Associated Press

"Unger's genius is in plotting the story so that the reader never knows what's coming next. . . . This is a read that will stay with you."
—*New York Journal of Books Review*

"Unger skillfully builds suspense . . . cleverly woven into the plot."
—*St. Petersburg Times*

"[M]ines the more intimate territory of family and community dynamics . . . In the style of Jodi Picoult, *Fragile* tells its tale through the real-time action and freighted recollections of a diverse cast of characters."
—*Boston Globe*

"Poetic at times, heartbreaking at others, and suspenseful throughout, this is easily the best book of the year and comes with the strongest recommendation we have."
—*New Mystery Reader*

"Lisa Unger writes psychologically in-depth stories with great characters. The plot is fast-paced and has many twists."
—*Daily American*

"While Lisa Unger shows amazing skill at plot development, pacing, and projecting a rich sense of place, her talent in characterization—in plumbing the depths of her characters' inner circumstances—is truly exceptional. . . . Shines with her signature talent."
—*Florida Weekly*

FRAGILE

LISA UNGER

FRAGILE

a Novel

Broadway Paperbacks

NEW YORK

Copyright © 2010 by Lisa Unger
Excerpt from *Darkness, My Old Friend* copyright © 2011 by Lisa Unger
Reader's Guide copyright © 2011 by Broadway Paperbacks, an imprint of the
Crown Publishing Group, a division of Random House, Inc., New York.

Originally published in hardcover in slightly different form in the United States by
Shaye Areheart Books, an imprint of the Crown Publishing Group,
a division of Random House, Inc., New York, in 2010.

This book contains an excerpt from the forthcoming book *Darkness, My Old Friend* by
Lisa Unger. This excerpt has been set for this edition only and may not reflect the final
content of the forthcoming edition.

Library of Congress Cataloging-in-Publication Data
Unger, Lisa, 1970–
Fragile : a novel / Lisa Unger.—1st ed.
p. cm.
1. Missing persons—Fiction. 2. Married people—Fiction.
3. Family secrets—Fiction. 4. Domestic fiction. I. Title.
PS3621.N486F73 2010
813'.6—dc22   2009037218

ISBN 978-0-307-39400-2
eISBN 978-0-307-59234-7

Printed in the United States of America

Book design by Lynne Amft
Cover design by Mumtaz Mustafa
Cover photography: © Robert Jones/Arcangel Images

10 9 8 7 6 5 4 3 2 1

First Paperback Edition

For my parents,
Joe and Virginia Miscione

We never understand what it means to be a parent
until we are parents ourselves.

I love you, Mom and Dad.
Thanks for everything . . . then and now.

PROLOGUE

When Jones Cooper was younger, he didn't believe in mistakes. He thought that every road led you somewhere and wherever you wound up, that's where you belonged. Regrets were for the shortsighted, for the small-minded. He didn't believe that anymore. That was a young man's arrogant way of looking at the world. And youth, among other things, had abandoned him long ago.

Jones felt the full weight of all his regrets as he pulled his Ford Explorer off the small side road and engaged the four-wheel drive to haul himself through the muck. Over the last week, the late autumn weather had been wild—hot one day, cold with flurries the next, then warm again. Now a thunderstorm loomed, as if heaven itself had decided to launch a protest against the erratic conditions. By morning, his tracks would be lost.

What had amazed him, what amazed him still, even after all these years, was how quickly he'd stepped out of himself. He'd slipped off every convention and moral that had defined him, a great cowl that fell to the floor with the unfastening of a single closure. The person beneath it was someone he barely recognized. He'd tried to tell himself over the years that the circumstances had changed him, that they'd forced him into aberrant behavior. But in his deepest heart, he knew. He knew what he was. He was weak. He was base. He always had been.

As he brought the vehicle to a stop, a white flash of lightning temporarily illuminated the area around him. He killed the engine and sat, drawing in a breath. In his pocket, his cell phone started vibrating. He didn't have to look at it to know it was his wife; after so many good years with a woman, you knew when she was calling, even what she would probably say. He didn't answer, but it set a clock ticking. He had about half an hour to call her back before she started trying other numbers. It wasn't his habit to be out of communication. Not at this hour, early evening, when her last session had ended and, if there was nothing big going on, he'd be wrapping up the day.

It was the thought of that, the lost normalcy, that set Jones to sobbing. He was surprised at the force of it, like a hacking cough that came from deep in his chest, buckled him over so that his head was resting on the wheel. His wailing filled the car; he almost couldn't believe the sound—animalistic in its agony—was coming from his body. But he couldn't stop it. He had no choice but to surrender. Then it passed, as quickly as it had come on him, and he was left quaking in its wake. As he wiped his eyes, a heavy rain started to fall. Another lightning flash, and he felt the rumble of thunder beneath his feet.

He reached under the passenger seat, where he kept his heavy yellow slicker. He donned it while still in the car, pulling the hood tight around his face. Then he stepped outside, walked around to the hatch, and pulled it open, taking cover beneath it as he peered inside. The bundle in back was impossibly small. It was difficult to imagine that its contents represented everything dark and ugly within him, every wrong road, every cowardly choice. He didn't want to touch it.

In his pocket, the phone started vibrating again. It broke his reverie, and he reached inside the vehicle to gather the thick gray plastic bag in both his arms. It no longer seemed small or insubstantial. It contained the weight of the whole world. He felt the horror of it all welling up within him, but he quashed it. He didn't have time for more tears, or the luxury of breaking down again.

With the bag in his arms, Jones moved through the rain and ducked lithely beneath the crime scene tape to stand on the edge of a gaping hole. A Hollows kid, named Matty Bauer, had fallen into the abandoned mine shaft, which opened beneath his feet while he was playing with friends. In the fall, he'd broken his leg. It had taken police and rescue workers the better part of the day to get Matty out as the hole kept breaking down around them, showering the boy below with dirt.

Finally, they'd managed to get a tow truck out there. Jones had been the first to volunteer and was lowered on a rescue stretcher to immobilize the victim so he could be lifted out. Even though Jones was just back on duty, recovering from an injury himself, he had wanted to go.

When he'd gotten to the bottom of the hole, Matty Bauer was quiet and glassy-eyed, shock setting in, his leg twisted horribly. Even as he'd lifted Matty onto the stretcher, whispering assurances—*Hang in there, kid, we've got you covered*—the kid hadn't made a sound. Then he'd watched as the stretcher lifted and lifted, spinning slowly like the hands of a clock against the circle of light above. He'd waited in that dark, deep hole for nearly twenty minutes, which seemed like hours, before they'd lowered the harness to lift him out. He'd done a lot of thinking down in that hole.

Take your time up there, guys.

Sorry, sir. Moving as fast as we can.

Which is apparently not very fucking fast.

But after the initial claustrophobic unease had passed, he'd felt oddly peaceful in the dark, some light washing in from above, voices echoing and bouncing down. He wasn't worried about the walls collapsing and being buried alive. He might have even welcomed the hero's death as opposed to the ignoble life he was living.

The shaft was scheduled for filling tomorrow at first light, the bulldozer and a great pile of earth already waiting. He'd left the station house saying to his assistant that he'd come here to check that everything was ready. He'd told her that he'd be here to supervise first thing in the morning. And that's what he was doing.

Can't have any more kids falling in that well. We're lucky Matty just broke his leg.

Jones Cooper was a good cop. The Hollows was lucky to have him. Everyone said so.

Without false ceremony or empty words, he let the bundle drop from his arms and listened a second later to the soft *thud* of it landing in wet earth. Then he went back to the SUV and retrieved the shovel he always kept there. He spent a backbreaking twenty minutes shoveling dirt into the hole, just enough to cover even what he knew could not be seen from the rim of the opening. As he worked, the rain fell harder and great skeins of lightning slashed the sky.

ONE
MONTH EARLIER

1

The sound of the screen door slamming never failed to cause a happy lift in her heart that was immediately followed by a sinking, the opening of a small empty place. Maggie could almost hear her son the way he had been once—always running, always dirty from soccer, or riding his bike and getting into God knows what around the neighborhood. He'd be hungry or thirsty, would head directly to the refrigerator. *Mom, I want a snack.* He was loving then, ready to hug her or kiss her; not yet like his friends, who were even then slinking away from their mothers' embraces, bearing their kisses as if they were vaccinations. He'd laughed easily. He was a clown, wanting her to laugh, too. Those days weren't so long ago, when her son was still Ricky, not Rick. But that little boy was as far gone as if he'd gotten in a spaceship and flown to the moon.

Ricky walked into the kitchen, standing a full head taller than she, clad in black from head to toe—a pair of jeans, a carefully ripped and tattered tank, high-laced Doc Martens boots, though the autumn air was unseasonably hot. Nearly stifling, she thought, but that might just be her hormones. She was used to the silver hoop in his nose, almost thought it was cool.

"Hey, Mom."

"Hi, baby."

He started opening cupboards. She tried not to stare. She'd been standing at the counter, leafing through a catalog packed with junk no one needed. Out of the corner of her eye, she watched it. Yesterday, he'd come home with a tattoo, some kind of abstract tribal design that spanned the length of his upper arm. It was hideous. And it wasn't done; there was just an outline with no color. It would take several more appointments to complete, and he had to earn the money to pay for it. *She* certainly wasn't going to pay for him to mutilate himself, not that he'd asked for money. The skin around the ink looked raw and irritated, shone with the Vaseline he had over it for protection. The sight of it made her sick with grief.

All she could think of was how pure and unblemished, how soft and pink his baby skin had been. How his wonderful body, small and pristine, used to feel in her arms, how she'd kiss every inch of him, marveling at his beauty. When she was a new mom, she'd felt like she couldn't pull her eyes away. Now she cast her eyes back at her catalog quickly, not wanting to look at her own son, at what he'd seen fit to do to his beautiful body.

The fight they'd all had yesterday was over; everything she needed to say, she'd said. He would be eighteen in three weeks. His body wasn't her responsibility anymore. *You have no right to try to control me,* he'd spat at her. *I'm not a child.* He was right, of course. That's what hurt most of all.

"Not a big deal, Mom," he said, reading her mind. He was riffling through the mail on the counter. "*Lots* of people have tattoos."

"Ricky," she said. She felt the heat rise to her face. But instead of saying anything else, she released a long, slow breath. It was a thing, like so many things, that could never be undone. It would be on him forever. Maybe she'd stop seeing it, like his hair, which was always a different color, jet-black today. He walked over and kissed her on the head.

"Not a baby, Mom," he said.

"Always *my* baby, Ricky," she said. He tried to move away, but she caught him and gave him a quick squeeze, which he returned.

"Rick," he said. He turned away from her and headed to the refrigerator.

"Always Ricky," she said. She knew she was being silly and stubborn. He had a right to say what he wanted to be called, didn't he? Hadn't she taught him to speak up for himself, to establish his boundaries, to have respect for himself?

"Mom." One word. It was a gentle admonishment, as well as a request that she lighten up a bit.

She smiled and felt some of her tension dissolve. No matter how sad, how angry she was, she and her son had the kind of chemistry that made it difficult to fight. They were as likely to dissolve into laughter as they were to slam doors or raise their voices. Unlike the chemistry Ricky had with his father. When her husband and son fought, she understood why world peace was impossible, why people wouldn't someday just learn to get along.

"How's the band doing?" she said. A change of subject would do them both good.

"Not great. Charlene and Slash had a fight; she smashed his guitar. He can't afford another one. We don't have any gigs lined up anyway. We might be taking a break."

"Who's Slash?"

"You know, Billy Lovett."

"Oh." Billy of the golden hair and sea green eyes, the charmer, the star soccer player, once upon a time the heartthrob of the fourth grade. He and Ricky were both seniors getting ready to graduate, unrecognizable by those fourth-grade pictures, taken when sunlight seemed to shine from their very pores. Now they looked more like they slept in coffins during the daylight hours. That Billy wanted to be called Slash was a new development.

"Sorry to hear that," she said. Honestly, their band was awful. Charlene's voice was middling at best. Ricky had been playing the drums since fourth grade. His technique was passable, but he didn't have any real talent for it—not that Maggie could hear. Billy, aka Slash, was a fairly decent guitar player. But when they got together, they emitted a raucous, angry sound that inspired in Maggie an awkward cringing.

"Wow," she'd said to them after she and Jones went to hear them perform last year at the school battle of the bands. They'd been in the final three but eventually lost to another, equally unpleasant-sounding band. "I'm impressed."

Ricky poured himself a glass of orange juice, managing to spill a few drops on the granite countertop and the just-cleaned hardwood floor. She grabbed a rag and wiped up after him.

That's the problem. You're always following him around, cleaning up his messes. He thinks he can do anything. Her worst fights with her husband had been about their son, their only child. Jones didn't seem to notice that their son, "the freak," as Jones liked to call him, had a 4.0 average and nearly perfect SAT scores. His early acceptance letters to Georgetown and New York University were hanging on the refrigerator, where she used to hang his crayon drawings and report cards. And those were just the first two.

What difference does any of that make when he doesn't even want to go to college? All that brilliance and all he can think to do is get his fucking nose pierced?

But Maggie knew her son; he wouldn't have gone through all the work of those applications as early as he had if there wasn't someone beneath the punk hairstyle and tattoo who knew what an education meant. He didn't want to work at the local music shop *all* his life.

"So are you and Charlene going to the winter formal?"

He flashed her a look, turning his too-smart eyes on her. They were black, black pools, just like her father's eyes had been. Sometimes she saw her father's strength, his wisdom, there, too. But mainly, she saw the twinkling before some smart comment or the flash of attitude. Like right now.

"You're kidding," he said.

"No," she said, drawing out the word. "I'm not kidding. It might be fun."

"Um, *no*, Mom. We're not. Anyway, it's not for months."

"You could do it your own way, with your own style." The rag still in her hand, she started wiping down things that didn't need wiping—the chrome bread box, the toaster oven, the Italian pottery serving bowl where they kept the fresh fruit, when they had any in the house—which at the moment they did not. She really needed to go to the grocery store. God forbid Jones or Ricky would ever pick up the list on the counter and go without being nagged for three days.

She wondered what "your own style" might mean to Ricky and Charlene. But all the other moms she ran into at the school or the grocery store were readying their daughters and sons for this high school event—shopping for dresses and renting tuxes already. Maggie could settle for gothic formal wear; she could handle that. She used to be cool a hundred years ago. She went to NYU, partied in the East Village—Pyramid Club, CBGB—wore all black. Her son's style didn't bother her as much as it did Jones. It was the whole college thing that kept her up at night. And Charlene, she worried about Charlene.

Charlene, a little girl lost, hiding behind a mask of black eyeliner and vamp red lipstick. She had an aura that somehow managed to be knowing but desperate, fiery yet vulnerable. She was the kind of girl who started wars, at once acquiescent and defiant. She'd spun a web around Maggie's son without his knowing it, without even perhaps her intention. Spider silk was stronger than chain if you happened to be a fly.

There was something in the pitch of his voice when Ricky had first told her about Charlene that had made her stop what she was doing and listen, something about the look on his face. She knew it was going to be trouble.

Maggie kept waiting for the death knell: *Mom, Charlene's pregnant. We're getting married.* But she was smart enough to keep her mouth shut, to welcome Charlene into their home, into their family as much as Jones would allow. She wasn't a bad girl. Maggie even saw a little of her younger self in Charlene. A little.

Maggie remembered how she'd railed and rebelled when her parents tried to keep her away from a boy she'd dated from a neighboring high school. Phillip Leblanc—with his punky hair and his paint-stained black clothes (he was an artist, of course), he was everything boys from The Hollows were not: cool, exotic, artistic. She did love him, in that way that teenage girls love, like a lemming. Which is not love, of course. Unfortunately, at seventeen, no one realizes that. And the only thing her parents accomplished with their endless groundings and tirades was to push her into his waiting arms. It was a big mess, from which she'd barely extricated herself. But that was another life. She still thought about him sometimes, wondered what became of him. Her random Google searches over the years had never turned anything up. He was a troubled boy, she realized now, and probably grew into a troubled man.

Even her mother had admitted recently, during one of Maggie's laments about Charlene, that they'd handled it all wrong. Maggie was surprised, because her mother was generally not one to give an inch. But Mom was long on self-reflection these days—when she wasn't obsessing about some noise in her attic.

Luckily, Jones recognized that when it came to Charlene, their son was standing on the edge of a cliff. Any sudden movement to help or control might cause a leap. They wouldn't get him back.

That girl is sleeping with our son, he said to her one night as they sipped wine by the pool.

I know, she said, not without a twinge of something angry or jealous or sad. She'd seen Charlene with her hand on Ricky's crotch just the day before. Somehow it made her remember changing his diapers and giving him a bath. She'd felt another lash of grief. Sometimes it seemed like that was all it was, motherhood—grief and guilt and fear. You said good-bye a little every day—from the minute they left your body until they left your home. But no, that wasn't all. There was that love, that wrenching, impossible love. It was all so hard sometimes, hard enough with two careers that they hadn't wanted another. But it was over so fast.

There's something not right about that girl.

I know it, she said.

Jones cast her a surprised glance over the table. *I thought you liked her.*

She gave a slow shrug. *I care about her because I care about Ricky. And he loves her.*

With a sharp exhale: *What does he know about love?*

Not enough. That's why it's so dangerous.

· · ·

"I'll pay for the tux and the limo," she said now. Was she begging?

"Come on, Mom."

"Just think about it. Ask Charlene. Even a girl as hip as Char might harbor secret fantasies about dances and party dresses." She tried for a smile but suspected she might just seem desperate.

"Okay, okay. I'll ask her."

He was humoring her, but she felt a little jolt of excitement just the same. She never thought of herself as *that* kind of mother. But there she was, pushing her kid to go to the stupid winter formal so she could have the pictures, join in with the other moms as they talked excitedly about gowns and flowers, limo services. It was embarrassing.

She went back to gazing through the catalog in order to appear nonchalant—a sensor alarm for the pool, a ceramic frog that hid a key in his belly, a floating cooler. She felt like buying something. Anything. She noticed her nails. She needed a manicure.

The screen door slammed again. When she looked up, her son was gone; her husband had taken his place, sorting through the mail. If they knew how alike they were in every way, they'd both burst into flames.

"Where's Johnny Rotten?" asked Jones without heat.

"He was here a minute ago." She closed the catalog and threw it in the trash.

"Heard me coming," he said. He opened the phone bill, glanced at it, and put it on the counter.

"Probably," she said. Then, "No more fighting today, okay?"

"What's to fight about, Maggie? The war is lost. Nothing left to do but surrender."

She felt her throat constrict. "It's not a battle. There aren't supposed to be winners and losers. He's our son."

"Tell that to him."

She looked over at him, but he was a locked box, staring down at the rest of the mail—more junk. She didn't know how to comfort him anymore, how to soften him. The years, the job, had made him harder. Not all the time. But his anger used to be hot. He'd yell and storm. Now he folded into himself, shut everyone else out. You didn't have to be a shrink to know this wasn't a good thing.

He glanced over at her. A quick up and down. "You look nice. Do something to your hair?"

"I had it trimmed a couple of days ago."

She tossed her copper curls at him, blinked her eyes in a teasing come-hither.

He moved over to her and wrapped her up in his big arms. She leaned into him, feeling his broad chest through the softness of his denim shirt, then looked into his beloved face.

"I can still drown in those blue eyes, Maggie," he said with a smile.

The years, parenthood, money worries, all kinds of stresses, had not robbed her of her love for him—though there were times when she feared they had. She still loved the sight of him, the smell of him, the feel of him. But sometimes she felt like they didn't always look at each other anymore. Like the gold watch his uncle left him, or the diamond earrings in a box that had been her grandmother's—precious things in the landscape of a life, cherished but barely noticed. Trotted out for special occasions, maybe, but most often taken for granted.

There were worse things. She'd seen her friends' marriages implode and dissolve, leaving massive emotional wreckage or just disappearing at sea, second marriages no better. She didn't always *like* Jones. Sometimes she ached to punch him in the jaw really hard, so hard she could split her own knuckles with the force of it. But she loved him no less totally than she did her own son. It was that complete, that much a part of her. He was half of her, for better or for worse.

"He's okay," she said, squeezing his middle. "He's going to be okay."

Silence. Jones took a deep breath, which she felt in the rise of his chest against hers.

Because that was what it was, wasn't it? Not just anger. Not a need to control in the way we most often mean it. Not a lack of love or understanding for their boy. It was fear. Fear that, after all the years of protecting his health, his heart, his mind, setting bedtimes and boundaries, giving warnings about strangers and looking both ways before crossing the street, it wouldn't be enough. Fear that, as he stood on the threshold of adulthood, forces beyond their control would take him down a path where they could no longer reach him. Fear that he'd be seduced by something ugly and would choose it. And that there would be nothing they could do but let him go. She believed they'd taught him well. Prayed they had. Why did her husband have so little faith?

"I hope so," he said flatly, like it might already be too late.

She pulled back to look at him, to admonish him, but saw by the clock on the stainless-steel microwave behind him that she had just five minutes until her next session. She didn't have time for a throw-down. She saw him notice her eyes drift, and then he moved away from her, unknowingly mimicking Ricky by opening the refrigerator and peering inside.

"Off to save the world," he said. "One desperate soul at a time. But what about her husband?"

"What about him?" she said, pouring herself a cup of coffee before heading down the hallway that connected her house to the suite of rooms where she saw her patients. "Is he a desperate soul?"

They were kidding around. Weren't they? When she turned to look at him, he was still gazing into the refrigerator, looking odd—too tired around the eyes.

"Jones?"

He turned to grin at her. "Desperate for some lunch," he said with a wink. Did it seem forced?

"There's leftover lasagna and a fresh salad I just made," she said, feeling a pang of domestic guilt for having eaten quickly without him even though she'd suspected he would pop home for lunch. She quickly quashed it. *I'm a wife, not a handmaiden. I'm a mother, not a waitress.* How many times had she said those two sentences? Maybe one of these days she'd start to believe it herself.

"My cholesterol?" he said, raising his eyebrows.

"Low-fat cheese? Whole wheat pasta? Ground turkey?"

"Ugh," he said, finding and reaching for it. "When did we get so healthy?"

"We're not healthy, Jones. We're old."

"Hmm."

She gave him a quick kiss on the cheek and left to meet her patient.

2

She loved him. She knew what that meant, no matter what anyone said. It was impossible not to recognize love, wasn't it? It was a dry brushfire, a shift of tectonic plates at the bottom of the ocean. It changed the topography of a life, destroyed and created. Her heart beat so fast and her throat was so dry before she saw him that it felt like panic. When would he get there? *Would* he ever get there? Did he really love her, too? Would he change his mind? That delicious worried waiting and then the meeting, flesh on flesh, the skin of his neck against her mouth, that deep exhale—passion like the relief you feel after releasing a breath you've held underwater. How could she not recognize love? She'd been with other boys, crushes. It hadn't felt like this.

"A moment of pleasure can lead to a lifetime of pain," her mother, Melody, had warned during one of her operatic lectures on action and consequence. Charlene felt sorry for her sometimes, wondered if her mother even remembered pleasure, if she remembered love. Or had she crossed so much time and distance that she'd forgotten the way, wouldn't remember the language even if she found it again?

There was an old photo album Charlene had found in her grandmother's house, at the bottom of a box in a dusty guest room closet. In the album, filled with images of people she didn't recognize, Charlene had unearthed a picture of Melody on her wedding day. Her mother was as slight as a reed, wearing a willowy vintage lace gown. She'd been just so *pretty*. But that wasn't the reason Charlene had slipped the photo from its plastic sleeve and put it in her purse. It was the expression on her mother's face as she looked at her new husband. She was lit up with bliss, a wide smile, glittering eyes. In all her life, Charlene had never seen her mother look like that. Never. The girl in the picture was a stranger, someone Charlene wished she knew. She looked funny and cool, like she'd make dirty jokes and drink too much.

Charlene had found the picture after her grandmother passed. They were cleaning the house, getting it ready to sell. Charlene wanted to keep the house, move in and sell the dump they lived in.

"No way," her mother said. "Do you have any idea how much work it is to live in an old place like this?"

But it was beautiful, three stories of lace curtains and hardwood floors, swirling banisters and rattling windows. Every stair had a unique song, every door stuck in the summer humidity. In the air, Charlene thought she could always smell her grandmother's perfume, a light floral scent that, for some reason, set her to humming "Rock-a-bye Baby."

But it was more than the work of living in an old house that had motivated her mother to sell; Charlene could see it on her face. It wasn't even the money, though she knew that was a factor. Charlene didn't know *what* it was, why her mother would want to sell her childhood home, let other people move in and "renovate"—strip the house of all its personality and history.

"You're too young to understand. Sometimes you just want the past to go away; you don't always want it lingering, tapping you on the shoulder, reminding you about things you'd rather forget."

"Like what? What do you want to forget? I thought you loved this house. "

"I do, and I know she'd want us to stay."

"Then *why*, Mom?"

"I'm just selling it, Charlene. We need the money. End of discussion."

And there was something so sad and strange about her mother that, for once, Charlene *did* shut up when she was asked. She had been thirteen at the time, filled with a big, ugly anger and a crushing sadness about losing her grandmother and the house she loved. But there was no talking to Melody about it. *Life is loss, Charlene. Get used to it. Was that true?* Charlene wondered. *Was that all it was?*

She'd lost her father already. She'd been too young to grieve for him; but she knew other girls had something she'd never understand. She wrote a song about it all, "Selling Memories."

The things you want to keep, go
The things you want to lose, stay
Sell your history
Sell your soul
You're still bankrupt, tired and old.
And the memories how they linger,
Wrap around you when you're cold.

The refrain was an angry scream, repeating the title over and over. It wasn't bad. Certainly no worse than some of the crappy covers they played over and over. She'd tried to get Slash to help her write some music recently. But he wouldn't.

Slash thought her lyrics, her poetry, tended toward the too flowery, overly ornate. As if someone who called himself Slash and wore black lipstick had any right to criticize *anything*. They fought about it, passionately and often. She disagreed. Her language was in line with her inner life. A drama queen, her mother called her. If pressed, she knew most of her friends—even Rick—would agree. She didn't care what they thought. Better to live loud, cause a scene, feel too much, than die a brain-dead automaton in a suburban wasteland.

If it weren't for Rick, she'd have left their stupid garage band ages ago. She was sick of singing covers at parties—other people's lyrics, other people's thoughts, badly imitated. Slash didn't have an original thought in his head. He could read music, mimic guitar players he liked, but he couldn't write an original chord to save his life. She hadn't meant to ruin his guitar when she grabbed it from him, but it had slipped from her hands and smacked against the wall, hit hard and in just the right way. She'd thought he might cry the way he looked at it. He just picked it up, its neck broken and dangling, the strings slack, and carried it out like a child in his arms.

"Nice, Char," Rick had chastised.

"I didn't mean it," she'd said, looking after him helplessly. She still felt bad about it, wondered how much it would cost to buy him a new guitar. This happened to her a lot. She acted out of passion, sometimes hurting people, and then felt horrible about it later. But she never seemed able to make things right again. She had a gift for creating damage that couldn't be undone.

She sat in her ticky-tack room, in her ticky-tack house, painting her nails iridescent green. She hated the tract house with all its perfectly square rooms and thin walls, identical to every third house in their development. It was like living in the box of someone else's limited imagination. How could someone reach the height of her creativity in a drywall cage? She couldn't. And she wouldn't. She would be eighteen in six months. After graduation, she was *so* out of here. College? Another four years of indentured servitude, living by someone else's arbitrary rules? No way.

Where do you think you'll go? her mother wanted to know. *You think you'll survive on minimum wage in New York City? Because without an education you'll be working at McDonald's.* But Charlene had an escape plan; it was already under way.

You can always stay here with me, Charlene, when you're ready. He'd promised her this the last time she'd seen him. *You can stay as long as you want.*

She was smiling to herself when she heard the slow rise of voices downstairs. She stopped what she was doing, poised the tiny, glistening green brush over her big toe and listened. Sometimes she could tell by the early decibels and pitch whether there would be a quick explosion of sound that ended with a slamming door and the angry rev of an engine, or whether it was going to be a slow movement, picking up speed and volume, moving from room to room until it reached a crescendo and someone got hurt. Might be her mother, might be her stepfather, Graham—might even be Charlene if she chose to get involved. Which she wouldn't today; after the last time, she'd promised herself never again. She'd had to cake makeup and black eyeliner over her eye for a week. She'd let them kill each other first. And it sounded like a bad one.

She couldn't make out the words, just that near hysterical pitch to her mother's voice. Charlene reached for her iPod, tucked the buds in her ears, and turned up the volume. The Killers.

She tried to sing along, to reach a place of blissful indifference. But her heart was thumping, and she could feel that dry suck at the base of her throat. She finished painting her nails with a hand that had started to tremble a little, then capped the bottle and put it down hard on the bedside table. She hated the mutinous actions of her body. Her mind was tough, not afraid of anything. But her body was a little girl shaking in the dark.

Charlene reached over and paused the music, listened to the air around her. She exhaled. Silence. For a moment, she was almost relieved. But the silence didn't sound quite right. It wasn't empty, void of energy. It was alive, hiding something. She got up from her bed, walked with her toes flexed and separated, mindful of the slime green polish. She listened at the cheap, thin door with its flaking gold knob. Nothing. Not even the television, which her mother had on *perpetually*—morning shows, game shows, on to soap operas, then the afternoon talk shows— Oprah, Dr. Phil. How could the woman even hear herself think?

Charlene found herself feeling the door, like they teach you to do if there's fire. If the door is hot, don't open it—they drill this stuff into you. Stop, drop, and roll. Endlessly, your entire school career, they sent you out single file with bells ringing. But the petty suburban abuses, a terrible marriage polluting the air you breathe, a stepfather's inappropriate glances and crude offhand remarks making you feel small and dirty, a selfish, silly mother who couldn't seem to decide between the roles of harsh disciplinarian and best girlfriend, leaving you wary and confused. Nobody tells you what to do about *those* things. Nobody rescues you with a big red truck, sirens blaring. You're supposed to live with it. But it hurts, damages, like a toxin in the water you can't smell or taste. It's only later that its pathology takes hold. You wind up on some shrink's couch for the rest of your life.

She was thinking this as she pushed the door open and walked down the hall toward the unfamiliar silence, wet nails forgotten now, leaving a smudge of green on the carpet with each step. At the top of the stairs, she stopped.

"Mom?" she called. There was no answer, but she heard something now. Something soft and shuddering, irregular in pitch and rhythm. Weeping. Someone was weeping. She moved slowly down the stairs.

"Mom?"

3

Marshall Crosby was sinking into depression again. Maggie could clearly see that. All the physical cues were there. His hair hung limp and unwashed over his thick glasses. It was one of the first things she'd noticed about him when he began his sessions with her, that he rarely bothered to brush the hair from his eyes. Instead he peered out from beneath it with a variety of expressions—disdain, defiance, shyness, or, like today, a kind of morose sadness. Something invested in itself. His bony shoulders slouched inside a threadbare navy hooded jacket; his knees were spread wide, hands dug deep into the pockets of his jeans. He had the purple shiners of fatigue under each eye.

"So how's it going today, Marshall?" Maggie said. She sat in the leather chair across from the couch where he sat. She smoothed out her skirt and laid her notebook on her lap.

"Good, I guess."

"You seem tired."

"Yeah. I guess."

"Up late with something? Or having trouble sleeping?"

A shrug. He turned to glance out the window as if he were expecting someone, then leaned back again.

"It matters," she said, trying to catch his eyes. But he stared now at the low coffee table between them. "We might need to alter your meds if you're having trouble falling or staying asleep."

"I was up late." Was there the slightest edge of impatience to his voice?

"Studying?" she said.

Marshall gave Maggie a sneer. "Studying is for pussies."

"Who told you that?" As if she had to ask. She knew Marshall's father well enough.

Marshall offered another shrug. She examined him for a moment, then let her eyes drop to the notebook on her lap. On the pad, she saw that she'd scribbled "Slipping away." She didn't remember writing it, but that was exactly how she felt about him.

Years ago, a frustrated teacher had pegged Marshall as learning disabled, and the label had followed him through grammar school, on into middle school and high school. For years, bored, miserable, abused at home, bullied at school, he'd floundered. Until Henry Ivy, Marshall's history teacher and the school counselor, recognized what everyone else had missed. Marshall was an abused boy presenting as slow. Henry offered Marshall a hand—some tutoring, some amateur counseling. Recent aptitude tests had revealed, to everyone's amazement, that Marshall possessed a near genius-level IQ.

Marshall's father, coincidentally, was arrested around the same time for a DUI offense. So Marshall had been living with his aunt Leila, uncle Mark, and two older male cousins, Tim and Ryan. Leila took Mr. Ivy's advice and brought Marshall to Maggie for evaluation and counseling. They'd all worked together to get him on track. The improvement had been nothing short of miraculous. Until six weeks ago, when Marshall's father was released.

"So how is it living with your father again?"

"It's okay, I guess. He's not much of a cook."

Marshall was given the choice to stay with Leila and Mark Lane; but he chose to return to his father. He'd been back at home just about three weeks, and now his grades were dropping, hygiene failing, blank expression returning. Maggie suspected that it was only a matter of time before Marshall went off his meds and started missing appointments. It made her angry, yes, but mostly it made her feel sad and powerless. After seeing Marshall last week, she'd been so overcome by those feelings that she'd called her own therapist.

"Therapy only works when the patient is a willing participant," said Dr. Willough. "That's true with adults and adolescents alike. The patient has to *want* help. And we have to recognize our limitations. Our boundaries."

Abused kids almost always wanted to go home. Sometimes you could stop it, sometimes you couldn't. Marshall's father was a cop. He was without a job after his arrest, of course, but not without friends. The judge who'd allowed Marshall to go home was Travis's longtime drinking buddy. Sitting in the courtroom, Leila, Travis's sister, had cried in Maggie's arms. *We've lost him,* she'd whispered. Maggie had hoped she was wrong. She still remembered the nasty sneer Travis had tossed back at them as he left with Marshall.

"Okay," she said. "So, if not studying, then what *were* you doing last night that kept you up late?" She measured her tone; light and easy.

"I was helping my dad." Marshall sat up a little straighter. There was a hint of a smile on his face. It's what every boy wants; to be close to his dad. She felt a little twinge about Jones and Ricky.

"Helping him with what?"

"He's a private investigator now, you know?"

"I heard."

Henry Ivy had told her during one of their frequent lunches that Travis Crosby had hung out his own shingle, though neither of them could imagine who would consider hiring him.

"I was helping him paint the office," said Marshall. "When I graduate, I'm going to be his partner."

There was so much pride in his voice; she wanted to feel happy for him. But she just nodded, staying neutral. He was a sensitive kid, picked up on her lack of enthusiasm. She saw his right leg start to pump. Anxiety. A second later his thumbnail was in his mouth.

"What about college?" she asked. "Mr. Ivy told me that, with your SAT scores, you have a shot at some good schools—Rutgers, Fordham."

He lifted a dismissive hand. "My dad says there's no money for that."

She tried to quash her own anxiety, stay level. She wanted to yell, *Get out of this town, Marshall. Get away from your father. Get an education. It's the only chance you have.*

"There are scholarships, grants, financial aid," she said instead. "We can help you with that."

His eyes dropped to the floor. She decided to change the subject. "How are things going with your mother?"

"My mother's a whore," Marshall said. His tone was mild, but the rise of color in his cheeks was telling.

"Why do you say that?" A low-level anxiety caused her to inch forward in her chair a little.

He pulled his mouth into a derisive sneer. "She has a new boyfriend."

Maggie forced herself to breathe in and out before answering, hoping the silence would let the exchange echo back at him. The sneer dropped, and he just looked inconsolably sad.

"That doesn't make her a whore, Marshall. When's the last time you talked to her?"

Maggie heard her son's car rumble to life in the driveway, then speed off. *Too fast. The kid drives too fast, and that muscle car doesn't help matters.* She got lost in her own thoughts for a second and almost didn't hear Marshall's response, something about his mother leaving him a message on Facebook.

"Said she missed me." He gave a bitter little laugh. It sounded bad on him, too old, too jaded.

"But no visits, no phone calls?"

"She said she doesn't have time. Too busy."

Maggie didn't know if that was true or not; it could have been that Marshall was avoiding her. Five years earlier, Angie Crosby had left Travis after a brutal beating (for which Travis was never charged, because he, too, had taken some blows from Angie). They then engaged in a vitriolic divorce and custody battle. In The Hollows, where they all lived—where they'd all grown up together—it was legendary. The rumors and gossip were endless; there was no function—not the precinct Christmas party or the annual pancake breakfast at the firehouse—where someone wasn't whispering about it.

"You were getting along really well, weren't you?"

"I guess."

When shared custody had been awarded, Angie disappeared. She
was eager to leave Travis behind, and it seemed she felt that meant leaving Marshall, too. If she couldn't keep him away from Travis, she'd admitted to Maggie recently, she hadn't wanted him. She'd refused to
attend a session with Marshall but had sent Maggie an e-mail explaining "her side of things." At age nine, Marshall had already been prone to
violent rages, had hit Angie twice and regularly invoked the vicious
names Travis had for her, she claimed. I have always been afraid of
Travis, even when I loved him. I am sorry to say that I feel
the same way about Marshall. I want a life where no one hits
me, where my son doesn't call me a bitch and a whore. Does that
make me a monster who abandoned her child? Maybe.

Maggie had been pleased to see them approach a tentative reunion
while Travis was away and Marshall was doing so much better. But
maybe when Travis came home and Marshall chose to return to him,
Angie withdrew again. Maggie made a note to call Angie and find out
what was really going on.

"Have you been taking your medication?"

Marshall nodded. She wasn't sure she believed him.

Maggie didn't always agree with the medication of children. It was,
as far as she was concerned, a last resort. She lost a lot of young patients
in her practice as a family and adolescent psychologist because she
wouldn't quickly call Dr. Willough for a referral prescription. But at
nearly seventeen, Marshall wasn't exactly a child anymore. And on his
first visit to her, he'd been severely depressed. Not bipolar, not ADHD,
not borderline—he'd had as many diagnoses over the years as he'd had
therapists. But she'd seen him as so clearly in the throes of a clinical depression that she'd prescribed a mild antidepressant, wary of the risks.

He seemed to have the right kind of supervision—an aunt who
loved him, an uncle who appeared equally fond of him and concerned
for his well-being, and, maybe most important, his cousins Ryan and
Tim, who were healthy and well-adjusted, and who were inclined to
take an interest in Marshall—bringing him to ball games, letting him
work on the old car they were trying to restore, coaching him on how to

approach a girl he liked. She'd educated them on the risks of a depressed teen on medication, what signs to monitor. But he'd responded well.

"Been in touch with Ryan and Tim?"

"Yeah, we hang." He looked above her now, not at her, still avoiding her eyes. He seemed to notice his bouncing knee and got it under control.

"Come on, Marshall. Let's cut through it, shall we? What's going on?"

He seemed to study the ceiling. When he looked back, he was smiling. She'd always liked his smile, sweet and boyish, as unexpectedly bright as a ray of sunlight through thunderheads. But this smile was ugly, sent a slight shiver through her.

He leaned forward suddenly, staring straight at her. "You know what, Doc?"

She gave him a tolerant, slow blink to show him that she was neither intimidated by him nor impressed by his shift in tone. It was striking, though, how his voice had gone from the dead, flat teenage monotone to something deeper, like a growl.

"What is it, Marshall?"

He issued a strange little chuckle. She fought the urge to shrink away from him, squared her shoulders and sat up. "I'm not sure I want you in my head anymore."

She put on her best cool smile, held his eyes, mineral green like a quarry lake.

"Whether you come here or not is, of course, your choice," she said.

Some kind of battle took place on his face, the acne on his chin and forehead blazing an angry red. The corners of his mouth fell in a pantomime of sadness. His eyes went wide, as if he was about to cry, then narrowed down, ugly with distrust and anger.

"Talk to me, Marshall."

She tried not to sound desperate, pleading. The mother in her wanted to sit close beside him, wrap him up and hold him tight. But she couldn't do that. He wouldn't be able to accept that kind of love, even if she could offer it to him.

He stood quickly then, raising himself to his full height, unslouching those perpetually hunched shoulders. She'd never realized how tall he was, always thought of him as a lean, lanky kid—never big or powerful, as he looked now. *He must be nearly six feet, close to two hundred pounds,* she thought with surprise. Involuntarily, she pushed herself back in her chair to rise. Her surprise must have registered on her face, triggering another battle on his. A nasty grimace won the war.

She'd never witnessed the tendency for violence in him, was startled by what she saw this session. What had happened? What had changed?

He bent over and picked up his battered backpack where it had rested near his feet, exiting without a glance back and closing the door quietly behind him. She sat for a full minute with her heart a turbine engine in her chest before she got up, walked over to her desk, and picked up the phone.

4

Rodents. They were everywhere. People didn't know. Didn't want to know. He'd seen colonies of mice, rats, squirrels, raccoons in attics, basements, inside walls, under toolsheds. Colonies that had lived beside humans, separated by an inch of drywall, for years. Living, breeding, dying, decaying to dust. There was a kind of beauty to them, their slippery bodies, their savage natures, their sharp little teeth and black eyes. The babies were cute, like the babies of every species. Tiny pink balls covered in downy gray fur, blind and squeaking.

The rat he had in his trap, a full-grown male, was definitely *not* cute. He'd died ugly, all bared teeth and reaching claws. He was big, too, maybe nine inches from nose to rump, weighing nearly half a pound if Charlie Strout were to hazard a guess. He'd seen them bigger, as big as a small cat. He'd seen them mean. He'd been bitten twice, once in an elderly woman's attic—she'd bandaged up the web of his hand and made him some tea. Ambushed. Once, he'd been bitten removing an animal he thought was dead from a trap. Careless. Mainly, they just ran from him, wanted to be left alone like everyone else.

He tossed the trap into the flatbed of his Ford. It landed with a *thunk,* and he covered it, along with two other bodies, under a thick canvas tarp.

"Catch anything?"

He turned to see the woman who'd hired him standing at the end of the path that led to her door. He was used to the look of revulsion, the wrapped-up body language. She had her hands firmly tucked in her pockets, her arms pressed tight to her sides, her shoulders hiked up. She squinted at him in the bright, late-afternoon light. It caught on the gold of her hair, glinted off the diamonds in her ears. She was pretty, a youngish forty-something. Women stayed attractive and girlish so much longer these days; he didn't remember his mom or her friends looking so good when he was the same age as his client's kid.

"I did, ma'am."

"Maybe the last one?"

"I started sealing off the exits. If there are any left, they'll get nervous, be more likely to go for the food in the traps when they get hungry and can't escape."

Her squint deepened. "But they can't get *in* the house?"

"No, ma'am, not likely." But they could. Of course they could. They were smart, stealthy. They'd come in holes she didn't even know were there, behind the entertainment center, maybe, up through the toilet if they could, through the central air vents if they found an opening and smelled food. "Just don't leave anything out. Make sure you take the garbage to the outdoor bin at night."

She nodded uneasily.

"We'll have you clear of this soon."

She gave him a grateful smile and walked over to hand him a folded-up ten. She was a good tipper, polite and friendly with him. "Thanks for all your help."

"No problem. And don't worry."

He felt a little bad; there weren't as many rats up there as the sales guy who made the first visit had probably led her to believe. He would have used words like *infestation. Well, I'm sure there aren't more than thirty up there.* Then he'd have talked about how bacteria from feces and decay could make its way into air vents and cause respiratory problems. The sales guy would have asked something like *Have you or your kids been getting more colds than usual?* By the time he was done, she'd agreed to two thousand dollars' worth of work for their "three-phase plan": trapping and removal, entry sealing, and cleaning up decay and feces, with their "patented formula" cleaner, which was really just some cherry-scented stuff they sprayed around. It was a total rip-off; most jobs took him about three hours—set the traps, remove the corpses, plug up a few holes, and spray the cleaner around. He'd space out his visits over a couple of weeks so it looked like more work than it was. But people would pay *anything* to be rid of rats, especially if they had kids. They all wanted humane trapping for the raccoons, moles, or squirrels. But no one cared about the rats, how they died. They didn't like to hear the snap of the trap or the squealing that might follow. Still, few asked for the rats to be removed alive and relocated.

He supposed it had something to do with the Black Plague—a bad history, over centuries and continents. Rats were regarded as the bringers of pestilence and death. In the projects of New York City, rumors abounded that they crawled into cribs and bit babies as they slept. He'd never seen anything like that in The Hollows. To him they were no different than the other animals people didn't want around. They were just critters, trying to get by.

He got into his truck. It was one of the nicer vehicles in the fleet the company he worked for owned. Wanda was working dispatch today, and she liked him, thought he was a gentleman, so she made sure he got one of the newer trucks with good air-conditioning and XM radio.

He cranked the air. October and it was still hot as a bitch. Global warming: that's what people needed to be worried about. They spent thousands for him to crawl around in their attics. But how many of those people had given a dime to save the rest of the planet? Not that he was any philanthropist. But he was making fifteen dollars an hour, not living in some 4,500-square-foot McMansion.

Driving out of the wealthy development past the towering faux Tudors and sprawling new Victorians nestled among old-growth trees, landscaping like botanical gardens, expensive, late-model cars lounging on winding drives, he wondered what people did to afford such opulent homes. How much did it cost to heat and cool these places, to clean, to maintain their yards and pools?

He'd always imagined himself in a nice house—a big corporate job, a pretty wife and well-groomed children. But thirty-five had come and gone, thirteen years since he'd graduated from university. Though he'd always been frugal, had some money saved, partially from a generous inheritance from his grandmother, he doubted he even had enough for a down payment on one of these places. And he had never come *close* to marriage.

His Nextel beeped as he was pulling onto the main road through town, heading back to the office. He pressed the button without lifting the phone from the center console.

"Hello, Miss Wanda," he said. "How's your day going?"

Wanda was a pretty woman who wore a little too much makeup, dyed her hair a red that was a bit too brassy. But still on the right side of forty, she had a tight little body and a sweet, sweet smile. And lately he'd been wondering if she might like to have dinner with him. With her he wouldn't have to dread the question about his work. It wasn't exactly a sexy job. Woman might purr when you say you're a doctor or a lawyer, or raise their eyebrows with interest if you tell them you're a professor or an architect. But tell them you're an exterminator, they literally recoil, wrinkle their noses in disgust.

Whatever got you into that line of work?

What a question. Most careers were just accidents, weren't they? You wound up doing something after school to bridge the gap while you decided what you really wanted to do, and thirteen years later, you still hadn't figured it out.

But what I'd really like to do is write, he'd add quickly. Some of the more arty ones might perk up a bit. But for a woman looking for some indication that success might lurk in his future, that was generally the last nail in the coffin.

"It's going all right, Charlie. Thanks for asking," Wanda said. He loved the shade of a drawl he heard on her words. Where had she said she was from originally? New Orleans, wasn't it? "How was your last call?"

"Big, nasty old critter," he said. "Dead as they get. Might be one or two more up there. We'll see when I go back next time. He could have been the last."

"Time for one more visit?"

Crap. All he wanted to do was go home and wash the stink off of him and open a beer, forget about his day, his life or lack thereof. He was even thinking he might try to hammer out a few pages on the novel he was writing, though he hadn't written a word in months. Of course, he was always thinking he might do that. Instead he'd go home, eat fast food in front of the television, and then go to bed.

"Anything for you, Wanda. You know that."

"You're a sweet talker, Charlie." Before he could flirt back, she rattled off an address. "I'll text it to you, and the directions. I wouldn't bother you this late, but the woman sounded really upset, and the sales team is gone for the day. She says there's something huge up there, making a lot of noise."

"Oh, really? Most things are pretty quiet during the day."

"That's what she told me."

"Well, I'll check it out." He decided to go for it. "So, Wanda. Will you still be there when I get back in?"

In the crackling silence that followed, he felt a wash of disappointment. He'd blown it. She was just flirting to be friendly. Not interested. Now he'd gone and ruined their easy working relationship. He was about to backpedal by asking her to sign his overtime form.

But then, "I *might* be, Charlie." There was that smile in her voice again.

"Something I can do for you?"

He cleared his throat. He knew his voice sounded too boyish sometimes. Women didn't always like that. He tried to modulate it slightly. "I was just thinking—um, wondering if you might like to get a drink."

When she spoke again, she dropped her voice down low. He knew she wouldn't want any of the other people in the office to hear. "I'd like that, Charlie."

He felt the first smile he'd felt all day, maybe all week. Hell, maybe all month.

"Then wait for me, Miss Wanda," he said. "I won't be long."

"See you soon."

In Charlie's experience, service people were almost invisible to the rich. And once he'd disappeared into the attic, they generally forgot about his existence entirely. Through the thin ceilings of shoddily constructed homes, he'd heard people say and do things—awful things, funny things, embarrassing things. Some of it he wrote down, hoping his observations might come in handy for his novel, if he ever sat down at his computer again and managed something more productive than downloading porn.

He'd heard a toddler call his mother a bitch; she'd slapped him—he'd heard the sharp smack of palm against flesh—and they'd both started to wail. While he was plugging up a hole mice had chewed through some drywall, he couldn't help but eavesdrop on a man having phone sex and jerking off in his garage while his wife cooked in the kitchen.

I love you. I hate you. Take me hard. Don't touch me. I miss you. What time will you be home for dinner? Don't forget to call your mom. He's away on business this week; I can't wait to make you come in his bed. Can you bring home some milk?

He was a silent witness to the full rainbow of the human experience, from the mundane to the tawdry. This condition wasn't informing his fiction, as he'd hoped. It was causing him to prefer the company of rodents.

"There's something up there. Something big."

The client was unapologetically old, with a snow-white head of tight curls, a face where skin hung like melting wax, but thin and alert. She had bright blue eyes that seemed to assess him from head to toe in a blink—not in a judgmental way. In the way of the wise, knowing, accepting what is. She wore a snug pair of jeans and a big sweatshirt that said ATTITUDE PROBLEM. Her Nike trainers looked like they'd seen some miles.

Wanda had said the old lady was upset, but she didn't seem upset to Charlie.

"I can't get to the attic anymore, or I'd find it myself and beat it to death with this." She glanced toward her cane, lifted it a little for emphasis. "I've had every critter imaginable up there—been in this house more than fifty years. Never heard anything like that."

She looked up at the ceiling, and he found himself doing the same.

"What did it sound like?" he asked. They'd climbed two flights of stairs together—in spite of the cane, she was fast—and now stood beneath the attic entrance. He was still catching his breath a bit. It was a

big, old house, a veritable museum of dusty carpets, mediocre oil paintings of nature scenes and stiff-looking people, heavy, ornate furniture. A
grand piano in a room filled with books, working fireplaces with mantels
covered in framed photographs. Beds with handmade quilts, dolls reclining in window seats. A real house, echoing with life lived—full of
memories and irregularly shaped rooms.

"Thumping, banging. Almost . . . *rhythmic*."

Probably not rats. Raccoons did a lot of thumping and pounding for
some reason.

"Okay, Mrs. Monroe," he said, reaching up for the cord that would
release the attic door and ladder. "Let's see what you have up there."

The door came down easily, and he unfolded the ladder until it
reached the floor. Mrs. Monroe flipped on a light against the encroaching darkness. He looked at his watch; it was already after six. He wondered if Wanda would really wait for him or if she was just being polite.
Maybe he'd go in and find a note—*Sorry, Charlie. I had to run. Another
time?* He wouldn't be surprised; he didn't have much luck with women.
After a few dates, they always seemed to want to be friends. He was already feeling the crush of disappointment before they'd even had their
first drink.

"You just be careful," Mrs. Monroe said. "And holler if you need
anything."

He hoisted his bag over his shoulder and climbed up, feeling the old
ladder groan beneath his weight.

The only light source in the attic was a small circular window at the
far end. But in the waning hours of the day, it just served to create a field
of shadows. He could stand but with an uncomfortable bowing of his
head and scrunching of his shoulders. He pulled out his flashlight and
shone the beam around, expecting to hear skittering, maybe something
knocked over in flight. But there was only silence. Boxes, an old rocker,
a small rolltop desk—a landscape of old and forgotten things. Why
didn't people just get rid of their junk? The old lady said herself she
hadn't been up here in years.

He looked around the floor for feces, lifting his nose to the air for
the telltale smell of urine. But all he smelled was dust and mold as he

made his way through the junk—an old radio, a box of rotary phone parts, piles and piles of books.

He was sniffling, holding back a sneeze, by the time he'd reached the end of the space. He looked out the window. He could see the roofs of other houses, the church steeple peeking through the gold, brown, and orange of northern fall on the trees—oaks, maples, some old pines and birch, aspen, sycamore. A Florida native, he loved the seasonal slide show of the North—the bright green springs and tawny autumns, the black-and-white winters. All he knew when he'd come up for college was the perennial summer, the swaying of palms, the white sand against green ocean. A beautiful single note that wavered only in extremes of weather—hurricanes, dramatic thunderstorms. Bright, hot sun and still, stifling air, or black skies and ferocious winds, sheets of rain. A couple months of perfect, dry, seventy-degree winter weather seduced the folks from Michigan and New York, only to leave them wilting when August turned to September turned to October and the weather still rivaled saunas and blast furnaces.

Walking back through the attic, he kept his eyes to the floorboards—still not detecting any critter presence by smell, sight, or sound. And then there it was, just as he was about to climb back downstairs. On a draft, he caught just the lightest odor of something foul, the curling, unmistakable scent of death.

He looked around a bit more, moving boxes, garment bags thick with old clothes, and accordion files bloated with yellowed papers, but the beam of his flashlight revealed nothing. If something had crawled up here and died, he'd have trouble finding it in all this clutter. He'd have to wait until the scent got worse. Luckily, the weather was warm. By tomorrow, late afternoon, it'd be ripe. He'd follow his nose.

He climbed downstairs to find Mrs. Monroe where he'd left her.

"Find anything?"

"Well, no. But I *do* smell something. So I'll set a couple of humane traps and come back tomorrow afternoon to see what we've got. I suspect raccoons."

She nodded but looked skeptical. She followed him down the stairs and out to the truck, where he got the traps. He should have been up-selling her, telling her she had an infestation, getting her to sign a contract for more service than she needed. There were bonuses in it for him if he did the sales job as well as the trapping work. But he just didn't have it in him. He didn't have that sales personality, that ability to see a need, a fear, or a desire, and then manipulate it. His father was a salesman, always knowing how to mold himself to please, to work a room, to schmooze with a client. But the gene didn't pass on to Charlie. He could only be himself.

Back at the office, he'd tell them that she was difficult and they'd leave her be. There were enough suckers out there. The difficult ones weren't worth it, especially these days, when people could post their discontent online. He'd come back and check the traps when he was done for the day tomorrow, write her a bill for the service.

In the late dusk, Mrs. Monroe didn't seem as tough as she'd appeared inside. She cast a worried glance back at the house, holding the paperwork he'd handed her.

"Don't worry, Mrs. Monroe. I'll get rid of whatever you have up there."

She gave a little laugh. "At this age, it takes more than critters in the attic to worry me."

But he could tell it was bravado. In the rearview mirror, she was just a tiny, frail shadow in the gloaming.

5

Maggie found the house dark and quiet. She closed the door that led from her office suite to her home and locked it, feeling a familiar mingling of relief and a mild flutter of nervousness. Closing this door and turning the dead bolt was something she made sure she did at the end of every day, a way of leaving her work behind. Some days this was easier than others. It was a door that she discouraged Jones and Ricky from walking through. They were to call her on the phone if they needed her. And they, surprisingly, respected that—though Ricky was not above pounding on the door when he'd seen a client drive away and knew there wasn't another patient inside. *Mom, I need some money! Mom, I can't find my Ramones T-shirt!* Jones liked to refer to it as the shrink zone. There was some resentment there, she knew, even though he had suggested that they build the addition rather than lease office space somewhere. Dr. Willough thought that she should have an off-site office, that a simple doorway wasn't enough to protect patient privacy, to achieve the crucial separation of family and professional life. But, especially when Ricky was small, Maggie found the convenience of being steps away from her home and family very comforting—between patients she could do a load of laundry, run a quick errand, read her son a story, and give the part-time babysitter a break.

"Hello?" she called, walking into the kitchen.

She'd expected to hear the television on, or the pumping bass from the stereo in Ricky's upstairs bedroom. She'd even thought she might see Jones sitting out by the pool, their bottle of wine already open, her glass waiting. But no. The sun had already dipped below the horizon and there had been no one home to turn on the lamps against the evening. She felt a low-grade anxiety, a nagging loneliness.

She moved through the rooms, flipping switches, filling the house with the light and warmth she needed, turning on the small, new flat-screen on the kitchen counter just to hear the sound of the local news. When the house seemed more alive, she felt better.

She peered into the refrigerator and fooled herself for a moment, thinking she might actually get creative and cook something. But since she hadn't been shopping and Jones had polished off all the leftovers—not just the lasagna but also the black bean soup she'd made earlier in the week—she gave up the idea quickly. The refrigerator offered only some wilting carrots and a bag of prewashed organic lettuce, a package of cheddar cheese, some tubs of Greek yogurt, and half a bottle of pomegranate juice. Of course, there were always the staples—milk, eggs, bread, butter, all varieties of condiments. She'd never allow the refrigerator to be *completely* empty. Her mother had never run out of these things, not once in Maggie's childhood. *Always be prepared to make an omelet or a grilled cheese sandwich. And always buy a roll of toilet paper when you do your shopping, even if you don't need it. That way you never run out.* Elizabeth's household wisdom: there was no shortage.

But it was good advice; Maggie had followed it, even in college. As a cook, a wife, and a mother, she held herself to at least that standard. Even now, she had cupboards full of more toilet paper than they'd ever need.

"Why do we have so much toilet paper everywhere?" Jones always wanted to know.

She picked up the phone and dialed his number, but her call went straight to voice mail.

"Where are you?" she said. "I was thinking of ordering a pizza and salad for dinner. Sound good? Call me."

Then she dialed Ricky. Voice mail again.

"What do you think about pizza for dinner? Maybe you want to invite Char?"

It was probably a bad idea given Jones's mood and the whole tattoo thing. But so what? If Ricky and Jones didn't fight about that, they'd

fight about something else. Maybe they'd be on better behavior with a
guest at the table. They could all have a meal in relative peace.

She ordered two pizzas from Paesano's (Jones and Ricky preferred
Pop's, but she thought it was too greasy), one plain, one pepperoni, and
a large Greek salad, got hung up on the phone exchanging niceties with
the owner, someone she'd gone to high school with, Chad Donner. She
might even have kissed him once—she had a fuzzy memory of some in-
discreet moment at an unsupervised Halloween party. At any rate, he always made goofy jokes and exuded a lonely energy when she stopped in
to pick up a meal or if she answered the phone at the restaurant, as
though he remembered something that was important to him but that
she had long forgotten. When she hung up, feeling vaguely bad, her
thoughts returned to Marshall.

When Marshall had left her office, it was as if he'd taken all the air with
him. She'd sat stunned and breathless, though she couldn't have said
why precisely. It wasn't as if he'd raged, or lost control, or even moved
physically toward her. But she'd felt a malice radiating off him in palpable waves. When he was gone, she'd called the high school and happened to catch Henry Ivy during his break.

"He hasn't been in school in a week," Henry said. "I e-mailed you."

"Did you?" she asked, opening her e-mail for the first time that day.
She scrolled through a flock of waiting messages and found Henry's,
sent late yesterday afternoon. She wasn't much for e-mail, hated the
impersonal distance of it. People used it to hide from one another.
It stripped communication of expression and tone, essential markers
for meaning. She avoided it when possible, preferring to pick up the
phone.

"Something's changed, Henry," she said. "We're losing him."

"What happened?"

She recounted the session in broad strokes, avoiding specific things
he'd said to protect Marshall's privacy and her oath. She focused instead
on his mood, the air of malice, and his abrupt departure from her office.

Henry was silent for a moment after she finished. If she'd been talking to Jones, that silence would have annoyed her. She'd have rightly assumed that he was multitasking, not quite listening to her. But with Henry, her friend since high school, she knew he was processing her words, turning the possibilities of the incident over in his mind.

"Maybe I'll stop over there on my way home," he said finally. "Check in with Marshall."

That was the problem with The Hollows—though maybe it wasn't always a problem. Everyone's relationship was complicated—your doctor was also your neighbor, maybe she'd gone to the prom with your brother. The cop at your door had been the burnout always in trouble when you were in high school. In this case, when Henry stopped by to check in on Marshall, Travis might not see his kid's teacher dropping in to check on a student. Travis might see the boy he'd mercilessly bullied for years, the one who'd finally—after a summer growth spurt—beat him down in front of the whole high school at a homecoming game. Beat him so badly that Travis had actually cried. No one was quite as intimidated by Travis Crosby after that—until he'd started wearing a badge and carrying a gun.

"Do you think that's a good idea?" she asked.

"I think it's my job." She detected a note of defensiveness, which reminded her of a question she'd held at bay for a while. How much of Henry Ivy's interest in Marshall had to do with Travis?

"You're a teacher, not a truant officer."

He blew out a breath. "Do you have a better idea?"

"Let's call Leila. She can send the boys over to connect with Marshall. It's less confrontational."

Another silence; in the background she heard the bell that announced the end of class, a sudden wave of voices and footfalls.

"Okay," he said. "You'll call her?"

"I will."

But she hadn't called right away. Her next patient had arrived early. There was a court-ordered evaluation she had to complete after that. And the next thing she knew, she was sitting in the dark of her office, the space lit only by the glow of her computer screen. She picked up the phone without bothering to turn on the light. Leila answered after just two rings.

"It's Maggie."

Leila expelled a tired breath. "I've been expecting your call."

Maggie told her about her last session with Marshall, suggested that she send Tim and Ryan over to reach out. But she didn't get the reaction she expected.

"I don't think so, Maggie. I'm sorry. We're overextended in this area to begin with. The boys—they haven't said much, but they've been keeping their distance from Marshall."

"But, Leila . . . ," Maggie began. When Leila didn't let her finish, Maggie felt a rush of something desperate. *When you feel that,* Dr. Willough warned, *you know you're over the line internally.* Maggie could almost see Leila lifting a hand and closing her eyes. Over the years, they'd been friends, rivals, and then friends again.

"You know Travis, Maggie," Leila said. "He's toxic. Like, you can't *touch* him—it burns. And Marshall. He's just different when his father's around. I hate to say it. I'm afraid of him. Of both of them. My own brother and nephew." She paused here, seemed to collect herself with a deep inhale. "I need to protect my boys from their . . . poison."

Maggie was quiet now. The thing was, she *did* know Travis and other men like him. Leila was right to protect herself and her sons. Maggie stopped short of saying so.

"I think my family has done everything we can for Marshall," said Leila when Maggie stayed silent. "He's almost an adult. We have to save ourselves sometimes, Maggie. You should know that."

"A boy like Marshall might not have the tools to save himself."

"I'm sorry," Leila said. Maggie felt as much as she heard Leila hang up the phone.

After that, Maggie called Marshall's mother and got her voice mail. She left a message, thinking that she heard doors closing, windows latching all around Marshall. This was what happened. Abused boys became dangerous men. Those around them with a self-preservation instinct—even the people who loved them—started to move away.

Maggie was thinking about all of this, staring at but not seeing or hearing the television, when the front door opened and then shut hard. She
heard heavy footfalls on the staircase. By the time she got to the foyer,
she saw only her son's feet at the top, turning the corner to his room.

"I ordered pizza," she called.

"Not hungry," he yelled back and slammed his door.

A moment later angry waves of thrash metal washed down the
stairs—high-speed riffing and aggressive bass beats. Sometimes Maggie
felt separated from her son by a wave of noise, harsh, ugly music she
didn't like and couldn't understand. Even when he was down in the
basement, pounding on his drum set, the sound kept her at bay. She remembered the music she used to listen to when she was his age, finding
herself—The Smiths, The Cure, Joy Division—characterized by the
typical angst and yearning, maybe even a bit of anger. Ricky's music
seemed so full of rage; she wondered what that said about him, if there
was a whole universe inside him that she just couldn't visit.

Jones had been an angry young man—furious at a father who'd neg-
lected and eventually abandoned him, resentful of a mother who smothered and clung to him in the absence of her husband. Maggie
remembered bar fights and road rage, a few on-the-job complaints, one
even making it as far as civilian review. But he'd mellowed over time,
even though she could still see that younger man when Jones and Ricky
went at it. Maybe it was hereditary, anger. Maybe it lay dormant in boy-
hood, the disease taking hold in late adolescence. Then it either burned
out before any damage was done, or took control.

She walked up the stairs, stood at the door, and put her hand on the
wall, feeling the textured sunshine yellow paint with her fingertips. The
wall vibrated with the sound coming from inside her son's room. She offered a tentative knock on his door. No response. She knocked louder.

"What?" he called from inside.

"Want to talk about it?"

"No. I don't."

The volume of the music increased. She could push inside or walk away. She could force a conversation, which might turn into a fight. Or just let him come to her when he was ready. She hesitated a moment, conflicted. Then she opted for the latter, moving quietly down the stairs, feeling that strange loneliness again. Uselessness, she thought, was the permanent condition of parenthood. In her office, with her patients, she always knew what do to, what to say. Why, then, with her own family did she so often feel at a complete loss?

For a while, she'd held on to some illusion of control. And then, right about the time Ricky gave up his afternoon nap, she finally understood that for all the schedules and consistency, the rewards and reprimands, ultimately it's the child who chooses how to behave. It's the parent's responsibility to provide the safe environment, the predictable rules, the loving discipline, and the healthy meals, but ultimately the child has to be the one to put the broccoli in his mouth, chew, and swallow. Jones still labored under the delusion that he could bend Ricky to his way of thinking, that with anger, hard words, and harsh punishment he could force their son to do and be what he wanted—in spite of all evidence to the contrary.

When Maggie reached the foyer, the twin beam of headlights swept across the far wall. She walked to the window and saw the pizza delivery car in her drive. She glanced at her watch, then went to the kitchen for her wallet. When she returned, the delivery boy was peering in one of the windows. She opened the door, was surprised by how cool the air had turned once the sun had set.

"Hey, Dr. Cooper." The delivery boy went on to say something else, something about a cold front moving in, but she barely heard him. Her eyes fell on a figure standing across the street. He leaned against a tall, old oak, washed in the glow of lamplight. It was too dim and he was too far, so she couldn't quite read his expression, though she recognized his bearing, those permanently slouched shoulders.

She stepped through the doorway and came to stand beside the delivery boy. She could smell warm pizza, cheap aftershave, wood burning on the air. She crossed her arms against the chill.

"Marshall?" she called.

She waited for a hand raised in greeting, or for him to start walking across the street. Maybe he felt bad about their session, wanted to talk about it. That would be a good sign. But he stood rooted.

"Marshall, is everything all right?"

She felt the quickening of her pulse when he still stayed silent. She was about to move toward him, to cross the street and bring him inside. She'd confront him head-on. She needed to show him that he didn't intimidate her, if that was what he was after. But then he took off at a run. She looked after him until he was just a pair of white sneakers, then was swallowed by the night. A moment later she heard a car door slam, an engine rumbling to life.

"Twenty-four fifty," the pizza boy said. "Dr. Cooper?"

"Yes. Sorry." She handed him thirty, told him to keep the rest, and he, too, took off at a brisk jog, toward his parked car. Just a kid, he looked barely old enough to be driving. He didn't seem to think much of the strange encounter, was only concerned with his next delivery. She held the hot pizza boxes and salad, still looking after Marshall. She had no reason to be afraid. But she found that she was.

An hour later, Maggie was still waiting on Jones. The pizza boxes sat one on top of the other on the cold burners of the stovetop. The salad was in the fridge. Ricky wouldn't come down. Jones hadn't answered at the station; his assistant, Claire, was obviously gone for the evening. There was still no answer on his cell phone. She tried not to worry. As a cop's wife, she'd learned not to. Jones had taught her early in their marriage that if there were something to worry about, she'd know right away. That was when he worked patrol. Now that he headed the detective division in a relatively small department, there was less reason to worry than ever.

The Hollows was a small, relatively affluent town, about a hundred miles outside of New York City. There were some challenged areas in the district, daily problems with drug dealers, domestic violence; there had been an armed robbery at a liquor store a few months earlier. Recently, a man had killed his wife and then himself, suffering a breakdown after learning she'd had an affair. There were the usual break-ins and petty crimes. It wasn't the kind of small town where everyone knew one another and nothing ever happened. But it was a relatively safe and quiet community. People who had grown up in The Hollows often returned after college to raise families. Doctors, lawyers, businesspeople who worked in the city commuted home by train on weekday nights. It had that quaintness to it, the kind that rich urbanites started to crave in their forties, when the glitz of the city ceased to glamour them. It was a nice place to live, with good schools, a lively center with trendy boutiques, an independent bookstore, a couple of nice restaurants, and The Hollows Brew, an upscale coffee shop that hosted a weekly poetry reading, showed the work of local artists on its walls, and had become a kind of general meeting place.

Maggie had never thought in a million years that she'd end up back in The Hollows. But she had. She didn't regret leaving the city behind and starting a practice here, in the town where she grew up. But sometimes, in a low moment, she wondered what would have happened if her father hadn't died, leaving her mother alone. Would she ever have come back here?

She picked up the phone and dialed her mother. It wasn't until the fourth ring that Elizabeth picked up. Maggie had noticed over the last couple of weeks that it was taking her mother longer and longer to get to the phone.

"Hey, Mom," she said. She tried to sound upbeat even though she knew it was pointless. Elizabeth always knew what Maggie was feeling, no matter how she tried to hide it.

"Hello, Magpie."

"How are your attic guests?"

"Quiet, too quiet," said her mother, mock-ominous. "And possibly raccoons."

"Did someone come out?"

"Yes, a young fellow. Laid out a few traps, said he'd come back tomorrow."

Maggie nodded but didn't say anything, half forgetting she was on the phone.

"What's wrong?" asked her mother.

"Probably nothing." She told her mother about Marshall Crosby lingering across the street, running off when she called his name.

"That boy was always trouble."

"You don't even know him." She knew her mother wasn't talking about Marshall.

"I meant Travis."

"Marshall is not Travis."

"Not yet."

Maggie felt the familiar rise of annoyance and defensiveness at her mother's superior, knowing tone. It bordered on imperious. Elizabeth Monroe thought that her seventy-five years of life, twenty-five of which she'd spent as the principal of Hollows High, had taught her everything she needed to know about human nature. Why had Maggie even bothered saying anything?

"Did you call your husband?" Elizabeth asked when Maggie didn't respond.

"Can't reach him."

Now it was Elizabeth's turn to keep her mouth shut. Between mothers and daughters, it seemed to Maggie, there was so much more meaning in silence than in any words spoken.

"And Ricky?" Elizabeth said finally. *Can't reach him, either,* Maggie thought but didn't say, *for different reasons altogether.*

"He's upstairs studying," she said.

"Well." A pause, a sigh. "Lock the door. If he comes back, call 911."

Elizabeth was always unemotional, pragmatic. Maggie had long ago stopped looking for tea and sympathy from her mother, had actually come to accept and even appreciate Elizabeth for exactly who she was—most of the time. Not easy work, not even for a shrink.

"I will." Maggie walked back over to the door, peered out. Just the quiet street, the glowing orange of porch lights, the sway of trees. "Good night."

"Maggie." Her mother's voice carried small and tinny over the air as Maggie took the phone from her ear.

"Yeah, Mom?"

"Call if you need me."

She felt a smile lift the corners of her mouth. Her mother was five foot two, a hundred pounds soaking wet.

"Would you come over and defend me with your cane?" Maggie said.

Elizabeth gave a throaty chuckle at that. "If I had to."

"Thanks, Mom. Good night."

"Good night, dear." Was there something wistful in her voice? Or maybe Maggie was just imagining things . . . her husband sounded strained and tense, her son angry, her mother lonely. Was she just projecting? When everyone close seemed to be suffering, maybe it was time to look in the mirror.

Just as she hung up the phone, Maggie heard Jones pull into the drive in his big government-issue SUV. It was a gas-guzzling maroon monstrosity, with big silver stars emblazoned on the doors. HOLLOWS POLICE DEPARTMENT. A rack of lights sat on top. At the door she watched her husband turn off the ignition and then just sit there a moment, looking straight ahead. In the light from the garage, she could just see his arm and the shadow of his head. She saw him put his hands to his temples and rub. She felt a gnawing sadness watching him there. Sometimes, even when they were only separated by feet or inches, he seemed so far away, untouchable. When did it happen? When did this strange distance grow between them, and why didn't she have the energy to open the door, walk out to his car, and bring him home?

6

It was one of the things Amber hated most about autumn, the early fall of darkness. Summer days reached lazily on into summer nights, stretching orange fingers against the encroaching black, then surrendering with a shrug. In autumn, the light snuck out early, like it was late for something, like it might not be coming back. After lunch, she started to feel uneasy, had a sense that the day was racing away and she was being left behind. Her mother said that she was too young to feel like that, that she had all the time in the world. But she couldn't shake the feeling when, even on the bus ride home, the sky was already growing dark.

It was dark now, as dark as it would be at midnight, and it wasn't even dinnertime yet. As she got farther from her house, she slipped a cigarette from the pack in her jeans and cupped her hand to light it. It wasn't until after she took the first drag that she saw him sitting there. She didn't know he had a car.

She heard him lower the window as she approached. She leaned down to look inside instead of walking by without acknowledging him, which she'd usually do if she saw him in the cafeteria or the hallway. Curiosity got the better of her.

"What are you doing here?" she asked.

She'd told her mom that she was going for a walk, the smokes shoved into her jeans, a lighter in her pocket. *Wear a jacket. And don't go far. Dinner's almost ready.* She wondered if her mother suspected that she went out for a cigarette. Anyway, what could she say? Every once in a while, Amber would find a cigarette butt pressed into the soft ground behind the pool house with her mother's lipstick on it. A little secret habit they both had. It would be just like her mother to pretend she didn't know her daughter was smoking, letting herself off the hook of forbidding and then punishing. Her mother preferred the surface of their life to be calm and harmonious, even when the depths were roiling.

He'd been parked down a house or two, just sitting there, smoking, as well. As she got closer, she saw a pack of Lucky Strikes on the dash. No filters. The sight of that red and white soft pack, one cigarette poking out a neatly ripped opening, and he suddenly seemed different to her, less dorky. It was a cool car, too. Old but tough, one of those muscle cars.

"Just chillin'. Waitin' on my boy." She hated it when white, suburban guys tried to talk and act like gangbangers, taking on the too-cool lope and apathetic, half-lidded gaze. He immediately sank back to dork in her estimation.

"Who? Justin?"

He gave a slow nod. She didn't know they hung out. In fact, she doubted it. She just couldn't see Justin Hawk, football quarterback, pot dealer, senior class heartthrob, throwing this guy a backward glance. Unless.

"You got some? Or are you waiting on it?" Amber asked. It would be nice to get high, even with a dork. Marijuana was the only thing that had ever taken the edge off the constant buzz of anxiety she had lately. It made her calm, relaxed her, made her laugh.

He gave a slow shrug. "Back at my crib, yeah, if you want some." *Crib. Come on.*

"I can't," she said, nodding toward her house. "My mom's cooking."

"You'll be back in twenty. I'm just a mile up the road."

Was that true? She didn't know where he lived. She didn't think he lived that close. Doctors, lawyers, hedge fund managers like her dad—those were her neighbors. She didn't even know what his parents did. Hadn't she heard his dad was in jail?

"Thanks," she said, trying to be sweet about it. "But I have to get back."

"Suit yourself."

Just like that he turned her off, tuned her out, and stared blankly ahead, as if she wasn't even there. She felt like she should say something, apologize. She'd have gone inside with Justin, or taken a ride with Brad if she'd seen him waiting in that sweet new BMW his parents gave him. She'd even have taken off for a few minutes with Ricky Cooper, gothic freak that he was. At least he had a band.

She started toward home, feeling a little bad. She knew he was thinking that she was a bitch, stuck-up. Everyone thought that. But it wasn't true.

"Hey, let me ask you something," he called after her. She stopped and turned.

"I gotta get my girl something. What's the best gift anyone ever bought you?"

She walked back over to the car, happy for an opportunity to end their encounter on a more positive note. He turned on the interior lights, and she moved toward the open passenger-side window. Closer, she saw that the upholstery was grimy, literally black along the edges and in the creases. Even from where she stood she could smell the reek of years—puke, cigarettes, fast food. She'd been about to lean into the car, but instead she found herself recoiling. Not at the filth, necessarily, but at the unpleasant unfamiliarity of it all—this boy with his ill-fitting clothes and bad skin, his old car, the ugly odor. She knew instinctively that she didn't belong in his world and was glad for it.

"Who's your girl?" she asked, moving back again.

"You wouldn't know her."

Figured. There probably wasn't any girl; she knew that.

"The best gift I ever got was a pair of diamond earrings, from my parents." She knew she sounded haughty, like the snob everyone thought she was.

"From a dude," he said with a sneer. "From your boyfriend. What's his name—Josh?"

The question made her a little angry, a little self-conscious. Every-body knew, didn't they, that she and Josh had broken up? She'd caught him flirting with another girl on Facebook, leaving sweet, sexy notes on her message board. I love your pix. You're such a cutie! Can I have your number? Josh swore it wasn't him, was still calling every day.

Just thinking about it made heat come to her cheeks. Everyone had been talking about the breakup all week. She was certain that even her best friends were gossiping about it behind her back, consoling her, then laughing about it together. Amber knew Tiffany had her eyes on Josh, too. Was he making fun of her?

"A locket," she lied. "A gold locket with his picture inside." It was the kind of gift she would have liked from Josh, something grown-up, something with meaning. But he always gave her drugstore teddy bears and supermarket flowers, boxes of candy she wouldn't dream of eating. Of course, she was always grateful. *Aw, Josh! You're so sweet. Thank you soooo much.*

He nodded. "That's cool," he said. "I like that."

He didn't say anything else, just kept his eyes on her. She noticed the stubble on his jaw, the size of his hands. He reached for the cigarettes, and she moved away from the car and headed toward her house again. She heard the engine start, and she broke into a run for home. She couldn't say for sure what scared her, but she didn't stop running until she reached her front door. She pushed on the great knob and walked into the tall, bright foyer. She could smell her mother's tomato sauce, heavy with garlic and basil. She locked the door and looked out the window. She watched him drive slowly by, then gun the engine and rumble off.

"Josh called. Again," her mother said from the kitchen. Amber thought tonight she might call him back. She didn't like not having a boyfriend. As she walked toward the kitchen, she wondered suddenly if Marshall Crosby had been there to see Justin at all.

7

Rinsing the dishes, Maggie cut her finger on a chip in one of the dinner plates, and she bled into the soapy water. It looked like nothing, little more than a paper cut, but she couldn't stop the bleeding. She put her finger in her mouth, tasting the salty sweetness of her blood, a little soap. The offending dish was a piece from the casual dining set they'd received at their wedding, a discontinued line of Royal Doulton stoneware. She wondered how it had chipped.

"You okay?" asked Jones, coming up behind her.

"Yeah," she said, showing him her finger. He lifted it to his mouth and gave it a little kiss. Then he finished loading the dishes in the dishwasher as she pressed a dry napkin against the cut until the bleeding stopped. She wiped the countertop with a tattered old dishrag that needed replacing, passing it quickly over the appliances, too, just like she would have had to do in her mother's home. *Keep on top of the surfaces and your house will always look clean,* her mother would say. Upstairs, Ricky's music had stopped. He'd never come down for dinner, and Jones had told her to leave him alone, let him sulk it out—whatever it was.

"Maybe we'll get lucky and Charlene dumped him," Jones said, starting the dishwasher.

"Jones."

"Well?"

He poured them each a glass of red wine, the merlot they'd opened last night, and she followed him out to the deck, even though she thought it was too cold to sit outside. She didn't like to miss their ritual if she could help it. Maybe it was the wine, or the semidark in which they sat, but in recent years, this place after dinner was where he was most open, most relaxed. Later, the television would go on and he'd blank out. Maybe she'd sit beside him and watch whatever he had on— usually something on the Discovery or History Channel; he wasn't into sports, didn't like other television shows, or even movies for that matter. Or maybe she'd go to bed and read or maybe, if she had a lot of paperwork, back to her office.

She'd told him about Marshall over dinner, the scene in her office, how he'd appeared across the street. She'd mentioned Travis as well, his new business endeavor.

"As if anyone in this town would hire Travis Crosby," said Jones. "You'd have to be the biggest moron alive to bring that guy into your business."

Her husband had always disliked Travis, though she remembered that in high school they'd played on the lacrosse team together, been occasional friends. They'd both joined the police department in the same year, Travis staying on the street, Jones moving over to the small detective division and eventually rising to head detective, a post he'd held for ten years.

Travis had been pulled over on the interstate, driving the wrong way at more than eighty miles an hour, blood alcohol over 0.2, his service revolver exposed on the seat beside him. Had he been in The Hollows, the incident would have been swept aside. But he was unlucky enough to run into a state trooper. It was his third offense in a decade, and this meant mandatory jail time, as well as the loss of his job.

"I don't know if that guy is more dangerous on or off the job. But I guess we'll see soon enough," said Jones.

"I'm worried about Marshall."

"You do what you can for him, Mags. But keep your distance. You're his doctor, not his friend. It's a professional relationship."

He was right, but she still bristled at the comment. She quashed the urge to snap at him. *You think I don't know how to keep a professional distance?* But after the fight last night, she was weary of angry words. It had started with Ricky about the tattoo, then morphed into something larger between the two of them. It was the old argument about how he was too hard and she was too easy, how she always took Ricky's side and he was always the bad guy. Thinking about it, she couldn't even remember who said what, the memory was just an angry blur, like a landscape seen through the window of a car driving too fast. They'd been up late arguing and finally come to grudging peace before bed. She didn't want another night like that.

He put a hand on her arm. "Don't be mad," he said. "I know you care about your patients. I just need you to protect yourself, too."

Her annoyance dissolved instantly. "I know," she said. "You're right."

She knew where the professional line was in terms of behavior, of course. But she didn't seem to have a stopgap internally, didn't always know when or how to stop caring on a personal level. It left her feeling drained sometimes, though she was better at protecting herself than she had been when she was younger.

"What about you?" she asked. She shifted in her seat, thinking the cushions were getting stiff and needed replacing. "Are you doing okay?"

There were leaves floating in the pool. They'd need to have someone out to clean and winterize, cover it for the season. Every autumn, she thought about her private promise to swim laps every day in the summer, enjoy the pool more on the weekends. And at the end of every season, she looked back with regret, thinking she could count on the fingers of one hand the times she'd done either.

"I'm just tired," he said. "Just really tired."

In the dim light, she watched him. He had his head back on the chair, looking up at the stars. She could already tell by the set of his jaw, the way his arms were folded across his body, that he wouldn't say more. She drained her glass and thought about another, then noticed that the cut on her finger had started to bleed again.

She got up to bandage it, and when she returned, Jones had already gone inside. She found him lying on the couch, the remote in his hand.

"Want to watch anything?" he asked. But she knew he'd just flip through the channels until he found something that interested him.

"No," she said. "Maybe I'll just catch up on some paperwork."

But he was already tuned out, just gave her a little nod. She stood in the doorway a minute, watched him settle in. She went upstairs and listened at Ricky's door, heard him singing along to something on his headphones. She worried that he hadn't eaten but figured he'd know there was pizza downstairs when he got hungry. Then she drifted back to her office, unlocking that door, moving through quietly, and closing it behind her.

Their house was *always* dark, not like at Leila and Mark's, where every light was always shining and there was a television going in one room, a radio playing in another. Everyone was always talking, yelling from room to room, his cousins were in and out, chatting on the phone, speaking in loud voices, laughing, arguing, goofing around.

Boys, *please*, Leila's eternal plea. The *noise*. But she never really sounded angry, not in the way he was used to. Even when she was scolding, she always seemed on the verge of laughing.

The refrigerator was always full to bursting; there was always something simmering on the stove. There was no room for dark or quiet or cold in that house.

"It's a three-ring circus over there," his father complained. "How did you stand it?"

"The circus is *fun*, Dad. People laugh and have a good time." He'd tried that good-natured joking around that was acceptable at his aunt's house. But it didn't work with his dad.

"The circus is for idiots." His father's words had the sting of a hard slap. Then, as if the slag weren't already implied, "You must have felt right at home."

Marshall *had* felt right at home. He really had. But when the judge had asked him where he wanted to live, he'd said, "I want to be with my dad." And he *had* wanted that.

"Why, Son?" the judge had asked with something like disbelief. He remembered that office, overwarm and dusty. The judge sat behind a giant wood desk that Marshall would swear was designed to make people on the other side feel small. The shelves were lined with books, matching leather-bound volumes. He remembered that a few years ago, this judge who looked so imposing now in his big black robe had slept on their couch, too drunk to drive home after a poker game. "Why would you want that?"

"Because he's my dad."

It was all Marshall could think to say. There was something deep within him that clung, held on tight. Even when he hated his father— and sometimes he really, really did—there was still a part of him that waited like a puppy for a bone. Anything—a smile, a pat on the shoulder. Anything.

Now he heard his father hammering in the basement. He flipped on the fluorescent light in the kitchen and walked over to the refrigerator. There were some dishes in the sink; the garbage was starting to smell. In the fridge, a six-pack of Miller Lite and the leftover Chinese takeout from last night sat lonely and uninviting. He let the door swing closed, then reluctantly walked down the hall and descended the stairs to the basement.

"You're late," his father said. Marshall sank onto the bottom step, wrapped his arms around his shins.

"Sorry."

His father didn't look up from what he was doing. "Where were you?"

Marshall didn't answer. Travis let the hammer drop and turned his gaze on his son. Something about the look on his father's face, and the hammer in his hand, made Marshall's heart beat fast, his throat go dry.

"I told you to stop going there," Travis said.

"I told her," said Marshall quickly. "I told her I didn't want her in my head anymore."

Even saying it now, remembering how she'd looked at him, he felt sick. He didn't tell his father how he'd hung around her house for hours, almost went to see her to apologize, then ran off when she came out and spotted him, too afraid, ashamed, confused to say what he wanted to say. All the words and emotions jammed up in his throat and his chest. All he could think to do was run.

Travis gave his son a nasty smile. "And what did she say to that?"

"She said it was my choice to come or not."

"Damn right it is," said Travis. He went back to his hammering, a slow lift and a heavy drop.

He was building shelves for his office. His father had a talent for things like that. The walls were painted, the new carpet laid. The office was starting to look good. They'd put together his desk, bought a computer on credit. They'd had a phone line installed and ordered a plaque: TRAVIS CROSBY INVESTIGATIONS. He was proud that he'd helped his father, even if Dr. Cooper didn't seem overly impressed. What did she know?

"So where were you all this time?"

"I went to see this girl I know."

"Oh, yeah?" Travis looked up at him, a crooked smile on his face. There was a shade of shared mischief there, the slightest hint of approval.

"And?"

"And we hung out. I took her for a ride in the car. She had to go home; she's got a strict mother."

"Is she a slut or a good girl?"

Marshall let out a little laugh at that. "I don't know," he said. He felt the heat rise to his face.

Travis gave him a look. "That was a trick question, Son. They're all sluts."

Now it was Travis's turn to laugh; it sounded more like a cough. Marshall looked down at the toes of his combat boots, which he'd bought from the army-navy shop in town. He had that feeling he always had with his father, like he'd failed a test he didn't know he was taking. No matter what answer he gave, it always seemed to be the wrong one.

"At least you're seeing a girl in the flesh instead of living your life on that box upstairs." His father meant the computer. Why he insisted on calling it a box, as if he didn't know what it was or what it did, was beyond Marshall. His dad wasn't *that* old.

"I didn't hear you complaining when we hacked into Mom's Facebook account," said Marshall. He brought this up as often as possible because it always made his father smile.

Predictably, Travis let out a laugh at the memory. "That *was* pretty cool. Did she ever figure it out?"

"Nah. But she's not seeing that guy anymore."

Marshall had a gift for figuring out passwords. It really wasn't that hard; most people were pretty lazy, wanted something easy to remember and then used that same password for everything. He knew his mother's password for the wireless router at her place was his name and the year of his birth. Marshall figured it was probably the same for Facebook, and he was right. Last week, he and his dad had logged in to her account and left a wall message on her boyfriend's page: I don't want to see you anymore. Your dick is too small. You've never satisfied me.

Marshall hadn't seen or called his mother since then. If his mother suspected him of hacking into her account, she didn't get in touch to say so. Marshall noticed that she'd "unfriended" the loser she'd been dating, and that her boyfriend (now *ex-boyfriend*) had done the same to her. Mission accomplished.

Josh, Amber's boyfriend, had been equally easy. His nickname on the football team was All-Star. Marshall guessed that was his password, and, again, he was right. Now the school was buzzing with Josh and Amber's breakup. But, of course, she still didn't seem that interested in Marshall, not even with the cool car and smokes. In fact, she'd practically run away from him.

His father went back to his hammering. It took Marshall a minute to realize that whatever nail Travis had been hammering was already sunk deep into the wood. Why was he still hitting it like that? Marshall stood and started to move back up the stairs.

Marshall didn't have a lot of good memories of his father. Dr. Cooper had asked him to think of some moments when he'd felt happy and safe with his dad. He wasn't sure what the point of that exercise had been, unless it was to make him feel more like shit than he already did. But he did come up with two occasions.

There was the time they went to the zoo together and his father had bought him an ice cream. He remembered that because it was his own cone; he didn't have to share it. They'd seen some tigers. His father had said, "Man, they're beautiful, aren't they?" Marshall remembered looking at his father's face and seeing something strange there—maybe it was awe. Travis had dropped an arm around Marshall's shoulder and squeezed him tight. Marshall remembered that his happiness had felt like a swelling in his chest.

Once, Travis took him to the beach. Neither of them had been wearing bathing suits, so they swam with their pants on. They'd jumped huge waves and laughed when they wiped out. They'd driven home wet and shivering, ordered a pizza, and watched a game afterward.

Also, it was always safe to be around Travis when he was busy building something. His temper didn't flare when he had his mind on a project, or when he was having a good time doing something. It was places like the dinner table or the couch that should be avoided, anytime Travis was idle and looking for someplace to direct his attention.

"Need some help?" Marshall asked.

His father shot him a look, a kind of up-and-down appraisal, ending in a sneer of disapproval. "An hour ago maybe. But not now."

Marshall stood for a moment, watching his father's thick arm lift and drop with the hammer. He wanted to say, *Dad. You got it. You can stop hammering.* But he didn't. Then, when it was clear his father didn't intend to look up again, Marshall turned and shuffled back up the stairs. He took the sack of egg rolls from the fridge, threw it in the microwave for a few seconds, and carried it upstairs.

Marshall closed the door to his room and waded through the junk on the floor—gaming magazines, clothes that needed washing. He accidentally kicked an empty Coke can, and it rattled under the bed. He sank into the tattered gray computer chair in front of his homemade desk—two planks of wood balanced between stacked red milk crates. The familiar sense of relief washed over him as the screen came to life and he entered his password.

Online it was all different. *He* was different. He could visit with people who wouldn't give him a second glance in real life. Like Charlene Murray. He logged in to Facebook and checked his in-box. It was predictably empty, though sometimes he heard from a girl named Maya, whom he'd met in a science fiction chat group on AOL last year. She had an impressive knowledge of the genre, but she used a picture of Hello Kitty as her image on all the social networks, which meant she was probably ugly or fat. Still, he enjoyed talking to her and was disappointed that she hadn't answered his last message.

He went straight to Charlene's page, as he always did, checking first for any new photos of her. Then he checked his status updates; there was nothing new. He reread the only message she'd ever sent him personally, after he'd added her as a friend and she'd accepted. Hey, Marshall! Thanks for the friendship. See you at the Nook on Friday?

He'd thought it was a personal invitation until he realized that her band was playing at the club that catered to the underage set, serving sodas and junk food rather than booze. She'd sent that message to everyone. Still, wasn't there something about the message she sent to him that was different? He thought so, though he couldn't say what.

You just have to talk to her, man. Get to know her, let her get to know you. That's all it is. Girls just want to talk. Sage advice from his cousin Tim. And it was good advice—if you were six feet tall, as blond and buff as a surfer, and every girl who met you fell instantly in love, if all you had to do was *choose.* But that was definitely not the case for Marshall. He was the kind of guy who disappeared in a crowd, the one you never thought about, who never said a word. Sometimes when he looked in the mirror, he almost felt like he couldn't even see himself. He could focus on certain things—his mousy hair, the acne on his skin, his thin arms and undeveloped pecs. But he couldn't get a sense of how all the separate parts of himself fit together.

When you work out, Ryan told him, *you get a better sense of your body. You'll get to know yourself better.* And when he'd been at Leila's, Marshall used to work out with them in the makeshift gym in the basement—they had free weights and an exercise bike, a weight bench and a sit-up plank. They told him what to do and he did it, though he had to admit he did not get off on the physical effort the way they seemed to. After working out, Ryan and Tim were pumped with adrenaline, ready and raring to go. Marshall just felt like lying down. Since he'd been back with his father, he hadn't even gone for a run. Any gains he'd made during his time with his cousins had quickly faded.

He looked in Charlene's notes for some new lyrics or poetry.

> *There's a secret place where we can be free*
> *Where the world will close its eyes to us*
> *And we can be*
> *Like the womb or the tomb*
> *We are alone . . . together*
> *It is a beginning and an end.*

He quickly went to her wall and left a note: Love the new lyrics, Char. You're so talented.

If he tried to say anything like that to her in person, he'd go red in the face, maybe even start to cough, make a total dork out of himself. But here he could comment on her updates, tell her what he thought about music and movies he knew she liked. She never answered him, but it was enough to know she was reading the things he wrote on her wall.

Last week he wrote to tell her about the car his dad had given him. "Lemme know if u ever need a lift!" He didn't tell her that it was his father's car and the only reason he'd given it to Marshall was that he wasn't allowed to drive for six more months as part of his parole. So Marshall had basically become his chauffeur, driving him everywhere even when he should have been in school.

But when he'd seen Charlene in the parking lot the last time he'd been to school, she'd called out to him, *Hey, Marshall, nice ride!*

He'd given her a wave, and she'd waved back. He understood that communication to mean that even if she wasn't writing back, she cared about the things he wrote. So he rushed to respond to every update, new photo, or note. Even though they barely exchanged a word—she'd wave as they passed in the hallway or smile when she saw him in the cafeteria— he *knew* her. He knew what she was thinking (Charlene is so sad today . . . for no good reason), reading (Charlene is loving the Twilight series!), when she was going to the mall (Charlene is meeting Brit @ the mall @ 2!!). He knew when the band was playing at a party, or when she was fighting with her mother. She posted all her new lyrics and poetry, and Marshall felt that this gave him a direct window into her soul. He *knew* Charlene Murray, maybe better than most because he could read between the lines. He thought maybe he knew her better than she knew herself.

"I went to high school with her mother."

Marshall swiveled around in his chair to see his father filling the doorway. He felt the skin on his face go hot, his stomach bottom out. He hated it when his father came into his room. It was a colliding of selves. He was a different person with his father than he was in here; these two parts of himself did not mingle.

"She was a whore," Travis said.

"Charlene's not," Marshall said quickly.

"No?" Travis walked over to stand beside Marshall, stared down at the screen. "I got news for you, Son. They're *all* whores."

Did he ever have anything new to say about women? It was pathetic. Travis had basically delivered the same wisdom downstairs. Still, Marshall felt the familiar internal storm—a sickening combination of anger and fear, a desire to connect, to agree and see his father smile in approval, and an equally strong desire to get away.

Now that Marshall was nearly the same height and almost as strong as his father, Travis didn't hit him often; Marshall wasn't physically afraid of his father. It was the things he said that lay like bruises on Marshall's skin, damaged his organs, poisoned his blood. That voice was in his head all the time. He just couldn't get it out. Even the competing voices—Aunt Leila, Mr. Ivy, Dr. Cooper—weren't loud enough to drown him out lately.

"She's a good person," he said quietly, turning away to look at her picture. She looked nice, not so much black makeup, smiling brightly.

"That's what I used to think about your mother. Of course, that was before I understood women. You'll learn the hard way. Like we all do."

Travis, chuckling now, started moving toward the door. Marshall knew he should just let him go. Travis already had a beer in his hand. If he sat down in front of the television, he'd drink until he fell asleep. And if his father slept in tomorrow, maybe Marshall could make it to school before his dad decided he needed a ride somewhere. But something dark within Marshall wouldn't allow his father to walk away.

"Dr. Cooper says that just because Mom has a new boyfriend, that doesn't make her a whore."

Travis stopped in the doorway and turned around. He had that dead, mean look on his face, those flat eyes.

Marshall felt the urge to rush to Maggie's defense; he didn't want to hear his father call her a whore, too.

"She's a good person," he said, realizing too late that he was repeating what he'd said a second ago about Charlene.

"She's a good person. She's a good person," Travis mimicked nastily. "If they were any good, Son? Trust me. They wouldn't want anything to do with you."

The words landed like a spray of acid, corrosive, burning through his skin. Anger deserted him, replaced with a tide of shame. Marshall felt his voice grow small inside his chest, a powerlessness settle over him. He was shrinking. He braced himself for a verbal battering, but instead his father deflated in the doorway. His eyes took on a kind of glassy quality, and he seemed lost in looking at something high above Marshall's head. Then he turned and walked away. Marshall didn't even feel strong enough to hate him.

He turned back to the screen and was surprised to see he had a new message. When he saw that it was from Charlene, he almost couldn't believe his eyes.

`Hey, Marshall,` it read. `Are you still good for that ride? Can you meet me on Persimmon and Hydrangea?`

When Charlie awoke, there was a moment before he remembered where he was and how he'd gotten there. He was aware of the sick pounding behind his eyes that came when he drank too much red wine. Then he was aware of the soft, clean bedding, so unlike the dirty, tangled mess he slept in at home. And then there was the measured breathing of a woman sleeping beside him. Slowly, the dawning, the memory of

the evening, crept into his consciousness. This would usually be the moment when he rooted around on the floor for his clothes, crept naked
from the bedroom, dressed hastily in the hallway, bathroom, living
room—wherever—and got out as fast as possible.

But he didn't feel the urge to do that. He turned instead to look at
her, the lines of her. The round of her shoulder, the swell of her hip beneath the sheet, the curl of her fingers and hollow of her palm resting on
the pillow beside her face. Oh, she was pretty, in a real way. She didn't
need to dye her hair or wear so much makeup. She didn't have the kind
of beauty that washed off, got stale, smeared on the pillow. She had
peaches-and-cream skin and washed-denim, kitty-shaped eyes. Maybe
in the first blush of youth she'd been a killer, a bombshell. But age had
revealed the mettle of her beauty; it would not fade with time.

Her breath smelled of peppermint, which told him that she'd gotten
up to brush her teeth after he'd drifted off. There was something about
that, something nice.

*There's something about you, Charlie. I always feel like I'm going to show
up for work one day and you'll be gone. You'll have gotten on to that thing
you've been meaning to do all the while you were doing this. Every day I see
you, I'm a little surprised. You know what I mean?*

She'd said it with a certain kind of wistful sadness that touched him,
that flattered him. He liked that she saw him this way.

I do know what you mean, Wanda.

So what is it? What is this thing you've been meaning to do?

I write. He looked down and cleared his throat. It was embarrassing,
as though he was in love with a movie star, or hoping to summit Everest.
I'm a writer.

When he looked back at her, she was smiling. Not laughing, not
giving him that *Good luck, don't quit your day job* derisive kind
of smirk.

I knew it, she said. *I knew it.*

He felt something shift inside him, something move and start to
grow. The look on her face made him want to be what she clearly
thought he was, someone with a secret talent, someone who was marking time until he got his big break.

In her sleep, she shifted closer to him. His bladder ached. He held it awhile, not wanting to break the spell of lying there beside her. But eventually, nature would not be denied. He moved quietly to the small bathroom. When he shut the door and turned on the light, he was greeted with his reflection in a full-length mirror. He was shocked by how bad he looked, how pasty and out of shape.

He could have lived with fat. You had a passion for food, you got big because of it. Whatever. He, on the other hand, took no enjoyment whatsoever from the garbage he habitually ate—bags of chips and tubs of soda, all manner of fast food, Taco Bell and McDonald's most often, Burger King in a pinch. And his physiology didn't allow him to get fat exactly—not big and round, not pink and portly. His torso looked like a spent white pillar candle, flesh drooping. In the light he appeared as underdeveloped as an adolescent, very little muscle tone, even in his chest or arms. He doubted he could run a mile, bench-press a hundred pounds.

In clothes, he looked okay. But naked, he could barely stand the sight of himself. A body in utter neglect. He looked away, turned on the water for privacy, and emptied his bladder into a spotlessly clean white toilet. At least he had a fairly decent-size schlong. Wanda hadn't seemed to notice his other failings, though she'd kept the lights low.

Lots of flowers everywhere in Wanda's house. On the shower curtain, a kind of retro floral print in pink and brown, matching rugs, towels, and accessories—soap dish, tissue box cover. Downstairs, he'd noticed it, too, when they drank wine on her couch. Everything was nicely put together, cozy throws and plush pillows, all coordinating. Not expensive things, but the kind of stuff you would get at Target. Her place was cute, with some thought behind it. She was a woman with style but a limited budget. He noticed these things, the kinds of things other men missed. The details told the story, revealed the person. The way she hung up her coat rather than throw it on the couch. How there was a little shelf on the table in the foyer where she put her purse. The way she didn't check her messages, even though the light was blinking. How everything was orderly, had a place, how her dishes and glasses all matched.

His mother had never been much of a homemaker, and his place was an afterthought. It wasn't a hovel or a pigsty; he was fairly tidy, cleaned occasionally. But Wanda seemed to devote a lot of energy to her home. He liked that she cared about herself, about where she lived. This was a good thing.

He quietly opened the medicine cabinet and found neat little rows of nail polish, shades of pink and red, a couple of tiny sample tubes of various moisturizers, a little jar of cotton balls, a bottle of aspirin, some pain-relief ointment, a plastic box of Q-tips. It was all so clean, so precise. Everything was carefully placed, labels facing out. Something about the colors of everything made him think of a candy shop. He'd done this before, opened medicine cabinets—in the homes of his clients, or women he'd slept with. The contents never failed to turn him off. He'd find all manner of remedies—antifungal cream, depilatories, hemorrhoid pads, sedatives, old, twisted tubes of unidentified lotions. Medicine cabinets, places where people were confident no strangers would ever enter, could be very telling. He wouldn't go so far as to say that the medicine cabinet was an allegory for the soul. But when he found things dirty, disorganized, the little shelves packed with expired medications and leaking containers, it made him wonder about the owner, what his or her inner life was like. His own medicine cabinet was a virtual biohazard—God only knew what was in there.

He heard something outside, a whisper. Quietly, he closed the door. Then he washed his hands, turned off the water, and shut the lights. He stepped back into the bedroom.

"When I woke up, for a minute, I thought you were gone."

"I'm still here," he said, standing by the bed. "Do you want me to go?"

"No," she said. "Don't." She patted the bed beside her, and he climbed back in beside the heat of her body, pulled her to him. She moved to him easily and wrapped her arms around him. Then his mouth was on hers; he felt the soft press of her breasts against his chest, grew hard and hungry for her again. His whole body shuddered when she climbed on top of him and then lowered herself onto him, began moving in slow, deep circles.

Watching her, the fullness of her breasts, the halo of her hair, he thought, *How did I get this lucky? This pretty, kind woman, so sweet and smart, seems to actually like me.* He took her breast in his mouth, and she released a throaty groan, a sound that rocketed through him, so nakedly did it reveal her pleasure. She seemed to him a gem in a jewelry store window. Somehow she'd been overlooked, her value diminished by the time she'd remained on display. He wanted to secret her away, claim her, before she realized her true worth and shunned the meager things he could offer her.

Later, she slept and he lay beside her charged with energy, filled with something he almost didn't recognize, it had been so long. Inspiration. Unable to drift off again, he pulled on his underwear and traveled downstairs, wandered into the kitchen and got himself a glass of water from the tap. He felt at home, as comfortable as if they'd been dating awhile and this was his regular habit. He wandered out the front door and sat on one of the cushioned chairs on the large veranda. It was way too cold to be outside mostly naked, but he didn't care. He was a furnace; the cold air made his skin tingle. He felt alive. A wind chime hanging by the door. Tiny bells. A rustling of leaves.

Then, some movement across the street caught his eye. There was a girl, with spiky hot pink and black hair a riot on top of her head, carrying a backpack. She stood beside some old muscle car with a faded green paint job. He could hear the powerful rumble of its engine.

He could see the pale skin of her neck, the top of her head. Her face was obscured by the landscaping surrounding the veranda.

She seemed to be talking to the driver. Curiosity lifted Charlie from his seat and brought him to the railing. Her voice carried across the street, but the words were lost in a wind that picked up and set the chimes to singing again.

He could see her face now. She was young, pretty—she didn't look afraid or angry, maybe a little sad. A fight with her boyfriend, he guessed. The poor guy was probably sitting in the car, begging her to get back inside. Charlie watched as the girl looked up and down the street uncertainly, then climbed inside the vehicle. He didn't know what time it was. Too late for a young girl to be out with her boyfriend, he thought. Of course, he'd have thought differently when he was sixteen or seventeen.

As the car disappeared up the street, he went back into the house. Wanda was sitting on the couch in his shirt, drinking a glass of water.

"You okay?" she asked with a little frown. "It's cold to be outside in your undies."

He patted his belly self-consciously and gave a self-deprecating laugh. "Lots of insulation," he said. She gave him a flirty glance under her lashes and a quick shake of her head. "You look good to me, cowboy."

He sat beside her, and she moved into him—so easy, so familiar. He dropped his arm around her shoulder. "To answer your question, I'm great, Wanda. I'm better than I've been in ages."

She gazed up at him and smiled wide. "Me, too."

In a moment, they were at it again—glass on the table, shirt on the floor. Just before he lost himself in another earthquake with Wanda, he noticed the time: 11:33.

8

There was something about the thumping that communicated to her, through deep layers of sleep, a sense of alarm. Even as she swam through the locks of consciousness, she felt the dawn of panic. A knowing. When she emerged into wakefulness, Jones was already up and pulling on the pants he'd left lying on the floor. The window was open, and the air had grown frigid.

"What is it?" she asked.

"Someone at the door."

They were parents. Jones was a cop, Maggie a psychologist. They were accustomed to interrupted sleep, the phone ringing at all hours. But this felt different. It was the door, not the phone, first of all. But more than that, the knocking was frantic, not measured and authoritative, as it would be had someone from the department needed to rouse Jones, unable for whatever reason to reach him on his cell or home phone.

Jones was out the bedroom door before Maggie had climbed from beneath the covers. As she was pulling on a sweater over her T-shirt, retrieving a pair of jeans from the floor, she heard him moving down the stairs.

"I'm coming. Take it easy," he called. Jones was not a man happily roused from sleep. He woke up like an ogre, cranky and groggy. This had better be good, or she felt sorry for whoever was at the door.

Before she followed him downstairs, her first instinct was to look in on her son. She pushed open the door to his bedroom and saw his sleep-

ing form sprawled on the bed, one long leg dangling off the side. He was
snoring deeply, had his headphones on.

She could hear the tinny sound of music carrying on the air; she saw
the undulating red and green lights on the stereo system beside his bed.
There was a surreal quiet to the moment. When she looked back on it,
she'd remember a kind of hum in the air. It was the last safe place. The
last moment when she could fool herself that any of them had a grip on
anything in this world.

After she'd closed Ricky's door and headed down the stairs, she
heard a woman's voice, talking fast, shrill with nerves.

"Is my daughter here? I've been trying to call. The line's been busy
for hours." Maggie heard an agitated laugh. "I never understood people
who take their phone off the hook."

Charlene's mother, Melody Murray, was a wreck—her blond hair
with dark black roots in a tousle, circles under her eyes, no makeup. Her
face was long with worry.

"Come inside," Maggie said. She reached the bottom of the
stairs and pushed past Jones to put her hand on the woman's shoulder.
Jones had been holding her at the door, almost seemed to have been
blocking her way with an arm, the door itself opened just a foot or two.
Melody looked behind her; she'd left her car running. Exhaust came
out in great plumes, glowing and strange in the red of the parking
lights.

"We fought," she said. "Charlene left, and I just assumed she
came here."

There was a flatness to her voice suddenly that didn't connect with
the frightened look in her eyes.

"When was the last time you saw her?" Jones asked. Maggie stepped
out onto the porch to stand beside Melody. The stone was cold beneath
her bare feet.

"She left the house around six, I think?" Melody used that question-
ing tone that seemed to be so popular with teenagers and sociopaths. It
was a tone that begged permission, understanding, elicited a nod of ver-
ification.

"We fought," she said again. Melody brought her thumb to her mouth and started chewing.

"What about?" Jones asked. Maggie read the expression on his face, his tone—disdain, suspicion. He didn't like Melody Murray, never had. Maggie suspected that was a big reason why he didn't like Charlene.

Melody seemed startled by the question, as if she'd forgotten that Jones was a cop, that by coming here she was essentially reporting her daughter missing.

"Melody, come inside," Maggie said. "Jones will turn off your car."

She gave her husband a look. He opened his mouth to say something, then clamped it shut. Then he obeyed like a good husband. As she escorted Melody inside, Maggie saw Jones take the cell phone from the pocket of his jeans while he moved toward the drive; he must have grabbed it when he got up, cop that he was. He was calling it in, a missing girl. Whether she was at a friend's house or had done something stupid like try to run away, she was, at the moment, a missing minor. Maggie suppressed a shudder.

"This is a nice house," Melody said, looking around. When Maggie glanced around her own home, all she could see were the flaws—the hairline crack in the ceiling, baseboards that needed dusting, the soda stain on the couch.

"Thanks," she said. "Come on in and have a seat."

With a hand on Melody's shoulder, Maggie led her down the hall to the living room. About halfway there, Melody stopped and turned around.

"Is she? Is she here?" Melody asked. She stared at Maggie with naked hope. In a formless long gray sweater and baggy sweatpants, Melody seemed waiflike and lost.

"No, she's not, Melody. I just checked Ricky's room before I came down. He's alone, asleep."

The woman visibly shrank, her shoulders sagging forward, her head dropping. "Oh, God. Where is she?" Maggie heard the anguish; it was a pitch that any mother would recognize, the acknowledgment that a thousand imagined horrors had shifted into the realm of possibility. Maggie felt the first finger of real fear poke her in the belly.

"What's going on?" Ricky stood bleary-eyed behind her. Jones walked back in the front door. He towered behind their son, hands on his hips. Jones's thick build and sunshine blond hair contrasted with Ricky's inky spikes and his lean, loping frame. Physically, they were opposites. But they both wore the same furrow in their brows.

Melody rose, pushed past Maggie, and ran to Ricky. "Where is she, Rick? Where did she go?"

Ricky shook his head. "Who?" he said. "Char? What do you mean?"

"Is she upstairs?" asked Jones.

Ricky turned to look at his father. When he answered, he sounded petulant and angry. "No."

"She's not," Maggie confirmed. "I checked his room before I came downstairs. She's not up there."

Jones seemed to debate a moment, ran a hand over his hair. Then he turned and went upstairs anyway.

"He doesn't believe me?" Ricky said, looking at Maggie.

"He's just checking."

Jones obviously didn't believe her, either, she thought with a rush of annoyance. They heard him pounding around upstairs. Then, a moment later, he returned with the cordless phone from Ricky's room in his hand.

"Why did you have the phone off the hook in your room?" he asked. He held it up to his son.

"I don't know." Ricky rubbed his eyes. "I was trying to reach Charlene. I must have fallen asleep without hanging it up. I don't know."

"Did you see her tonight?" Jones asked. He sounded more like a cop than a father, someone ready to believe the worst before anything had even happened.

"No. She stood me up. I was supposed to meet her at seven at Pop's."

"Oh, God," said Melody.

"Does she have access to a vehicle?" asked Jones. He turned to Melody.

"No," she said, issuing a sob. She covered her mouth with her hand. "Then she left on foot."

Melody nodded, and Maggie led her to the couch.

"Did you follow her out?" Jones asked. He trailed behind them. "When she left, did you see which way she walked?"

Melody shook her head again, sank down into the suede cushions. She grabbed one of the soft throw pillows and clutched it to her middle.

"Okay," said Maggie. "Let's all try to be calm a minute, think about this. If she was on foot, would she have gone to a neighbor's house, a friend nearby?"

"I've called everyone. No one's seen her."

"Could she have used her cell phone to call someone, to have someone pick her up?" Maggie glanced up at Ricky. He looked at some point above her, his mouth slack and eyes wide. Who else would Charlene call but her boyfriend? She'd called him before when Graham and Melody were going at it. He'd told Maggie as much.

"She doesn't have a cell phone," said Melody.

But she did. Maggie had seen it, even had the number programmed into her own phone. She looked over at her son again; now he was staring at the floor. Did he know where Charlene was? She remembered him storming in, locking himself in his room, blasting the music. The phone was off the hook in his room. He looked up to see her watching him, and quickly cast his eyes away.

"She does have a cell phone, Melody," Maggie said. She walked to the kitchen and took her phone from its charger. She scrolled through the numbers until she found it.

"Ricky," Maggie said. "Call Charlene from the home phone right now."

"I've been trying all night," he said.

"Try again," said Jones. He handed Ricky the cordless unit that he'd been holding, and the boy dialed.

"Put it on speakerphone," said Jones, and Ricky obliged with a sullen glance at his father. The call went straight to voice mail. "This is

Char. Leave a message—or don't. What do I care?" Then a heavy strain of punk rock blasted out. Ricky looked around self-consciously.

"Uh, Char, it's me. Where are you? Your mom is here. Everyone's pretty worried. Call me back."

He ended the call and kept his eyes on the phone in his hand.

"If you did't get that phone for her, Melody, where did she get it? She doesn't have a job, right?" asked Jones.

Melody seemed distracted; she was staring out the window into the backyard.

"I don't know," she said. Her voice sounded weak and small.

They all looked at Ricky.

"How should I know?" he said, lifting his palms. "Everyone has a cell phone. I figured her mom got it for her."

"You need a credit card to open a mobile account," said Jones. Maggie waited for him to go on, but he was already walking off, his own cell phone in his hand. He turned back.

"I need that number," he said to her.

Maggie handed him her phone with Charlene's number still on the screen. He took it and walked off again. She heard him giving the number to someone on the other end. A few moments later, there was a knock at the door, then male voices in the foyer.

"Who would she have called other than you, Rick?" Maggie asked.

He gave a slow shrug. "I don't know. Maybe Britney?"

Melody shook her head vigorously. "No. I already called."

Maggie watched Ricky stare at the ground, shifting from foot to foot. Melody had a shine to her eyes. Jones stood grim-faced in the entrance to the living room, two uniformed officers behind him. Thinking purely as a professional, Maggie thought each of them was off pitch. Melody was too unhinged, considering Charlene had run off in a safe neighborhood after a fight, not for the first time. Ricky was vacant, looking anyplace but into her eyes. Jones was stern and angry, when he should have been helpful and concerned. Even she felt oddly disconnected, floating above the scene. The tightness in her chest was the only sign of the fear and tension she felt.

She was suddenly aware of the ticking of the old grandfather clock in the foyer—a housewarming gift from her mother. She didn't even like it but found a general inertia when it came to getting rid of it. It had stood in its place, marking time, for more than a decade. As she walked to the closet, prepared to go out and look for Charlene herself, the clock issued a single chime, announcing the half hour. It was 11:30 P.M.

9

The watercolor sky—silver fading to blue fading to black, the high slice of moon and glimmering stars—reminded her that she'd always wanted to paint but didn't know how, was in some ways afraid of the idea of putting brush to canvas, of making a mark that couldn't be erased. The idea that she might create something that was laughable, pitiable, or silly had stopped her from ever taking a class or even buying paints. Foolish. It was foolish. If she had a patient tell her such a thing, she'd ask him why he would hold himself back from something that might give him pleasure and peace. Who constituted this imaginary audience of ridiculers and detractors? How might he defend his desire to create something beautiful just for himself? And what, just what exactly, was so horrifying about making such a harmless mistake as a mark on paper that couldn't be erased? But she didn't bother asking herself these questions. She just made false promises to herself. Years ago, she would tell herself that she'd have time when Ricky was older. Now it was when Ricky left for school, or when she and Jones retired.

Her father had been an artist. Her mother had an attic full of his oil paintings and watercolors—landscapes, portraits, still lifes. When Maggie was a girl, there had always been a work in progress on the easel he kept in the dining room, where he liked the light, the position of a mirror that gave him a different perspective.

In the evenings and on weekend afternoons, he'd stand there, fussing and musing over this detail and that. Sometimes she'd watch him. More often, she'd just walk past, knowing he saw little and heard less when he was engaged in a canvas. She could set the house on fire and he wouldn't notice until he was engulfed in flames, maybe not even then. As a teenager, she took full advantage of the freedom this absorption offered her. She didn't remember ever resenting it, or wishing for more attention.

Often, out in the garbage, she'd find a canvas her father had spent weeks working on—a beach scene, a stand of trees, an apple and vase placed just so on the table—discarded with the rest of the trash they generated. And when she did, she'd feel a rush of anxiety and sadness, have the urge to rescue the canvas, hide it in the attic—which she often did. She remembered thinking it was like throwing away time, time he'd have too little of anyway, time spent with his back to his wife and daughter. It wasn't even as if there was any joy or passion to it, not that she could see. Because, for her father, it was all about the end result, the precision, the skill, getting it right. And if it wasn't "right," it belonged in the trash, away from his exacting gaze. Art was about more than getting it right, wasn't it? And even though she knew it was, she couldn't bring herself to put a brush to canvas.

The air inside Maggie's Lincoln Navigator was thick with heat and tension. Melody gnawed at the skin on her thumb, stared straight ahead blankly. She'd been shivering when they climbed into the car, so Maggie had cranked the heat. Now there was a sheen of sweat on her brow. She reached to turn it down a bit, noticed that the dash had a thin layer of dust. She hated it when the car wasn't spotless. Jones's car was always filthy—soda spilled in the cup holders, crumbs in the creases of the seat, the reek of fast food. She didn't know how he could stand it.

Melody hadn't said a word since she listed off the names of friends Charlene might have run to, people she claimed to have called already. Tiffany Crowley, Britney Smith, Amber Schaffer. Maggie knew them all. Britney had struggled after her mother's second divorce and had spent a year seeing Maggie once a week, but was doing better now. Ricky had taken Tiffany to the movies once in junior high. Amber was a gifted child who'd been in all Ricky's advanced placement classes, whom she'd seen at various parties of Ricky's and parents' nights at school. A nice girl. More like the kind of girl she'd hoped to see Ricky dating.

Someone who would not be missing on a school night after a fight with her mother. She knew their mothers, too. They'd all attended Hollows High together.

Melody and Maggie had had an English class together as juniors in high school. Then, Melody was regarded as a burnout, someone who hung around the breezeway smoking. She wore her hair long, almost to her waist, and seemed to have an endless collection of rock concert tees. Someone who'd slept with a couple of the popular boys, was generally regarded as trashy but could still be found at all the cool parties, might be seen with one of the beefy, beautiful football players leaning against her locker. She'd lived in a rambling old house with her single mother, a hippie artist who everyone knew dealt weed on the side. Maggie remembered envying Melody a kind of freedom she seemed to have, a lack of concern about the opinions of others. She carried herself with a pride uncommon in teenage girls, as if she already knew who she was and didn't need to look about for validation. But somehow the years had robbed her of that. Now she wore her hair in a suburban, middle-aged bob and dressed without care in formless old sweaters and T-shirts, faded, tapered denims. Years of smoking had caused the skin on her face to crack and sag. The woman who sat before her seemed defeated by her life, withered and sick of it all. She bore no resemblance to the free spirit Maggie remembered.

"You're so lucky to have a boy," Melody said. "Can I smoke?"

Maggie nodded, pressed the button on the center console to lower Melody's window. She didn't mind the smell of smoke so much. It reminded her of other days, city nightclubs and bars, even her father hiding behind the toolshed sneaking a cigarette away from the watchful eyes of her mother. The smell of it made her oddly nostalgic, made her remember the time before she really understood the power of consequence, the fragility of the human body.

Melody rooted around in her purse, pulled out a pack of Marlboro Lights and a red lighter. She held the pack out to Maggie, who hesitated just a second before shaking her head.

"You used to smoke, once upon a time," Melody said. A slight, knowing smile turned up the corners of her thin lips. And Maggie saw her then, the girl that Melody had been.

"A long time ago," Maggie said. She found herself smiling, too, a little.

"You can always take it back up. Keeps you thin."

"No, thanks."

The comment made her feel a little self-conscious. Was it a dig? Her skirt *had* been a little tight when she buttoned it this morning. Extra weight always went to her bottom first. And she *always* gained during times of stress because she was a comfort eater. Although she wouldn't say she'd been stressed about anything in particular lately. She'd just been feeling edgy, out of sorts.

Melody took the pack back sullenly, tapped out a cigarette, and lit it in one practiced motion. The deep inhale, the crackle of paper and tobacco; Maggie could almost feel the smoke filling her lungs, the surge of nicotine in her blood. She almost changed her mind. Then she glanced over and thought that Melody looked like a witch in the glow of that cigarette. Her shoulders bony and hunched, hands gnarled, deep shadows on her face.

"So what did you and Charlene fight about, Melody?" she asked.

Melody exhaled a cloud of smoke, turned to look out the window. "This is it," she said. "This is Britney's house."

Maggie pulled into the large circular drive and killed the engine, was about to climb out when Melody said something she didn't quite hear.

"I'm sorry. What?" Maggie said.

"Do you remember her?"

"Who?"

"Sarah."

The name caused Maggie to draw in a sharp breath of surprise. She just stared at Melody, who was watching her closely. The cigarette was forgotten in the other woman's hand, the ash starting to dangle.

"Of course I do," Maggie answered.

"She was my best friend."

"I know that. Why are we talking about this now?"

"She had a fight with her mother on the phone. Remember? She missed the bus—again. Her mother was mad, thought she'd just been screwing around. She told Sarah to walk."

"It wasn't far," Maggie said. She could remember the narrow road that ran past the school. About half a mile down, a rural road intersected it and ran off into the woods. Sarah's house was back there, near Melody's. The Meyers had a big, beautiful home, different from the tract homes that characterized the developments at the time. Sarah's parents—her father a poet, her mother a painter—had designed the house, had it built. There was a long, winding, treacherous drive that was occasionally impassable in winter until the hired plow got to it.

On that day, Maggie remembered riding the late bus home after drama rehearsal and seeing Sarah along the side of the road, her backpack looking heavy. She was limping a little, as if one of her shoes hurt. It wasn't Sarah's bus, but the driver stopped all the same. It was getting late, the sun sinking fast below the horizon. The early spring air was still cold. There weren't many kids on the bus—a few boys from the science club, and one of the three Asian kids who attended the school.

"I can drop you off, Sarah. No problem," Maggie heard the driver say.

Maggie could make out Sarah's voice but not her words. Maggie saw her point at the road that was just a few feet away. Her house wasn't more than half a mile through the trees.

"All right. Watch yourself, you hear?"

And the bus hissed and lurched forward, leaving Sarah behind. Maggie looked back to see her turning off the main street and making her way toward the tall stand of trees. It seemed like a hundred years ago.

"Don't go there, Melody," Maggie said. "This is not the same."

"How do you *know*?" The other woman turned pleading eyes on Maggie. She seemed to remember the cigarette then, tossed it out the open window.

"Because it's not." Maggie couldn't think of anything more convincing to say. The fear on Melody's face was a contagion.

"Does Jones ever talk about it?" Melody said.

"Jones? No. Why would he?"

The other woman just shrugged and shook her head, glanced away from Maggie. Melody might have been about to say something, but the front door to Britney's house opened then, and her mother stepped onto the porch. Denise was as petite and pretty as she'd been in high school. Good genes, old money, married rich—twice. It showed. Even in velour sweatpants and bare feet, baggy pink sweatshirt, obviously roused from dozing on the couch, she was a perfect ten.

"What's going on? What's wrong?" she asked. She hugged herself against the cold.

"Is Charlene here?" Melody asked, stepping down out of the car.

Denise shook her head. "Not on a school night. Brit has a test first period. She's sleeping."

"Can we come in?" asked Maggie, walking up the steps to the porch. "I think we need to talk to Brit. Charlene is missing." There it was, the word spoken and out there, floating on the air. She regretted it, should have been more vague. She should have said something, anything, else. She couldn't take it back.

Denise looked stricken, moving back toward the house and pushing the door open. "Of course. Come in."

It didn't take long for tensions to build. The three of them—the pretty cheerleader, the sexy burnout too old, too knowing for her age, the geek with gothic leanings—they were all there, these representatives of the perennial high school subcultures, squirming and pink beneath the shells of their adulthoods. Maggie thought that childhood things would be left behind, these silly groupings would fade and become meaningless, but they never were. Not in a town like this. Those teenage girls, each awkward and unsure in her own way, never left The Hollows.

Brit stood sleepy before them now, every bit as beautiful as her mother. Maybe more so. Also with no trace of the high school angst and insecurity Maggie remembered so well. The girls of Ricky's gener-ation knew their power better, didn't seem to be casting about as much for approval and validation. Though, of course, Brit had her own set of problems, occasionally throwing up after bingeing, reacting to some terrible pressure she claimed she didn't really understand herself. *I'm not perfect,* she'd said to Maggie in a session. *That's what they think, but I am so far from that.*

"I have no idea where Char is. I'm sorry." She huddled in close to her mother, was half-hidden behind her. A protective posture.

"You didn't hear from her at all tonight?" asked Melody. "She didn't call to tell you she'd left home?"

Brit shook her head quickly.

"Brit," her mother urged, nudging her gently with a soft shoulder.

"What?" the girl snapped, moving away from Denise. "I don't know where she is." Denise hung her head and moved away, traced a circle on the floor with a perfectly pedicured toe.

Britney and Charlene were unlikely friends. Brit, the athlete scholar, not a cheerleader like her mother but a track star, the fastest girl Hol-lows High had ever seen, a record breaker, and one of three girls in a heated competition for the valedictorian spot. The girl before Maggie was a textbook overachiever.

And Charlene, the resident gothic queen, singer in Ricky's band, smart enough in her own right but not inclined to academic achieve-ment, pouring her energy into her music—she sang and wrote lyrics. She was a talented, intelligent girl, artistic and wise beyond her years but not cast from the same mold as Brit. They were as different as two girls could be but had been friends since the third grade.

"This is not the time to be protecting Charlene, Brit," Maggie said gently. "We know she's your friend. But this is serious. If you know her plans, or you know where she is, you need to tell us."

Brit released a sigh, lifted her eyes to the ceiling.

"Please," said Melody. "I know you guys think you're grown up, that you know everything. But she's just a girl. The world is not what you want it to be. It's an unforgiving and dangerous place. Some conse-quences are forever."

Maggie flashed on Sarah's lean form, a hundred years ago, walking into the tall, black woods, the sky a slate slab above her. From Melody's pleading tone, Maggie expected to see her tearing. But her face was grim, a stone mask of tension.

"Sometimes home is not a safe place, either," said Brit, looking pointedly back at the older woman.

Melody blinked and shook her head as though she'd been struck. "What is that supposed to mean?"

Britney narrowed her eyes. "You know."

The eruption was quick and fierce. Melody moved in to Britney, shouting something unintelligible, her face gone from stone to fire, flushing a hot red. Denise stepped forward to put her body between the two.

"Stay away from her, Melody," she said firmly. "Stand back."

When Maggie put her hands on Melody's arms and pulled her back, Melody began to sob. It started low, then turned to a wail. She doubled over with the force of it. It was a terrible sound, something that frightened Brit, caused her to go white, her face to go slack. The sound connected to a place in Maggie's center. Denise felt it, too, Maggie could tell. A mother's fear for her child. Denise moved to Melody and put her arms around the other woman, led her away.

"What was she afraid of at home, Britney?" Maggie asked. They were good with each other; she knew Brit trusted her, knew that Maggie understood and accepted who she was, flaws and all. *You're everything you need to be,* she'd told Britney in a session. *It's enough to just be who you are.*

Britney looked up at the ceiling, then back at Maggie. "She was afraid of Graham," she said.

Melody's wailing grew louder; Denise had taken her to the couch in the sunken living room off the foyer. *Calm down, Mel. It's okay. We'll find her. We'll find her.*

"How so?" Maggie asked. She was trying to be the measured and even one; but the stress of the situation was starting to get to her, too. "Did he hit her?"

Maggie remembered the shadow under Char's eye a few weeks back. She'd asked the girl about it, but Char had laughed it off. Hit her head on the faucet in the tub when she bent down to pick up a dropped bar of soap. Silly. Stupid, she'd said. It didn't ring true, but Maggie hadn't pushed. Charlene didn't present like an abused kid. Maggie knew Melody wasn't a perfect mother, and Graham Olstead wasn't anyone's idea of an ideal stepfather. But what did an ideal parent look like? She wasn't arrogant enough to think she knew.

Britney shook her head, seemed to measure her words. "He was *inappropriate* with her. Crude. Suggestive. She thought it was only a matter of time."

"Until what?"

"Until, you know, he hit on her or something. Tried to touch her."

Maggie looked back at Melody, not far from where they stood. If she heard Britney, she didn't make any protestations. She had her head in her hands, was rocking slightly back and forth.

"But he'd never touched her before?"

Brit shook her head. "He said things to her—like, told her that she looked good, in a dirty way. Or he'd come into her room wrapped in a towel after his shower. Things like that. That's what she told me."

Maggie was aware suddenly of a terrible tension in her shoulders, a clenching in her stomach. She realized that Melody had never answered the question she'd asked on leaving the car.

"The stepfather thing is not always cool, you know, Dr. Cooper." Britney had lowered her voice to a whisper and leaned in close to Maggie. Brit was remembering her own stepfather, Maggie knew, Denise's second, very rich husband. There'd never been any hint of abuse, just a sense Brit had that he didn't want her around, that she was a nuisance in his marriage to her mother. But Denise had divorced him years ago, never married again. *I have money; I don't need a husband,* Maggie remembered her saying. *I just want to be myself for the first time in my life.*

"Was she here tonight, Britney? I need you to be honest with me now. Have you heard from her?"

Denise had joined them again. "No one's going to be mad. Okay, Brit?"

Britney looked at her mother. Denise's beauty was maturing—fine lines and a softening around the jaw didn't diminish her prettiness; Britney was blossoming—her face narrowing, losing its childish fullness, her prettiness becoming something more luminous. Maggie could see their closeness as Denise snaked an arm around Brit's middle and the girl rested her head on her mother's shoulder.

"I got a Facebook message from her earlier," she said finally, pulling away from her mother. "I'll show you."

They walked through the house, Britney and Denise leading the way to the computer room, Maggie and Melody close behind. The long hallway was a photo shrine to Britney—the little blond cherub morphing into a fairy princess, at Disney, in Paris, climbing on a jungle gym, on her grandfather's shoulders at the Macy's Thanksgiving Day Parade—the privileged life of an adored child.

"What did you and Charlene fight about?" Maggie asked Melody again.

"What *don't* we fight about, Maggie?" It wasn't an answer. Maggie detected a stall. But she didn't press; Melody was getting a glassy, haunted look that Maggie didn't like.

Brit sat at the computer, and her fingers started dancing expertly on the keyboard. Some low music came from the monitor, and Maggie leaned over Brit's shoulder.

"She updated her Facebook page. So I got an alert, but that's it. She hasn't called or sent me a personal message. So I don't know where she is right now."

"What does it mean that she 'updated her page'?" said Maggie. She was annoyed with her own ignorance on this subject. Ricky had been urging her to get more current, even to create a page for herself. *You could connect with your old friends,* he'd said. *I'm too connected to them as it is,* she'd countered. *Your patients will think you're cool. I don't need my patients to think I'm cool.*

"There's a box on the top of your page where you can type in what you're doing at the moment. Like mine says, 'Brit is studying for her biology exam and wishing she was watching *American Idol*!'"

"What does Charlene's say?" Melody asked.

Brit pointed to the list of status updates on her page. It read: `Charlene is getting out of Dodge. Finally.`

"I sent her a message to ask her what she was talking about." She clicked over to her mail page and showed them the message: `What's wrong??? Call me!!!` They were all looking over her shoulder; Denise had put on a pair of glasses. Melody was squinting at the screen.

"But she hasn't answered," Brit went on. "She updated at 7:09, and I sent her a note at 8:04. I tried to call her, but the call went straight to voice mail."

"Is it unusual for her not to get back to you right away?" Maggie said. It was something Jones might ask.

Brit nodded, gave a slight shrug. "A little."

Melody started to cry again. Then there was a loud, authoritative knock at the door, followed by an urgent, staccato ringing of the doorbell. Denise startled at the sudden sound and went quickly toward the door.

Maggie found herself following. As she moved from the hallway into the grand foyer, there was an odd, disconnected moment where she took in the triple-height ceiling, the marble beneath her feet. A round table stood in the center of the space, topped by a gigantic vase of flowers that gave no noticeable scent.

What had seemed opulent on entering suddenly felt disturbingly fake, the studied and purposeful display of wealth. She detected an emptiness beneath the beauty, a new-money cluelessness about taste; rooms chosen from a catalog or choreographed by a decorator but not reflecting the true style of the owner. But it was just a moment that passed and was forgotten when the room filled with cops, Jones first in the crowd, looking grim with purpose.

"What are you doing here?" she found herself asking her husband. But of course he would be there. There was a missing girl; she'd said the words herself. He was head detective at the Hollows Police Department. She didn't hear his answer, but when they locked eyes over the escalating noise, she saw something foreign on his face, a look she'd never seen before and couldn't name.

It was 12:32 A.M.

10

I t's nice of you to do this," she said. Her voice caught in her throat, and she sounded like she was crying. But she wasn't, not anymore. There was a heavy scent in the air, cigarettes and something else unpleasant. Her sinuses were swelling, her head starting to ache from it.

"I want to."

"Most people wouldn't. It's a long drive."

"I'm not most people."

She looked at him and smiled, but he didn't take his eyes off the road to look back at her. She nodded.

"Well, thanks."

She dug through her purse for a pressed powder to fix herself up. She knew she must be a wreck. She found it and popped open the mirror. Even in the scant, intermittent light from the passing streetlamps, she could see that she had raccoon eyes, her eyeliner and mascara making dark, wet smudges.

"I'm a mess," she said, digging for a tissue and then wiping away the makeup. The white Kleenex came away black.

"You're beautiful, Charlene."

He was looking at her now. She gave him a weak smile.

"You're sweet," she said. Something about his gaze made her squirm.

She saw his jaw clench at that, eyes back on the road. He was a weird one, always had been. But what did she care? He was her ride out of this life, once and for all.

Gotham waited. She felt a clench of excitement mingled with an

unexpected fear. Hadn't she been waiting for this? Didn't she have plans?
A place to stay? She wasn't some clueless runaway.

She was sorry about Rick, about standing him up and leaving him
behind. But he was such a baby in so many ways. Such a mama's boy. For
a while he'd acted like he might take off with her, not go to college, try
to break into the music business with her. He was a good drummer,
could be great if he devoted any real energy to it. But in the end, he'd
balked. He looked cool, like a punk rebel. But on the inside, at his core,
he was a good boy. And she was *not* a good girl. Most definitely not.
They were wrong for each other. She'd take him places he didn't really
want to go. He'd hold her back. They'd wind up hating each other. He
was a Hollows boy, just like his father. Or just like his mother. He'd leave
to go to college, but eventually he'd come back. Charlene was never
going back. She couldn't. Not after tonight.

"So do you have a plan? Is someone expecting you?"

"Oh, yeah. I've been seeing someone in the city."

"I thought you were with Ricky Cooper."

"We're just friends. No strings."

He gave a sharp little laugh. "Does *he* know that?"

Charlene felt her face flush. And that smell was starting to make her
feel queasy. Sometimes, on a long ride, she'd get carsick, start to feel that
gray wobble of nausea, that expanding unwellness. All she needed was to
get sick in this guy's car.

"Can you pull over a minute?"

"Why?"

"I think I'm going to throw up."

He pulled over quickly, and she got out into the chill of the night.
She walked off the shoulder to the grass and sat, put her head on her
knees. She could hear the rush of traffic, people racing toward whatever
next event of their lives. Just like her, moving on, moving forward. She
willed herself to be solid, to not fall apart by the side of the road. But it
was no use. She managed to keep it off her clothes by getting on all
fours, but she vomited until she was retching. It seemed to go on forever.
When it was over, she sat sobbing.

"Are you all right?" he asked from behind her. She hadn't heard him get out of the car, had forgotten about him altogether.

"Do I look all right?" she snapped. Then she remembered that he had gone out of his way for her, was her ride. "Sorry," she said more gently. "No. I guess I'm not."

She felt him just standing there, not saying anything. Finally, she got up and faced him. He was taller, bigger than she thought of him— when she thought of him at all. He opened the door for her, and she climbed back inside. The stink of the old car made her feel sick again almost immediately. She rolled down the window.

"I know it's cold, but I need some air," she said as he started driving again.

"It's fine." But he'd gone grim and sullen. Just like all men the minute you stopped being a sweet little flower. The second you ceased to please, they got shitty. Some of them, like Graham, got violent. She felt another wave of nausea at the thought of her stepfather, but she pushed the events of the evening away—a bad B horror movie she'd rented and turned off before the bloody conclusion. If she didn't think about it, it wasn't real. She could do that. Always had been able to. But her body was disloyal, puking by the side of the road, sobbing. Now her hands were shaking, adrenaline pumping for no good reason.

"Sorry," she said again. "I'm not having a good night."

But he didn't say anything, just kept driving. *Well, fine, fuck you, too,* she thought. When the cold air got too much, she rolled up the window and leaned her head against the glass.

"Should we put on some music?" she asked.

"Radio's broke."

Her mother insisted that there was no way Charlene could remember her father. He'd died when she was very young, in a car accident on his way home from work. But she did remember him—how it felt to hold his hand or ride on his shoulder. She knew his face, a lot like hers, from the photographs she had of him. But that was not how she remembered him. Nor were there particular events in her memory of him. It was an essence, a feeling—just a good, warm feeling, a safe, secure happiness. When she was younger, she could access that feeling simply by holding his picture to her chest and closing her eyes. But as she grew older, she couldn't do that anymore. It became elusive, a shadow slipping around the corner while she gave chase. How could she ever get it? That wonderful feeling? The safety of being loved by someone who didn't want to violate you in return, who didn't want to *take* something that didn't belong to him?

She'd thought Graham was all right at first. She was nine when he and her mother married. There were fun times—a trip to Florida and Disney, a baseball game at Yankee Stadium. She couldn't say she'd ever loved him; but she remembered feeling okay when he was around.

But Charlene had gotten her period when she was ten and started developing early. By age eleven, she'd needed a bra. He'd started looking at her differently then, averting his eyes, shrinking from her embraces. She felt the sting of a rejection she didn't really understand. Around the same time, his marriage to her mother started to go sour. The good times were over; there were only fights and tears and slamming doors.

Then a few years later *it* happened. She awoke in the night and went to the kitchen in her underwear and a tank top to get a glass of orange juice. On the way down, she passed by the family room without even glancing inside. She might have done the same on the way back if he'd been quiet, but as she passed by the darkened room, she heard a low moan. The sofa bed was out, and Graham was on top of the sheets, wearing just a T-shirt, his bottom half exposed. He was masturbating. She stood staring, stunned. When she looked at his face, he was watching her. He didn't try to cover himself. He just continued pumping his hand, watching her. She couldn't read his expression— something between need and anger. She felt her face start to burn and her throat go dry. She backed away until she hit the wall behind her. It must have been seconds, but it felt like hours that she stood there, mouth gaping—disgusted, ashamed, and oddly fascinated.

Finally, she broke into a run for the stairs and locked herself in her bedroom. All night she waited for him to try to turn the knob and get in, but he didn't. She thought about telling her mother, but she couldn't imagine the conversation, the words she would use to say what he had done. Her mother was so sad already, so unhappy. Charlene knew she remembered Dad, too. *I shouldn't have bothered trying to marry again. I was lucky to have love like that once. I didn't deserve him in the first place, the things I've done.*

The next morning, Graham was sitting at the kitchen table with his paper and a mug she'd given him one Father's Day—WORLD'S GREATEST DAD. She hadn't even meant it when she bought it; she was just trying to be nice. Now she wanted to smash it across his stupid face.

"Good morning, Charlene," he said. His expression, when he peered at her over the paper, was a dare.

"Want some eggs, baby?" her mother asked. A cigarette burned in the ashtray, the coffeepot gurgled, and morning show hosts bantered on the television. Outside, there was a depressing drizzle.

"I'm not hungry," she said. "I may never eat again."

Graham held her eyes.

"Oh, stop it," her mother said. "You're a skinny minny. Toast?"

"Sure, fine. Toast. Thanks."

Her mother popped the bread in and then went upstairs to get ready for work. For a few minutes, they sat there. Graham pretended to read; Charlene listened to the television but stared at the wallpaper.

"I was thinking on the way home tonight I'd pick up a DVD player, get rid of that old VCR."

She'd been begging him for one for months. You could only get VCR tapes from the library. It was embarrassing not to have a DVD player.

He put the paper neatly on the table in front of him and folded his hands over it. His hair was still wet from the shower. The denim shirt he wore brought out the blue of his eyes. She shrank back from him when he leaned toward her slightly. She saw remorse on his face, something sad.

"What do you think about that, Charlene?"

What was he offering her? Was it an apology? A bribe? She was nearly fourteen at the time; she knew what he'd done was wrong. Her mother would leave him. He could go to jail. She was old enough, smart enough, to know these things. You learned about it in school, what was okay, what wasn't. So why did *she* feel dirty and small inside? Why did *she* feel ashamed and afraid? She kept thinking of him lying there, that hungry look on his face. But if she told her mother, the whole world would come crashing down around them. It wasn't as if he'd *touched* her.

She turned her eyes to his and held his gaze, even though the act made her stomach cramp with nerves.

"That would be great, Graham," she said. "But we really need a new television, too."

Now the road stretched before them, and Charlene watched it disappear under the hood of the car. She found it hypnotic, the way the car filled with orange light when they passed beneath the tall highway lamps, then went dark again for a time. After a while, adrenaline abandoned her, leaving her weak and exhausted.

She dozed once, nodded awake with a start, feeling suddenly, deeply afraid. But she willed herself to be calm. *He's waiting for me,* she thought. *He got my message and he'll be waiting. Everything is going to be fine.* She thought of Kat Von D from *LA Ink,* who'd left home at fourteen and now was on TV, a famous tattoo artist. Everything had turned out all right for her. With those thoughts, she started to drift again.

A bump in the road brought her back. It was dark, except for the glow of the dashboard lights. It took a few seconds before she realized that they'd left the highway, were driving along a deserted rural road. Not a streetlamp, not a house in sight. Just the black shadows of trees against the sky. She felt a thump of fear.

"Hey," she said. She tried to sound casual. "Where are we? Where are we going?"

The old analog clock on the dash, lit in a dirty yellow light, read 12:32 A.M.

11

Jones Cooper had been a beautiful boy—lacrosse star, straight-A student, crown prince of Hollows High. And Maggie Monroe, though she'd never have admitted it, had spent her high school years admiring him from afar. His body was a study in perfect form. He was fast, agile, powerful—every inch of him exactly as it should be.

But this wasn't why Maggie found herself daydreaming about him, watching him secretly from beneath the bleachers. It was because beneath all those golden layers, there was a place where the sun didn't reach. There was a place within him that *saw*. He knew that there was a world beyond The Hollows, the town that stood in his thrall. And that it could be ugly and frightening. There was something dark about him, or maybe just something that acknowledged the darkness.

At least that's what Maggie thought she saw when she watched him. She was the geek in black, with black fingernails and eyeliner, the brain, the poet, the freak. His eyes had never rested on Maggie in high school, though he claimed differently now. *I always noticed you. I thought you were too smart for a stupid jock like me.*

But Maggie remembered his gaze always drifting over her to the prettiest or most popular girls, girls who shone a bright reflection back at him. Maggie didn't mind. He was a star in the sky; she never expected to touch him, only to gaze at him in admiration and wonder.

Anyway, she didn't have time for boys. She needed to study, to do well, knowing that an education was her only ticket out of the town she hated. The Hollows, to her teenage mind, was a hell mouth, a social

and cultural void populated by the petty and small-minded—those
kings and queens of high school cum pizza parlor waitresses, gas station owners, and desperate housewives. The Hollows was only a hundred miles from New York City, but it might as well have been on
another planet. Maggie always knew on an instinctive level that she
would need to fight The Hollows's powerful gravitational pull if she
wanted to get away.

But ultimately it was Jones who drew her back. She'd never have
believed it when she graduated high school and moved into the city to
attend NYU. During college she never came home for more than a
weekend. Even summers, she managed to find work or internships,
places in the city where she could stay cheaply. She went straight on
to graduate school, working toward her Ph.D. in psychology. With
her demanding studies, work, then her residencies, sometimes a year
would pass, with Maggie seeing only her parents when they came
into the city to take her to dinner, visit a museum with her, maybe see
a show.

"You never come home," her mother complained over the phone
one night. "People wonder about that."

"I'm sorry, Mom."

But the thought of that town, that old house, her parents' low-
grade, continual bickering, the headaches that always plagued her on her
return, kept her away.

"Jones Cooper asks about you."

"Really?" The name was pleasantly distant. Jones Cooper. Like a
song she'd loved but one for which she couldn't quite remember the
tune. "Under what circumstances do you bump into him?"

"The town is changing. We've been having some problems at the
school with drugs. One boy brought a gun last month. Jones Cooper has
been in my office quite a few times."

"*Really?*" It was hard to imagine guns and drugs at Hollows High.
Kids had snuck cigarettes, got fake IDs to buy booze, maybe smoked
some weed when Maggie was a kid.

"Yes, really," Elizabeth snapped, annoyed. "Over the last two years, we've developed a meth problem. It's a nationwide concern, especially in rural areas like this."

Maggie knew this, of course. But she always, for some reason, had thought The Hollows was immune to such deterioration. She didn't like to think of her mother, always a petite woman, then in her fifties and getting smaller every time Maggie saw her, walking among drug users and gun-wielding thugs. Sometimes tough talk wasn't enough.

"Do you think about retiring, Mom?"

Elizabeth released a disdainful snort. "They'll carry me out of here."

Stubborn old woman, Maggie thought but didn't say.

When Maggie was finishing her doctorate at Columbia University, her father was diagnosed with late-stage lung cancer. In the months that followed, she found herself back in The Hollows every spare moment, helping her mother to care for her father as he fought the disease admirably but deteriorated quickly, then died horribly.

In Maggie's memory, the period was an awful blur of sadness and exhaustion. But it was also a time of fierce intimacy; she'd never spent so much time as an adult with her parents—helping, comforting, just *being* with them. Both Maggie and Elizabeth were changed by the violence of her father's passing, but they were closer than they'd ever been.

At the gathering that followed her father's funeral, Maggie managed to separate from the crowd and stand alone on the back veranda, looking out at the expansive property, the weeping willows, the thick woods of beech and ash beyond. It was a gray, muggy day; a misty rain made everything glisten. She felt a hand on her shoulder.

"I'm sorry about your father, Maggie. He was a good man."

She turned to see Jones Cooper. He was thicker than she remembered, premature fine lines around his eyes. His blond hair was a shade or two darker. None of it diminished his beauty. He was still washed in that same golden light. Still with that same shadow at the core.

"Thank you," she said. Heat rose to her face with the rush of chemical attraction.

She found she didn't feel awkward or uncomfortable around him at all. If he had spoken to her in high school, she would have burst into flames. That afternoon, they stood side by side and stared out into the yard in a comforting silence.

Then Jones said, "You got out of here. Never came back."

There was something wistful in his voice that surprised her. She'd never thought of him as someone with a dream to leave The Hollows.

She nodded, a knot of guilt in her center. She'd spent more time with her father as he lay dying than she had in the years since she'd graduated from high school. She might have known her father better as an adult if she hadn't so persistently stayed away. For some reason, she found herself saying this to Jones, even though she was sure he'd just come to offer platitudes. But he listened, kept his eyes on her.

When she was done, he said, "Your parents wanted you to have your own life. They raised you to be independent and move away from here. Your mother has said as much. He knew you loved him. You were here when they needed you. That's a lot."

She was used to offering others solace and advice; it surprised her to receive it, to be grateful for it. She found herself crying. She put her hand to her eyes and then felt him wrap his arms around her. In a way, after that moment, she never left The Hollows again. The years grew over that embrace like a vine.

Now they were fighting—again, which unfortunately was their way in times of stress. Each was a safe place for the other to blow off steam. It had started when they'd stepped outside, Jones telling her to go home, he'd handle it from here.

"Where's Ricky?" she asked, glancing at Jones's SUV, for some reason expecting to see their son sulking in the passenger seat.

"At the house with Chuck." Chuck Ferrigno, one of the other detectives on the squad.

"What do you mean? You don't mean to ask questions about Charlene?"

A raised female voice inside caused them both to look at the door for a moment, then look back at each other.

"Of course," he said.

"You left our minor child with a cop, no parent or attorney present, to be questioned about a missing girl?"

"Come on. He's a cop's son. We're not calling in an AMBER Alert here. This is a runaway situation. Not an abduction."

For some reason, she heard Melody's plaintive question, *How do you* know?

Everyone had thought Sarah had run away as well, after that fight on the phone with her mom. Trying to get even. Trying to make everyone worry. There were recriminations later that the police didn't act quickly enough. But that was another girl, a lifetime ago.

"What's wrong with you, Jones?" she said, lowering her voice to a whisper. "Don't you have an instinct to protect your son?"

He drew back as if she'd slapped him. Before he had a chance to return fire, Melody burst out the door, rushing toward Jones. She looked harried, pursued by demons. When she spoke, it was a barely intelligible wail.

"Are you going to find her, Jones? Are you going to do something besides stand around with that superior look on your fucking face and find my daughter?"

"Melody," said Jones, his voice surprisingly calm and gentle. He placed a hand on each of her shoulders. "Calm down. We'll find her."

Melody started to weep again, her face morphing from a mask of rage into a caricature of misery; then she collapsed against Jones, who supported her weight and led her back into the house. A light blinked on in an upstairs window of a neighboring house. Maggie heard a door open. It wouldn't be long before everyone knew what was happening.

Denise stood in the doorway, on her face an expression of pity battling disdain. The homecoming queen. Jones practically dragged Melody up the three steps to the front door. The jock and the burnout. The other cops, too, Tony Jackson and Mark Albright, bit players from the same every-East-Coast-high-school production—the science nerd, the fat kid. And finally Maggie, the goth who couldn't wait to get away but wound up coming home. And yet they were all so much more than that, weren't they?

The only one of them who was not allowed to be what she would become was Sarah. And she *was* there, on everyone's mind. How could she not be? They all remembered her. She'd never left this place, either.

1 2

Sarah had stood among them but always, somehow, apart. She didn't belong there—in The Hollows, in that school, and she knew it. Everyone knew it. And yet no one could accuse her of being a snob or stuck-up in any way. It was her gift that kept her separate; maybe she didn't even want it that way. But how could someone who knew the passion and discipline of an artist before she was fourteen stand anywhere but apart from the rest of them, who barely knew who they wanted to be or what they might be good at?

Music had claimed Sarah when she was too young to know anything else. Maggie saw that clearly, looking back. When Sarah played the violin, she disappeared, became a portal through which her prodigious talent passed. Maggie remembered the way Sarah's face would contort, her eyelids flutter, her head move willowy and slow; she was utterly unself-conscious with a violin beneath her chin and a bow in her hand. She was lost and found. It was a special thing, an uncommon thing. And everybody, even those who would normally taunt and tease, torture a thing they didn't understand, kept a reverent distance.

Her parents had moved from the Pacific Northwest so that Sarah could have proximity to New York City but chose the suburbs so that they could keep her safe from all the threats and temptations of an urban environment. Sarah was absent every Friday, when she commuted to Juilliard for the day with her mother for the precollege program. Sometimes they spent the weekend, returning Sunday afternoon. It was impossibly glamorous, yet she sat in the same cafeteria, failed to climb the rope in gym class, got detention for passing notes to Melody during study hall. Among them, but apart.

Maggie hadn't thought about Sarah for years, not in that way. She didn't remember often the way Sarah had lived, who she had been. Sarah was forever defined by the way she died. She was every parent's nightmare, a warning, a cautionary tale. She was proof that everything parents feared was possible, even in this quiet, not quite suburban, not quite rural town. The worst happened, even here.

Maggie was thinking this as she watched Ricky slumped on the long suede couch of their great room. The large stone fireplace on the far wall was flanked by shelves filled with books and photographs, Jones's old sports trophies, Ricky's various art class creations—an ashtray, the sculpture of a frog. The high, beamed ceiling gave it a spacious feel, but it was a warm room, a real room, where they ate pizza and watched movies, spilled soda on the carpet—nothing like the showplace where Denise and Britney lived. It was designed for comfort with the sectional and plush carpet, a cozy love seat, a new flat-screen hanging on the wall.

"If you know something, Son," Chuck was saying as Maggie walked into the room. Both man and boy raised their eyes to look at her, but neither acknowledged her. Chuck kept talking. "Now's the time to let us know before this gets out of hand. If she's taken off and you know where, you're not helping her by keeping it to yourself."

She sat beside her son. "Do you know something, Ricky?"

He offered a shake of his head, kept his eyes blank and staring at the ground. He was a charismatic kid when he wanted to be. When he didn't, he was a locked box with the key inside. Just like his father.

"I told you," he said, an annoyed edge creeping into his voice. "Charlene stood me up tonight. She didn't answer any of my calls. If I knew where she was, I'd tell you. Especially with her mom so upset."

"Let's go through it again. You were supposed to meet her where?" asked Chuck.

"At Pop's Pizza."

"How was she going to get there?"

"Her mom was going to drop her off, I guess. I didn't ask."

"You didn't ask? Didn't offer to pick her up?"

"Char's not allowed in the car with me. Her mom doesn't want her to ride in cars with boys."

Chuck issued a conspiratorial chuckle, a kind of *I remember how it was* smile, and a roll of the eyes. She saw Ricky smile in return.

Then, "So you never drove anywhere together?"

"No, we did," Ricky admitted. "All the time. But her mother doesn't know that. I don't pick her up at the house."

Chuck nodded slowly. He was a heavyset guy, with a thinning head of dark brown hair, a round, sweet face. He always had a slightly disheveled look about him, even more so now, as he'd clearly been roused from sleep, the shadow of stubble on his jaw, the back of his head matted. He had a demeanor that seemed to encourage people not to take him too seriously. But Maggie knew it was a mistake not to.

"What else doesn't her mother know?" Chuck asked.

"That's enough, Chuck," Maggie said. "Are you interrogating him? Do we need a lawyer?"

"Come on, Maggie. There's a girl gone missing."

"And Rick says he doesn't know anything." She didn't like the pitch of defensiveness she heard in her own voice.

"Well," Chuck said. He glanced over at her son, who seemed to be sinking deeper into the couch. "I think he does."

In the silence that fell between them, Maggie heard the ticking of that old grandfather clock. She and Chuck locked eyes. He hadn't grown up in The Hollows. He was a beat cop from New York City who'd moved to town after his second son was born. His wife didn't want to wait up nights for him, worried sick, wondering when two of his buddies would come to the door with the bad news. He drove patrol in The Hollows for two years, was promoted to detective last year after scoring high on his exam.

"She broke up with me, okay?" Ricky said. His voice was faint in that way it always was right before he was about to cry. "She stood me up, and then I got a message on Facebook."

Maggie turned to look at her son. The blank outer shell had dissolved; he looked the way he had when his best friend in kindergarten had moved away, or when Patches, their dog, had been hit by a car and died in his arms. The profound, unapologetic sadness of youth pushed down the corners of his mouth, sloped his shoulders; it crushed Maggie to see it on his face. It also ignited a flash of anger at Charlene—a silly, selfish girl who had caused all this drama, all this pain, because she had a fight with her mother.

"What did her message say?" asked Chuck gently. "Let's take a look at it."

They followed Ricky upstairs to his computer. Jones hadn't wanted Ricky to have a computer in his room. Jones had wanted it left in a common area so that they could monitor Ricky's online activity, keep him safe from the Internet predators, prevent him from downloading porn. But when he'd turned sixteen, they'd decided to give him his privacy, considered him trustworthy and smart enough to be granted that small privilege.

In the mess of his room, rock posters covered every inch of wall space. A shelf held a slew of soccer trophies he'd won in middle school before he fell in love with the drums. A hamper overflowed with dirty clothes. A cup sat filled with some congealed liquid. The room held the scent of sweat and old food. *Onions*, Maggie thought. *It smells like onions in here.*

Ricky sat in front of his computer and showed them the screen; her message was already open, as if he'd been reading it over and over. Maggie looked over his shoulder, just as she had done with Britney earlier. Chuck stood behind her.

```
I'm sorry I didn't meet you. Something happened at
home. I can't go back there tonight. Maybe never.
It's better if we say good-bye anyway, Rick. I've got
to go my own way. You've got to go yours. Go to col-
lege and be a good boy. Maybe our paths will cross
again someday. I do love you. I'm sorry.
                                            Love,
                                            Char
```

"Where would she go?" asked Chuck, backing up to let Ricky pass as the boy stood up from the chair.

Ricky sank onto the bed and put his head in his hands. "I don't know. She always said she was going to the city. She said she had friends who could get her into the music business. But I don't know who."

"You never went to the city with her?" said Chuck. "You never met any of these friends?"

Ricky looked at his mother. "We've been to the city to see bands and stuff. But I never met anyone she supposedly knew. Honestly, I thought she was making it up. She makes stuff up, you know, to make herself feel better."

"She lies, you mean?" said Chuck.

"Yeah, but just, like, stories. You know, dreams. She hates it here, hates her stepfather. I always thought of them as kind of escape fantasies."

"Britney said Charlene was afraid of Graham," Maggie said. She sat beside her son and draped an arm around his shoulders. She was surprised when he moved in closer to her, didn't squirm away from her embrace. Chuck stood, dominating the doorway now. He was a very big man, with a protruding belly and a barrel for a chest. Intimidating now that he was frowning.

"*Was* she afraid?" Chuck asked.

"She wasn't *afraid*, exactly. I would say she distrusted him. She said he was *inappropriate* with her. That's the word Charlene used. He'd hit her mom, but she'd hit him a bunch of times, too. It's a violent relationship."

Chuck issued a sigh, bent his head and rubbed the crown. A chime coming from somewhere on his person caused him to reach for his phone in the pocket of his jeans, pull it out, and glance at the screen.

"Okay, Son," he said, distracted, still looking at the device in his hand. "When you hear from her—and I think you will—you need to let someone know. Try to get her to come home. A girl can get herself into a world of trouble out there."

"I will," said Ricky.

Maggie felt a flutter of panic now for Charlene, her anger dissipating, and she followed Chuck as he descended the staircase.

"So what now?" she asked him at the door.

"Everyone's looking for her. The whole department will be putting in hours tonight knocking on the doors of neighbors and friends. We'll find her."

"She could already be on a train to New York, if that's where she's headed."

"We'll put out a tristate runaway bulletin, enter her name into NCIC and DCJS." Maggie knew these were information databases, but she couldn't remember what the initials stood for. "We'll contact the Center for Missing and Exploited Children, get a picture up there. You know the stats, Maggie: seventy-seven percent of runaways come home within the week."

She knew the statistics, of course. But numbers didn't mean anything when you were talking about a girl you knew, someone you cared about. There were people—predators—waiting out there for someone like Charlene, a girl with big dreams, not sure if anyone really cared about her, afraid of her stepfather, fighting with her mother. The anger Maggie had felt toward Charlene had passed. Left in its wake was something like fear. The worst happened, even here.

When she closed the door on Chuck and turned to go back to her son, to comfort him, the grandfather clock read 1:05 A.M. She hadn't heard the hour chime.

The day would come. He'd known that it would, of course. That it had to come. Because even then, when he was young and clueless, he knew you couldn't bury that much wrong and make it right. And though there was no real reason to suspect that today was the day, he knew it was. It was Melody's face, that terrible contortion of rage and misery. Her face, her voice—it brought him back. You shouldn't have to bear witness twice. He should have left The Hollows long ago, gone away to college like Maggie but never come back. But he didn't.

He had a laundry list of excuses—a bad knee had derailed his hopes of a scholarship, the old cliché; his mother was sick, couldn't be on her own; he'd always dreamed of being a cop in the town where he grew up, of giving back. All of these things, all noble, with kernels of truth at their centers, were lies. The reality was that he hadn't needed a scholarship; there was money. Anyway, he'd never been as good as all that; he'd just been better than his below-average teammates. His mother *was* sick, mentally ill, unstable—it shouldn't have been his job to watch over her and then to watch her die. But he'd taken it on, even though other family members had offered a hand. He *did* like the idea of policing The Hollows, a way of atonement, he supposed. But it wouldn't have been enough to keep him here. No, the truth was that he was afraid to leave. He was a coward.

Not a run-from-battle kind of coward—not afraid of heights or airplanes or small, enclosed spaces. He was not afraid of duty or responsibility. All of that was easy. What he feared were the long, empty spaces between those things where life was lived.

Melody's wailing had turned to a low whimper. They were driving through the neighborhood around her house while the other guys knocked on doors and made phone calls. As he drove, his eyes scanned the sides of the road, looking for a dropped book bag, a shred of clothing, anything; he'd asked Melody to do the same. In a busier jurisdiction, there wouldn't be the manpower or the time to pay so much attention to a kid who'd run away before and probably would again. It wasn't even protocol. But in a town like The Hollows, where most people knew one another, it just seemed like the right thing to do.

"Where's Graham?" Jones asked.

"How should I know?" Melody snapped. There was an edgy defensiveness about the way she said it that made him take notice.

"Didn't you call him to tell him Charlene was missing?"

"Of course I did. His phone was off." When he didn't answer, she added, "He said he might go hunting this weekend."

"It's after one in the morning and you don't know where your husband is?" The words sounded hard, judgmental.

"Not everybody has a *perfect* marriage like you and Maggie," she said. She had a nasty smile on her face as she drew a pack of cigarettes from her purse.

"Can't smoke in here, Mel."

She lit the cigarette anyway and lowered the window. He fought the urge to grab it from her and toss it out onto the street. She had always been a rude, inconsiderate bitch, and he didn't think Charlene was much better. Smarter, maybe. Better looking than Melody had ever been. But really Charlene was just out for herself, a con looking for a mark; if he'd suspected it before, he knew it now.

They took the road that ran out of the development and wound toward the more rural farm country. Then he took a right onto an unpaved passage that passed over a stone bridge into a thick area of woods. It was a link of wild land between two development neighborhoods, a twenty-acre strip that ran in back of the more expensive homes, so city folks could think they were in the country.

Where Melody and Charlene lived, Whispering Acres was more lower middle class. Back at the precinct house they called it Whimpering Acres because of all the domestic violence calls—an angry husband answering the door, a woman crying behind him. These days you didn't need the wife to press charges, because they almost never did. But cops rarely hauled the husband away unless they had to, unless the woman was so obviously battered that you couldn't get around it, unless you knew the next time you came you'd be calling an ambulance or the coroner's office.

Patrol had been out to Melody and Graham's plenty of times. Sometimes he was bleeding; sometimes she was. It was always a neighbor who called to complain about the noise. Jones knew what it was like to grow up like that. He felt an unwanted twinge of empathy for Charlene. At least she had the guts to run away from it; he never had. Finally, it was his father who left and never came back.

The Acres wasn't a bad neighborhood; the streets were lined with average ranches and split-level tract houses. You might find the occasional junker in the drive up on blocks, or clotheslines in the back, a rusty old shed, a side yard cluttered with toys, twisted bicycles. Acres folks didn't have the time or money to pay much attention to landscaping or to chipping paint or weeds poking through the sparse gravel on the drive—they were working two jobs to make ends meet.

By contrast, in The Oaks, a mile south, the single-story dwellings of
The Acres were replaced with towering houses—four or five thousand
square feet—surrounded by old-growth trees, meticulous yards, late-
model vehicles in three-car garages. Trash cans disappeared as soon as
the garbage truck had passed. Driveways were paved with multicolored
bricks. Mailboxes stood in carefully groomed flower beds. These were
the doctors, the lawyers, the financial professionals who commuted into
the city for work each day. During the day, the neighborhood was abuzz
with activity, a parade of service professionals—nannies, maids, land-
scapers, pool cleaners—most of whom lived in The Acres, or in one of
the outlying areas around the high school.

Jones's family didn't live in either of these neighborhoods, having
chosen instead the hipper area off the main square. They called it SoHo,
short for South Hollows, which Maggie always found funny, because to
her there was only one SoHo and that was in Manhattan. Their restored
Victorian sat on a quiet, tree-lined street, just a few blocks from shops,
restaurants, the library, a yoga studio. Maggie needed that, having left
her life in the city to be with him here. She wanted to be near what little activity the town had to offer. He liked it, too, though initially he
didn't want to live that close to the precinct house. But now that he was
watching his weight, it was easy for him to stroll home and eat a healthier lunch. With his total cholesterol over 250 and his weight not far behind, there were no more Philly cheesesteaks, fries, and a large soda
sitting in his car with one of the guys. Now it was turkey lasagna at
home alone. He wondered if a longer life was worth living if you
couldn't eat whatever the hell you wanted to eat.

Melody released a hacking cough and tossed her cigarette out the
window.

"The world is your ashtray, right, Mel?"

"Shut up, Jones. When did you turn into such a self-righteous
prick?"

In between The Acres and The Oaks, on the dark, unpaved road,
Jones stopped the car. He rolled down the window and took in the cold,
quiet air. He could hear the babbling of the little creek that flowed
through town. Somewhere deep in the woods, something moved light

and quick. A deer, fleeing the sound of the engine, the high beams. Maybe something else.

"What are you doing?" Melody asked.

"I'm just going to look around here a minute."

He flipped on the rack of lights on the roof, and the area around them flooded in harsh white. Everything beyond the beam disappeared.

He stepped out of the car and looked into the black around them, listened to it. Then he walked down the slope to the bank of the creek, peering under the bridge.

"Why are you doing this?"

Melody had exited the vehicle and came to stand above him, leaning on the stone edge of the bridge.

"This is where they found her body. You remember?"

When he looked at her, she was as white as death.

"*Why* are you doing this?" she said again. Her voice was a raspy whisper, her face melting in fear and grief. He felt a little jolt of regret. He hadn't done it to hurt her or to frighten her. He just wanted someone to remember with him, wanted not to be alone with it for once. He saw how wrong that was now.

He shoved his hands in the pockets of his jeans, stared at the black water, the slick stones beneath. "I'm sorry. I didn't mean— She's *fine,* Melody."

But she had already turned from him and gone back to the SUV. The slamming of the door bounced and echoed all around him. It would have been an ugly thing, a dark and hateful kind of poetry, to walk down here and see Charlene. Was that what he thought he'd find?

Back in the SUV, Melody was weeping again. He climbed in the driver's side and closed the door, cranked the heat. He'd been sweating this afternoon. Now the air was frigid. Winter was settling over The Hollows.

"Am I being punished?" she asked. He had no urge to comfort her, to apologize again. He just wished he hadn't offered to drive her around. He wished she would stop crying.

"Do you ever talk to Travis?" she said when he didn't answer her.

"Don't," he said. "I didn't mean—"

"You feel it, too. I can see it on your face. You look like you've seen a ghost."

"Stop it." He put the vehicle in gear and started to drive. "Pull yourself together."

Jones and Travis Crosby had never been friends, exactly. No, never that. But something magnetic and irresistible drew them together over and over, either in conflict or in complicity.

Travis's dad was the Hollows police chief, a grim and sour man who retained his post for almost thirty-five years. During his tenure, crime in The Hollows was well below the statistical average. And revenue from parking and moving violations was higher than anywhere else in the state. But his cruelty, his rages, were well known. And everyone knew that Travis got the worst of it.

Jones's father, before he disappeared just shortly after Jones's thirteenth birthday, had worked at the dairy just out of town, a family farm where kids would ride their bikes to the ice cream shop on summer afternoons or for the questionable entertainment of cow tipping on moonless nights. Once upon a time, town legend held, their fathers had been friends. But some rift had placed a distance between the two families. In spite of this, or maybe because of it, or because of some unspoken, shared hatred of their fathers, Travis and Jones wound up killing time together now and again. Almost always getting into trouble when they did.

That afternoon, lacrosse practice had gone late. They were in the play-offs the following weekend, and the coach was busting their balls every afternoon. Jones walked to his car in the near dusk, legs shaking, feeling light-headed from exertion. He didn't see Travis sitting on his hood until he was just feet away.

"Nice ride," said Travis.

"Birthday gift from my mom." It was a restored '67 Mustang, fire-engine red, mint condition, custom stereo and speakers. Jones loved it but was embarrassed by it, by the attention it drew, by its cherry shine. He hated it a little, too, because of how she lorded it over him all the time. *Aren't you lucky to have a mom who would buy you something like that? You better be nice to me. Don't leave me like your father did.*

"Must be nice to be filthy fucking rich."

Jones gave a little laugh. Nobody in The Hollows was rich, not back then. A few new residents were building nice houses in the hills. But people who came from The Hollows were descended from German settlers—they were peasant stock.

"My uncle restores antique cars," Jones said. "I don't think it cost that much. Just a lot of hard work on his part."

Travis gave a slow nod, ran his hand along the hood. "Seriously, man. It's nice."

"Thanks."

"Can I get a ride?"

Travis still bore a red half-moon scar under his eye from the beating Henry Ivy had given him at the homecoming game. It seemed to have humbled him a bit, that beating. Jones, like everyone at Hollows High, was glad for it. Travis was a bully and an asshole. Though Jones couldn't help but feel a little bad for the guy, too. It was the ultimate humiliation to get beaten down in front of the whole school by someone who had previously been regarded as the biggest geek on Earth.

Jones nodded his chin toward the car and walked over to pop the trunk. They both dropped their lacrosse gear inside.

He often thought about how normal everything was that afternoon, how right everything was with the world. They were just two ordinary kids. Each had his sets of problems; both were children of dysfunction. But it was a cold, pretty evening. They were well exercised, sober, healthy. They weren't aimless or needing to blow off steam. They were both tired from school and practice, and Jones couldn't wait to get in the shower. Any other day, each would have been home within the half hour. Jones would have eaten with his mother, then gone to his room to do homework—because if his grades fell, he couldn't play.

But as they pulled out of the school parking lot and made the left turn to go home, they saw a late bus stop briefly in the distance, then start moving on its way. And then they both saw her, her thin form weighted down by a heavy backpack, a violin case in her hand. Sarah Meyer walked with slow determination.

"She walking?" asked Travis.

"Looks like it," said Jones. He didn't know her at all. Once he'd walked past the music room and heard her practicing. It didn't sound that great to him; he wasn't sure what the fuss was all about.

"You know what I heard about her?" said Travis. He'd dropped his voice low though they were alone in the car.

"What?"

"That she gives great head."

Jones laughed, but at seventeen, just the thought of it caused his crotch to ache a little. Of course it was a lie. Because Travis was a liar, always making up the craziest shit just to get a reaction.

"No way." Sarah was a small girl, skinny, with fine, mousy brown hair, forever clad in corduroy pants and some girlie sweater her mom had obviously picked out. She had this distracted air about her; even in class he'd sometimes notice her staring out the window, daydreaming.

"I'm not kidding. She sucked Chad Donner off under the bleachers after school last week." Travis let out that hoot of laughter he was famous for, was getting himself all excited.

"Whatever."

"He said she liked it. *Loved* it. No, no. He said she was *crazy* for it."

"Shut up, Travis." Jones regretted giving him a ride. This happened all the time. He'd find himself hanging out with Travis and wondering why he didn't remember from the last time that he didn't like the guy at all.

"What? You don't believe me? Let's ask her."

By the time they reached her, Sarah was just about to turn off the main road and head up the unpaved drive that led to her house. It was nearly a mile long, running first through a field and then into a thick wooded area. Wasn't she scared, Jones wondered, in the gathering dark? She didn't seem to be, her shoulders square, her pace steady.

"Slow down, slow down," said Travis, as he rolled down the window. Then, "Hey, Sarah," he called. "Want a ride?"

. . .

But Jones didn't allow himself to blame Travis for what had happened on that very normal evening. There had been decades to marvel at the minutiae, the little things that had led them all there: if Jones hadn't dawdled in the locker room, reluctant to go home to his waiting mother and endure her smothering attentions—or if he'd lingered longer; if Travis's car hadn't been in the shop; if Sarah hadn't missed her bus; if Melody hadn't come strolling up from her place to meet Sarah on the road, having seen her from her bedroom window.

But there was another part of him, too, that suspected none of it could have been altered, that no matter what any of them had done that day, they all would have arrived together at the same point in time. That there was no way to have avoided the moment when their unique combination of energies, desires, and fears unified to create something awful.

Thinking that kept him from remembering that he was the one with all the power, literally the one in the driver's seat. All he would have had to do was keep going, endure whatever ribbing Travis had to offer up. *Aw, you always were a pussy, Cooper.* He could have ignored Travis's directive and taken them both home. Except he didn't.

1 3

Henry Ivy got suspended for a week because of the beating he gave Travis Crosby. But he didn't care. It had been a long time in coming. Travis had been terrorizing him since middle school. Looking back now, as a school counselor with a master's degree in childhood development, Henry saw what a troubled kid Travis had been, could even muster some compassion for him. But at the time, after years of humiliation—tray dumping, towel snapping, locker graffiti *(Henry Ivy is a faggot, gay boy, cocksucker)*, once a bloody nose in gym class after Travis threw a football in his face—Henry only saw him as a tormentor. He didn't know why; he'd never done anything to Travis. Travis had merely pegged Henry as an easy target, one unlikely to retaliate, and with a kind of lackluster determination took whatever opportunity presented itself to make a fool out of him.

For years, Henry endured. He didn't tattle. He didn't fight back. He just made himself as small as possible inside and waited for whatever it was Travis was inflicting to pass. More humiliating, if less painful than the actual event, was the wake of attention from his classmates. *Henry, are you all right? You should kick his ass, man.* One of his equally geeky friends—because Henry *had* been a major geek, with big, thick glasses, plaid shirts, and corduroy pants—would walk with him to the nurse's office, offering solace and advice. But most humiliating of all was when Maggie was the one to walk with him.

"He's a jerk," she'd tell him. "And a loser. One day you'll be making millions and he'll be pumping gas."

"I know," he'd say. He didn't know any such thing. He was just wish-

ing one day she'd look at him without pity in her eyes. One day he
wanted her to look at him with awe and pride, maybe even with love.
But that had never happened, though she'd always looked at him with
the affection and acceptance of enduring friendship. That was something. That was a lot.

These days, he'd like to think that the type of systematic torture he'd
suffered at the hands of Travis Crosby would not be tolerated. It would
be noticed and addressed, because educators should know by now how
toxic was the relationship between bully and victim, how it might turn
deadly.

But then, a kind of "boys will be boys" attitude allowed Henry's torture to continue without much interference. Once he even saw the PE
teacher smirk at one of Travis's favorite activities, stealing Henry's
underwear and towel while he was in the shower and hiding them so
that Henry was forced to walk wet and naked to his locker while everyone laughed.

That was more than twenty years ago, but as he pulled in front of
the Crosby home, it might as well have been last month. He felt the
surge of adrenaline in his hands as he parked the car and shut the ignition. Whatever Henry's history with Travis, Henry cared about Marshall. Maybe because he saw more of himself than he did of Travis in
the boy. Maybe because he recognized Marshall as another of Travis's
victims. Or maybe there was something deeper, something less noble
than caring for the welfare of a troubled boy. A kind of desire to salt the
wound of their past.

In high school, Henry had loved Maggie Monroe. He loved her like
an ache, a terrible pain in an organ he couldn't place or name. An illness
for which there was no cure. She hadn't loved him, of course. But she
was the reason, in his junior year, that he bulked up, got contacts, convinced his mother to take him shopping for some less dorky clothes. She
was the reason he'd beaten Travis in front of the entire school, in response to the most minor of assaults. As they'd passed each other on the
bleachers, Travis had growled low and mean, "Fucking faggot." It was
just loud enough for the other guys in Travis's group to hear and start
to laugh.

There was no flash of rage; he was not overcome by emotion. He just turned quickly and put a hand on Travis's shoulder, spun him around.

"Say it again," said Henry.

Surprise widened Travis's eyes for a second, but then he smiled. "What? Are you deaf, too? *Fucking faggot.*"

While Travis's crew was still laughing, Henry brought his fist out so fast and so hard that Travis fell back to the ground with the impact as it connected with his jaw. Henry thought it would be loud, like in the movies, his fist falling with a satisfying smack. But no, flesh on flesh was a soft sound. His own hand hurt so badly that he pulled it back to his chest, surprised at the heat rocketing up his arm.

He almost apologized, so chastened was he by the pain. But then there was something about Travis down, his hands up, his friends standing slack-jawed with shock, there was something about that momentary hush when everyone around them stopped what they were doing to look on, that caused Henry to drop to his knees, straddle Travis, and just start punching—face again, abdomen, ribs—until someone pulled him away, still swinging. He hadn't lost himself to anger; he was aware. He didn't feel good or triumphant. In fact, the physical effort, the pumping adrenaline, made him nauseated. Then he heard a girl weeping. "Stop it. Stop it. Please. Stop."

But it wasn't a girl. It was Travis. He didn't feel good, then, either. He looked down to see the other boy crying, lying on his side, curled into a fetal position. He felt relief only, mingled with something dark, a knowledge that he'd let the likes of Travis Crosby bring him low. He, a straight-A student with a perfect attendance record, was suspended.

"I'm surprised at you, Henry," said Mrs. Monroe, Maggie's mother and the school principal. "You're bigger than that. The smarter among us must use our intellects to resolve conflict. We can't let the Travis Crosbys of the world drive us to violence."

A month before, he'd have been crushed to earn her disapproval, anyone's disapproval. On that day in her overwarm office, Henry found he just didn't care. He remembered all the details—a pretty picture of Maggie as a little girl, the smell of coffee brewing somewhere, his student record open on her desk, a pencil holder shaped like an elephant, flecks of dust floating in the bright sunlight. But what he remembered most was the calm he felt. *This is what it feels like to do the right thing that others will think is wrong. This is what it feels like to stand up and fight back.*

"Sometimes the Travis Crosbys of the world don't understand anything else, Mrs. Monroe." Back talk! He'd been taught better. He thought he'd get one of the legendary Monroe tongue-lashings. But when he looked up at her, she just frowned and shook her head. She agreed with him; he saw it in the pale blue eyes behind her thick lenses.

"Suspension, Mr. Ivy, though it does pain me. One week."

He accepted his punishment and happily spent the week eating junk food and watching television, while his mother fretted about his "permanent record."

"What will the college people say?"

His father, a research scientist who barely visited the real world, so lost was he in his own gray matter, surprised Henry by saying, "I have confidence that you did what you had to do, Son."

"You do?"

"Sometimes the bullies of the world need a little humbling," he said, echoing Henry's own feelings. His dad was a good man, a bit absent-minded but always there when he was needed.

In Marshall Crosby, Henry saw himself but without the benefit of loving parents. Someone smart but lacking a sense of worth, abandoned by his mother, abused by his father. Someone being victimized by Travis Crosby. He'd wanted to give Marshall a break no one else had seemed willing to give.

As he got out of the car and crossed the street, he thought that Maggie was probably right. It wasn't a good idea to visit the Crosby home, a run-down two-story in The Acres. The white paint, graying and chipped, some of the black shutters askew on their hinges—the whole place had an aura of neglect. The lawn was patchy, overgrown in some places, dead in others. The garage door stood open; it was so filled with old junk that there was no room for a vehicle. The old Chevelle that he'd seen Marshall driving around in sat in the driveway, its engine

clinking as if it had recently been running. He stepped on the gray porch
and felt the wood creak beneath his weight.

Henry didn't just have Marshall on his mind. The news of Charlene Murray's disappearance had rocketed through the school. There
was an aura of worry and excitement in the hallways, klatches of girls
gathered whispering, dramatic. He picked up snippets as he walked the
halls. *She ran away to New York City. She had a fight with her mom. She
was afraid of her stepfather. I heard she has a boyfriend in Manhattan. I
thought she was with Rick Cooper!* The big news when he left the school
that day was that she'd updated the status bar on her Facebook page:
`Charlene is large and in charge, living in New York City! The
Hollows SUCKS!`

An early-morning meeting at the school, with police and some of
Charlene's friends and their parents, had yielded nothing. Rumors
abounded about a boyfriend in the city, someone she'd met at a concert,
but no one knew a name or address. Calls to her cell phone went straight
to voice mail. Other than the status bar update, no one had heard from
her since early evening yesterday. Melody Murray looked cored out by
worry, dark under the eyes; her voice was quaking. But the attitude of
the police, Jones Cooper in particular, was that Charlene Murray was a
runaway.

"She'll come home when she runs out of money," he'd said. "Or
nerve."

Maggie had shot her husband a look; then her eyes fell on Henry.
After the meeting, Maggie told him about Marshall's visit to her home,
about her conversation with Marshall's aunt.

"I feel like everyone's backing away from him," she said. "That's
what happens."

Then, "Maybe you *should* stop by there, Henry. If you think you can
keep your cool with Travis."

Maggie was a person who cared too much. It was one of the reasons
why he still loved her. Maybe he always would.

.   .   .

Henry lifted a hand and knocked on the door. It was flimsy, the glass in square panes rattling with each knock. The air had lost all the warmth and humidity it had held yesterday and taken a hard dive into winter. The lawns around him were a litter of fallen leaves, the trees already turning ashen fingers against the sky. No answer. He knocked again.

Just as he was turning to leave, he heard footsteps inside. A moment later Travis, thick-jawed and barrel-chested, opened the door. The two men regarded each other.

"What do you want, Ivy?"

Henry still remembered Travis lean and handsome. The man before him had deep lines at his eyes and around his mouth, a grayish cast to his skin. He was a bad facsimile of himself, had a chewed up, defeated aura.

"I'm looking for Marshall. Are you aware that he hasn't been in school in a week?"

Travis offered an exaggerated shrug, took a sip from a big mug of coffee he held. "News to me."

Henry felt a tingle of anger, a little flood of adrenaline. Travis leaned against the door frame.

"He told Dr. Cooper that he was helping you paint your office," Henry said. He tried to subtly peer into the house behind Travis, but the big man filled the doorway.

"True. In the afternoons and at night, though. Not during the school day."

Henry calculated that Travis had about fifty pounds on him. But he reeked of cigarettes. Henry ran five miles a day, lifted weights, even took a yoga class now and then. He was in good shape, just five pounds heavier than he'd been as a senior in college, and that was hard-gained muscle.

"Do you know where he is right now?" Henry glanced over at the car.

"You're telling me he's not in school, then I don't know."

Narrowed eyes, slack posture, a muscle clenching and unclenching in his jaw, Travis radiated a lazy meanness. It was an attitude he'd cultivated as an adolescent and then perfected as a town cop. Now that Travis had been stripped of his uniform, Henry thought the guy looked more dangerous than ever. It chilled Henry to think that Travis was no longer bound even by the code of the department.

"Look, Travis," said Henry. "Marshall's been doing really well. He's been on medication, studying hard. I think he has a good shot at a school like Rutgers or Fordham. But he needs to keep it up, come to class. You want what's best for him, don't you?"

Travis dug his hands into his pockets and rocked back on his heels, seeming to consider Henry's words. And Henry thought for a moment that he'd been heard. But then a derisive sneer spread across Travis's face.

"And you think you know what's best for him?" he said. "A bunch of head shrinking, pills, and history lessons?"

Henry felt his fist clench, felt the urge to take a step back and prepare to fight. But he kept his cool, thinking of Maggie, and held his ground.

"I do think some psychological help—medication combined with talk therapy—and a good education are the right things for Marshall, yes," he said. "And most people would agree with me."

"Well," said Travis. "I'm not most people. And Marshall is *my* son. So I'll decide what's best for him. And you, my sister, and that shrink can all fuck right off."

Instead of anger, Henry felt a kind of resigned sadness close around him like a curtain. He remembered how unsatisfying it had been to beat on Travis, how much it had hurt. Turned out Mrs. Monroe was right after all. *The smarter among us must use our intellects to resolve conflict.* He'd find another way to help Marshall. Henry offered a deferential nod, the lift of a hand.

"When you see Marshall tonight, ask him to come to school, to finish out the year and get his degree. After that, it's up to him."

He didn't look Travis in the face again, knew he couldn't see that nasty grin without being moved to do something he didn't want to do. So he turned and walked away.

At the bottom step, he heard Travis whisper, "Fucking faggot." And he thought, but couldn't be sure, that he heard Marshall, or someone, laugh in response. Henry Ivy kept walking.

Marshall thought he might throw up, but he pasted a wide smile across his face, so that when his father turned back from the doorway that's what he saw. The effort of holding up the corners of his mouth felt like it would break his face in two.

"I told you he was a pussy," said Travis.

Marshall tried to laugh, but it sounded strangled. He was so tired. He didn't remember ever being this tired before. He pushed himself off the bottom stair and went to stand by the side of the window by the door. He watched Mr. Ivy hesitate by his car a moment and look back at the house. Then Mr. Ivy climbed inside and closed the door. It was another minute before the engine started, as if he was watching the house, waiting. He was giving Marshall a sign. *It's not too late; if you come out now, I can take you away.* Marshall rested his hand on the knob just as Mr. Ivy pulled the silver Honda into the street and drove away. Marshall felt a part of himself go with him. He wanted to run into the street and wave his arms. *Mr. Ivy, help me!*

"What are you looking at? Is he still out there?"

Marshall watched the street, hoping that he'd see the car come back . . . maybe this time with the police. Maybe they knew who he was and what he'd done. Maybe they'd come back and take him away. In the fantasy of this, where they broke down the door and led him away in handcuffs, he only felt relief, a blessed, knee-weakening relief. Something like the feeling he'd had when he'd seen his father led away from the courtroom in handcuffs, knowing Travis would be in jail for six months, and that Marshall would be staying with Leila and Mark. He'd been scared; he'd been sad, too. But he'd also felt something inside him relax and expand. He wouldn't always be steeling himself, preparing to ward off blows. He could put down his guard.

"No. He's gone."

He felt his father's hand on his shoulder. "Why don't you get some rest? You've had a hard night." His father sounded almost *nice,* almost like he imagined other fathers sounded when they talked to their sons.

He turned to look at Travis. "But—," he started.

His father lifted a hand. "We'll deal with it later. Go on upstairs."

He couldn't bring himself to argue, didn't want to ruin it by starting a fight. And he *was* so tired; he could barely keep his eyes open. He headed up the stairs. When he turned around, he saw that his father was shouldering on his plaid wool jacket, something it seemed like he'd been wearing forever. Marshall was about to ask where he was going, but the words wouldn't come. Travis couldn't be going far because he wasn't allowed to drive. As he reached the landing and turned for his room, he barely registered the door opening and closing.

In his room, everything in the space around him, everything that had occurred in the last twelve hours, seemed fuzzy and indistinct. He found himself grasping at memories that slipped away like water through a cupped hand. He lay on his bed and stared at his computer.

The screen saver was a racing galaxy of stars; a doorway to that other universe. He had so much control there. In the real world, life was so messy, so many variables—things spun out of his grasp. Even inside himself, he seemed to have so little control over his emotions. And once his emotions took over, he split in two. There was the watcher within him, the creature without. The watcher could only look on, its desperate commands, pleas, and warnings ignored while the creature acted.

We don't choose where we come from, Marshall. And we often have little to say about what happens to us. But the adult understands that he and he alone is responsible for his life. You have choices now, choices that will affect your future. Let me help you make the right ones.

It was one of the first things Mr. Ivy had said to him. And the words had seemed strange at first, because no one had ever said anything like that to Marshall. He actually, for a moment, wondered if Mr. Ivy was making fun of him. When Marshall was called to anyone's office, it was for a reprimand or for the delivery of some bad news—like he was being held back a grade or was being switched to a lower-level class, one of those small rooms with one or two other students and a teacher who spoke very soft and slow, repeating the same stupid shit over and over. But Mr. Ivy never treated him like a moron or a mental case. He'd treated Marshall with respect, offered him a hand up from the swamp he was wading through.

Through a kind of mental fog, he heard a car door slam outside. He went to the window, wondering if Mr. Ivy had come back. But instead, Marshall watched his father climb into a taxi, saw the car pull up the street. *Where was he going?* He couldn't imagine his father calling for a cab, paying for a ride. A low-level anxiety started to buzz inside him. There were some flashes of memory—his mother crying, Charlene on all fours puking by the side of the highway. His head ached. It ached so bad he was nauseous from it.

He stumbled to his computer and, as he moved the mouse, the screen came to life. Charlene's page was open in front him; he read the list of comments from her last posting: "Charlene is large and in charge, living in New York City! The Hollows SUCKS!"

Even if she hadn't told him her password, it wouldn't have taken him long to figure it out. *Rockstar.* They were all living inside their heads, weren't they? They were living on dreams because life didn't quite measure up, and even in their teens they already had the vague sense that it never, ever would.

He started to laugh then. It came from a deep, dark place inside him. He thought of Mr. Ivy, Dr. Cooper, his aunt and uncle—all the people who believed in him, who put themselves out because when they looked at him, they saw something that wasn't there. His father always thought that he knew better, that he was smarter than everyone else. *If they were any good, Son? Trust me. They wouldn't want anything to do with you.* As it turned out, his dad was right.

It felt like laughter, ripping through him in great uncontrollable peals. But when the screen went dark, he saw himself. The boy in the re-flection was weeping.

Charlie floated through the day on the memory of Wanda's perfume; he imagined that the unique scent of her body and the floral melody she wore still clung to his skin. The sense memories of their night together kept coming back to him in flashes as he drove from job to job, as he crawled around in attics, carried traps to his truck. He barely noticed the hours pass. He kept hoping to hear her voice on the Nextel. But Old Joe was on dispatch today; it was Wanda's day off.

"I'll cook dinner for you tonight, Charlie, if you don't have any plans." She'd said it shyly, as though she worried about seeming too forward, too eager.

He didn't care about seeming too eager. Hell, he *was* eager.

"I don't have any plans, Wanda. And if I did, I'd cancel them." He could still hear that mellifluous giggle.

He'd intended to knock off a bit early, pick up some flowers and a nice bottle of wine before going back to Wanda's. But as he was finishing his last call, he remembered Mrs. Monroe and the traps he'd left in her attic. He'd promised he'd go back to her today. Remembering her standing there watching him leave, he couldn't bring himself to let her down. He called Wanda from his cell, her home number on a folded sticky note in his pocket. He wondered if she'd be angry, or annoyed. Most women would be.

"That's what I've always liked about you, Charlie," she said. "You're a kind person. A man of your word. Trust me, it's a rare, rare thing. You take your time."

"Wanda," he said, a rush of feeling pulsing through him. "I'm dying to put my arms around you."

There was a moment of silence, when he heard her breathing. He wasn't worried that he'd said the wrong thing. They were past that awkwardness already.

"I'm waiting for you, Charlie," she said. Her voice sounded breathy and sweet.

He let out a little moan. "Okay, I better go before I come racing over there right now."

"Go take care of Mrs. Monroe. And then get over here and take care of me," she said and hung up with a playful laugh. He thought of her perfect breasts and parted lips and was glad he had a ten-minute drive to Mrs. Monroe's to get his pants under control.

As he pulled up to the old house, he saw Mrs. Monroe standing in the big bay window over the porch. She stepped back quickly when she saw him turn in the drive, maybe embarrassed to be caught waiting. She greeted him at the door.

"I thought you forgot about me. I called your dispatch," she said. "The guy who answered the phone was a moron, not that nice girl on the phone yesterday."

"Oh, no, Mrs. Monroe. I wouldn't forget."

She waved a hand. "People today forget everything. They even forget to take care of their children." She wasn't crotchety, not complaining. She just seemed sad, wistful.

He wanted to disagree with her, to say something positive to change her mind. But too large a part of him agreed with her. He wondered if he was the only one who felt frightened and agitated watching television—the terrible programming, the manipulative advertising. *What is this doing to our culture?* he'd wonder. But on some nights, he was too tired to turn it off. And suddenly everyone was driving like they were mildly drunk—people pulling out into traffic without really looking, weaving in their lanes. Inevitably, he'd glance over to see someone entrenched in conversation on a cell phone, oblivious to everything else. People did forget everything. They even forgot themselves.

"Well, I'm not one of those people."

"A throwback," she said with a smile, giving him a pat on the arm.

"I guess so."

He made his way toward the staircase. "Any noise last night or today?"

"Not a peep." She stayed at the bottom landing. "Forgive me if I don't follow you up. My arthritis."

"No problem. I remember where the attic access is."

But the traps in the attic were empty, the bait untouched. He moved some of the junk around but still saw none of the usual signs—no feces, no evidence of gnawing. The scent he'd caught yesterday was gone. Maybe it had been his imagination. Or hers. He entertained the notion that the old lady might be losing it, hearing things that weren't there. But no, she didn't seem the type. Still, what he'd smelled yesterday was an odor that only intensified with time. If there was something dead up there, it should only smell worse today than yesterday. Maybe the cool weather had slowed the decay. He'd leave the traps one more day, come back again tomorrow.

He found Mrs. Monroe on the couch watching the news. On the screen, a picture of a missing girl—a pretty girl, thin with fair skin and jet hair, dark brown eyes. *An assumed runaway. Police encourage anyone who has seen her to contact them immediately,* a male voice-over declared grimly.

"Mrs. Monroe," he said. The old woman gave a little jump of surprise. "I'm sorry. I didn't mean to startle you."

"Oh," she said, pointing at the screen. "That girl, she's a friend of my grandson's. They're all very worried. No one's spoken to her since last night."

"I'm sorry. I hadn't heard the news today."

The old woman pushed herself from the couch with effort, waving away his attempt to help her.

"Find anything up there?" she asked. When she finally rose, she steadied herself with her cane.

"Afraid not. I'll come back tomorrow and check again." Her shoulders seemed to sag a bit with disappointment; she drew in a weary breath.

"All right." She handed him a rolled-up bill. "I appreciate it."

"Oh, no—," he started to decline. But she pushed the money into his hand.

At the door he said, "I hope she's all right. Your grandson's friend."

"I do, too," she said with a shake of her head. "She's a troubled girl. Problems at home, I think."

"I'm sure she'll turn up."

He wasn't sure of this at all, of course. In high school, a friend of his—a girl friend he'd secretly loved—had run away. Lily. The memory of it caused a surprising catch of sadness in his throat. It was something he seldom thought about anymore, had willed away from conscious thought. No one ever saw her again. Ever. He didn't share this with Mrs. Monroe.

It wasn't until he was back in his truck and driving toward Wanda's that Charlie remembered the girl he'd seen last night, the one with the punky hair who'd climbed into the old muscle car. Could it be the same girl? Should he call the police and say something?

Thinking about her standing there on the street, looking uneasily around her, caused him to remember Lily and that ugly, frightening time in his life. The memories were so vivid, so powerful—the smell of her skin, the sound of her voice, the fear, the dread, that indescribable unknowing. The sadness came on him so forcefully that he had to pull over on the shoulder of the highway and rest his head against the wheel. It was so many years ago, and there was still so much pain.

His phone rang then, startling him, and he answered it quickly. "Hello."

"Charlie?"

"Wanda."

"Are you all right?"

"Yes," he said, forcing brightness into his tone. "I'm just on my way. Sorry about that."

"I'll put the chicken in."

There was something sweet, comforting about that sentence. Something that smacked of a domesticity he had craved without even realizing it. He let the feeling wash over him, rinse away the memories that had come back to call. He'd do what he'd planned, pick up some wine and some flowers and spend the evening with a beautiful woman who seemed to really like him. He'd tell her what he saw, ask her what she thought. Maybe he'd even tell her about Lily, a girl he'd loved a lifetime ago who haunted him still.

14

When his mother died, Jones had used all the emotions that rocketed through him to put on a powerful display of grief. What he felt, in fact, was a shuddering relief, as if at the easing of unbearable pain. He felt rage. He felt strangely unmoored, as though he'd been tied to his life only by the obligation he felt to care for his mother. But he did not feel grief. He would not miss her. Still, he might have been found weeping at her bedside in the hospital or at her graveside during the funeral. It wasn't an act.

Poor Jones. He was so good to her. He spent his whole life caring for her.

He knew that's what they all thought. It wasn't true. He'd spent his whole life tending to her, appeasing her, pandering to her. These things were very different. Very different.

When his mother was buried and all the proceedings were finished and he was left alone for the first time in his life, the silence almost deafened him. It filled the house and washed over him. While Abigail had lived, there was never quiet. There was always her constant talking— gossiping, complaining, explaining, reprimanding, directing. And then there was the television, on morning, noon, and night, quiet only when he went into her room at night and turned it off after she fell asleep. Sometimes she'd wake up and turn it back on. He'd hear it when he got up in the night to use the toilet—the melodramatic strains of music from old movies, tinny laugh tracks.

He'd wondered if there was something wrong with him, not to feel grief for his mother. Maybe there had *always* been something wrong with him, maybe he lacked some human capacity to feel. Like now, for instance, as Melody Murray sat weeping (again) in his office, he felt nothing but a low-grade annoyance. She had the same aura about her as Abigail had, that self-dramatizing near hysteria, always seeking comfort and pity from those around her, giving nothing. Charlene had it, too, that willingness to cause any amount of discord and pain as long as it drew attention to herself. He'd wanted to explain it to Ricky, to tell him why he didn't like the girl, but he found he didn't have the words for it. Anyway, Ricky wouldn't have listened. That kid had never listened to a word Jones had to say.

He'd watched as Maggie spent the day comforting and cajoling, trying to gently draw information from Charlene's friends, their son, Melody, anyone who had any connection to Charlene. He'd felt relief that she was around for this. She could be all the things he was not—yielding, comforting, encouraging. Watching her, he had been reminded that Maggie was the one who'd saved him. If she hadn't returned to The Hollows when she did—shortly after Abigail's passing—if she hadn't seen something in him to love, he wasn't sure what would have happened to him.

His wife couldn't have been more different from his mother; Mags was sensible, practical, giving, loving, understanding. Though Maggie would have hated to hear him say so, in those ways she was truly Elizabeth Monroe's daughter. Although Maggie also possessed the soft gentility of her father, lacked Elizabeth's hard edges and sharp tongue.

"Where's Graham, Melody?" asked Jones. "Have you been able to reach him?"

She looked up at him sullenly. "No."

There were a number of things bothering Jones. The fact that Graham was nowhere to be found was chief among them. The whole hunting thing just didn't ring true, especially since none of the morons Graham usually hung around with had gone with him. Graham wasn't the type to go off by himself in the woods and get meditative, to hunt and reflect. He was the type to go off into the woods with his buddies under the pretense of hunting and get drunk, pass out in the blind, never fire off a round.

Other things were bothering Jones, too. According to Charlene's phone records, she hadn't used her cell phone since late afternoon yesterday. Admittedly, the modern teenager was a bit of a mystery to Jones. But he did know one thing: they were wired together like the Borg, constantly calling, e-mailing, texting, social-networking. If Charlene was involved in some kind of drama that led her to run away, she'd have called or sent text messages to *everyone*.

Then he'd discovered that the credit card attached to Charlene's mobile account was in Graham's name. Graham had purchased that phone for her, paid the bill every month, even though her mother didn't know and hadn't wanted her to have one. But Charlene had told everyone who'd listen that she was afraid of him, that he was "inappropriate" with her. It was a word all her friends and even Ricky had used independently of one another, as if she'd told them each precisely the same thing, using the same phrasing. Which didn't mean it wasn't true. He could see the potential in Graham, especially as Charlene grew older, her beauty eclipsing Melody's completely. Still, if it *was* true, and Graham was using gifts to manipulate his relationship with Charlene, and now they were both missing, what did it mean?

"You still haven't told us what you fought about," said Jones. Melody responded with a sigh, her weeping subsiding. She was all dressed up in a neat red sweater and black skirt, pumps. She'd put her face on and done her hair for the local afternoon news.

"Char," she'd said, playing the role of good mother for the camera. "Just come home, honey, we'll work it all out. I promise. And if anyone knows anything or has seen my girl, please call the hotline." He had to hand it to her. She pulled it out when the cameras started to roll. He remembered that about her.

"The truth is," she said, making a show of rubbing her temples, "I don't even remember what started it. Something about what she was wearing. It exposed her navel, and I told her to change her shirt. I told her she looked like a tramp. Things just got all crazy from there. The next thing I knew, she'd packed a bag and was walking out the door. Not the first time. I figured she'd be back in an hour. Or call and we'd make up. That's how it is with us."

Chuck stood in the corner of the office. He'd been silent for about fifteen minutes, staring out the window. But Jones knew he was present, listening. They'd set it up this way, eliminated all the people she was leaning on—Maggie, Char's friends and their mothers. Sent them all home one by one. They didn't want it to seem immediately like an interrogation.

"We have a few questions, Ms. Murray," said Chuck, walking from his place by the window and sitting in the chair beside Melody, across from Jones's desk. Melody didn't look up at him, kept rubbing at her temples, her eyes closed.

"Mel, that phone of Charlene's?" said Jones. "Looks like Graham got it for her."

Melody opened her eyes and looked at Jones. "No."

"It's his credit card on the account."

Melody didn't say anything, looked down at her cuticles.

"It might be nothing," said Chuck. "But the last charge on his card was late yesterday afternoon. Twenty-three dollars and change at the Safeway. Around the same time as Charlene's last call. When did you say he left for his hunting trip?"

The pale white of Melody's skin, the lines around her eyes, the sagging of her jowls got Jones to thinking about his mother again. It was the stroke that finally did Abigail in. After decades of threatening to become an invalid, a lifetime of imagined illness, and pointless trips to doctors in an ever-widening radius around town, he'd come home from work one night to find her on the bathroom floor, stinking of urine. For a moment, he thought it was an act.

"Mother. Mom?" he said from the doorway. She'd been complaining about terrible headaches for days, but he'd paid her no mind.

Take an aspirin, Mom.

That's what I love about you, Jones. You're the soul of compassion.

No doubt she would have loved the idea of him carrying her around, bathing her, changing her diapers like an infant. But even he had his limits.

"Graham and I . . . haven't been getting along," said Melody softly. "I mean, he hasn't been coming home every night for a while now."

"So, he didn't go hunting?" asked Chuck.

"He said he might go hunting. But I haven't been able to reach him."

"Where might he go hunting if that's what he did?"

"How should I know?" she snapped. She sat up suddenly from the grief-stricken slouch she'd been in. "What do I know about hunting?"

Chuck gave her an empathetic nod, and Jones was grateful he was there. He liked the other man's big-city cool, an aura that he'd seen and heard it all, was surprised by nothing. Jones wanted to throttle Melody, could feel the itch in his hands, though he'd never struck a woman in his life. He tilted back in his chair, feeling it tip, finding his balance. He kept his eyes on Melody, who was getting squirmy and agitated. Outside his office, Jones heard someone laughing, smelled something vile cooking in the microwave.

"I think you ought to be out there looking for my daughter instead of sitting around here talking to me."

"I hear you, Mrs. Murray," said Chuck. "And I assure you we haven't lost our focus. But there are some things that concern us. We've heard from several people that Charlene was afraid of Graham. What do you make of that?"

Melody blew out a disdainful breath. "That's bullshit. That's Charlene making a show of herself. Trying to get people to feel sorry for her."

"But he hit her," said Jones. "Several people saw her black eye. She told my son and Britney that he hit her."

"It was an accident," she said, looking away. "She got involved in a fight between me and Graham. He was swinging at me."

Nobody said anything for a moment. Then, "I'm not *saying* it was right. I'm just saying he didn't mean to do it. After that, I asked him to leave. That's why he hasn't been sleeping at home much."

"So how would you characterize their relationship, then? Why would he buy her a cell phone and keep that from you?"

"Charlene has a way of getting what she wants," she said with more than a shade of resentment. She let out a little laugh. "It's funny, all those girls saying that Graham made these subtle advances. But it was Charlene who was always half flirting, wearing revealing pajamas when he was around, batting her eyelashes. Graham is a lot of things. Subtle is not one of them."

"So you think she could have convinced him to get her that phone?"

Melody nodded. "Or she could have lifted his card. Graham wasn't good with money. He might not have noticed for a while."

Jones and Chuck exchanged a look, both picking up on her use of the past tense. Not that it meant anything necessarily. It could just mean that she considered their relationship over.

"Could she have convinced him to go away with her, Melody?"

Jones saw something flash across her face, he couldn't say what. Was it calculating? She wasn't a stupid woman, though he was tempted—had always been tempted—to think of her as such. She'd been a mediocre student, gone to community college, like he had. She held a good job doing something administrative at the big oil company that had some offices in a town nearby. She wasn't an intellectual. She had what he thought of as survival smarts. She'd be what she needed to be to get by.

"Is that what you think?" she asked, a shrillness creeping into her voice. She gripped the arms of the chair. "That they ran off together?"

Chuck lifted a hand. "Nobody's saying anything yet. But no one seems to know where either of them is at the moment. Could just be a coincidence."

"Graham didn't show up for work today," said Jones.

"What else is new?" said Melody with a snort. "He's had four jobs this year alone."

Jones saw it then. Melody Murray hated her husband. Nothing so unusual about that. Hateful feelings could crop up in a marriage, like weeds pushing their way through concrete. If you weren't vigilant, they took over quickly, like kudzu, depriving love of light and air until it withered and died. It was a slow, silent death, impossible to imagine in the heat of new love.

She rose from her seat, and neither of them moved to stop her. She walked over to the couch behind her and picked up her jacket and purse, moving slowly.

"I don't know what you two think you're getting at," she said, pulling on her coat. "But Charlene did *not* run off with Graham. She hates him."

"But that might not have stopped her from using him for a ride. In which case, Graham is in a lot of trouble."

"I don't give a shit about Graham," she yelled suddenly. "You get that? Just help me find my girl."

Chuck stood, put up two placating palms. "There are detectives at your house right now, going through Charlene's room, looking at her computer, trying to figure out where she might have gone."

Melody looked confused for a minute. "At *my* house? I didn't give permission for that."

"When we realized that Graham was missing, that the credit card on Charlene's account belonged to him, that her friends seemed to feel she was afraid of him, we obtained a warrant from a judge. We don't need your permission, Melody," Jones said.

He might have handled someone else differently. Someone he liked, trusted, respected. Someone he didn't know as well as he knew Melody Murray. He might have asked her permission before obtaining a warrant. Most parents of runaways would throw open their doors. But he didn't ask. Whether he'd acted on instinct or bias, he couldn't be sure.

He felt her eyes on him, and he looked back at her, daring her to open her mouth in front of Chuck, who was looking back and forth between them. Chuck was too smart, too canny, not to be picking up on the subtext. But Melody didn't say anything else; she just turned and stormed out, slamming the door hard enough to rattle the thin walls.

Jones got up after a beat and pulled on his jacket. He'd follow her home, see what the other detectives had found there.

"Lots of history in this town, huh?" said Chuck, trailing behind.

Jones didn't feel inclined to answer.

15

She wouldn't write that, Mom."

"Then who did?"

"I don't know. But think about it. 'Charlene is large and in charge'? She would never use such clichéd language."

But Charlene was a cliché, a living cliché, though Ricky and Charlene herself were both too young to realize it. Maggie didn't say as much, of course. And he was right; it didn't really sound like Charlene. She didn't say that, either. The day was starting to take its toll. She had a low-grade ache behind her eyes, a fatigue-induced nausea.

"Ricky," she said, sitting down at the kitchen table. It was a small banquette, tucked into a window seat. Behind them outside, leaves fell in streamers of red, orange, gold, and brown. They'd sat together at this table since he was a baby, first in a high chair, then in a booster seat, then beside her. She remembered all the milled vegetables she used to make—peas, carrots, squash. Then it was grilled cheese, peanut butter and jelly, macaroni and cheese—the happy, clean, innocent foods of childhood.

Now he sat across from her, watching her with the same intensity he'd had since he was a child. When he wanted something from her, he was relentless. Right now, he wanted her to tell him that Charlene had not broken up with him and run away to some imaginary life in New York City without so much as a backward glance. At the moment, he wanted to believe that something had happened to *take* her away. Even though Maggie was certain he didn't understand the ramifications of wishing such a thing. He didn't really know what that would mean.

"The best thing we can do right now is avoid jumping to conclusions. We need to keep the lines of communication open for Charlene so when she does reach out—and I believe she will—we're here for her." With her thumbnail, she chipped away at some dried piece of food on the wood surface of the table. It was only the three of them. Why was it so hard to keep things clean?

"But what if she *can't* reach out? I mean, everyone has assumed that she ran away, but what if something else happened to her?"

He seemed to have forgotten altogether about the message she'd written him. Maggie thought about reminding him, but then decided against it. She reached across the table and put her hand on his. Her eyes drifted to the tattoo. It still looked red and inflamed. She looked away and tried to catch his eye.

"Your father and the rest of the department are looking for her. They're not just blowing her off as a runaway. They're investigating the disappearance. We have to trust them to do their jobs well." She stopped short, too, of telling him about Graham's being missing as well, about the credit card on Charlene's cell phone account. It wasn't yet public knowledge anyway, and it would only hurt or frighten him further.

He started kicking the bottom of the banquette with his heel. It made a hollow knocking noise. He'd always done this absently, when he was reading or thinking. It drove Jones crazy.

"He hates her," he said.

She felt a flash of something; her cheeks went hot. "No, he doesn't. Of course he doesn't."

"You know he does."

"You don't understand your father," she said. She released a tired breath. "Sometimes he doesn't know how to show fear or concern. It just comes off like anger or judgment. He cares about people. He helps them. That's who he is."

Her son turned angry, dark eyes on her. "Maybe you're the one who doesn't understand him."

He got up from the table before she had a chance to respond.

"He's probably *glad* Charlene's gone," he said, his voice cracking.

"Stop it," she said. She reached for him as he moved toward the door. He slipped out of her grasp. In the turned-up corners of his eyebrows she saw the depth of his sadness. It wasn't just about Charlene. She felt her heart clenching.

"He doesn't care about people," Ricky said, his voice coming up an octave. "He doesn't care about Charlene. He doesn't even care about me."

"Your father loves you." It sounded lame, and she hated having to say it. She shouldn't have to convince him; he should know it. Why didn't he?

He turned in the doorway. "I know you believe that, Mom. I guess the problem is that I don't."

"Ricky," she said. But he was already heading fast down the hallway. By the time she reached the front door, he was getting in his car. She walked out after him, bracing herself against the cold air. The sky was a flat, dead gray. The air tingled with the promise of snow, though just yesterday they'd all been wilting, wondering if fall would ever come.

"Where are you going?" He was sitting in the car Jones had helped him buy for his birthday, a restored Pontiac GTO. Ricky bought the gas, paid the insurance. She couldn't keep him from leaving. She felt small, weak, unable to control anything in her life, including her own child.

"I have to work," he said.

That was a relief, at least, a sign that he was not going off the rails. He'd been working at the same music store since he was fifteen. Sound Design sold CDs, books, high-quality instruments; it had been there since she was a kid, sitting in a strip mall off the main highway that ran through town. She still thought of it as a record shop, which made Ricky laugh. He was helping them to design a website to keep the store more current, to keep it from going the way of all small businesses being dwarfed by Internet giants. She'd gone to school with the owner, Larry Schwartz, who'd inherited the store from his father.

For a second she'd thought Ricky was headed out to find Charlene. And there would have been nothing she could do to stop him. That was exactly what they'd feared, that chasing Charlene would lead him off the path, into the woods. She put a hand on his arm.

"I know how hard this is. I'm afraid for her, too," she said. "Just try to stay calm. Don't do anything crazy," she said.

"Like what?"

"Just stay put, Ricky. She'll come back when she's ready. She'll call you."

Warm air drifted from the car. She heard a mournful strain of music she didn't recognize from the radio.

"And what if she can't? What if something has happened to her?"

She shook her head, took a deep breath. "They're looking for her. If something's happened, they'll find out."

He nodded uncertainly, then shifted the car into reverse. She stepped back, stuck her hands into the pockets of her jeans. She hadn't changed her clothes since she got dressed last night. She'd canceled all her patients today, trying to do what she could for Melody and for Jones.

"I love her, Mom." In the split second before he completed the sentence, she thought he was going to say *I love you, Mom.* She felt that familiar rise of happiness, and then the fall of disappointment. It seemed like forever since he'd said that. *I love you sooo much, Mommy,* he used to say, offering exuberant embraces, unembarrassed kisses.

"I know you do, sweetie. I know. It's going to be okay. You'll see."

It was a false assurance, and they both knew it. But he smiled at her just the same. She watched him drive off until his taillights disappeared around the corner. She felt the urge to cry, but she fought it back. No time for that.

Back in her office, she sorted through voice messages and e-mails, many of them asking about or related to Charlene. News had spread like a cold virus. There was an e-mail notice about a town meeting at eight, at the school, organized by Henry Ivy—to brainstorm about Charlene, where she might have gone, and organize information to help the police. Anyone who knows Charlene is urged to attend. That's what she loved about Henry, he was always the first responder, getting people together to help when there was a crisis.

The local women's club, too, had organized a search party; neighbors were walking the area around Charlene's house, others were making calls. Any help is welcome, even just the forwarding of this e-mail message. The message contained the most recent school picture of Charlene.

Maggie remembered this about The Hollows, now that it was happening again. How those who had lived here generation after generation rallied in a crisis. Meetings were called, food was made, people reported for any task that might help. There was an invisible net that could be seen only when tears were shed.

It had been the same when Sarah was missing, years ago. Initially, she, too, was suspected to have run away, trying to punish her mother. But Maggie also remembered a strange energy, a dark current of knowing that something awful had happened. Even the next day, when the air was buzzing with a kind of excited, gossipy fear, much like today, there was something ugly hovering. Even Maggie and the other kids seem to sense that Sarah wasn't just going to turn up, sheepish for having caused so much trouble.

They found Sarah's body hours after the first snow of the season started to fall. The school was called to assembly, and Travis Crosby Sr., the Hollows police chief at the time, delivered the news in a soft, wobbling voice. Maggie remembered the heavy silence that fell, a collective hush of disbelief, and then the wailing started, first low and singular. Then a cacophony of weeping sounds, a chorus of pain.

She'd just felt gutted, numb. She hadn't really known Sarah well, wasn't sure how to feel other than afraid. She saw her mother up onstage and, unthinking, went to join her. Her mother took her in her arms, and they stood like that while Elizabeth told students to return to their homerooms, said that parents would be called and the counselors would organize in the cafeteria for anyone who needed to talk and to run a study hall for children whose parents couldn't get away from work.

· · ·

Maggie listened to her voice mail: her neurotic was calling to cancel his appointment for tomorrow because he was afraid it might rain (he didn't think he was going to get away with that, did he?); a lawyer she knew needed a consult; her mother, who often confused her office number with her cell phone, was calling to find out what was happening with Charlene. Three more messages were hang-ups, something that always made her uneasy. During her residency at Columbia, a young woman she'd been seeing ended her life with a bottle of painkillers. When Maggie got to her office that morning, her machine was filled with messages, each just the sound of soft, measured breathing and then a sudden hang-up. Later that day, she learned about her patient's suicide from the detective who was called to the scene. That breathing stayed with her; she thought of it as the sound of despair, of reaching out to find no one there. She heard it sometimes in her dreams.

Of course, that was in the days before everyone had a cell phone and caller ID. Her patients could reach her now if they needed her in the night. She could see who was calling and hanging up on her, make a proactive phone call in return. She scrolled through the numbers on the phone's digital display. Unknown caller. A low agitation was setting in, that feeling she had when something, someone, she cared about was in crisis and she was powerless to help. Then, the phone in her hand started to ring. Unknown caller. She picked up quickly.

"Dr. Cooper," she answered.

There was just silence on the line, a distant crackle. She took a wild guess. "Marshall? Is that you?"

"How did you know?" he asked, sounding young, frightened.

"I was hoping, Marshall. I've been concerned about you. How are you? Let's talk."

"I'm sorry," he said. "For the way I acted yesterday." She felt a wash of relief. He had come back; he still wanted help. She knew what to do here.

"I understand," she said. "You're under stress. There are better ways to cope, and we can work on that."

"I just want to know something."

"What's that?"

"How do you know if you're a good person? I mean, how do you know if you're *not*?"

She'd had this kind of existential conversation with him before. She answered him the way she always did.

"I don't think anyone is only good or only bad, Marshall. People are multilayered with qualities and flaws."

"Right," he said quickly, almost sounding annoyed. "But some people are bad. They do bad things to other people. They hurt people."

There was a lump of dread in her center. *Who was he talking about?*

"True," she said carefully. "But even those people often have something that redeems them." A silence followed, went on too long. She thought maybe he'd hung up. Then, "I'm not sure I believe in redemption."

"Then what? We're defined by our mistakes, our bad qualities? One false move and there's no forgiveness?"

"It depends on what we've done, doesn't it?"

"What are we talking about here, Marshall? Have you done something?"

His breathing came ragged, as though he was crying.

"Whatever it is, we can talk about it, work through it."

"I have to go," he said. "I'm sorry."

And the line went dead.

"Marshall," she said pointlessly. She quickly moved to her desk, looked up his number and called back, but the line was busy. She hung up and tried again. This time the line just rang and rang until she gave up.

She felt that familiar wash of anxiety again and thought of her mother. When she'd told Elizabeth that she wanted to be a psychologist, that she wanted to go on to graduate school for her doctorate in psychology and go into private practice, she hadn't gotten the reaction she'd expected. Elizabeth had looked more worried than excited or proud. Maggie never forgot what she'd said, so surprised and disappointed had she been at the words.

"You can't save the world, Magpie. You've been trying all your life, bringing home every stray and broken thing. Some things can't be fixed."

Maggie couldn't remember now where they'd been. Maybe Telephone Bar on Second Avenue, her parents in for one of their frequent visits. Someplace in the city, she knew that. She remembered the smell of vinegar, the lightness she felt drinking red wine with her parents.

"But some can," she'd said quietly. "And how do you know the difference unless you try?"

"But why do *you* have to be the one to try?"

"Elizabeth," her father had admonished. "It's wonderful, Maggie. It's a wonderful choice." He'd put a comforting hand on her arm.

She hadn't argued further with her mother. She knew it was pointless to try to bring Elizabeth around to her way of thinking. Dinner had continued with discussions about money, what there was for graduate school, what Maggie would have to earn, what loans and grants they should try to acquire. On the surface, it was all very calm, practical, optimistic. But Maggie hadn't eaten another bite, her insides a brew of sadness and disappointment, anger at her mother for her—what was the word?—her *distance,* her know-it-all attitude about everything, even what Maggie chose to do with her life.

Later, after becoming a parent herself, Maggie understood her mother's worry better. She saw it in Ricky, this desire to shelter the fragile things he found, like Charlene, and his willingness to sacrifice himself for others. He didn't know how vulnerable he made himself. She remembered the baby squirrel he'd found in their backyard. He'd built a bed out of washcloths and tried to feed it milk from a dropper; it had died the next day. He was six at the time, and sometimes she still remembered how he'd cried, with the tragic hopelessness of the young. It had caused her a physical pain to see him so sad, because she knew how much it hurt to try to save something that could not be saved.

Now she walked over to her desk, called Henry Ivy on his cell phone, and got his voice mail.

"I had a strange call from Marshall," she said. "Call right away. I'm really worried."

Then she dialed Leila, Marshall's aunt, and also got voice mail. She left a similar message. She didn't expect to hear back, but maybe Leila would relent and send one of the boys over there. As a last resort, she looked up Angie's number and called her, was surprised when she answered.

"This is Dr. Cooper," Maggie said.

"I've been expecting your call." Why did everyone keep saying that?

"You have?"

"I should have called you when Marshall went back to Travis. But I . . . ," she said, letting the sentence trail.

"I'm worried about him," Maggie said when the other woman didn't go on. "He seems in a very dark place."

"He's vile, Dr. Cooper," she said sharply. "He's cruel, he's abusive. He's Travis times one hundred. Just like Travis is worse than his father is, none of the old man's code. Every generation, the gene gets stronger."

Maggie was surprised into silence by the venom in her voice.

"At least the old man never hit a woman," Angie went on. "He'd beat the crap out of Travis, but he never hit Travis's mother or sister."

Police Chief Crosby still lived in The Hollows, getting more cantankerous and meaner as he got older. Maggie would expect to see him at the town meeting tonight. He was always right on the spot when there was trouble, his role as town cop dying hard.

"Angie—"

"It's our fault. I know that. Marshall saw violence—terrible, awful violence—before he was old enough to even talk. There was never a warm minute in our house. Never. And I'm sorry for that."

It occurred to Maggie then that maybe Angie had been drinking, her words tumbling, her tone wavering between angry and maudlin.

"Has something happened between you and Marshall?"

She heard Angie start to cry.

"Has he been violent with you, Angie? We need to address it if he has, because up until now, he hasn't been violent. And a sudden change in his behavior could suggest a crisis point."

"I don't want to get him in trouble, Dr. Cooper. I just want him to stay away from me. Tell him that, will you? Just tell him to stay away?"

The line went dead, and Maggie really wished people would stop hanging up on her. The whole family had a serious problem with abruptly ending unpleasant conversations. Looking at the phone still in her hand, Maggie felt her frustration reach its peak, and she started to internally back away. She was worried about Marshall, but she was equally worried about Charlene, and her own son. She thought about calling Jones, alerting him to the problems with Marshall, but everyone was so focused on Charlene at the moment that she doubted her call would amount to much. She could almost hear Jones. *What do you want me to do, Mags? Bring the kid in because you had a worrying phone call? I've got a missing girl here.*

Maggie decided to turn her focus back to the immediate crisis. She walked over to her computer and opened up Facebook, entered the log-in and password Ricky had left for her on a yellow sticky note on her computer screen. He'd wanted her to look at Charlene's page, see the status bar update that had him so worked up.

The page loaded slowly, Maggie's computer being old and cluttered with too many files and applications that she had neither the know-how nor the inclination to manage. Eventually, her screen filled with Charlene's image and a list of comments from friends, all of them on-screen from that day. Where are you, girl? We're all so worried! Hope you're livin' it up in NYC! You rock! I always knew you'd get out of here! Each message was accompanied by a thumbnail image of the sender, most of whom Maggie recognized, all of them vamping or clowning around for the camera. She scrolled through until she found Ricky's image, where he was doing his best to look arty and haunted. But to Maggie, he just looked like her baby dressed up for Halloween, a little silly and self-conscious. She supposed that was why teenagers never wanted their parents around; parents only saw the children they knew, not the adults they were trying to become. Come home, Char. This is uncool, read Ricky's message. Please.

Something caught her eye in the left-hand corner of the screen, an area labeled "Mutual Friends." Charlene and Ricky had nineteen friends in common; Maggie clicked on the "see all" link, feeling very proud of her technical prowess. She expected to see familiar faces, and she did—Britney, Tiffany, Amber. Cursory glances at their pages showed the usual—messages from friends, favorite books and music, pictures from parties and school events. No indications of the drugs, or alcohol abuse, or teenage sexual depravity that the media would have everyone believe was going on, no seedy underbelly to Hollows High.

But many of the people listed she didn't recognize. They looked older, though they shared Charlene and Ricky's gothic chic. She started clicking on pictures and found musicians, nightclubbers, an East Village bar owner, the owner of a seedy-looking recording studio. She knew Ricky and Charlene had been sneaking into the city for a while now, going to shows and clubs—his guilty admission to Chuck was not exactly news to her. She'd done it herself as a kid. Were these the people they were hanging out with? They looked hard-edged and strange, too old for the scene but still hanging on. One young woman had a tattoo on her face, a trail of tears. One pale, too-thin man brooded with a cigarette dangling from his mouth, dark circles under his eyes.

Maggie leaned her head back against the leather of her chair, the brightness of the screen bothering her because of her fatigue and the headache that was increasing behind her eyes. Ricky had given her access to his account. Had he, on some level, wanted her to see these people? He couldn't have thought she'd just look at Charlene's page and not explore his. Hadn't he told her that he didn't know Char's friends in the city? That he thought she'd been lying?

Maggie found herself somewhat guiltily scrolling through her son's in-box, reading messages from friends and acquaintances. There was nothing that caused her concern. All the messages were from friends she knew well, concerning homework or band gigs, gossip, plans for the weekends. Even the notes between Ricky and Charlene were pretty PG-rated, almost, she thought, pointedly so. She'd always warned him against considering his online activities private. He'd obviously taken her advice to heart. Or, knowing that he'd given away his password, he'd cleaned up his in-box.

At the bottom of the list of mutual friends, she saw an image she didn't expect: Marshall Crosby. She clicked on the picture, a dark photo, obviously taken in poor lighting by his computer camera. He looked slouched, and ghoulish around the eyes; the room behind him was a mess of books and tossed clothes, stacks of video games, soda cans in a line along a dresser, rock posters covering the wall. As his page loaded, she saw that most of the fields, like favorite books and films, were blank. Even the profile area glowed white, empty of the details she expected to see. The only area where he had seen fit to enter information was the status bar, and what he'd written there, thirteen minutes earlier, caused a cold finger to trace Maggie's spine: `Marshall thinks bad people should be punished.`

In Maggie's memory, it had snowed for days. But it hadn't really. In fact, there was just the initial light snowfall that coated Sarah's newly dead body so that when Chief Crosby first saw her, he thought she was a fallen branch, so thin and still and dark was her form. The days that followed were characterized by freezing precipitation—sleet, a light rain— the tentative spring abandoning The Hollows as the shock of it all settled and everyone found themselves shuffling stunned and stricken from assembly to counseling, if they wanted it, then to the horrifying open-casket wake and grim burial.

Maggie found that she could hardly take it in; none of it seemed quite real. Even now, she remembered it only in snapshots—Sarah's mother collapsing at her daughter's grave, her own mother clinging to her in a way she never had before or since, maintaining a grip on wrist or shoulder or elbow for days, it seemed. She remembered Sarah stiff and bloated in her casket, a waxen image of herself, not a girl filled with music, not a girl at all. The mortician had filled in the cuts on her face with some thick kind of makeup, but still you could see them there, a faint spiderweb of lines, like the cracks in the face of a porcelain doll that had been broken and glued back together. Her face looked painted on, hideous, a death mask. Maggie could still hear Sarah's mother wailing if she thought on it, could feel the sound of it reverberating in her own chest.

She'd been younger than Ricky was now, in her sophomore year at Hollows High. She'd been sheltered, her schedule strictly maintained by Elizabeth. Home right after school unless she had an extracurricular activity, have a snack and relax, homework, then play with friends or watch television. Dinner was always at 6:30, bedtime no later than 9:00. She'd railed against all the rules, felt smothered by her mother's constant questions. Rebelled by doing things to her appearance, like dyeing her hair, getting multiple piercings in her ears. Elizabeth had reminded her of this, not without a tiny bit of glee, when Ricky started his descent into gothic punk. Maggie realized she was every bit as on top of Ricky as Elizabeth had been on top of her, constantly talking, asking questions, maintaining routine. *Well*, she thought, *there it is. I've become my mother.*

"Do you think you would have been able to walk out the door after a fight?" her mother was saying as they drove to the meeting. She looked as tiny as a child in the huge passenger seat of Maggie's SUV. Again, the heat was cranking; Elizabeth had always hated the cold. "That I would just let you walk off and not go after you? Ridiculous."

"I know." Maggie had called her mother after she learned about the meeting, and Elizabeth wanted to attend. She'd phoned Ricky at the record shop, and his boss had agreed to let him go so that he could be there, too. He was planning to meet them at the school.

"That girl," Elizabeth said. Maggie knew she was talking about Melody, not Charlene. "There was always something about her."

"She's not a girl anymore, Mom. She's a mother whose daughter is missing. She needs our compassion and our help."

Elizabeth snorted. "You're such a shrink, Magpie," she said, mock-crotchety.

"Mom," Maggie chastised, but she felt a smile turning up the corners of her mouth.

Her mother took a tissue from her purse and blew her nose.

"What do you remember about that time?"

"What time?" her mother asked, not turning to look at her.

"You know what I'm talking about," Maggie said, annoyed that her mother was being purposely obtuse. She always did that when she didn't want to talk about something.

"I knew you'd bring that up."

"How could it not come to mind?"

"I remember everything about it. Every detail. Every ugly minute. It was the worst thing that ever happened to this town."

Maggie waited for her mother to go on. Then, "They say your memory fades when you get older. I wish it were true. You forget things like where you put your keys or your glasses, you space out on doctors' appointments. But the bad stuff stays, Maggie. The old things you'd rather forget, those memories move closer, grow more vivid."

"Like what? What do you remember?"

They were stopped at a light. It changed to green without Maggie noticing until someone behind them leaned on his horn. They both jumped a little, and Maggie lifted a hand in apology, moved forward.

"Everyone's in a big rush," said Elizabeth.

Maggie figured that her mother was just going to ignore her question, that she'd have to press. And she was prepared to press. She wanted to talk about Sarah, for some reason. Since Melody had brought it up, she hadn't been able to stop thinking about it. *Does Jones ever talk about it?* Melody had asked. Why had she wanted to know that? It was such a strange question.

Maggie was about to push Elizabeth to answer, but her mother started talking.

"Of all the terrible feelings and awful memories from that time, you know what bothers me the most?" she said.

"What's that?"

"I never believed that he killed her."

Something about the way she said it gave Maggie a strange little jolt of dread.

"He confessed, Mom," she said.

"I know he did," Elizabeth answered, her voice flat. She cleared her throat and looked down at her lap. She smoothed out her skirt with two flat palms, a determined little sweep of her hands; it was a familiar gesture to Maggie, something her mother did when she wanted to avert her gaze.

"You never told me this."

"What's to tell? It's just a feeling. I knew that boy. I just never did believe he had it in him. It's always bothered me."

"If not him, then who?"

Elizabeth released a breath. "Now, the answer to that might just be what kept me from asking the question in the first place."

Maggie didn't say anything, taking in her mother's words.

There was never any doubt that Tommy Delano killed Sarah. There had always been something wrong with him. Everybody said so. Since he was a boy, he'd been unnaturally quiet, occasionally prone to blank but terrifying rages. As an adult, he had often been seen slinking about the garage where he worked, lurking in corners, watching in that quiet way he had. Or he might have been spotted walking aimlessly through town, or hanging around the arcade or the pizzeria where the younger kids gathered. When people mentioned him, they used words like "creepy," or "odd." They said he had a way with cars, though. That he was a talented mechanic, a tireless worker. They said all those things about him, and so they were all true.

They also said that he killed his mother. It was an accident; a terrible fall from a steep staircase into the basement. His father found them. The boy sitting mute at the top, his mother in a heap on the floor below, neck broken, blood pooling. What precisely happened or how long he'd been sitting there was not clear. But the incident followed him through grade school, middle school, high school, and beyond. The story was whispered behind his back over two generations. He became a kind of bogeyman to some. *He walks the woods behind the school, watches the girls. Watch out. Tommy Delano's waiting for you.*

But when Maggie saw him, she just thought he was a sad man, fixing the buses that sat broken in the yard. He didn't seem frightening, with his narrow shoulders and grease-stained coveralls, barely raising his

eyes from the ground. He *was* in the woods behind the school sometimes, smoking cigarettes.

Sometimes the senior boys would gather around the bus yard fence
and taunt him. *Why'd you kill your mom, Tommy boy? How horrible,* Maggie remembered thinking, the children of people he'd gone to school
with taunting him over an accident that had killed his mother. As a girl,
she just didn't understand cruelty, didn't understand why some people
felt good about making other people feel bad. Even now, she didn't
understand it much better. Maggie never saw Tommy react. Sometimes
he'd just go inside one of the buses until the boys went away on their
own or were reprimanded by one of the teachers.

After the first twenty-four hours passed, and Sarah didn't return
home and it was clear she wasn't hiding out at the homes of any of
her friends, Maggie noticed a palpable shift in energy; the twittering
nervousness waxed to cold fear. Maggie spent an entire English class
distracted by the empty seat near the window that would have been
occupied by Sarah. It struck her as so frightening and strange that
someone was missing and that Miss Williams still stood at the head of
the class, giving her lesson about metaphor, and Vicki and Michelle
were passing notes, and Trevor was doodling in his notebook. Maybe
it was just a trick of memory, but by the second day—when the squad
cars were parked in front of the school and the students were dis-
missed early—she remembered knowing on some deep level that Sarah
wasn't coming back, and that everything else would move forward
anyway.

Maggie couldn't remember when suspicion turned to Tommy
Delano, but it was at some point after the psychic arrived. Eloise
Montgomery looked just like anyone's mom, with a plaid shirt and
high-waisted jeans, a brown faux-leather purse clutched to her side.
By lunch, the popular girls had already gathered to make fun of her
hair, a blunt, unflattering cut that looked like a helmet. There was
nothing else notable about her, not a searing gaze or a glowing aura.
On her way to biology class last period, Maggie saw the psychic sitting
in the music room, talking to Sarah's teacher. The woman listened in-

tently to whatever it was that Mr. Landtz was telling her, nodding slowly.

Maggie remembered dining alone that night with her father, who wasn't much of a cook. They had fast-food hamburgers, eating them off the wrappers without plates. Since Sarah's disappearance, her mother had come home late and left early—helping the police, consoling the family, and organizing volunteers. Maggie just wished Elizabeth would stay home.

"How are you doing with all of this?" her father wanted to know.

"I don't know. It doesn't seem real."

"Hmm," he said. "I know what you mean. Things like this never do, I guess."

The next day Tommy Delano was taken into custody. The evidence against him was circumstantial. Sarah's mother regularly brought her vehicle into the garage where he worked for service, often with Sarah in tow. Delano had been in the school office, collecting payment, and had had opportunity to hear Sarah's phone call to her mother saying she'd missed the bus. They found a collection of newspaper clippings about Sarah in an envelope under his bed. Then, in the trunk of his car, they found a pair of underpants, which Mrs. Meyer identified as Sarah's. By the evening, he'd confessed, just as that late spring snow began to fall. Then he told Chief Crosby where to find her body.

No, there was not a doubt in anyone's mind that Tommy Delano killed Sarah. That he was waiting for her in the wooded area between Melody's house and her own. *We met in the woods. She was glad to see me.* That he'd lured her into a vehicle and held her for more than twenty-four hours, hiding with her in an abandoned hunter's cabin deep in the woods by Old Creek, confessed his love, repeatedly raped her. *I made love to her. She wanted me to.* He cut her face. *I punished her for talking mean.* And then, when her terror and rage started to feel like rejection, he killed her. *She hit me,* he reportedly told Chief Crosby with hurt and indignation in his voice. *I only wanted to love her.*

Tommy Delano was sentenced to life in prison, his time to be served without the possibility of parole. And The Hollows breathed a collective sigh: *It's over.*

Maggie had waited to feel that sense of relief everyone else seemed to feel. But instead she just kept noticing, all year, that someone else came to fix the buses now. He was a big guy, with broad shoulders and close-cropped hair. The senior boys had nothing to say to him. And Sarah's seat was empty and the world went on and on without her, as though she'd never been there all.

"You never said anything about this before," Maggie said now to her mother.

Elizabeth didn't answer, just kept looking out the window at the people moving slowly into the school.

"Mom?"

She waved a hand at Maggie. "Don't listen to me. I'm just being silly and maudlin."

But Elizabeth was not, nor had she ever been, silly or maudlin. Maggie's mother wasn't prone to drama, or to listing off regrets. But she did have a habit of forming cement judgments about people and never, even in the face of overwhelming evidence to the contrary, changing her mind. And even if those judgments were rarely wrong, it was still not a quality Maggie appreciated in her mother. People changed. She knew this to be true, had witnessed it in others and even in herself. Still, something about what Elizabeth said bothered Maggie, caused an uncomfortable ache, made her remember something she couldn't *quite* remember.

"It doesn't matter anymore," Elizabeth said. "They're both gone now. At peace, I hope."

"The evidence was clear."

"Yes," Elizabeth said. "Of course it was."

They pulled into the high school parking lot and moved toward the entrance near the auditorium, where the meeting would be held. There were fewer cars than Maggie would have imagined. She'd expected the lot to be full, people milling about outside. But the doors were closed, though she could see people in the hallway through the small square window. She found a spot near Jones's vehicle and parked.

"It's snowing." Maggie helped her mother out of the car. Elizabeth had railed at help until her last fall, which had fractured her hip and left her limping and relying on her cane. Now she grudgingly accepted the assisting hand, the proffered arm.

"So it is," said Elizabeth. "So it is."

16

Elizabeth Monroe had a secret. A thing she'd never told another living soul. It was a place within her, a whole other dimension to her memory that she rarely visited. It was a cold, dead region, which she could forget about altogether, like her husband's grave. What foolishness it was to visit that place where his poor body was laid. He wasn't there; his soul didn't linger. She knew that, but she did her duty to the plot, tended it, laid flowers on the appropriate days: anniversaries of death and marriage, his birthday. Maggie liked to go on Father's Day (another load of rot, if you asked Elizabeth, these greeting card–generated occasions). Her husband, the only man she'd ever loved, was gone. And visiting his grave did not make her feel closer to him. At all. People, no one tells you when you're young, fade as time passes without them—all the little qualities and tics, the happy times, the sweet moments, become blurry and vague. It's the bad things that stay with you, the ugly things that nag.

Nighttime, not the late hours but the gloaming, when the sun was setting and dinner must be prepared and the long evening stretched out before her—that's when the loneliness settled in like the ache in her hip on a rainy day, when the regrets, the bad memories, sometimes came to call.

She was glad for nights like this, even though the occasion was grim. It gave a purpose to the evening, something outside her own needs. When Maggie had called, she'd invited herself along to the meeting, though she couldn't be of much help, maybe just a little support for Maggie and Ricky. God knows where Jones might be in all of this, following up leads, playing the good cop, the town hero. Everyone loved Jones Cooper, always had.

She'd taken her seat toward the front and tried not to eavesdrop on Maggie and Jones.

"I sent a car out to the Crosby home," he was saying. "There was no one there. Patrol has their eyes open, though I'm using most of the guys for Charlene at the moment, so we're pretty light out there tonight. And we'll have someone at the school tomorrow."

"Okay," said Maggie uncertainly.

"It's probably nothing."

"I know. Except whenever anything awful happens, there are always these clues that seem to have piled up that someone's about to snap. Clues that no one sees, or brushes aside. I don't want that to happen here."

Elizabeth's son-in-law towered over her daughter, had an attentive hand on her arm. "We won't let anything happen," he said.

They were perfect for each other, cops and shrinks always on the front lines trying to save a world that doesn't want to be saved, that tends inexorably toward entropy no matter what anyone does.

"Why are you frowning, Mom?" said Maggie, coming to join her. Elizabeth heard the edge of annoyance in her daughter's voice.

"What?" said Elizabeth. She felt immediately defensive. "Now you're policing my thoughts?"

Maggie released a sigh, pressed her mouth into a line. Elizabeth clutched her bag on her lap and squared her shoulders. At a certain point your child starts to think she can tell you what to do, how to be, everything you did wrong your whole life. Maggie was always on Elizabeth for being sour and judgmental. But there was no one on the face of the earth more judgmental of Elizabeth than her own daughter. The irony of this seemed lost on Maggie. She was so open and compassionate, giving and patient with everyone, even strangers—but when it came to her own mother? Maggie gave Elizabeth a hard time even when she managed to hold her tongue—which admittedly wasn't often.

"Hey, Grandma."

Ricky slid past her to sit on the other side of Maggie. He leaned in and offered her a light kiss on the cheek as he passed.

"Hello, baby boy."

Maggie and Ricky immediately started talking about something to do with the computer, and Elizabeth found herself tuning out, scanning the room. Where was everyone? There were about twenty-five people, all gathered in little klatches, leaning in close, gossiping. Henry Ivy stood on the stage; he'd created a time line of events since Charlene's disappearance. Elizabeth supposed there would be more urgency if Charlene weren't suspected of running away. But it was a mistake to be so blasé. It was a mistake they'd all made with Sarah. Elizabeth thought it was a kind of innocence back then, a different idea about the world and how things might unfold. Now maybe it was a desensitization; so many things were wrong and violent and frightening, people just couldn't react properly to everything.

It was Chief Crosby—he was still that to her, though it had been a dog's age since he wore the shield—who got her thinking about her secret. She saw him sitting there in the front row, eyes trained on Henry Ivy's time line. He leaned back, pushing his big belly forward almost with a kind of pride at its girth. His legs were spread wide, his arms folded over his chest. As if sensing her eyes on him, he turned and looked straight at her. She held his gaze, lifted a hand in greeting. He gave her a slow nod.

They were so different than they had been, both of them. They were unrecognizable from the young people they had been together. Elizabeth, for one, was surprised when she looked in the mirror and saw an old woman looking back at her. When did it happen? Chief Crosby was no less deteriorated, though he didn't seem to be shrinking, as she was. He just seemed to be getting wider and rounder. But his eyes were exactly the same—small, mean, and, worst of all, knowing.

What gave her comfort when she did choose to walk that dark terrain, follow the trail of what-ifs and if-onlys, was that she wasn't the only person in The Hollows with ugly memories and buried secrets. Not by a long shot.

She gave Chief Crosby a cool smile, and he did the same before turning back around as Henry Ivy called for order.

"Maybe people don't think a runaway is a reason to call a town meeting," said Henry Ivy, standing on the stage of the auditorium. He spoke softly, but there was something about him, a quiet way he had, that always commanded attention. Maggie felt the familiar rush of affection for him. She respected and trusted Henry, his motives, his caring for the young people of The Hollows. She often wondered why he'd never married, never even, as far as she knew, dated. For some reason, in their friendship, it was a question she could never bring herself to ask. She sensed that he wouldn't want to answer.

"But when one of our children goes missing, no matter whether she has run away or is taken from us, it's reason for concern. Many of you suspect that Charlene has left for New York City. A Facebook message has told us so. For some of you, the youngest among us, this seems like a very romantic notion. But it's not."

Someone coughed, and there was a murmur of activity toward the back of the room. Henry looked into the gathering—Charlene's friends and their parents, mainly, one of Charlene's teachers, a few people Maggie didn't recognize.

"Is Melody here?" Henry asked.

Jones walked to the top of the center aisle. "Melody is helping some of our men look through her home for any evidence about where Charlene might be headed," he said, purposely vague.

But even that was enough to cause a few heads to lean together, some whispering. Maggie saw Amber pull out her cell phone and start tapping on the keyboard. She turned to look at her husband. On her arrival, he'd updated her briefly about Graham, about the search at the Murray home, but he wouldn't mention that here, knowing that the information would spread quickly, become unmanageable. Maggie herself didn't know what to make of it. It was inconceivable that Charlene and Graham would have run off together. And, loser that he was, Graham still wasn't the type to abscond with a minor. But Maggie had known Graham forever; he was really just a buffoon, harmless. Or so she'd always thought.

"So what I'm asking now is, Does anyone have any information on where Charlene might have gone? New York City is a big place; police there have been notified. But the chance of an officer randomly spotting her is unlikely. So what do we know about places she might have frequented, who she might know, where she might be staying? And don't think you're protecting her by keeping secrets. Charlene could be in very big trouble."

He looked out at the crowd. Maggie watched Britney reluctantly rise.

She turned around to look apologetically at Ricky, then said to Henry, "She said she had a boyfriend in the city. All I know about him is that he plays guitar and his name is Steve."

Maggie looked at Ricky, but he was staring blankly ahead. Elizabeth reached over Maggie and gave Rick a comforting pat on his thigh, but he didn't seem to notice. That anger at Charlene started to simmer again.

"Do you know anything about him? A phone number, e-mail? Is anyone his friend on Facebook?" Henry asked.

Britney shook her head. "No one knows him. No one's met him. Honestly, we all thought she was making him up."

"Who were those Facebook friends of yours, the ones you and Charlene had in common?" Maggie whispered to her son.

"Who?" he asked. Just like Elizabeth, stalling with obtuse questions.

"The older ones from New York, Rick," she said, failing to mask her annoyance. "You know who I'm talking about."

He shrugged. "They're just people we met. The guy who owns the studio, Markus, said he'd help us record our demo tape. We met him at a club."

"Does he know you're only seventeen?"

Another defensive shrug, the gesture of choice among teenage males. "I don't know."

"Have you been in touch with them since she disappeared?"

"What do you think?" he snapped. Then, more gently, "Of course. No one's seen her."

"And these were not the people she claimed to know, the ones who could get her into the music business?"

"No. I told you. I never met those people. Or the other guy she was supposedly seeing."

"You know about him?"

"We had an open relationship."

"Oh. Great. That's great."

Maggie noticed Henry was looking at them, raised her hand in apology.

"Do you have anything to share, Rick? You were closest to Charlene," Henry said.

Ricky stood up. "I don't believe Charlene left that message on Facebook, the one about being 'large and in charge.' She would never use language like that; it's not her voice or her tone. I think she was making things up about who she knew in New York, her supposed other boyfriend."

"So where do you think she is, Rick?" asked Henry. Everyone had turned to look at Maggie's son. He stood strong with head and gaze straight at Henry. He was tall and proud, so like Jones, composed, not allowing himself to be overcome with the emotion she knew brewed within him. *I'm not a child*, he'd said to her the other night. He was right.

"I don't know. I've talked to the people we both knew in New York, and no one's seen her. She hasn't been in touch with anyone, including me, since early yesterday evening, and I think that's suspicious. Because if there's one thing Charlene needs, it's an audience."

"But that's assuming the Facebook message didn't in fact come from Charlene. If she did send it, then she's being true to form," said Henry. "Someone would need her log-in and password to send it from her account."

"Lots of people know that. I do. Her friends might."

"I think it sounds just like her." Britney was standing now, looking at Ricky. "She's doing what she always does, making a show."

Ricky shook his head. "You don't understand her."

"No, Rick," said Britney softly. "It's you who doesn't understand.

She uses people. She used you; she'll use whoever she went to be with in New York."

The air went electric with an awkward tension. Maggie heard someone laugh, but when she looked around, she couldn't see who it was.

"I thought you were her friend," said Ricky. He looked more sad than angry. Maggie heard a little catch in his voice.

"I *am* her friend," said Britney. She started to tear up, dug her hands into the front pocket of her pink Hollows High sweatshirt. "I see her for who she is and care about her anyway."

Denise stood up and put a bolstering arm around her daughter. Maggie resisted the urge to do the same for Ricky; he wouldn't want that. Didn't need it.

Ricky looked away from Britney and back at Henry.

"I think something bad happened last night. Something more than a fight with her mother. Charlene fought with her mother constantly; they never got along. It wouldn't be a reason for her to run away, not like this."

"Like what?" Henry said. "What do you think might have happened?"

"I don't know," Ricky said, seeming deflated. Maggie turned around to look at Jones, hoping he would step forward to support their son. But he was gone from where he'd stood by the door. She knew that he had a job to do, that something important had called him away. But she felt angry and disappointed anyway.

"I may have seen her. The missing girl."

"May have?"

"It was dark. I'd had some wine."

"Where and when was this?"

"Last night around eleven thirty. I was at my—," he said, stumbling over the word. "At my girlfriend's house on Persimmon Way. Well, she's not really my girlfriend. We just started seeing each other. But, um, anyway . . . she was asleep and I went to the kitchen to get some water, went out on the veranda to drink it."

"It was cold last night."

"Yes, it was."

"So why go out to the veranda?"

Charlie cleared his throat. "You know, just to get some air."

"And?"

"I saw her—this girl with pink and black hair—standing on the sidewalk, talking to someone in an old car."

"What kind of car?"

Charlie shrugged. "I don't know. I'm not good with things like that. It was green, big. Like a muscle car, but I couldn't tell you the make or model."

"Okay."

"Then she got in and the car pulled away."

"She got in of her own free will?"

"It appeared that way. She didn't seem afraid or upset. Maybe a little sad. But she opened the door and climbed inside. I never saw the driver. I mean, he—or she—never got out of the car."

The detective was writing things down on his pad. Charlie felt an uncomfortable dryness in his throat, a slight shake to his hand. He felt guilty, edgy, as though he'd done something wrong and was trying to hide it. He always felt that way when cops were around, like they were looking at him, seeing a secret guilt he couldn't acknowledge himself. Maybe it was because of Lily.

Now, at the police station, with Wanda sitting in the waiting area reading a paperback novel, he could feel a sheen of sweat on his brow. He wanted to wipe it away, but he didn't want to call attention to the fact that he was sweating in the first place. He kept talking.

"I heard about the disappearance late today at a client's house. I didn't know about it before then."

"A client?"

"I work for a pest removal company."

Charlie waited for some show of disgust, but the detective just nodded his head. The guy was slightly overweight, slightly balding. But there was something virile and intimidating about him, something in the set of his brow, in his cool, level gaze. His shirtsleeves were rolled up to reveal muscular forearms covered with dark hair. The leather shoulder holster made him look beefy and strong. Charlie felt small and boyish in comparison, weak somehow.

"I'm not sure it was her, actually. But my girlfriend thought I should say something, just in case."

The detective was still writing. What was he writing? Charlie knew he hadn't said enough for all that writing. He looked around the room; it wasn't how he envisioned a police station. He thought there would be big oak desks facing each other, some kind of chalkboard with a list of open cases, old rotary phones, a cell for holding criminals, flickering fluorescents. But it looked like the inside of any modern office building, with cubicles, fax machine, watercooler. The detective's desk was faux wood and metal; a brand-new computer gleamed on its surface. Even so, he was writing on a notepad balanced on his crossed leg. A southpaw, pushing his hooked hand awkwardly across the page. His broad shoulders partially obscured a riot of crayon drawings tacked to the walls: a city scene, a stick figure in hat and badge standing next to what looked like a squad car, a family of four with enormous heads lined up beside a tiny house.

Charlie felt the urge to tell the detective about Lily, but he knew that was a stupid idea. It was irrelevant, ancient history. Bringing it up would just seem weird.

"Did you see what she was wearing, Mr. Strout?"

Charlie thought about this. He shook his head. "I want to say she was dressed in black? But I can't be sure about that. Like I said, it was dark and I was on the veranda; there's some landscaping that kept me from seeing clearly."

Again, the slow nod. Charlie waited for the detective to turn those hard eyes on him. But when he finally looked up from his notepad, his gaze was polite, easy. Beside him was a picture of himself, a pretty woman, and two children, all grinning wildly.

"Can you remember anything else, Mr. Strout?"

Charlie shook his head. "I don't think so."

The detective slid a business card across the desk. CHUCK FER-

RIGNO, DETECTIVE. There were several numbers—an office phone, fax, and mobile line. There was also an e-mail: cferrigno@hollowspd.ny.gov.

"I'm going to ask you to think about that vehicle, Mr. Strout. Maybe you know more about cars than you think. If you can remember a make or a model, fantastic. But any other distinguishing marks—a noticeable dent, a bumper sticker. Anything like that might help, as well."

"Okay," said Charlie. "I'll think on it."

"And call anytime. Even if you remember something and you think it's insignificant, just call or drop me an e-mail. Let me be the judge."

"Okay."

Charlie sat a moment before he realized the interview was over and felt a rush of disappointment as he stood. Had he expected to be offering the clue that would break the case, send the detective running for the door? Maybe. He had been watching a *lot* of crime shows on television.

The detective offered a hand and, maybe sensing Charlie's hesitation, said, "Is there anything else, Mr. Strout?"

"Uh, no," said Charlie. "I'll think on that vehicle."

"Great."

Wanda was waiting for him when he pushed through the exit door. It was a quiet night in The Hollows, he guessed. She was the only one sitting in a long row of plastic chairs against the wall.

"How'd it go?" she said, rising.

"Good. He took the information." He zipped up his jacket.

"See?" she said, looping an arm through his. "I told you it would be fine."

"You were right," he told her. He was glad she was there. He felt calmer, more stable, just looking at her. "He wants me to think about the vehicle. I just don't know much about cars."

"I do," said Wanda, with an excited little inhale. "My daddy worked for Ford. He was a clay modeler. He knew *everything* about cars. Maybe I can help?"

He held the door open for her, and they walked out into the cold.

He felt like they'd been together for a hundred years, he was so comfortable, so sure of what he needed to do to make her feel good. Outside, he laced his fingers through hers, noticing her square, perfectly manicured nails, and they walked to his car.

"You don't mind?" he said. "Talking it through with me?"

"No!" she said, squeezing his hand. "It'll be like our own mystery to solve."

He opened the door for her and waited until she slid inside, then closed it gently. He walked around to the driver's seat, already thinking about what he'd seen last night.

"It was green," he said, when he'd climbed inside. "Big, you know? A gas guzzler."

He started the engine. He was suddenly glad he'd sprung for the new Prius a couple of months ago, that he had something nice to drive Wanda around in, not the old Volkswagen he'd beaten into the ground. The Prius wasn't exactly a manly car. But it looked nice inside, and he thought it said something about him, that he cared about the world enough to sacrifice a little speed, a little of the cool factor he might achieve from the new Charger or maybe a Mustang. He had some money saved, had inherited quite a bit when his grandparents passed on. He could have had a sexier car. But he was glad to have something more sensible for Wanda. He thought that was what she was looking for— safe and sensible.

"Okay," said Wanda, putting on her seat belt. "Do you remember a hood ornament?"

"Um, no. Well, maybe. Maybe there was something."

Wanda let go a little gasp. "You know what we should do?"

"What?"

"We'll go home and get on the computer. Look at pictures of old cars. Maybe that will help."

Home. She'd said *home.* Could it happen this fast? You work with someone for more than a year, finally get the guts to ask her out, and the very next night you feel like you've loved her forever? And she was using words like *we* and *home.* Maybe they were just that right for each other. And just that lonely.

"That's a great idea."

He reached over and put his hand on her thigh. Then she placed her hand on top of his.

"Wanda," he said, and he was surprised at how thick with passion his voice sounded. He found he couldn't look at her, kept his eyes on the dash. The flood of emotion, the wash of gratitude he felt just not to be alone right now embarrassed him.

"I know, Charlie," she said softly, squeezing his hand. "I know."

He put the car in gear and started to drive. A light snow was starting to fall.

Blood cannot be cleaned. Not totally. The proteins react to heat and certain chemicals, tending to bind. Even if the stain is removed, those proteins might remain, making them easily discoverable with today's forensic technology. But it generally didn't take fancy police work or high-tech equipment, just an unyielding gaze. Blood splatter is insidious, hiding in the doorjamb or on the baseboards or where the light switch cover meets the wall, any place stressed and tired eyes might miss. And, in Jones's limited experience with such things, people in general weren't that smart, thorough, or calculating. Maybe it was just The Hollows. The five homicides that had occurred on his watch had been predictable and easily solved.

In the case of the Murray home, it wasn't just the three large spots of blood on the outer gasket of the refrigerator door. It was the Google history on the computer—"how to clean bloodstains"—that told the tale. But Melody Murray wasn't talking. She'd taken to a silent rocking that Jones didn't find quite sincere.

"Melody," he said, standing in her living room near the arched entry. She reclined in a ratty old La-Z-Boy, her eyes glassy, gaze distant.

"Whose blood is that? What happened here?"

"What blood?" she asked, dreamily. "There's no blood."

Seeing her like that made him think of Sarah's funeral. Melody had gone silent and traumatized like this in the days her friend was missing and was virtually catatonic when Sarah's body was found. Even then, though she had plenty of reason to lose herself to grief and fear, he didn't quite buy it.

In the laundry room, Jones had seen a baseball bat leaning beside the dryer. He walked away from Melody now, went over and picked it up with a gloved hand, stood for a moment feeling its heft and width. An open box of fabric softener on the shelf above released the lightest scent of lilac into the air. Her house was clean, which surprised him. He would have predicted it to be a pigsty. But it was orderly, floors and surfaces free from collected dust.

Jones could hear the two other detectives moving around upstairs. Katie Walker, the town's only crime scene tech, a graduate of John Jay College in Manhattan, had already photographed the blood and the position of the bat and now sat at the kitchen table labeling items in crime scene bags—some rags from the washing machine, a pair of dishwashing gloves from the garbage can on the side of the house. She glanced up at him as he passed with the bat. Katie, another graduate of Hollows High, had moved back home to be near her sister, who'd just had twins. Jones liked her; she was quiet, thorough, into details. She didn't make assumptions, just collected evidence and coolly analyzed it. Of course, they didn't really need her in The Hollows, not often. But there was money in the budget for a part-time tech. So when Katie asked the Hollows police chief, Marion Butler, for a job, she got it. Tonight, he was glad for it, glad not to have to call in the state police.

He stood in front of Melody, who was staring at the television with the volume all the way down. Melody looked up at him, her eyes falling on the bat in his hand.

"Graham play?" he asked.

She laughed a little. "That lazy shit? I wish."

Jones forced a smile. "What's the bat for?"

"Protection."

"Protection?"

She tucked a strand of hair behind her ear. "In case someone breaks in or something, you know."

Jones nodded. He sat on the couch next to her chair, carefully put the bat on the coffee table. It rolled a bit; he steadied it with a finger.

"It must be rough, Mel. Graham is not an easy man to be married to, I'm sure. Can't hold a job. Always running around. Drinking with his boys."

She kept her eyes on him, looking a little less blank.

"And then, of course, if you suspected he had his eyes on Charlene . . . That would be enough to make anyone go off the deep end."

She offered him a slow blink, and it occurred to him that she'd taken something. He'd found a bottle of prescription painkillers in the medicine cabinet upstairs. All the heat she'd shown in his office—the indignation, grief, fear—was gone. She had that hazy look he remembered from high school, when she was always stoned.

"No one would blame you for trying to protect your daughter," he said.

She put her head in her hands, seemed to fold into herself, and after a moment her shoulders started to shake.

"Just tell me, Melody," he said, after she'd released a few shuddering sobs. "What happened here last night?"

But when she looked up at him, she wasn't crying, as he'd thought. She was laughing.

"You always did think I was stupid, didn't you, Jones?"

He felt a lash of anger so intense he stood up and walked out of the room, her nasty cackling following him down the hall. He stopped to collect himself.

"You done, Kate?" he called back, leaning a hand on the oak banister. His chest felt like someone had a rope around him and was pulling tight, making it difficult to breathe. Maggie was always warning him about the speed and intensity of his anger, reminding him to take deep breaths when he felt stressed, suggesting yoga and meditation. What he *needed* was for people to stop *fucking* with him. Then he'd be more relaxed.

"Just about," she said. She sounded wary, picking up on his tone.

"We need to get that blood to a lab, compare it with the other DNA samples we've obtained here. Find out who it belongs to before the night is out."

He was afraid she was going to say, "But that's going to take weeks." They didn't have a lab here in The Hollows. Evidence would have to be sent by squad car to Albany; they'd wait in line behind every other homicide that had come in before them, not that they were even calling it a homicide yet.

Instead, smart girl that she was, Katie followed his lead. "Yes, sir," she said briskly. "Right away."

.He heard her push her chair back, start gathering up her things. Melody stopped laughing. He waited in the hush that fell, his chest releasing, his breath coming more easily.

"Jones," Melody said, that pitiable tone creeping back into her voice. "Wait."

"I don't need a ride. My house isn't far."

Sarah kept walking, but Jones saw a little smile turn up the corners of her mouth, as if she was embarrassed by the attention but liked it a little bit, too.

"Oh, we don't mind," said Travis. "You shouldn't be alone here. It's getting dark." Travis had this way of modulating his voice to make himself sound so sweet, so innocent. Jones could never do that, could never mask his intentions or emotions. Even with coaches and teachers, Travis could wheedle himself out of trouble with charm.

Jones followed her slowly, the gravel of the road crunching beneath his tires.

"I'm not supposed to ride in cars with boys," she said, still not looking over at them. She picked up her pace a little bit.

Travis chuckled. It sounded light and amiable, though it was anything but. Jones watched Travis's knee jump in a slow, tense rhythm. "We won't tell."

Jones was starting to feel uncomfortable. She clearly didn't want to get in the car; it was disrespectful to keep pushing, he knew that even then. But Travis had never learned that. In all his life, he never did learn that. No one ever taught Travis that when a woman said no, sometimes she meant it.

Jones said nothing, though, did nothing, just continued to follow her slowly. Up ahead, he saw a dark, narrow form making her way down the unpaved road. Even from that distance, he knew it was Melody. Her house was not a tenth of a mile away. He could see the cupola through the trees. She'd probably spotted them from her upstairs window. Melody Murray had always made him uncomfortable, awakened within him some combination of desire and disdain. He'd touched her breast once at a keg party. In a dark closet, they'd rubbed and groped. Then he'd slid his hand beneath her dress and sought the warm flesh of her breast under the silky bra she wore. He could still remember what it felt like, small and soft, oddly heavy in his hand.

"Here comes trouble," said Travis. Rumor was that Travis had popped Melody's cherry in her parents' bed. Jones didn't know if it was true or not.

Sarah looked ahead and gave an enthusiastic wave, then started moving quickly, almost jogging, toward Melody. Was she frightened of them? Did she feel the energy of Travis's intent, that he wasn't just offering her a ride? Here again, Jones might have turned around, listening to Travis bitch and moan but then being rid of him for good. But when he brought the car to a stop, considered turning around, Travis got out.

"Crosby, get back here."

But Travis didn't listen; he approached the two girls, hands in his pockets.

"Hey, Mel," Jones heard Travis say, sugary and sly. "Why don't you guys come for a little ride?"

Jones stayed in the car, watching the three of them. He remembered Sarah stepping back, Mel leaning in toward Travis, familiar and at ease. Then—whatever was said he couldn't hear—the three of them were walking toward the car.

"Pop the trunk, Cooper. Sarah needs to put her stuff back there."

Then they were all in the car together, the heat blasting, Robert Plant on the radio. Travis and Melody were in the back. Sarah sat beside him, smelling nice, like soap and flowers.

"Where are we going?" she wanted to know. He noticed how she edged away from him, trying to push herself toward the door. She had her hands folded primly in her lap. She didn't want to be there. Why had she agreed to come? He was about to ask if he should just take her home when he heard the *pop* and *hiss* of a cigarette lighter from the back. The sharp, tangy odor of marijuana drifted up to the front seat. He looked in the rearview mirror to see that Melody had lit a joint, was taking a deep drag.

"Melody!" said Sarah, turning around. "What are you doing?"

"Come on, Sarah," Melody said as she released the smoke she'd been holding. "Don't be such a *prude*." Travis and Melody started to laugh as she handed him the joint. Sarah turned around and didn't say anything else, looking tense and pale. Jones didn't reflect on it for long, just put the car in gear and started to drive. He knew a place they could go and not be bothered.

The meeting resulted in little more than hurt feelings and frustration. Henry always had good intentions. But there was some resentment that a meeting had been called at all; an abduction was one thing, a runaway quite another—which might explain why attendance was so poor. As Maggie walked with Elizabeth back to her car, she overheard Britney talking to her mother.

"Why does everyone buy into her drama all the time?"

"Britney," Denise said. "This is a serious situation. Charlene is only seventeen."

"But she *wants* to go to New York."

Denise released a little laugh. "She's too young to know what she wants, and she's *certainly* too young to know what she needs. New York City is a dangerous place, in more ways than you even know."

Maggie didn't hear the rest of the conversation as the two climbed into their vehicle, a gleaming black Infiniti now covered in a light dusting of snow. But even if they hadn't moved out of earshot, Maggie would not have been able to hear over Elizabeth complaining about Chief Crosby. "Can you believe that old coot, just sitting there all fat and smug? I never could stand him."

"Mom."

Ricky had parked beside them, his green GTO looking more blue under the yellow parking lot light. Maggie didn't like the car, though the old steering column had been replaced with one of the safer, new ones and the glass was new as well. So it wasn't as unsafe as an old car could be. But it was still too powerful, encouraged her son to drive too fast, and burned too much gasoline. It was loud, too, always woke Jones when Ricky came in late. Naturally, that wasn't a problem for Maggie, since she always dozed on the couch until her son came home.

"I mean, *really*." Elizabeth was still talking. "What did he think he added to that meeting with all his rambling?"

"Maybe he was just showing his support."

Her mother just grunted as Maggie helped the old woman into the car. "And where was that girl's mother? And her useless stepfather?"

"I don't know, Mom."

Maggie shut the door, glad for a brief moment of silence as she walked around to the driver's side. She started the car and turned on the heat, waiting for Ricky to show up at his car, which he did a few minutes later. She rolled down the window and he leaned in.

"That was a huge waste of time," he said.

"It helped establish a time line at least," said Maggie. "It might be useful in ways that aren't clear now."

Why did she always feel the need to do that—to bring up the positive, to look for the silver lining? And why was she surrounded with people who had the opposite tendency? Sometimes it could be truly exhausting.

"What happened to Dad?" asked Ricky. She saw the same hurt and disappointment on his face that she'd felt when she noticed Jones gone.

"He got a call," she said, though this was just an assumption. "He said they were working on a lead. He'll get in touch when he knows something. Don't worry."

"Yeah," Ricky said with a nod. He looked down and moved a rock with his boot.

"I have to bring your grandmother back to her house," Maggie said. "What are you going to do?"

"Go home, I guess. What else can I do? Maybe Britney's right. Maybe Char wants to be gone from here. Maybe she did write that status update and I'm just kidding myself. Denial, you know?"

She put a hand on her son's arm. "I'll come home after I drop off your grandma," she said. "We'll talk some more. Brainstorm."

"Okay," he said, moving toward his car. "Bye, Grandma."

"See you, kid. Hang in there."

"Rick," Maggie called. He turned to look at her. "It's going to be okay."

Her assurance sounded hollow, even to her own ears. She couldn't—shouldn't—offer that guarantee, of course. What she was trying to say was, "I'll take care of you, no matter what happens." But the truth was she couldn't really take care of him any longer. She couldn't bandage his knee and give him an ice cream; she couldn't even hold him when he cried. Because he didn't bring his wounds to her anymore, and he didn't cry, either. And there wasn't enough ice cream in the world to soothe the pain of love lost.

"I know." He climbed into his car. She watched him drive away before she did the same.

Maggie always entered her mother's house with some combination of nostalgia and claustrophobia. The very scent as she walked through the door brought a melee of memories, not of events, necessarily, but of feelings. She wondered if there was any human emotion she had not experienced within these walls—from love to rage, from joy to grief.

"Want some tea?" her mother asked, shedding her coat on the bench by the door and moving into the kitchen. Jones had taken to calling her the three-legged tyrant, claiming that the cane had made her bossier than ever.

"Sure." Maggie didn't want tea; she wanted to go back to Ricky. But Elizabeth needed her, too. She hadn't spent any real time with her mother in a while and thought a cup of tea wouldn't take long. Ricky had probably holed himself up his room, music blasting.

"Do you think something's happened to that girl?" Elizabeth asked when Maggie entered the kitchen. She noticed that there were dishes in the sink and that crumbs had gathered at the baseboards around the cabinets. The sight gave her pause. Her mother was a meticulous housekeeper, always had been.

"I don't know. I really don't know."

"When she ran off before, how long was she gone?"

"Not overnight. Usually she was just with a friend. A few hours maybe."

Rather than say anything about the dishes, Maggie moved over to the sink. They'd bought Elizabeth a new dishwasher, but she seemed disinclined to use it; Maggie always noticed the drying rack on the counter. She got the soap and sponge from under the sink and started washing.

"Why don't you use the dishwasher?"

Elizabeth didn't answer, taking cups from the cupboard beside Maggie.

"We made mistakes, you know, with Sarah. The police didn't act for over twenty-four hours. There were a lot of wrong assumptions, bad information."

"Jones isn't making that mistake. He's being thorough. Following up leads, checking stories." Jones had asked Maggie not to say anything about Graham, and she wouldn't. *Not even to Elizabeth, especially not to Elizabeth.*

"You know something."

"No," Maggie lied, scraping something hard and dry off a plate. "He promised to keep us posted, and I'll keep you posted. I promise."

The kettle started to whistle, and Maggie thought about how she usually made tea in the microwave and it never tasted right. She made a mental note to get a kettle with a whistle when things settled down. A red one.

While her mother poured the hot (not boiling) water into the flowered porcelain pot and stared at it as if she could will the tea to steep faster with the power of her gaze, Maggie finished the dishes, got the broom from the pantry, and swept the floor.

"We could get someone in to clean, Mom."

"No," Elizabeth said sharply. Maggie could see that she was embarrassed. "I can't have that."

"Why not?"

"Because it's . . . *frivolous.*" She spat the word, as if she couldn't stand the taste of it on her tongue.

"Oh, heaven forbid," Maggie said, raising her palms in a gesture of mock horror.

"Maggie, please."

"Sit down. I'll pour the tea."

For once, Elizabeth obeyed without a wisecrack or protest. As Elizabeth moved into the dining room, Maggie noticed for the first time that evening how stiff her mother's movements were, how carefully she lowered herself into the chair.

"Mom, did you fall again?"

"No," Elizabeth said too quickly.

Maggie poured the tea and carried the cups over. They both drank it without cream or sugar. She sat across from her mother at the table where she'd shared dinner with her parents most evenings of her growing up. The old oak piece, which nearly spanned the length of the long dining room and comfortably sat ten, had belonged to her grandmother. It had been stripped and refinished only twice in its life, had been so lovingly cared for that its surface still gleamed in the light. It felt as solid and permanent as a mountain, as if it could never be moved from the place where it stood, where it had stood as long as Maggie could remember.

"Tell me," Maggie said. She watched her mother and thought how delicate she seemed suddenly. This titan, this woman full of confidence and attitude, was getting old. Maggie felt a little shock of fear. The child in her still thought of Elizabeth as immortal.

Elizabeth took a sip of her tea.

"It was nothing," she said. She put down the cup, touched the rim. "I just, you know, lost my balance when I was trying to load that damn dishwasher. I should have washed the dishes by hand—like I *always* do—but Jones made such a damn fuss the last time he was here about how expensive it was and how much time and trouble it would save me." She paused to take a breath. "Anyway, I'm fine. Just sore. Too sore to stand and do the dishes, or to sweep."

"You have to tell me these things," Maggie said. She felt a rush of sympathy and sadness for her mother. "We'll go see the doctor tomorrow, have an X-ray."

"Look, if I'm still sore tomorrow, I'll let you know. You have enough on your plate, Maggie. Too much."

"Mom—"

Elizabeth lifted a hand to indicate the end of the discussion. "I promise, I was going to call tomorrow anyway if it still hurt. I swear."

Maggie knew the impossibility of arguing with her mother, so she just got up, went into the small bathroom down the hall, and got some Advil. She noticed that the bathroom was so clean it made her own seem like something you'd find in a youth hostel. So she figured Elizabeth was being honest about the timing, that she'd felt bad for only a couple of days. Her mother scrubbed the bathrooms religiously once a week; it was a chore Maggie had always dreaded in childhood. But now she did the same at her own house.

Maggie brought a glass of water and the Advil to her mother. Elizabeth took the pills and downed them with the water, gave her daughter a smile.

"I promise," she said, reading Maggie's worried frown. "See? I feel better already."

Maggie rested her hand on her mother's; it felt tiny and fragile until Elizabeth turned her hand to squeeze Maggie's, and then she felt her mother's strength. Maggie smiled back.

"Ah," said Elizabeth suddenly, looking up at the ceiling. "There they are! Do you hear it?"

"What? No, I don't hear anything."

"Listen!"

Maggie listened and heard only the silence of the old house.

"They stopped," Elizabeth said, looking disappointed. "You didn't hear?"

"No," said Maggie. "I'm sorry. I didn't." She felt a slight tingle of worry for her mother.

Elizabeth glanced over the table at Maggie, then down at her fingernails. "Well," she said, draining her cup and standing up. "That boy is supposed to come back and check his traps again tomorrow. Never mind."

Her mother moved stiffly back to the kitchen sink, and Maggie wondered when Jones had come by and why he had given her mother a hard time about the dishwasher, but she stayed focused on the matter at hand. "If they're a nuisance," she said casually, "why don't you come sleep at our place?"

"No," Elizabeth answered with a dismissive wave of her hand. "I'm not going to let critters run me from my home."

"We'd love to have you, Mom. Just a visit until the problem is gone."

When Elizabeth had hurt herself earlier in the year and Maggie had suggested that her mother move in with her, the old woman had coolly informed her that she would never consider that as an option. "I'll have my own home until the day I die, Maggie," she'd said. "Don't imagine me any other way."

Elizabeth's harshness on the matter had hurt Maggie. She was annoyed by her mother's lack of consideration for the rest of the family, not to mention her lack of foresight about the future. Elizabeth was unwilling to talk about alternatives to living alone in a gigantic old house that she might not be able to manage one day, the care of which would fall to Maggie and Jones. But Maggie was in no mood for a battle, so she backed off even on this small matter. The time for battles would come soon enough. She got up and took her cup to the sink, rinsed it, and put it in the rack.

"Okay, Mom. I'd better get back to Ricky. Do you need anything before I go?"

"I'm fine," her mother said stiffly.

Why did she have to be like this? So brittle and uncompromising? This was a question Maggie had been asking about her mother for as long as she could remember. She was beginning to think that there wouldn't be an answer in either of their lifetimes.

Even though he was only seventeen, Rick Cooper knew that love could exist even though it was starving and unrequited. It didn't need love in return to survive. In fact, maybe he loved Charlene more, harder, because he knew she didn't, couldn't, love him back. Charlene could never love something that stood at her doorstep; she could only love something far away and hard to get, something that didn't want her. Somehow he'd known this about her from the beginning, but it didn't keep him from falling for her.

"We're just friends," she'd tell him as they lay in the backseat of his car together, as he kissed her neck and felt her body beneath his.

"Okay," he'd say as she wrapped her arms around him, put her warm mouth to his.

"You're not my boyfriend," she'd tell him. "I don't want that." But she'd hold his hand and whisper in his ear that she loved him. And he knew she meant it, in a sweet way, in a true way. She'd touch him all over, make him feel things inside and out that gave him a fever. His hands had roamed her body, the soft swell of her breasts, her heart-shaped bottom. But still, she'd held herself from him. For all her sexy cool, she'd seemed childlike, innocent. He barely thought of anything else.

She wasn't like the other girls, the girls his mother would like to see him dating. She wasn't frivolous and bubbly, wearing pink bubble gum lip gloss and carrying Hello Kitty notebooks. She didn't have the coyness of Britney, that look that said she knew a little about prettiness and power but not quite enough to wield it well. Charlene wasn't the kind of girl who teased, then got scared of the reaction she invited. She wasn't pampered or sheltered. She already knew the hard edges of the world, knew that life disappointed and that most people's dreams never did come true.

She was hungry and melodramatic, impossible to predict or control. She did things that made people angry, like smashing Slash's guitar at practice. It was wrong. It was silly. But it was in moments like those that he loved her the most, when he was almost crazy with the desire to shelter and protect her.

He pulled the car into the garage and sat, toying for a moment with the idea of closing the door and sitting there with the engine running until he fell asleep. He imagined his father finding him, roaring with grief. He fantasized about Charlene hearing about his death. The dark romance of it would appeal to her. She'd use the pain to write a song about him.

Love survives
even when it's wrong,
even when we're strong.
It holds on to us with its teeth,
tears us down to the bone.
It won't let go
until we give in
or bleed to death.

But it was just a moment, a childish indulgence. He wasn't suicidal; if he were, he thought, Charlene would probably like him better. If anything, at the moment he was numb. He'd felt something that he imagined was close to grief last night, an aching hollow in his center, a trapped and quiet raging in his chest. Most of the day had been spent in a state of controlled panic, making phone calls, trying to connect with the people he knew in New York. After he learned that no one there had seen or heard from her—or so they were saying—something inside just powered down. His neck and shoulders ached. The new tattoo on his arm—Charlene's idea—burned.

The only thing he knew for sure right now was that Charlene hadn't written those status updates on Facebook. But what it meant, he didn't know. Maybe someone had her against her will, was using the updates to keep people thinking she'd run away. Or maybe it was her new boyfriend, this guy Steve everyone was talking about. He could see her doing that, giving him her password, letting him write whatever he wanted, knowing that Rick alone would know it wasn't her. Just rubbing it in. There was the anger, too. It lived beneath the surface of all the other emotions, pacing its cage. *She uses people. She used you.* It was true, what Britney had said. He knew that.

He shut the engine and walked into the house, through the laundry room and straight to the refrigerator. His early acceptance letters stared at him. That he'd applied to colleges at all had been the final nail in the coffin with Charlene. "You're a good boy. You'll go to school and be a doctor like your mom, help people. That's you. You should be proud of that."

But he wasn't proud. He wanted to be bad, like whoever it was she'd gone off into the city to be with, if that was what she'd done. He took a carton of orange juice from the refrigerator, drank from it, and put it back, slamming the door. The letters and the magnets that held them fell to the floor with a clatter.

"Are you even going to go?"

Rick jumped with a jolt of fear that felt like an electric shock. His father was sitting in the dark dining room, a looming black shadow at the table.

"Go where?" he managed. "Christ, Dad. You scared the crap out of me."

"To college."

Great, the old college conversation. Perfect time to discuss it. "I don't know," he said.

He expected some sarcastic comment or light insult. But instead his father said, "You have to go, Rick. Don't stay in this town your whole life like me."

Rick snorted his disdain. "I wouldn't." He hadn't meant it as an insult to his father, but that was what it was. He felt like he should say something to soften it, but then he didn't, he just leaned over and picked up the letters and magnets, placed them on the counter by the phone. His father didn't say anything, either. Rick walked into the dining room and turned on the light. He sat down at the table.

"What's happening with Charlene? Where did you go during the meeting?"

"We're searching the residence," his father said. "I got a call."

"What did you find?" Rick felt a lump of dread in his belly. His father looked strange—tired, sad around the eyes. He wanted to say, *Are you okay, Dad?* But there was, as ever, a glass wall between them through which nothing soft or tender could pass. Only angry or loud words, heavy things thrown with force, could shatter it.

When he was very young, Rick used to slip into bed with his father. His mother often slept elsewhere—on the couch or in the guest room across the hall from his room. He was too young to wonder why then. But when he heard her move softly down the stairs or quietly close the door, he'd wait a bit, then pad down the hall and slide in beside his dad. His father's breathing would be even and deep. Rick would try to match his breath to his father's, but he could never quite do it.

"We found blood, Rick."

"Blood?" Rick felt his hands start to tingle.

"Melody claims that she and Graham had a fight last night and that she hit him with a baseball bat in self-defense. She claims he left, saying he wouldn't come back. Afterward, Charlene and she fought about that cell phone. Turns out Graham got her that phone. Melody says she found the bill; that's why she and Graham fought."

"I thought Mrs. Murray said last night that she didn't know about the phone."

"She lied."

"Why?"

"I don't know. Anyway, she claimed that she took the phone from Charlene. That's why they fought. That's why Charlene left. Melody claims she smashed it, threw it in the trash that was picked up this morning."

"That's why no one's been able to reach Charlene," said Rick.

His father nodded. "There's something else."

"What?"

"There's a witness who saw Charlene—or someone matching her description—climb into what's described as a big green muscle car last night and drive off."

"Where?"

"Persimmon and Hydrangea, around eleven thirty."

"It wasn't me."

His father kept hard eyes on him. "Ricky," he said, finally. "I can't help you unless you tell me the truth."

"Dad. I was here, sleeping. You know that."

His father shrugged. "I went to bed at nine; I was beat. I didn't wake up until Melody came knocking."

The strangeness in his father's expression had deepened. He looked haunted and afraid. The look was contagious. Rick started to feel edgy, guilty, as though his father was seeing something within him that he didn't know was there.

"The car wakes you up when I come and go."

"Not always."

The grandfather clock marked the quarter hour, and Rick heard the refrigerator start to run, making ice cubes. He stared at the facets of the stained-glass lamp that hung over the dining room table. When he was a boy, he'd thought it was the most beautiful thing in the world, the way the colors glowed in the light. Lately, it just looked old and tacky.

"Dad. What are you asking me?"

"I need you to tell me what happened last night."

"I did tell you. There's nothing more to say."

They both fell silent as the front door opened and closed. Rick felt nearly weak with relief to hear his mother's voice.

"What's going on?" she said. She came into the dining room, shed her coat, and draped it over a chair.

Jones told Maggie everything he'd told Rick. As his dad spoke, his mother sat in the chair beside him. Rick saw it, triumphantly, as a taking of sides. Normally, Jones would sit at the head of table with Maggie in the chair to his right and Rick in the chair to his left. Head of the table, man of the house, Rick would always think mockingly. But now his father sat across from them. His mom put her hand on Rick's leg.

"There are a lot of cars like that around, Jones," she said. "The boys around here like those old GTOs and Mustangs. I saw an old Chevy the other day. It's a trend."

"It's quite a coincidence, though, don't you think?"

There was that tone, that smug, condescending tone that Rick hated more than anything. The one that said: *I'm smarter than you. I'm better than you. I know more than you'll ever know.*

His mom didn't say anything for a moment, just looked down at the table. Then, "If you want to ask him something, why don't you just ask him?"

His dad said, "Did you pick Charlene up on Persimmon last night?"

"No. I didn't. I was here sleeping. I fell asleep trying to call her after she stood me up. I have told you this a hundred times. Why don't you believe me?"

But his father *didn't* believe him. Rick could see it in the set of his mouth, in the narrowing of his eyes.

"I'm telling you the truth," he said. He got up from the table, pushed the chair back with more force than he intended. It scraped loudly on the floor. The crystal glasses in the china cabinet sang.

"Ricky," said his mother, grabbing hold of his hand.

"Right now, I can help you, Rick," his father said. He leaned forward across the table. There was an urgency in his voice that Rick didn't understand. And for a moment, he thought he saw his father's eyes fill. "If this thing goes any further, there's nothing I can do."

What did he mean by that? What did he think? Did he think Rick had done something to Charlene? He didn't trust his voice to ask the questions, and a part of him didn't want the answers. Instead, with his parents' rising voices crashing behind him like a wave, he got up and left them.

By the time they reached the front door, he was in his car, backing out of the drive. As his father stood on the step, his mother looking small behind him, Rick drove off, not thinking about where he was headed or what he was going to do, just glad to be away from the person he saw reflected in his father's eyes.

Maggie watched her son disappear down the road, guilt, fear, and anger a chemical brew in her stomach.

"You *don't* think he's capable of hurting Charlene," she said when Jones came back inside and closed the door. He moved past her without saying anything and climbed the stairs. She followed him to Ricky's room, where he flipped on the light, stood scanning the area.

"Answer me, Jones." She felt the old, familiar anger. He forced her to side with Ricky. He always had. They'd battled about everything from nap time to curfew, from television viewing to phone privileges. Jones always felt like he had to take a hard line. And she had no choice but to soften the edges. Who else was here to defend Ricky against his own father? Sometimes she really hated Jones for it, for putting her in this impossible place.

"Maggie," he said, turning to her. "Anyone is capable of anything, given the right circumstances, the right motivations."

She felt a rush of disbelief, an unsettling chill at his words. "You don't mean that."

"Don't I?" he said. He sat down at Ricky's desk and started going through his drawers. "Would you kill to protect Ricky? Of course you would."

"That's different."

"Why?"

"Don't be obtuse, Jones. To defend my son, yes, of course I would. What does that have to do with anything?"

"We're talking about motivation. How do we really know what motivates people to do what they do? Why do people rape and kill? Why do people abduct young girls? Maybe they think their motivations are good and pure, like a mother defending her child."

She tried to summon her patience. Something about the conversation reminded her of the helplessness she'd felt on the phone with Marshall earlier.

"The actions of a parent to defend her child are reactions to threats. Not a lack of impulse control or an appetite to be sated. Not the selfish actions of a sociopath or a psychopath. Are you saying that you think our son raped and killed Charlene? That he abducted her?" She could hear her own voice going shrill with anger and panic.

"The girl is *missing*. She's gone. A witness says he saw her get into a green muscle car. But our son, who drives a car like that, claims to have no idea where Charlene is. I don't know what to think. I really don't."

Maggie held his eyes, though she wanted to look away, wanted to *run* away from him and his craziness. She saw something working on his face, something she didn't understand. She remembered the expression she'd seen at Britney's house.

"What are we really talking about here, Jones? *What* is going on?"

He seemed to deflate in the chair. Then he put his head in his hands.

"When I got the call from Chuck about the witness who saw the car," he said through his fingers, "I just felt sick."

"What kind of car?" She had an awful thought, then. *What if Ricky was lying?* She knew he couldn't hurt Charlene or anyone. But what if he did take her someplace? Helped her to run away?

"The guy didn't know," said Jones. "He claimed not to know much about cars."

"Okay," she said. "Okay. So we *can't* assume that it's Ricky. We can't assume that, at best, he's lying about knowing where she is or, at worst, he's done something horrible. That's way too big a leap. You know him, Jones. He's our boy. Our *baby*."

She came to kneel beside him. She controlled the part of her that wanted to throttle him, to get in her car and go after Ricky. *You're too hard, too unyielding,* she wanted to yell. *You drive him away. He was waiting for me to come home so that we could talk. What happens now is on your conscience.* But in the war between her husband and her son, she'd always tried not to take sides, to comfort and mediate instead. She tried, even though she almost always failed.

"I *don't* know him," Jones said, looking up from his hands but not at her, at something past her. "I look at him with that hair, that nose ring, that tattoo. I don't know him."

"Then don't look at those things. Just look at his face."

"I can't even talk to him. Every time I try, we just end up fighting."

She shook her head. "You might try to come in softer, with less anger and more love."

"I *do* love him," he said, finally meeting her eyes. "You know that. *He* knows that. Earlier you said that I had no instinct to protect my son. Maggie, nothing could be further from the truth."

"Then believe him."

Jones released a long breath, took her hands. "But what if he really has done something awful? Let's just say he has. I can protect him now, if he's honest with me."

"How do you think you can protect him?"

He stood up, and she sank back to her heels as he walked over to

Ricky's closet and opened the door, peered at the mass of clothes and shoes, boxes of books, games, towers of CDs.

"What are you doing?"

"I know how things happen," he said. "I know how a moment can spiral out of control. How the consequences of one careless action can cost you everything."

From where she sat on the floor, she watched Jones going through boxes on the floor of Ricky's closet. Somewhere along the line they had stopped talking about Ricky and had started talking about Jones; she could see that, but she didn't understand it all.

"What are we talking about, Jones? What's going on?"

He gave a quick, dismissive shake of his head. "If there's something here that incriminates Ricky, I need to find it now. You get that, right?" He turned around and looked at her again. "Because if someone else finds it, there's nothing I can do."

"And if you find something, then what? You're planning on destroying evidence, covering up a crime?"

He didn't answer her, moved over to the bed and lifted the mattress, peering underneath. He seemed disorganized, almost frantic.

"*What* are you looking for?" Her voice sounded desperate and pleading. Once upon a time this room had been a nursery, with clouds painted on baby blue walls, stars on the ceiling, plush animals on clean white shelves. She'd sit in the room and nurse her son and think that when it came to her baby and the room she'd made for him, she'd done everything right. She hadn't felt that way in a long, long time.

"I'm looking for the truth about our son, Maggie. You'd do well to help while you still can."

"You're not making any sense. I get it about the car. I understand why that worried you. But what does anything you learned at the Murray residence have to do with Ricky? What has you so frantic?"

He started pacing the room, finally sat down at the computer and booted it up.

"I don't know," he said to the screen. She could see his face reflected there. "I don't know how it all adds up."

"So why do you think he had something to do with all of this?"

"Call it an instinct," he said, getting up again, seeming to forget the computer and continuing his search of the closet.

Like the instinct you had that he was using drugs when you found a pack of cigarettes in his backpack? Maggie had been just barely able to prevent Jones from having Ricky secretly drug-tested by their family doctor. *Like the instinct you have that he's a loser who will amount to nothing, in spite of good grades and excellent test scores?* She admired her husband and would be the first to admit that his instincts were, like her mother's, rarely mistaken.

But when it came to his own son, he was usually dead wrong. He seemed eager to believe the worst, was blind to all the good. What did it say about him? In her work, she often found that people who couldn't connect with their children had trouble connecting with themselves, had a core of self-loathing. Was this true of her husband? she wondered as he continued ransacking Ricky's room and she watched, helpless, clueless as to what to do. And if it was true, why had it taken her so long to confront it?

Wanda was dozing on the couch, and Charlie's eyes were starting to ache in the glow of her computer screen. He'd been scrolling through a classic car site for hours, and all the cars were beginning to look the same. He'd never been a guy who knew about cars, though he had always wanted to be. Wanda, it turned out, *was* one of those guys. And it didn't seem to bother her much that he didn't know a fin from a fender. He'd seen a few barely suppressed smiles, but then her attention had started to wander, and eventually she'd drifted over to the couch, commenting from there until she fell asleep.

At this point he was pretty sure that the car he'd seen was a Chevelle. Or maybe it was a Pontiac GTO. Or maybe it was a Mustang. The truth was, it had been dark, he'd been a little sleepy, a little high on Wanda.

He stood and leaned back, listened to a series of cracks from his spine. The flowers he'd bought her earlier sat proud and purple in the vase at the center of the table. He didn't know any more about flowers than he did about cars.

"Lilies!" Wanda had exclaimed. "They're my favorite, Charlie. How did you know?"

"I don't know," he said. "But when I looked at them, I thought of you." It wasn't a lie or a line. He'd never been good at that. It was the truth. He was rewarded with a tight embrace.

After dinner, he'd helped her clean the dishes. Not the kind of half-assed help his father used to offer his mother, that kind of befuddled, mystified carrying of a few dishes from the table to the kitchen only to quickly retire to the couch to watch football or the news. He'd helped her load the dishwasher, and then to wipe the table, put the place mats and cloth napkins in the laundry room.

Then, over a glass of wine, he'd told her. About the girl he saw last night. About Lily. When he mentioned her name, he saw Wanda's eyes drift over to the flowers. He found himself reading her thoughts. Maybe that was why, on some subconscious level, he'd chosen them. But she didn't say anything about it. Just listened and then offered the advice that had brought them to the station.

He looked at Wanda, who turned over in her sleep, putting her back to him. He moved to her, took the cozy throw blanket from the couch, and draped it over her slim body, admiring the rise of her hips, the dip of her ankle. She sighed in her deepening slumber.

He stepped out onto the porch. The light snow had stopped and not accumulated at all. The air was still and cold, the wind chimes silent. Empty planters hung, bereft until spring. There was an old ceramic cat by the door. On impulse, he lifted it and found a key. Without thinking, he pocketed it. He'd give it to her later and tell her he didn't think it was safe, even in a safe town, to leave a key outside the door.

He looked out toward the street. Had it just been last night? He imagined the scene, watching her standing there with her punk hair and uncertain expression. Because that was what he saw on her face. It wasn't fear, exactly, just uncertainty, as if she were doing something against her better judgment. Except this time, he called out to her, *Hey, do you need any help?* Maybe she would have said no, or flipped him the bird. But maybe she would have said yes. Maybe just that one sentence from him would have been enough to keep her from getting in the car.

He stepped onto the sidewalk. In the bay window of the red house across the street, the blue light of a television flickered. There was a heavy bass thump of music being played too loud somewhere. On the wire above him, a mourning dove cooed, low and inconsolable.

He walked across the street and stood approximately where the girl had stood and looked back at Wanda's house. From where she'd been standing, she wouldn't have been able to see him through the trees in

Wanda's yard. Across the street, an upstairs light glowed. Somewhere a car coughed to life, then roared off. The way the sound carried, he expected the car to approach and pass, but it never did.

What was she thinking as she stood here? Where is she now? He remembered asking himself those questions about Lily, standing like this in the place she was last seen. But it was the second question that hurt the most. *Where is she now?* His imaginings on the subject were grim and wild. Every year or so, he'd drop Lily's mother an e-mail, ask how she was doing, really just wondering if there was any news of Lily. Even her skeletal remains would have offered some kind of relief after nearly two decades of dark wondering. She hadn't answered his last message.

"She's sick," his mother had told him. "Cancer."

"Cancer? That's awful."

"Is it any wonder?" she'd said, her voice nearly a whisper. "Grief like that can kill you, Charlie. A missing child? It's an unimaginable horror."

In the street, he noticed a slick, gleaming puddle. The fluid had a rainbow sheen to it. He felt a little jolt of excitement. The car he'd seen had idled there, and it had definitely not sounded healthy. He put his toe to the edge. The liquid was sticky, nearly dry. It was possible, wasn't it, that it had leaked from the car he'd seen? Even though maybe a hundred cars had passed that way since last night. But it could be something. Was it enough to call that cop?

"Charlie?"

Wanda had come out after him. Just the way she looked beneath the amber glow of the streetlamp, so pretty even disheveled from sleep, even with a little worried frown on her forehead, made him think he was going to ask her to marry him.

"What are you doing out here?" she asked him.

"Look," he said. He pointed to the liquid in the road.

"Hmm," she answered. She bent down to squint at it. "Transmission fluid."

"The engine of that car sounded pretty bad."

"And to leak that much fluid in one spot, it would have had to idle here awhile. Not just any passing car would dump that much. The stop sign on Hydrangea is a good twenty feet away."

"So what does it mean, when a car is leaking that much transmission fluid?"

"Well," she said. She put a hand to her chin. "It means that it didn't get very far."

"We should call that cop," he said. He kept his eyes on the stain on the road. "Do you think we should?"

"Definitely," she said with a nod. "Yes."

"It's kind of late." He glanced at his watch, a cheap Timex with a black leather band and roman numerals he'd bought at a drugstore nearly ten years ago. If some future version of himself (an out-of-shape pest control technician, no less) had appeared the day he bought it and told him that he'd still be wearing it almost a decade later, he'd have laughed in his own face.

When he looked back at Wanda, she said, "I don't think people are getting much sleep when a girl is missing."

He'd be embarrassed if he called that cop and then he said something like, "That could have come from any car in the last twenty-four hours." He'd look like one of those buffs, guys who watched so much crime television that they thought they knew as much as detectives. Or worse, he'd look like someone guilty, someone who was trying to insert himself as a helpful person into the investigation in order to exert some control. He knew how it felt to be under suspicion.

"What?" Wanda said. She placed a hand on his arm and gave a little rub. "What are you thinking?"

"I just don't want them to get the wrong idea about me, you know?"

"Why would they?" she said.

He issued a breath and sank to the curb. "There was a time, after Lily went missing, that suspicion fell on me."

She sat beside him. "Really?"

"They did a locker search at school and found this notebook I kept. I had written her all these poems and love letters, things I'd never given her. We were friends; that was it. I knew that. But it didn't keep me from dreaming."

He rubbed the back of his neck, where a dull ache had settled.

"For a while, not for long, they had questions for me, for my family.

They searched my room at home and found a scarf of hers. Something she'd left at my house. I kept it, even though I knew she was looking for it, slept with it in my pillowcase because it smelled of her. They thought I was obsessed with her, that maybe I'd hurt her because she didn't love me, or whatever. Even though I was cleared, that suspicion followed me. I left town for college up here and never went back, except to visit my parents every so often."

"I'm sorry, Charlie. That's awful," she said. She stared at the ground between her feet.

Too much baggage. He was dumping too much on her, too soon. They hadn't even been together forty-eight hours. God, what was wrong with him? He was too embarrassed to even apologize for being such a mess.

"I still think we need to call," she said. "It could be relevant. Better to be wrong and embarrassed than right and . . ." She let the sentence trail with a sad shake of her head. Then she stood up quickly, and he thought she was going to walk away from him. Instead, she held out her hand. When he took it, she pretended to use all her strength to haul him to his feet.

"Come on, cowboy. Let's call," she said, tugging him toward the house. He remembered how he'd felt last night over dinner, how he'd realized that she thought he was something special, and how he'd desperately wanted to be that for her. He would be that. He knew he could be.

Inside, he called the detective. He got voice mail and left a message, telling him about the stain on the road and how he'd narrowed it down to three possible car models. Wanda watched him from the couch, seemed to have something on her mind.

"That story," she said when he came to join her on the couch.

"What story?" he asked, although he knew what she was talking about.

"About Lily. You should write about it."

He settled back and looked into her eyes. He thought, *Wanda, will you marry me?* She'd say no, of course. *Charlie, it's too soon. I've been hurt before. Not without a ring.* Something like that. But one day, she was going to say yes.

He said instead, "Wanda, I've been trying to write that story for twenty years."

She made an affirming noise, as though she knew all about waiting for something.

"I have a feeling the time is now."

"Are you satisfied, Jones? I mean, what did you think you were going to find—a bloody shirt, a smoking gun?"

No answer. He'd stopped talking about twenty minutes ago, which was probably a blessing. They'd arrived at that place in their argument where every word they uttered was designed to hurt and inflame. They were in the garage now. Jones was riffling through the garbage can, which simultaneously angered and disgusted her.

The tsunami in her chest made her think of the time after Ricky was born, when she thought she might ask Jones to leave. Parenthood was a crucible. The pressures revealed truths, resurrected buried childhood memories, unearthed hidden aspects of the personality. She'd seen it in her practice—couples changed so much by their new roles as parents that they were no longer compatible. She'd been afraid it was true for them. That dark place in Jones that she'd always found so intriguing was no longer attractive. In fact, it was repellent. The mother in her identified it as a threat. Sometimes, she actively hated him.

But the thought of leaving him had filled her with sorrow; so she'd stayed. And eventually a new marriage had unfolded. It was not as light and full of romance as it had been before Ricky. But there was something more true, more solid about loving someone through change. She thought maybe when marriage survives that shift from romance through friendship to partnership, it's stronger. Maybe that's when you go from being a couple to being a family.

"This search is more about you than it is about him. You realize that, right?"

He shut the lid on the trash can and turned to face her. He stripped the gardening gloves from his hands, put them on the workbench by the door. She'd bought the bench and a full set of tools for him two years ago. Once upon a time, he'd liked working with his hands, building shelves and things for the house . . . a coffee table, an Adirondack chair, a curio cabinet for the upstairs guest room. It brought him some kind of peace. When they'd learned about his high cholesterol and he'd started experiencing tightness in his chest, Maggie thought that it would help to get back to that old hobby, that it might lower his stress level. Everything still hung gleaming on its designated hook. He'd never touched it.

"What is that supposed to mean?" he said.

"It's about your desire to control rather than to have faith."

"Faith?" He practically spat the word, as if it tasted bad in his mouth. "What, like faith in God? Faith in the *universe*?"

She shook her head, released a disgusted breath. "Faith in our *son*. That we've taught him well, that he's a good person. That he'd never hurt anyone's *feelings*, never mind hurt anyone physically."

Something sad flashed across her husband's face, and she felt a flood of relief. He'd heard her. He buried his face in his hands. She moved closer to him and put a hand on his arm.

"He's always been a good boy, Jones," she said. "And he's grown into a good man. You should have seen him tonight—strong, articulate, sincere. He's just like his father."

When he took his hands away from his face, his expression was so haunted and strange, she almost took a step back from him. She felt a black flower of dread open inside her.

"Jones. *What is it?*"

Then the doorbell was ringing and he moved away from her quickly. By the time she'd followed him to the door, he was shouldering on his jacket. Chuck was standing in the foyer, the dark circles under his eyes that she'd noticed earlier looking deeper. There was a ketchup stain on the collar of his barn jacket. She couldn't be sure, but she thought he was wearing the same clothes he'd been wearing yesterday.

"What's going on?"

Chuck looked at the ceiling above her. She followed his eyes to that hairline crack that always bothered her.

"A lead of sorts," he said. "Might be nothing."

She thought Jones might leave without saying anything to her, but instead he walked back and kissed her lightly on the mouth.

"Jones."

"Keep looking," he whispered, and then he was gone.

"You should have gone over there right away," said Jones, climbing into the passenger seat of the vehicle. He didn't let the other guys drive him, but he didn't mind riding shotgun with Chuck for some reason.

"It didn't seem like a priority." Chuck's tone was easy, not defensive. "Strout saw what he saw. There didn't seem to be much else to it until I had other information."

"You could have talked to the neighbors. Maybe someone else saw or heard something."

Chuck gave an affirming nod. "It didn't seem important at the time."

They sat in the driveway, the car idling.

"What did seem important then? What other information?" Jones asked, rubbing at his eyes. He was so tired that his vision was blurry. His chest felt tight and uncomfortable again. He shouldn't have had that double cheeseburger at lunch. It was *not* on the diet recommended by his doctor.

Chuck didn't look like he felt much better. In the light shining from over the garage, he looked pasty and gray. They were both too old to be pulling all-nighters.

"After Strout left, I got access to Charlene Murray's Facebook account and her e-mail. Her friend Britney had the log-in and passwords. She remembered she had them written in an old notebook, searched through and found them, gave me a call."

"And?"

"I found a message that Charlene wrote, the last one on her account, asking Marshall Crosby if he could meet her on Hydrangea and Persimmon. She told him she needed a ride. This confirms what Strout saw."

The news gave Jones a little rush of energy. He felt some strange combination of relief and dread.

"That was her last communication?"

"Yeah. After that, no other messages. If you don't count those status bar updates."

"Was there a message back from Marshall?"

"No." Chuck held back a sneeze by squeezing his nose. He reached into the pocket of his coat for a tissue that looked overused already.

"So we don't know if he read it," Jones said.

"No, but we do know his father owns a green 1968 Chevelle."

Jones knew that car well. Why hadn't he thought about it before? Travis had been very proud of it, showing it off in the parking lot the day he got it a couple of years ago, taking some of the girls for a ride. But it was always in the shop with this problem or that. Just the other day, Jones had seen Marshall sitting in the driver's seat, idling in front of the grocery store. Travis came out with a grocery sack that looked like it contained only a six-pack, climbed into the passenger seat.

Ricky drove a 1966 Pontiac GTO. It was a similar color; the body type *might* look like the Chevelle to someone who didn't know about cars, but their GTO was mint; Jones knew that for a fact. For Ricky's birthday last year, they'd researched the purchase together and finally driven to New Hope, Pennsylvania, to pick up the car from a guy who restored them for a living, just like Jones's uncle had.

Jones remembered how excited he'd been about his Mustang when he'd turned sixteen. He could see that same thrill in his son. The guy who sold it to them had a few piercings, too. So Jones hadn't felt self-conscious about Ricky's hair and getup. It had been a good day for the two of them. They'd had fun, no fighting at all. It was the only day like that he could remember since Ricky had reached adolescence.

"How's the transmission on the GTO?" Chuck asked. His tone was light, his attitude carefully casual.

"It's in good shape," Jones said quickly. "We just had it in for a tune-up last week. Everything in that car is brand-new."

That's why he came here instead of calling, Jones thought. *That's why he came here before going to Crosby's or to check out the area where Strout spotted Charlene.* Jones just wasn't sure whether Chuck had come out of loyalty or suspicion. He was sure Chuck had inspected the driveway before even ringing the bell.

Chuck rubbed his sinuses. "Good."

Jones told Chuck a little bit about Marshall Crosby, about his problems, some of the things Maggie had told him, like the status bar update. *Marshall thinks bad people should be punished.*

"When Charlie Strout left a message about the fluid on the street, I thought I'd go check it out after I stopped by the Crosby house to talk to Marshall."

"Let's split up," said Jones. He reached for the door and pushed it open. "Get in touch with Katie, have her get a sample of that fluid. You go talk to Strout again. Knock on doors around the neighborhood."

"Okay." Chuck wiped his nose again.

"What was your read on him?" asked Jones.

"Strout? He seemed okay. A little jumpy. I ran a check on him. He's squeaky clean, not even an outstanding parking ticket."

Jones stepped back out of the car and closed the door. Chuck rolled down the window.

"I'll go with you," he said. "Strout can wait, right? Katie can get the sample without me."

He had that look, as if Jones had asked him to fetch the water when he was good enough to pitch. They both knew Chuck deserved to go to the Crosby house. It was the more compelling lead, especially now that they had the information Maggie had provided, combined with the message Chuck had found. And really Chuck had been doing all the heavy lifting since Charlene disappeared. But Jones just couldn't give it to him. If one of the Crosbys was involved in this, Jones needed to know first.

He knew Chuck would do what he was asked; that was one of the things he liked best about the guy. The younger detectives were all so full of themselves, mimicking attitudes and things they heard on television, always wanting the job to be something that it wasn't, always mouthing off like there was a camera rolling somewhere. Chuck was a real cop, a quiet and careful observer, with an eye for detail and an ear for lies.

"I'll call you if I need you," said Jones.

Chuck opened his mouth, then snapped it into a tight line. "Okay," he said.

The light snowfall had stopped as quickly as it began, nothing accumulating, though the driveway looked glassy and slick. Jones stepped carefully to his vehicle and waited for Chuck to pull out of the driveway, then followed him until their paths diverged at the next intersection.

20

Something woke Elizabeth, suddenly and totally. She sat up quickly, her heart thumping, senses straining. What was it? The familiar shapes of the room revealed themselves in the dark, the mirror over her dresser, the posts of her bed, the rolltop desk in the corner, the wing chair and ottoman. She pushed back the covers and reached for the light. The cane she had balanced on the nightstand clattered to the floor.

With the light on, she saw the mirror's reflection of a frightened old woman in a silly nightgown with frills at the cuffs and neck, little flowers everywhere. And she was about to have a chuckle at herself when the thumping began, startling her again.

"Hell's bells."

She tried to reach her cane from the bed, but it was just out of her grasp. So she lowered her feet to the cold wood floor and steadied herself on the night table, using it to push herself back upright, not without a considerable amount of pain. It took a moment, once she was standing, for the pain to pass. And after it was gone, she felt quite exhausted by it. Maggie was right. She'd been foolish not to let someone know about her fall. But she couldn't stand the humiliation of it all—the prodding and poking at the doctor's office, the pitying looks.

Again she heard the thumping. It was louder, more frantic than it had been, like something trapped, something panicked. She slid her feet into her slippers.

"That's it," she said. She knew she should call Maggie or Jones and have someone come get her. When Maggie had offered to bring her home earlier, she had wanted to say, *Yes! I don't want to be in this old house with all its memories and critters in the attic.* But instead she'd been stubborn and even a little rude. Maggie had left angry with her, she knew.

When Elizabeth was a younger woman, she used to wish to grow older. She wished for the gravitas and respect she thought would be awarded naturally with age. She thought there would be a freedom in no longer worrying about pointless things like your figure or your hair—older people didn't worry about those things, did they? Surely not. And it was true that she didn't worry about those things any-more. When your hair was shocking white and your face looked like a raisin, only the most foolish and vain women still pretended that anything they wore or did to themselves would give them any sexual allure.

But what she hadn't realized was that this imaginary respect she craved was only granted to older *men*. She hadn't understood that when her body started to weaken and sag, when her beauty faded, she would become invisible. That people would treat her like a child again, with-out the kindness that is generally extended to children. Doctors, check-out clerks at the grocery, even some of her former students, *even* Jones and Maggie, sometimes spoke to her either loudly and slowly, as though she were hearing-impaired, or with a kind of brave patience, as if she were terribly tiresome or very slow to comprehend. The only one who didn't occasionally treat her like a doddering old biddy was her grandson.

If she'd known how old age really was, she'd have appreciated her strong body and attractive features, the small amount of respect her job had afforded her, while it all lasted.

Thump. Thump. Thumpthumpthump. Thumpthump. Thump.

She walked out of her room and stood a moment beneath the attic access. She hadn't been up there in years, sending Jones or Ricky up when she needed this or that—an old painting of her husband's that she'd suddenly remembered and wanted to see again, some photo albums, a lace tablecloth her mother had made. She reached up with her cane and nabbed the loop with its crook. With a two-handed effort, she pulled down the door, the ladder unfolding easily and coming to the floor with a gentle *thud*.

Now the house was perfectly silent as the attic exhaled a breath of mold and mothballs, decades of abandoned and forgotten things. It might be nice to see some of the things up there—her wedding dress, some old records. What else? She didn't even know. She stared at the yawning darkness above her and couldn't help but think about her secret.

"I've had enough," she announced to whatever had decided to make its home up there.

She stood her cane against the wall and climbed the ladder slowly. What did she intend to do once she was up there? she suddenly wondered. With that thought, about halfway up, the pain began, a rocket from her hip down the back of her thigh. It took her breath away, left her clinging to the ladder rungs.

Thump. Thump. Thump.

She looked up and half expected to see her visitors peering at her from the dark doorway, eyes gleaming at her stupidity. But no, there was nothing, just that gaping emptiness reaching into the past. She wasn't more than a few feet off the ground, but she felt paralyzed, frozen—afraid of the pain, afraid of losing her grip and falling again. But already she was starting to shake with the effort of holding herself in place.

Thump. Thump.

When she finally lost her grip, she slid more than fell to the floor, where she lay for a moment before she started to cry. She thought of all the things Maggie had wanted—to bring Elizabeth to her house, to get Elizabeth a bracelet with a button to press if she fell. All things she'd refused, stubborn with her own pride. Now there wasn't as much pain as regret.

The cane stood against the wall. If she could reach it, maybe she could pull herself up. But her limbs suddenly felt full of sand, so she just rested her head on her arm and let the tears come.

It seemed like a hundred years ago that Elizabeth had gone to see Tommy Delano, left work early to drive the hour and a half to the facility where he was being held until his sentencing hearing. She didn't—couldn't, really—tell anyone where she was going. The parents of her students wouldn't have liked it. And even she had to admit that it would have been unseemly. He'd already been tried and convicted in the minds of all the citizens of The Hollows, thanks to Chief Crosby blabbing to everyone who'd listen about the boy's gruesome and depraved confession. There was no room for compassion or sympathy where Tommy Delano was concerned. He was a confessed child killer. End of the worst story told in The Hollows.

But it wasn't some grand capacity for sympathy or compassion that compelled her to drive out of town, to take the highway four exits and cover the desolate miles to a squat gray building in the middle of nowhere surrounded by razor wire, its perimeter guarded by armed men in turrets.

The thing was that she'd always really *liked* Tom, which was not something she could say about all of her students. He was a skinny kid, with a drawn face and watery brown eyes. His clothes, always the wrong size, cuffs ending at his forearms or hems dragging on the floor, were never quite clean. He was a straight-C student, though Elizabeth suspected he could do better. He wasn't funny or charming. But he had a sweet smile, spoke in soft, respectful tones. When she looked at him, she saw kindness, something purely good, even a quiet, twinkling sense of humor.

Once, many years before Sarah's murder, when Tommy had been a student at Hollows High, she'd driven him home. So terrified had he been of the bullies on his bus, that he'd lingered until the bus was gone.

"Dad," she'd overheard him say from the pay phone in the school office. "I had detention and missed the late bus." She knew he hadn't had detention.

"Okay. I'll wait in the library. I'm sorry, Dad. Yes. I'm sorry."

She just couldn't reconcile the boy who'd rather tell his father he had detention than ride the bus with bullies with the image of Sarah's killer, the knowledge of what had been done to her.

"I'll speak to those boys," she'd told him as she drove him that late afternoon to save his father the trip. It was right on her way.

"No," he'd said quickly. "Please, Mrs. Monroe. You'll just make it worse."

She'd stared at the road ahead, not knowing what to say to that.

"Thanks, Mrs. Monroe. But there's really nothing you can do. It's just the way it is."

Of course, that was years before Sarah's murder. A lot can happen to a person in a decade. Maybe a lifetime of torment and misery, the festering wounds left by his mother's death, could transform a timid, quiet person into a killer. But she just couldn't see it. Could she have been *that* wrong about him?

At the prison, she'd waited alone in a gray, cold room before Tommy appeared behind the glass in an orange jumpsuit with his hands cuffed. When he sat, the guard who'd escorted him removed his handcuffs. Tommy looked at her with a sad, confused frown.

"Fifteen minutes," the guard said.

Each picked up a receiver.

"Mrs. Monroe, what are you doing here?"

What *was* she doing here? Coming had been a foolish thing to do. Had she come to ask him if he'd really killed Sarah? Had she come to prove herself right about him? To prove that she really did recognize the difference between good and bad? She found herself at a loss for words, stared down at her wedding ring and twisted it for a second.

"I wanted to see you, Tommy," she said finally. "I just *can't* believe you killed Sarah."

His body seemed to sag. He turned his face from her and rubbed at his neck as if it was itching. When he looked back at her, there was something blank, something cold on his face.

"Well, you're the only one in The Hollows who doesn't believe that," he said. His tone was at once bitter and resigned. His voice had gone much deeper in adulthood, a bit gravelly from smoking. She realized that even though he was in the office regularly, she hadn't really spoken to him in years—maybe just a quick hello or good-bye. She still saw him as a boy, a student at her school. She hadn't updated the picture in her mind's eye. She fixated on his hands. They were cleaner than she'd ever seen them. Usually they were black at the nails, grease caked into his calluses. She tried to imagine those hands, those dirty, hardworking hands, doing terrible things, dipped in blood. She couldn't.

"You confessed," she said.

"Yes." She was a little surprised to hear it. Maybe she had expected him to tell her that he hadn't confessed, that it was a mistake or a lie.

"And you confessed because you did—," she said, stumbling over the phrasing. "Because you killed her."

"Because I—," he started, then didn't finish. He just stood up and hung up the phone. He called for the guard. When the handcuffs were around his wrists, he raised them to her—in a gesture of resignation or farewell, she never did find out.

She hadn't known what to say when he left her so abruptly. She'd had the urge to call after him, to press him. In the end, she'd just watched him go and then left as well, feeling selfish and wrong about the visit. But she'd also left convinced that she'd been right about him, that he didn't have it in him to torture, mutilate, rape, and kill a young girl. And she'd vowed to do something about it, though she didn't know what.

Thump. Thump. Thump.

She'd drifted off on the floor; she didn't know for how long. Now that the door to the attic was open, she wasn't even sure the sound was coming from up there. It seemed to come from the air all around her, inside her own head. She wondered how long she'd have to lie here like this before someone found her. She thought she'd try for the cane again when she felt less tired. But for now, she found herself content to wander through the attic of her life. She wanted, no *needed*, to visit those dark places and examine all the things she'd done and hadn't done, and to make amends where she could—before she lost what fragile hold she still had on it all.

21

Travis opened the door for Jones and offered him a beer, which Jones declined in spite of really, really wanting one. There was a yellow light glowing over the kitchen sink, a nearly full ashtray and an open bottle of beer on a table in the room's center, as if Travis had been just sitting there, smoking and drinking, staring off into space. The room was devoid of decoration, just clean Formica countertops and old appliances. The only decorative touch was an old calendar hanging on the fridge, still on December of the year before, every square blank, a topless woman stretching over the hood of a Cadillac.

"Marshall home?"

A quick shake of his head. "What's he done?"

"I don't know. Maybe nothing. I just want to talk to him."

Jones told Travis about Charlene, about the message she'd sent to Marshall, about the witness who'd spotted the car. Travis took a seat at the table, lit a cigarette. The smell made Jones sick, but he didn't say anything. Cigarette smoke reminded him of Abigail. He barely had a memory of her that didn't include a cigarette in her hand or dangling from her mouth. More brand cigarettes—long and brown like shrunken dead fingers, crooked and pointing, piles of them in ashtrays all over the house. When she died and he sold the house, the real estate agent had made him strip the curtains and the wallpaper, even rip up the carpet. Everything was yellowed and stiff, reeking of smoke.

"He said he took some girl for a ride the other night. But that was early in the evening," Travis said. "Anyway, I didn't believe him. He lives in his head on that computer upstairs."

He said it without heat. Jones nodded, walked over to the refrigerator, saw a magnet from Pop's Pizza. He thought about his own kitchen, cluttered with every possible gadget, colorful ceramic bowls, at least one pile of catalogs and mail, a little gathering of cute salt and pepper shakers that Maggie had haphazardly collected over the years—little Eiffel Towers, dancing pigs, an egg and a yolk. She was always complaining about the lack of counter space. *Get rid of some of this junk,* Jones would say. *It's not junk, it's life,* she'd answer.

"I saw your boy last night," said Travis.

"Where?"

"At Pop's," he said, gesturing toward the magnet as if that was what had made him think of it. "He was sitting there, looking like he'd dropped his ice cream cone on the sidewalk."

"Alone?"

"Yeah. Stood up from the looks of it. Checking his phone, dialing and hanging up."

Jones felt something loosen in his chest. If Ricky had told the truth about that, maybe he was telling the truth about everything. When relief passed, guilt rose in its place. *This search is more about you than it is about him,* Maggie had accused. Maybe she was right.

"Charlene is Ricky's girl, isn't she?" Travis said.

"Yeah," said Jones, sitting across from Travis. The other man took a long draw from his beer. They were easy together, always had been, even with, or maybe because of, the past they shared.

"That must kill you, Jonesy. It must keep you up at night."

Travis was already over the line Jones had seen him cross too many times. They'd all go out for a drink, a bunch of guys from the precinct, and the rounds would start coming. By about round three, Travis would start to change. Depending on his mood, he'd get rowdy, or maudlin, or just plain mean. His face would turn a particular shade of red, his voice would take on a certain pitch. And soon a few of the guys who couldn't handle it would beg off for the night. Usually, someone would wind up taking Travis home. Often it was Jones. Travis didn't bother Jones as much as he did some of the other guys. Jones understood him, knew the size and shape of the baggage he carried, how much it all weighed.

"She wouldn't have been my choice for him," said Jones, smiling in spite of himself.

Travis took another swig off his bottle. "She looks like her mother."

Jones gave a snort. "Mel never looked that good."

"Come on. *You* fucked Melody Murray."

"No, man. I never. That was you."

Travis laughed again; this time it took on a hooting quality. "Now, *that's* true. I popped her cherry—in her mama's bed."

"That's what I always heard."

They both chuckled for a bit. For a minute they were just two middle-aged guys who'd known each other nearly forever.

Then, "So where's Marshall, Travis?"

"He took the car a while ago. Pissed at me, as usual. Said he was going to sleep at his grandpa's. He actually seems to like the old bastard."

"You and your dad still not talking?"

Travis cast his eyes to the ashtray and ground out his cigarette. "You know, the DUI, losing my job. I disgraced him, he says." Travis started to laugh a little then, but Jones could see there was no humor in it. "*Disgraced*. Like he's the queen of England."

Travis started tapping his fingers on the table, beating out a nervous rhythm. Then he lit up again. Jones could see yellow stains on his index and middle fingers.

"I'm going to need to talk to Marshall, Travis. Like, right now. Tonight."

Good humor abandoned Travis's features, and that familiar darkness settled in around his eyes and the line of his mouth.

"How's the transmission on your vehicle?" Jones asked.

Travis gave Jones a slow blink. "Needs work."

He stood up quickly, and Jones did the same. It was never a good idea to be sitting when Travis was standing. Travis left the room and returned a moment later with a beat-up denim jacket.

"I'll come with you," he said. "To find Marshall."

That was the last thing he needed, Travis along for the ride. But there was something about the way the other man looked that ignited a

familiar feeling of pity within Jones. It was that same thing that always
drew them together. Besides, Marshall was a minor; Jones couldn't really
talk to the kid without a parent around anyway.

"Suit yourself."

The sky outside had turned quickly and totally from dusk to night. Jones
and Sarah looked anyplace but at each other—Sarah looking at her
knees, Jones messing with the radio—while Travis and Melody rocked
the car in the backseat, laughing, moaning, until finally it stopped. Jones
flipped through the stations; they only got a few back then, whatever
happened to carry in from bigger cities that day. Sometimes on 712 AM,
The Hollows Wave, the night DJ played some decent stuff. But that
night all Jones could get was an alternative station.

"Oh, I love this song," Sarah said. Jones had no idea what the song
was or who was singing, but he didn't want to seem uncool. She didn't
say anything else.

"Are you two just going to sit there?" asked Travis, popping his head
between the front seat headrests.

Neither Jones nor Sarah answered; they just exchanged an embarrassed look. She definitely didn't act like a girl who enjoyed giving
head, not that he'd ever met a girl like that. Really, most girls—in his
limited experience—didn't want anything to do with what was going
on in your pants. Most of them just wanted to kiss, maybe do a little
rubbing. Most of the girls he knew balked at even putting their hands
down there.

"There's no point in pretending you're a prude, Sarah," said Travis.
"We all know the truth."

Sarah frowned, turned to study him and Melody. "What's that supposed to mean?"

Melody started to giggle. "Come on, Sarah. Lighten up."

Travis and Melody were both stoned stupid, now laughing like idiots. Finally, Travis pushed open the door and the two of them tumbled
out, ran screaming into the woods. They left the door open, and the cold
air quickly filled the car. Jones got out and closed it, could still hear their

voices off in the distance, like the calling of barred owls. He returned to the driver's side.

"Can you just take me home?" Sarah asked. "My mom is going to be really worried. And *really* mad." She looked like she might cry, eyes wide, corners of her mouth turned down.

"Yeah, okay. Sure," he said. "They'll be back in a minute and we'll go."

He noticed that some of the tension in her shoulders released with a breath. And her arms, which had been wrapped firmly around her middle, relaxed a bit.

"What did he mean 'We all know the truth'? What's he talking about?"

"Don't listen to Travis," Jones said. He felt embarrassed. "He's got problems."

"No, really. I want to know."

He should have told her that he had no idea what Travis was talking about, just left it at that. But there was a small part of him—a young, stupid part of him—that wondered if the whole innocent thing *was* just an act she was putting on. Maybe, he thought, if he just told her what he knew, she'd relax. Maybe it was even true.

"Travis says someone told him that you give good head." The words sounded clumsy, felt awkward on his tongue.

She stared at him blankly but slowly started to shrink away from him again. She looked down at her knees. "I don't know what that means," she said.

He felt his face flush. "Uh, you know."

"No," she said, getting angry now. "I don't."

Jones found himself gripping the wheel, wishing he'd never listened to Travis, wishing he could be anywhere but where he was. Finally, he left the car.

"Crosby!" he yelled into the darkness. "Let's go. Let's get out of here. I have to get home."

He heard the car door open and close, and then determined footsteps on the ground.

"What does it mean?" she asked. He turned to face her. She was tiny, much smaller than he was, but somehow her direct and powerful stare cowed him.

"Oh, God," he groaned, looking up at the starry sky. "You know, like a blow job, okay? That you suck cock."

She stepped away as if he'd slapped her, and he felt like he had, he was so ashamed in that moment. She was a nice girl. She *was* innocent.

"I want my stuff out of the trunk," she said. Her voice was faint.

"Why?" he asked. "You can't walk from here. Your house is miles away, and it's dark."

He'd driven them out of The Hollows and down past the dairy farm to a state park that closed at dusk but where no one ever bothered to pull the gate shut. They were three miles from town, surrounded by nearly five hundred acres of yellow poplar, hemlock, American beech, iron-wood, dogwood, red and white oak. Kids from school came here a lot, sometimes to play, sometimes at night to drink or make out. He came here often to walk or run the five miles of trails; sometimes he did his homework on one of the picnic tables or down by the rushing Black River just to be away from his mother, from everyone.

"Look," he said, raising his palms. "I'm sorry. Let's just wait for those guys and then we'll all go."

She shot him an annoyed glance and then walked to the head of the rocky path that led into the park. "Melody!" she yelled. "Let's go. I have homework."

Her voice bounced off the rock walls of the glacial ravine, came back sounding haunted and strained. But she stayed there, looking into the park even though no one called back to her.

"I'm sorry," he said again, coming up behind her. "I shouldn't have said that. I'm a jerk."

He could see that she was shivering, so he shrugged off his varsity jacket and draped it over her shoulders. She seemed to consider refusing, then offered a weak smile, pulled it tight around her. He noticed then the sweet turn of her nose, the wide, full shape to her lips. Her eyes were heavily lidded, almost sleepy, but their color—hazel with flecks of green and gold—shone in the amber light.

"Who says that?" she asked him, after a moment. "Why would they say that about me? I don't—I haven't."

Jones kicked at a stone by his foot; it skipped off into the brush.

"Forget it," she said.

Jones shrugged. "You know what? Probably no one said that. It was probably just Travis being a tool. He's, you know . . . troubled." He made a looping motion with his finger and pulled a funny face. They both laughed then, and he felt the awkwardness between them pass. But the next second, Travis and Melody emerged from the path.

"What's so funny?" Travis snapped at them. Melody wore a deep frown, looked as if she were fighting back tears.

"Let's get out of here," she said, brushing past them, headed for the car. "I want to go home."

"What happened?" asked Jones.

"Melody's a little prick tease. That's what happened," said Travis, staring at her hard. He was clenching and unclenching his fist.

Melody spun around. "Shut up, Travis," she shrieked, and the sound of it echoed around the park.

"What's wrong with you?" asked Sarah. She strode over so that she was standing right in front of Travis.

The exact sequence of events, who said what, was always nebulous here. Jones remembered a chaotic rise of voices, like gulls on a beach fighting over food. He remembered himself as apart, watching, even considering going to the car until they got it all worked out. He remembered Melody saying that she wasn't a slut, or something like that. And Sarah asking why he'd spread rumors about her, she didn't even know him.

But more than anything he recalled the electricity of rising anger, their pulled, pale faces.

"You're a loser, Travis Crosby. A born loser."

She couldn't have known the charge of that word, what it would mean to him. She couldn't have known that he'd heard it a thousand times, in a hundred ugly ways, from a father who'd never had a kind word for his son. It was just the word a girl who wasn't accustomed to calling people names would choose. She said it dismissively and turned to walk away.

"What did you call me?" His voice was white-hot.

Jones saw her turn back to look at him, to say it again. Travis's back was to Jones, so he didn't know what she saw on Travis's face that made her own expression go slack with fear, her eyes widen.

"Okay," said Jones, "that's enough."

But then Sarah was running, casting Jones's varsity jacket to the ground. Did she start to run and he gave chase? Or did he move toward her, causing her to bolt? Jones couldn't tell. But Travis was after her. She disappeared into the dark of the path, her footfalls loud and echoing, with Travis on her heels. Melody and Jones exchanged a look, and then they followed.

"Leave her alone, Travis," Melody yelled.

When they caught up with Travis and Sarah, the two were in a standoff. Sarah had picked up a heavy branch and stood with her back to a long pathway that led into the river valley below.

"Stay away from me," she said, crying, lifting the branch like a baseball bat. "Get away."

Behind her yawned the steep and twisting path down, the individual steps just stones lined in the earth, jagged gray teeth in mossy gums.

Jones grabbed Travis by the shoulder. "Let's go. This is finished."

But Travis turned and swung on Jones, catching him hard in the jaw. Jones fell back with the shock and pain of it, a warm gush of blood traveling from his nose over his lips onto his shirt. He didn't see what happened next; Melody and Travis always said different things. Travis said that Sarah came after him with the branch and he fended her off. Melody said Travis turned from the swing on Jones to go after Sarah. Whatever happened, the end result was that Sarah fell. And her head hit a sharp stone jutting from the ground. That was the next sound Jones remembered hearing. And then there was absolute silence. Everything in the forest around them—the wind in the leaves, the singing of spring frogs and crickets—seemed to stop. Jones got to his feet and saw her lying there between Melody and Travis. Melody dropped to her knees beside Sarah, who was so still.

"Sarah," she whispered, as though trying to rouse her from sleep. "Sarah?"

Then she looked up at them, her face a mask of sorrow and fear. Her words were just an exhaled breath. "She's—she's not breathing."

"No," said Jones. "That's not—No."

He went to kneel beside Sarah as well and saw the unnatural angle of her neck, the strange stillness, the odd cast to her skin.

"Oh, my God." He felt the first grip of true fear he had ever known. "I never touched her."

They both turned to look at Travis, who started to back away, his lips parted, head shaking. Then Travis took off in a sprint, disappeared up the path to the main road.

It was that night that Jones realized your body was a thing that could be broken on impact through careless action, broken like a branch left in the road. She was wrecked before him, ruined, ended. There was just one moment between her life and death, just one breath drawn and not released. He thought about the sound it made . . . that final, soft noise of flesh on stone, the crackle of breaking bone. It was so quiet.

Then, years later, there was a dawning, a slow and terrible dawning that he, too, would die. Even he would one day draw a breath and not release it, or release a breath and not draw another. He would cease to exist, cease to draw the world in through his senses, though it would go on without him. A grim dread, accompanied by a petulant rage, settled on him. It was all so damn fragile. It shouldn't be. Something so important should be stronger. How were we all supposed to bear it? he wondered. How could anyone really live, knowing that they were going to die? What was the point?

That night, and every awful thing that followed, was there between them in the Explorer as they drove to find Marshall. It was always there, wasn't it? But the years had buried it all deep, covered it with the fallen debris of ordinary days. Jones wanted to say, *Is it still with you? Do you still dream about it?* But he didn't. He knew the answer, could see it in the shattered expression Travis had worn that night and how that face, hollowed with fear and regret, was just beneath the surface of every other face he wore. That's what Jones saw when he looked at Travis, not the fearsome bully everyone else seemed to see.

Travis lit another cigarette without asking, rolled down the window, letting the cold air sweep in. Jones drove from The Acres and took the main road through the center of town, passed the coffee shop and the independent bookstore, Pop's Pizza and the Om Yoga Studio. A sharp right after the last light put them on Old Farmers Road, which started as a paved road but devolved into little more than a rocky path, completely impassable after a heavy snowfall.

Chief Crosby (everyone still called him that, thought of him that way, though he'd retired long ago) owned the surrounding hundred acres, thick with hemlock and pine. Rumor had it that he'd had offers from developers—huge offers—that he'd summarily turned down. Every winter Jones fully expected to have to find a way to haul the chief's giant corpse out of there. But every spring he emerged in his big red pickup truck, looking a bit slimmer, like a bear emerging from hibernation.

"My old man is never going to sell this land, not even a sliver of it," said Travis. "It's worth a fortune."

"He won't live forever," said Jones.

"We'll see," said Travis, flicking his cigarette out the window.

As they turned onto the drive, Jones saw Marshall's car parked on an angle beneath the glow of a spotlight that shone from the garage. There was a low crescent moon, and a field of stars he didn't usually get to see in the brighter light of town. The Crosby house was built from fieldstone, a massive chimney reaching up through the red and white pine; it was still and dark, sure of itself to the point of being contemptuous, like the old man himself.

Off down to their right, a stone carriage house tilted in the landscape, its boards splintered and gray, its roof caving in. Jones exited the vehicle and approached the Chevelle, got stiffly to his knees, joints and lower back protesting, and spotted the dark puddle on the ground beneath it.

When he stood up again, he was surprised to see Travis directly behind him. He hadn't heard the door open and close, had assumed the
other man was still sitting in the warmth of the vehicle.

"What are you doing, Crosby?" said Jones, taking a step back. He
felt the urge to rest his hand on the gun he carried in a shoulder holster.
He knew, though, that a move like that, slipping your hand inside your
jacket, was one of antagonism for another cop. He didn't want to over-
react, but the sight of Travis unnerved him. Shadows had settled on the
hollows of Travis's face, in the valleys under his eyes, in the deep lines
around his mouth.

"Do you ever think we should have just owned up to what happened
that night?" Travis said.

Jones drew and released a deep breath. Here it was, clawing its
way up from the dirt beneath their feet. "Why are we talking about
this now?"

Travis turned up the corners of his mouth in a mirthless grin.
"Come on, Cooper. We all died that night. We're just ghosts in our lives,
aren't we? Everything is rotten, decayed."

"Speak for yourself."

"It was an accident. I didn't mean to hurt her. Not . . . *kill her.*" His
voice shattered on the last words.

"I know that. I do."

"I just keep thinking that if it had just stopped there, if I'd just had
the courage to own it . . . ," Travis said. He let the sentence trail and his
eyes drift over to the old house, the place where he'd grown up. "The
thing is, I *wanted* to be a better man than my father, a better father than
he was. I just never knew how. You can't build a house without the right
tools, you know."

Jones saw the other man begin to cry and cast his eyes away. He
didn't want to see Travis break down. His hand was itching to reach for
the gun in its holster. *It's too late for all of this, Travis,* he wanted to say.
*We're too far gone. All our mistakes, everything we've done wrong. It is just
part of who we are now. There's no such thing as redemption. Two people are
dead because of all the things we did and didn't do. Your tears mean nothing.*

But he was pretty sure that was not what Travis needed to hear. He wished Maggie were here; she'd know what to say to him. She always had the answers.

"I know I can't undo the things I've done. I can't go back and be a better father. But I can protect my son right now. I can do that."

When Jones looked back at Travis, the other man had a gun in his hand, a .38-caliber Smith & Wesson, his old service revolver.

"What are you doing, Travis?"

"What I have to do."

"What's he done, man? We can work it out."

Jones thought about Maggie and the things she'd said, how angry she'd been at him tonight, the accusations she'd leveled against him. And he saw now that she was right about everything. And Travis was right, too, about them all being ghosts in their lives—not living right, not at rest or at peace, just howling at the fringes.

"Hiding the truth isn't the same as protecting someone." Even as he said it, he knew what a sad hypocrite he was. "What good did it do any of us?"

But Jones could see the blank determination in the other man's eyes. He knew instinctively that he wouldn't have time to draw his weapon now. He'd waited too long.

He lifted his palms in a gesture of surrender; when he saw Travis relax, Jones rushed him, hoping that Travis's reaction time was slow because he was drunk. But before he could reach Travis, the explosion of the firing gun opened up the night.

He was a coward. Charlene was right about him. He was a mama's boy, because that's where he wanted to be, at home with his mom. Instead he was driving around The Hollows, flirting with the entrance to the interstate that would take him into the city. But he couldn't quite get himself to drive up the on-ramp. He'd passed it three times already. He could drive to New York, and then what? Go to a club, hope to bump into her? He didn't know where anybody lived. Would he wander the streets, looking at every girl who passed?

He ran one hand through his hair. It felt as hard and spiky as Astro-Turf from all the gel he used to create that carefully messed-up look. The action caused his arm to ache. He wasn't sure a tattoo was supposed to hurt this much; the skin beneath the ink looked red and raw. He'd dabbed away a little pus. That was all he needed, for the stupid thing to get infected. That would really send his parents off the deep end.

She uses people. She used you. Earlier he'd been so sure that something had happened to Charlene. But now he wasn't sure of anything. Whose car had she gotten into? Where had she gone? Why did his father believe he'd done something to hurt her? Or that he was lying? On the seat beside him, his phone started ringing again. Mom calling, the screen blinked anxiously. He didn't answer. As much as he wanted to pick up and talk to her, he didn't.

He was tired, pulled into a deserted gym parking lot. He'd already been through the drive-through at Taco Bell, had an Enchirito and nachos while he drove. Then he went through Starbucks and got a venti Peppermint Mocha Frappuccino with extra whipped cream and chocolate sauce. So, for a while, he was wired, his mind buzzing with one grand plan after another. Now, crashing hard, Rick just wanted to go home. But he couldn't stand the thought of them—his father's accusations, his mother's worried frown. If he went home, they wouldn't just leave him be; they'd be up all night fighting. He wondered what it was like to live in a family where people didn't feel compelled to talk all the goddamn time about every little thing. Not that this was a little thing. It was a big thing, the biggest thing. The girl he loved was missing. His father thought he had something to do with it.

He brought the car to a stop and killed the engine, sat in the deserted parking lot. It was after midnight, and he hadn't seen another car in an hour. He rested his head against the window, started to doze, and immediately began to dream. He dreamed that he was swinging a bat, and as it connected with a ball pitched to him by his father, it made a sharp crack, the bat splitting in two. The sound startled him awake. Then he heard it again.

Carried on the night air, it sounded like the firing of a gun. His dad had taught him the difference between gunfire and the backfiring of an engine. The sound of gunfire had a crack to it, a report, whereas the sound of a car backfiring was more explosive. He listened for it again, but he only heard the wind through the leaves. He rolled down the window and caught the scent of cut grass and something else, the faintest odor of skunk. He kept listening for a while, hoping to hear it again, but there was nothing. Then his phone started ringing again.

Sitting there listening to it, wondering if he should finally answer, Rick felt his fatigue and sadness become unbearable. He couldn't sit alone in the dark anymore. He turned the key, and the engine rumbled to life. He knew where to go, someplace where he could rest and be left alone.

He drove back through town and made a right, followed the road past Hollows High, and turned onto Blacksmith Bluff, his grandmother's street. He pulled into her driveway, putting the car in neutral and drifting in the last fifty yards, like he did at home not to wake his dad. But as he stepped out of the car, he noticed that the light in his grandmother's bedroom was on.

He used the key he had on his ring and pushed the front door open, stepping into the foyer. He flipped on the light and moved inside.

"Grandma?"

He saw a light shining down the stairs from the hallway on the second floor. He didn't want to give her a heart attack. He didn't want to wake her if she was sleeping, either. But when he heard a low and distant moaning, he broke into a run up the steps. Elizabeth was on the floor beneath the attic access, her cane toppled beside her.

"Grandma," he said, kneeling beside her.

"Ricky," she said. "You need to tell them."

She looked pale and withered lying there, so helpless. Beneath his hand, her shoulder felt tiny and frail. It scared him. She was a power-house, as strong and permanent as the old oak tree out in the backyard.

"Grandma, it's okay." He pulled the cell phone from his pocket and dialed 911, though his first instinct was to call his mother. He knew enough not to try to move his grandmother, though he could easily have scooped her up in his arms and carried her to the bedroom.

"You have to tell them, Ricky." She clutched his wrist, her grip urgent.

"I need an ambulance at 173 Blacksmith Bluff," he said to the dispatcher. "My grandma fell. She's hurt."

"Ricky," Elizabeth said. "She was already dead when he found her."

Rick didn't know what she was talking about, tried to focus on the dispatcher's voice while giving his grandmother a comforting rub on the arm.

"She's disoriented," Rick said, holding her gaze. "Can you contact my father, Jones Cooper? He's the head detective at the Hollows Police Department."

The dispatcher told him to stay on the line until the ambulance arrived. Rick tucked the phone between his ear and his shoulder.

"It's okay, Grandma." He heard the dispatcher requesting the ambulance. *Arrival in four minutes. Hang in there.*

"She was already dead, Ricky. He didn't kill her."

"Grandma . . . I don't understand." He felt a tingle of panic. Was she talking about Charlene? Did she know something? "Grandma? What are you talking about?"

But her gaze was glassy and distant, staring through him. She released a sigh and relaxed her hold on his arm. In the distance, he heard the wailing of sirens.

After calling Ricky several times to no avail, Maggie found herself at a loss. She considered calling her mother and then, when she noted the time, decided against it. She wouldn't "keep looking," as Jones had urgently requested, nor would she go out after Ricky and drive aimlessly searching for him. She couldn't think of anything more crazy-making.

So she found herself paralyzed, staring at the cordless phone in her hand, trying to figure out an appropriate course of action—one that was reasonable and productive, not the unhinged move of a frantic mother, or the fearful action of an overly obedient wife. Even if Jones didn't know their son, she did. He would call or come home, and he would do it sooner rather than later. Or so she hoped.

But then the phone was ringing in her hand. She answered it without glancing at the caller ID.

"Hello?"

"Dr. Cooper?"

Her heart sank to hear an unfamiliar voice. "Yes, this is."

"It's Angie Crosby." In the current chaotic context, it took Maggie a moment to place the name. Marshall's mother.

"Oh, Angie." Maggie's worry about Marshall returned to the forefront of her mind for a moment. And she was ashamed to note that she was almost glad for it, the distraction from her personal crisis.

"It's late," said Angie. "I'm sorry."

"No, it's quite all right. I'm up," Maggie said. "What's wrong?"

There was silence on the other line and then a muted weeping.

"Angie?" Maggie said. "What is it?"

"I'm sorry I hung up on you before. I didn't want— But now I've been thinking."

"What's happening?" Maggie felt a flutter of fear and something else she wouldn't have admitted, the relief of being on solid ground, of knowing what to do, what to say.

Angie issued a few more shuddering breaths, then, "He came here earlier today."

"Okay," Maggie said. "And something happened between you. Tell me about it."

Stop shrinking, Jones would say to her. *You use those benign questions and leading statements as a shield, Maggie. Always calm, always in control, always looking for a way to "help." But where are* you? *What do you need? What do you feel?* He was right, in a way. It was always so much easier to help others than it was to help yourself. But what was wrong with that? It was her job.

"Something's happened to him," Angie said. "He's changed."

Maggie opted for silence. Sometimes that was a better way to draw things out than the affirming statement or coaxing question.

"He said that Travis was right," Angie went on after a moment. "That all women were whores and users. Especially me."

Maggie realized she was gripping the phone, leaning so hard against the table that the edge was digging into her rib cage. She forced herself to lean back and breathe. When the other woman didn't continue on her own, Maggie said, "Did he hurt you?"

More muffled crying. "He pushed me, hard against a wall of shelves. I hit my head on a corner—hard enough to black out."

"I'm so sorry, Angie. Are you all right?"

"I am. But when I came back around, Marshall was gone."

Maggie wanted more details about how the encounter had started and what had happened to make it escalate to violence, though she saw from Marshall's actions in her office earlier that there was a simmering rage there, just waiting for an opportunity to boil over.

"When I talked to you earlier, I was upset about what happened between Marshall and me," Angie went on. "I figured I'd change my locks and not be so quick to answer the door to him next time. I didn't want him to get in trouble, you know. So much of what's wrong with him is my fault, Dr. Cooper. I know that. I left him to Travis."

Angie started crying again. Maggie felt her own eyes tear; she could hear so clearly the pain and frustration in the other woman's voice.

"So what's changed since last we talked?" Maggie asked. "Did he come to your house again?"

"No, no. After I talked to you and pulled myself together, I had a horrible thought. I keep guns here in my house. A revolver and a semi-automatic weapon. I have a license and am trained to use them."

"Angie."

"They're gone, Dr. Cooper. Marshall stole my guns."

The words made Maggie feel sick, as if she couldn't draw another breath. The thousand incredulous questions she wanted to ask—*Didn't you have them locked up? How did he know you had those guns and where you kept them? When was this and how long did it take you to call me?*—lodged in her throat. The best she could do was to say, "Oh, my God, Angie. Did you call the police?"

Maggie heard Angie blowing her nose. Then, "No."

"What?" she said. "Why not?"

Another sniffle. "I didn't want to get him in trouble."

Maggie issued a long, slow breath. "Okay. What you need to do, right now, is hang up the phone and report the theft to your local police department. You need to tell them that Marshall is unstable and that he is armed."

"I don't want to call the police on my son, Dr. Cooper."

"You don't have a choice. This is not just about Marshall anymore."

Maggie found herself staring at a picture of Ricky, Jones, and her that hung on the opposite wall. Ricky was maybe three at the time. They were all dressed up, smiling. She used to think when Ricky was small how hard it was to protect him—from falls, from disappointments—how she worried about things like what he was eating and whether he was watching too much television. Compared with the things that came later, that time seemed idyllic and innocent. It was amazing how many different ways you could fail your child without even realizing it.

"Angie," said Maggie, trying for a tone that was calm but stern, "report the guns stolen and alert the police in your area, in case he's still nearby. And I'll do the same here in The Hollows."

The other woman was silent; Maggie could hear her breathing. "Angie."

"I thought you would want to help him," she said, sounding petulant and angry now. *Poor Marshall,* Maggie thought. *Did he ever have a chance with parents like this?*

"This *is* helping him. We're helping him not to hurt others or himself." Was it not obvious?

"Okay," Angie said. "Thanks. Thanks a lot."

Maggie heard Angie slam the phone down hard and fought back a tide of anger.

She dialed Jones first and got no answer, left a message on his voice mail. Then she called the nonemergency number at the precinct and alerted Cheryl, the woman who answered, to the situation with Marshall. Then she called Chuck, for lack of any other options. His number was posted over the phone.

"Ferrigno," he answered. He somehow managed to infuse fatigue and annoyance into the syllables of his name.

"It's Maggie."

"What's up?"

She told him about Marshall and the stolen guns. "Does Jones know about this?" asked Chuck when she was finished.

"No, I can't reach him."

"Okay. I have to go."

"Why? What's happening?"

"Just stay put, Maggie. I'll call you in a while."

He ended the call then without another word. In her frustration at being hung up on again, Maggie slammed the phone down on the table, releasing a little roar of anger. She got up and grabbed her purse from the counter. She couldn't just sit there waiting for a phone call for the rest of the night. She had to do something. She didn't know what. She dug around for her cell phone and, when she found it, realized that it was dead. She'd charge it in the car.

But before she headed out the door, something made her turn around and pick up the phone again. She glanced at the clock as she dialed the number she, for whatever reason, knew by heart, though she rarely had reason to call Henry Ivy at home. Maybe it was because he'd had the same number since he was a kid, living in the house where he grew up, though his parents had long ago retired to Florida. He answered quickly, sounding alert and wide awake.

"It's Maggie."

"Maggie. What's wrong?"

"I'm coming to get you. I need your help."

She heard the squeaking of his mattress, the pushing back of sheets. "Okay," he said. "I'll be ready."

2 3

The sky above them was a field of stars. Jones stared up at the sway-ing tips of the towering pines. If he just kept looking up, maybe when he looked down again, it would all be a dream, a mistake, a horri-ble imagining. But no. Melody sat cross-legged beside Sarah, holding her white hand. She was rocking, singing something softly.

"We have to get out of here," she said when she saw him watch-ing her.

"We have to call the police," said Jones, rising. He realized that he was crying, that his face was wet with tears. He wiped at them with his sleeve, but they just kept coming.

"Did you kiss her?" Melody asked, apropos of nothing.

"No." He looked at Sarah's body and knew that they were all stand-ing before a chasm of pain and grief, that life as they knew it had ended. He'd see her again and again over the years, every time he looked at a corpse lying crooked on the ground. It was always the same feeling, the pointless rise of wishing things were different, of knowing that things could not be undone, that these were the last peaceful moments before someone, somewhere, would be crushed by sorrow.

"We have to go," she said. "He'll find a way to pin the blame on us. He'll bring his father back here, and they'll find a way. He weasels out of everything."

Jones was about to protest. But Melody interrupted.

"It's your car. You picked her up. I brought the weed. I'm high right now. We have to leave. Sarah's gone. There's nothing we can do for her."

Looking back now, he remembered that she was level, logical even, far beyond her years. He felt near hysteria, about to shake apart at the seams. She stood and started leading him away from Sarah's poor, broken body.

"We can't just leave her here," he said. "We'll call the police and tell them it was an accident. It *was* an accident."

"We have to go. I don't want my life to end here tonight, too."

Later, during the one and only conversation they had about that night, Melody would swear that it was he who wanted to leave, she who wanted to stay and call the police. Melody would claim that he was the one who dragged her toward the car, while she protested loudly. But Jones didn't remember it that way. As he remembered it, they both walked back to the Mustang. He opened the door for her, as he'd been taught to do, and she climbed inside. They left Sarah. They left her there in the woods, in the dark, alone. Jones fought the rise of bile all the way back to Melody's place.

"Follow his lead," she said. "If we follow him, we'll be all right."

He agreed. Even as she left the car, the events of the evening seemed distant and strange, as if it were something he'd watched on television as he drifted off to sleep—fuzzy, indistinct, unreal.

When he pulled into his driveway, his mother was waiting at the door. She was always waiting at the door, or at the window, as if she expected daily for him not to return home.

"You're late," she said. She pushed the screen door open for him. "I kept a plate warm."

"Sorry," he said. "I gave Travis Crosby a ride home."

"Where's your jacket? It's cold."

Where was his jacket? He remembered, then, wrapping it around Sarah's tiny shoulders. She'd cast it to the ground when she ran from Travis. He'd forgotten it. He didn't remember seeing it in the parking lot when they returned to the car. But he didn't remember much; he'd left there in a shocked daze. Did Travis take it? That's when he remembered that her things—her book bag, her violin case—were still in the trunk of the car. He felt his knees start to buckle with the weight of it, and the next thing he knew, he was kneeling by the stairs, his head in his hands.

"Jones! What's wrong? What is it?"

He told her. He told her everything that happened from the minute he picked up Travis until he dropped off everything. And when he was done, he sagged with relief. His mother had come to sit beside him on the staircase, pulled her knees up inside her tattered white housedress. He was afraid to lift his eyes from his hands to look at her face. Instead he looked at the papery skin of her ankles, all the millions of purple spider veins along her legs. When he found the courage to lift his eyes, she was staring at him, the look on her face unreadable.

"Mom. We left her there. She's still there," he said.

"How could you do this?"

"I don't know. I don't—," he said. "What should I do?"

"After everything I've done for you. How could you do this to me?"

He stared at her, incredulous. "To you?"

"They'll take you away from me."

"Mom." He couldn't believe what she was saying.

She had a crazed light in her eyes. "You'll do what that girl said. You'll keep your mouth shut and follow Travis Crosby's lead."

"But—," he said. The ground beneath his feet felt like it was made from fog; he couldn't find firm footing. "She's still out there."

His mother came to kneel beside him and grabbed him by the shoulders. Her breath in his face reeked of cigarette smoke.

"You listen to me. She's dead and gone. There's nothing you can do for her. Do you want to flush your whole life down the toilet?"

But they both knew it wasn't about him or about his life. Somehow it had become about his mother and what he had done to her, how this might ultimately take him from her. He looked at her, her hard, dark eyes, her thin line of a mouth pressed tight, her white skin flushed with emotion. She didn't care about him, or about a girl left dead in the dark.

"It's not right." The words sounded weak and lame because he stayed rooted on the stairs.

But she didn't seem to hear him anyway. "If it ever comes down to it, I'll swear you came right home. Who do you think they'll believe—that little druggie tramp and that delinquent Crosby kid, or me?"

He just sat listening to her go on. She ranted as she ushered him into the kitchen and put a plate of food before him. It smelled vile.

Abigail was a horrible cook, everything either overseasoned or under-cooked. He pushed his food around his plate, swallowed a few bites to appease her.

The rest of the evening passed in a blur—a shower, homework, then to bed like any other ordinary night. Except he was still in the park with Sarah, and she was alive, and he kissed her. And maybe he'd ask her out for Friday night. She was a nice girl; he liked the way he felt when she was sitting in his car. He wondered what it would be like to hold her hand. And then she was lying on the ground, stiff and growing cold.

After his mother went to sleep, he looked out his window to see that a light snow had started to fall. He couldn't take it anymore. He couldn't leave her there. He grabbed a coat from the closet and left the house, letting the Mustang roll in reverse from the drive, starting it only when he was in the street. Even so, as he drove off, he saw his mother's bed-room light come on.

When he got to the park, the lot was covered in a brittle layer of glitter-ing snow. The vehicle gate had been closed and locked. In all the years he'd been coming there, it never had been before. He left the Mustang at the gate and easily climbed over. He felt the cold prickle of snow on his face, neck, and hands.

He expected to see his jacket by the trailhead where Sarah had shed it in her run from Travis. But it was gone. He followed the trail to the stone staircase. He stared at the place where they'd left her. But Sarah's body wasn't there.

With the light snow covering the ground, there was no evidence that any of them had ever been there. He felt a lift of hope in his heart. Had they been wrong? Had she gotten up from where she lay and found her way home? He walked to the edge of the staircase and looked down. He could see all the way to the bottom, but no one was standing there. He walked up the trail awhile, looking in the brush, wondering if, disoriented maybe, she'd gotten up and walked farther into the park. But he was alone. Finally, after a while, he left, the snow crunching be-neath his feet, the wind picking up and moaning through the trees. As he walked back through the lot, the falling snow was already covering his tracks. By the time he'd returned to his car, his footprints were nearly gone.

It took a second for Jones to realize that he was on the ground, outside in the cold. He immediately reached for his gun, but his holster was empty. His hand flew to his waist for his cell phone next. That was gone, too. He felt more angry than afraid. How could he have turned his back on Travis Crosby? And then there was the pain—a burning ache in his side, a terrible tightness in his chest. He wondered coolly, *Is this it?* Would he meet his end as Sarah had, alone on the cold ground, miles from anyone who loved her? He knew he didn't deserve better. But no, he wasn't going like this. No way.

The Explorer was just twenty feet away. Inside the vehicle was the radio, of course. In the hatch there was a rifle, hidden in a locked compartment beneath the carpet. He heard voices, distant, outside. They carried up on the trees and into the air. It was hard to know from which way or how far. Then he heard a slicing scream, rage or agony, male or female, he couldn't be sure. But it electrified him, shot adrenaline through his system, and he was up on all fours, crawling for the SUV.

Somewhere, he heard a cell phone start to ring; it sounded like his own. He didn't have the time or the strength to try to find it. Travis must have tossed it into the woods nearby. Radio or gun? He decided to go for the gun first.

When he reached the back of the Explorer, he used the bumper to pull himself to his feet. The whole world tilted with his pain. His breath came ragged, and even that caused his chest, back, and abdomen to ache. His shirt and coat were soaked with blood. But he suspected that the bullet had just grazed the flesh of his belly. There were some advantages to being fat. He pulled the keys from his pocket and, with effort, pushed open the hatch. He flipped back the carpet easily and unlocked the compartment, removing the loaded gun. In his weakened state, it felt impossibly heavy. If he had to fire it, the recoil might do him in.

Now that he was armed, he was about to head to the radio, request backup. But another scream sliced the night, and Jones felt a chill down his spine, a painful throbbing in his chest. In its wake, the air seemed preternaturally quiet. Then, the sharp crack of a gunshot. Then another. Then nothing. Jones gripped his own gun and headed off into the woods behind the Crosby home.

Maggie watched Henry exit his front door and lock it behind him. She wondered how many times she'd watched him do that over the years of their friendship. He didn't have a car in high school; she was always driving him somewhere in their senior year, often picking him up on her way to school. She felt a familiar wash of affection for him—and gratitude for their enduring friendship. Sometimes, like tonight, she felt closer to him than she did to her own husband.

I always thought you'd marry him, Elizabeth had said to Maggie just before she married Jones.

Henry? No.

Why not?

There's no heat, Mom. No chemistry.

That's what young people don't understand. You don't need heat. In fact, you're better off without it.

What? You and Dad didn't have heat?

Oh, we had heat, her mother said with a mischievous grin.

Mom!

At the time, Maggie had thought it was a ridiculous thing to say, that you don't need passion. She was smart enough to know that chemistry didn't sustain a marriage, but without it there was nothing. Even an eternal flame needs an igniting spark. But nearly twenty years into her marriage and her practice, she understood what her mother meant. Some people thought the spark was everything, kept wanting it again and again, leaving behind a wake of failed relationships. Her patients would have these steamy affairs, leave the relationships they were in, only to find that once real life—bills, blending families, work—crept in, it was the same old thing.

Henry jogged to the car and got in the passenger seat.

"What's going on?" he asked. He reached over and fastened his seat belt.

She told him everything—about Jones and Ricky, about Angie Crosby's claim that Marshall had stolen her guns. He took it all in with a careful nod, looking down at some point between them.

He was quiet for a moment after she'd finished. "So what are we going to do?"

She studied him, noticed the lines under his eyes, the gray at his temples. She thought he was better looking now than when they were kids, as though he had settled into his looks. When he looked up at her, she glanced away, embarrassed that she was thinking anything of the sort in a moment like this.

"I was hoping you'd have some ideas."

Henry tugged at each cuff on his jacket.

"Well, I went to the Crosby residence earlier today." He told her about his encounter with Travis. She could tell it had disturbed him, stirred up old memories and feelings. But he kept his recounting neutral, and she didn't dig.

"Marshall wouldn't be with Leila and her family," said Maggie, when he was done. "They're distancing themselves from him. If he'd come to her, she'd have called me."

She remembered her cell phone then and rooted around in her purse for it, plugged it into the charger that dangled from the cigarette lighter.

"I don't know whether to look for Ricky or to look for Marshall," she said, staring at the phone's screen. The charge was so low that, even plugged in, it wasn't coming on right away.

"Rick is smart and solid," said Henry. "He's not going to do any-thing stupid."

She was grateful to hear him say it. She trusted her son; she was happy to know it wasn't just a mother's denial.

"Marshall, on the other hand, is in major trouble," said Henry. "If the police find him with guns, that's pretty much going to be the end of him."

"Henry," she said, looking at her friend. His brow was creased with worry. "The police finding him with guns is the best-case scenario. I'm worried about what will happen if they *don't* find him. Soon."

"Okay," he said, rubbing his eyes. "The only thing I can think to do is to go to Chief Crosby's house. The property is totally isolated. It's late. I know Marshall has a relationship with his grandfather. I can't think of where else he would go."

It made sense, though she dreaded an encounter with the chief. There was something about those milky blue eyes that always made her want to run from him. Maybe it was just her mother's passionate dislike for the man. Maggie always found her mother's opinions contagious. She started the engine.

"I was thinking Ricky might have gone to my mother's house," she said. She was really just thinking aloud. "But I can't imagine him disturbing her in the middle of the night. And if he was there, she'd have called."

Maggie put the car in reverse and backed out of the drive. Henry put a hand on her shoulder. "He's okay," he said. "Maybe he snuck in there and went to sleep. Should we drive by and look for his car?"

It was tempting, but Elizabeth's house was on the other side of town. If Ricky was there, he was safe. The urgency to find Marshall was high. Maggie said as much.

"Where's Jones now?" asked Henry.

"I have no idea." She didn't mean to sound clipped and angry. But she *was* angry. Why should she have to lean on her friend in this crisis? She should be with her husband.

"This is all going to turn out all right," he said. "You'll see."

But the stone in her gut told her something different.

24

The voices he'd heard were gone. And he was alone with the sound of his own breathing as he made his way through the woods. The only light came from the sliver of moon above him. Down by the lake, he saw the old boathouse. It tilted against the night sky, looked about ready to fall into the water. He knew the chief kept a boat, an ancient cabin cruiser. He remembered taking it out onto the lake with Travis, drinking and fishing, lying on its bow. Last time he'd talked to the chief, the old man said that it was still seaworthy, that he still fished off it.

He stood and tried to quiet his breathing, to ignore the pain in his side, in his chest. Above him, he saw the shadow of a large bird circling. A barred owl was using the scant light to hunt. The next thing he knew, he was on his knees again. If he believed in God, he'd use the opportunity to pray. But he didn't believe in God. He didn't believe in anything, not even himself.

After he'd discovered Sarah's body gone, Jones drove to Crosby's house next. He saw Chief Crosby's big red pickup parked in front of the carriage house. Before Jones killed the engine in the drive, Travis was out on the front step moving toward him. He had his hands pressed deep in his pockets, his shoulders hiked up like a vulture. Inside the screen door, Jones could see Chief Crosby's formidable frame. As Jones exited the Mustang, he heard the engine pinging, cooling in the night air.

"What are you doing here, Cooper?" Travis came up close to him.

"Where is she?" Jones asked.

"Who?" said Travis. He narrowed his eyes in what seemed to Jones a caricature of menace. All he saw when he looked at Travis was fear.

"Sarah."

"I don't know what you're talking about." Travis leaned back and looked up at the sky.

"Travis. Come on. It was an accident."

Chief Crosby stepped out of the house then. Jones stared at him, felt the familiar dread he had whenever the chief was around. The man was a ghoul, a monster. Jones would see that later. But then, he was a titan, somebody everyone in The Hollows looked upon with respect and admiration. The sight of him shut them both up.

"Boy," the chief said. "It's done. Walk away and keep your mouth shut."

"No. Where is she?" Jones's whole body quaked—with fear, with anger. The expression on Travis's face was a mirror of his own heart.

The chief came down off the step and strolled toward them easily. "You left your jacket," he said. "It's got her blood all over it."

And Jones remembered again that Sarah's things were still in his trunk. Chief Crosby must have seen the understanding dawn on Jones's face, because he let out that hooting Crosby laugh, a laugh Jones would hear every time he heard Travis laugh.

"Well, I can see you're not stupid like your old man," said Chief Crosby. "Question is, are you a coward like him?"

The words sliced Jones to the bone. In that moment, all his righteous anger, even his fear, deserted him. All he felt was a crippling shame. And it was in that place of shame that he made the decisions he made that night, and every decision that followed.

It took Jones a second to differentiate Marshall from the tree he leaned against. The boy sat on the ground, a gun in his hand. In the moonlight he was ghostly pale, looked as limp and weak as a scarecrow off his pole.

It was so strange to see Marshall there that, for a second, Jones thought he might be hallucinating. This strange mingling of the past and the present had him badly off-kilter. If Jones had been standing, not kneeling, he might have walked right by Marshall. The kid was so still and quiet.

"Are you hurt, Son?" Jones asked.

Marshall didn't seem to hear him, appeared dazed and not present. Jones stood and approached him slowly, reached down, took the gun from his hand. The gun, a semiautomatic, was warm to the touch, recently fired. He could tell by the weight that it was loaded. The boy let it go without resistance, let his arm flop to his side. Jones tucked the gun into his empty shoulder holster.

Marshall turned his face to look up at Jones. "How do you know if you're a good person or a bad one?" he asked.

Jones didn't know the answer. How could he? He thought about his wife again. If Maggie were here, she'd know what to say to Marshall. Maggie was sure about these things. She knew the answers to the hard questions.

"I don't know," said Jones. He had a sense that the situation called for honesty, and that was about as honest as he could be. "I really don't know."

Marshall gave a slow nod and looked at him with something like gratitude.

"What's happened here, Marshall? Talk to me. Where's your father?"

But Marshall had the glassy gaze of someone slipping into shock. Jones leaned in close, but the boy didn't seem to be injured. There was no blood, no outward sign of trauma.

"Did you bring her here, Marshall? Is this where you brought Charlene after you picked her up?"

Marshall nodded absently. "I'm sorry. I'm sorry for every bad thing."

"Marshall," said Jones. He bent down to pick up the rifle he'd dropped when he fell to his knees. "Where is she, Son?"

Jones thought he saw a flash of light then and heard the approach of a vehicle. He hoped it was Chuck. It wouldn't be too far a logical leap for him to go to Travis's house after Strout's, then proceed here in the search for Marshall. Chuck would see the vehicle in the drive, notice that the rifle had been removed from the hatch. Chuck would move into the woods, gun drawn, good cop that he was.

Why hadn't he told someone where he was going or called for

backup? Jones could tell himself that it was urgency, a rush to get to Charlene if she was, in fact, here. But really it was just arrogance, a lack of foresight. The same personal flaws that had allowed him to turn his back on Travis, that would allow him to proceed to the boathouse, rather than turn around and get help first.

He looked at the boy on the ground, though he wasn't really a boy anymore, with stubble on his jaw, at least as tall as his father. If Jones still had his handcuffs, he'd have made Marshall lie on his belly, secured his hands behind him. But those were gone, too. He had a hunch the kid wasn't going anywhere.

"Marshall, stay where you are. Don't move until I come back for you."

"Yes," Marshall said. But Jones felt as though he was answering a question Jones hadn't asked.

Jones left the Crosby property that night so many years ago. And just as he was told, he never said another word to anyone about what happened to Sarah. When he returned home, his mother had been near hysteria—Where had he been? What had he done?

"It's over," he'd told her. "It never happened." And so it was.

He'd kept Sarah's belongings locked in the trunk of his car for a few days, while the storm of her being declared missing and her body discovered miles from where he knew she died raged around him. He was ready for the police to come with that jacket, to kiss his life and all his hopes good-bye. In fact, he almost hoped uniformed men would walk through his front door and take him away.

On the night her body was found, Jones moved Sarah's things deep into the attic of his mother's house. She never went up there, and even if she did, she'd pretend not to see, because that's who she was.

He knew he should have been rid of those things, burned them or driven them far from The Hollows, somewhere they'd never be found. But he didn't. He couldn't. As long as he held on to them, he could hold on to hope, too. Hope that he might find the courage to do the right thing, to be the man he wanted to be, the man he should have been. But that day never came. He was a coward. He had always been that, just like his father. His father couldn't manage the simplest thing, just to be around for his family. He didn't have the strength for even that. Why should his son be any different?

Jones never said a word. Even when the psychic fingered Tommy Delano and he told them where the body was, so far from where Sarah had actually died. Even when he learned that someone had mutilated Sarah, cut her with razors, sexually violated her, he stayed silent. Who had done those things to her? He thought of her, so pretty and so sweet, so strong and honest. He could barely stand to think of her as he'd seen her in the open casket, gaping wounds in her face filled with putty, bloated, unnatural. He knew how Sarah had died. Travis hadn't violated her. Unless . . . unless he'd come back later and done those things to her while she lay bleeding? But he wasn't that, was he? He couldn't have done those things, could he?

Jones never understood Tommy Delano's role in it all, why he'd say he killed her when he didn't. Through the confession, the trial, the sentencing—they all stayed quiet. Only once, after Sarah's viewing, did Jones and Melody Murray ever discuss the horror of it all. She was waiting by his car. He'd parked far down the road from the funeral home, and she stood in the dark by the trees.

"What do you want, Mel?" he said. He didn't look up at her, just unlocked the car door.

"I need a ride." He opened the door, considered getting inside and driving away without a word. He didn't want to be close to her, to talk to her. But he couldn't leave another girl alone in the night.

"Get in," he said. And she did.

He pulled onto the road; behind him people milled out of the funeral home, returning to their cars, going home stunned and horrified.

"Why would they have her like that?" Melody asked. "Why did they want us to look at her face?"

She looked sunken, wrecked by grief and fear.

"Where's your mother?" he asked.

"Where's yours?" she shot back.

Then there was quiet, a horrible quiet between them, when they both realized how alone they were with their dark knowledge.

"Who did all of that to her, Jones? Who cut her that way? Who raped her? Tommy Delano didn't kill her. Did he do those things?"

"I don't know," he said. "I don't know."

"I heard there are over two hundred cuts on her body."

"Stop it."

"We did wrong by her, Jones. We left her there."

"You *wanted* to leave her there." He pulled over to the side of the road and stopped the car.

"No." She shook her head. "No." Then she started to cry. "I was so scared," she wailed. "I was so scared."

He took a deep breath and, for an ugly moment, wished that Melody had been the one to die that night, that Sarah was sitting beside him. *She* wouldn't be hysterical; *she* would be strong, brave. She'd have done the right thing, the good thing, that night. She wouldn't have left her friend behind to be scavenged and violated. But the truth was that the only one of them who was any good at all was gone forever.

"Don't ever talk about it, Melody. Don't ever tell a soul. And don't ever bring it up to me again. She's gone. Nothing we do will change that now. Nothing."

Melody looked at him with such naked despair that he looked away. Every time he looked at her again over the years, that was the expression he saw. It was always there, right beneath the surface. But she never talked about Sarah again, not to him.

Later, when Tommy Delano hanged himself in prison, his death created a seal that could not be broken.

The Crosby boathouse was in worse shape than the carriage house had been, on a dramatic tilt to the left. When Jones entered, he saw that the roof was riven with holes, the sky visible in jagged patches. The wood beneath him groaned under his weight. The lake water lapped against the dock, and the boat, loosely tied, knocked a slow beat against the rubber bumper surrounding the slip.

"Crosby," he said, making his voice boom. "You missed. A bad shot even at point-blank range."

His voice bounced back at him. He sounded strong, powerful. But he was scared, heart hammering. Everything was shadows; Travis could step out, gun drawn, from anywhere.

On the dock, down by the stern, Jones saw what looked like a pile of sailcloth. As he moved closer, he realized that it was the chief, his giant chest and belly rising like a mountain. Jones heard a horrible wheezing, a deep rattle coming from the old man. In the dim light, the blood spilling from his center was black.

Jones knelt down beside him. He knew that blank look, the stare of eyes that were already seeing something the living cannot. He put his hand on the old man's shoulder. He knew he should be feeling something—compassion, regret, sorrow—something other than the cold indifference he often felt in the face of suffering.

"Where's my jacket, old man?" Jones asked.

It was all he could think to say. The other man moved his jaw, as if to say something, but then he just sighed. And Jones could swear that, just before Chief Crosby released his final rattling breath, he smiled. Then he felt something, the bile of rising hatred. Hatred for Chief Crosby and what he'd asked all of them to do years ago, and hatred for himself for having done it.

"Is he dead?"

Jones spun around with the rifle. There was a dark form at the entrance to the boathouse.

"Don't move," said Jones. "Put your hands in the air."

The figure quickly complied. "Jones, it's me. Henry Ivy."

Jones felt a wave of relief. "What are you doing here, Ivy?"

"I came with Maggie."

He said this as though it should make some sense. There was a mist descending around Jones. He found himself hyperfocusing on the sound of the water hitting the dock, the strange scent coming off the chief. *Why was Ivy riding around with his wife in the middle of the night?* But Jones found himself nodding. Of course she wouldn't wait alone by the phone. She could never do that. And who else would she call to ride shotgun but Ivy? Her childhood friend who she was too naïve to know had loved her for decades.

"Where is she?" Jones asked, lowering his gun. "Where's my wife?"

"With Marshall," Ivy said. He moved into the light. "Are you hurt, Jones?"

"Is she okay? Is Maggie all right?"

"She's fine. She's taking care of Marshall. Is the chief . . . dead?"

"Looks that way," Jones said, glancing back down at the body.

He wondered if Ivy had heard the question he asked of the chief, wondered if it would mean anything to him if he had. Ivy was staring at the body on the dock, his expression blank. Jones wondered if anyone would cry for Chief Crosby, and if it was his son or his grandson who'd killed him.

"I need you to call for backup," said Jones.

"Already done. As soon as we saw your vehicle, we called 911."

Jones could hear the wail of sirens then.

"You don't look well, Jones. Let me help you."

"Travis shot me."

Even as he said the words, it didn't seem quite real. It seemed like something that had happened so long ago the details had gone blurry. The solid things around him were disappearing; the dock beneath him, Henry Ivy standing in front of him. He was starting to see bursts of white light.

Ivy moved toward him, saying something, reaching out to help him. But Jones didn't hear. He was thinking about Charlene, thinking that if Marshall was going to hide her on this property, it might be on the boat. It was isolated from the house; any sounds would be carried out and over the water. He wondered if, like always, he had too little to give and was too late to give it.

Jones managed to stumble off the dock and onto the boat. It pitched with his weight, and he almost lost his balance. *Don't fall,* he told himself. *If you fall now, you won't be getting back up.* He heard Ivy calling after him, the sirens growing louder, but Jones just walked to the narrow stairwell that led to the cabin and, with effort, moved down.

And there she was. For a second he thought he was looking at another corpse, someone broken and left for dead. She was still and pale, bound at the wrists and ankles, her head tilted to the side. A piece of gray electrical tape covered her mouth. He felt that terrible sense of loss that he'd felt in the park that night, that familiar helpless rage at a thing that could not be changed. But then she opened her eyes and saw him there. He'd expected her to writhe and scream at the sight of him. But instead she just closed her eyes again and started to cry.

He moved to her quickly, unbound her ankles, and took the tape off her mouth. When he got to her wrists, she wrapped her arms around his neck and sobbed. He found himself sobbing, too. Not just for Charlene, or for the pain in his chest that was threatening to shut him down, but finally for Sarah and for the part of himself that had died with her.

"Marshall, tell me what happened." Maggie knelt beside the boy.

She took off her coat and wrapped it around him. He was pale and shivering. She kept glancing back at the trees into which she'd watched Henry disappear to follow the sound of Jones's voice.

"Crosby," she'd heard him boom. But she didn't hear the rest.

Marshall grabbed her hand and held on tight. She fought the urge to pull away. Something about his desperate grasp, the crazed look in his eyes, frightened and drained her, as though he could suck the very life from her. She tried to draw back a little, but his grip on her arm was too strong.

"He was right," Marshall said. He pulled her closer. "He was right about everything."

The way he said it, a growl through gritted teeth, made her shiver.

"Who?"

"My father."

"Marshall, no."

But in the next moment, Henry was carrying Charlene from the trees, a slim, bruised, and filthy rag doll in his arms, and Jones was trailing behind them. Maggie could see the unnatural gray-white to Jones's skin. She used all her strength to break from Marshall's grasp and got up and ran to her husband.

"I'm sorry," he said when she reached him. In her arms, he lost the last bit of physical fight he had in him, and his weight brought them both to the ground, hard.

"I'm so sorry," he said, again.

Then, dreamlike, the Crosby woods were filled with light and people she knew, people she'd known forever, all in the various costumes of their adulthood—paramedics and police officers—like some kind of somber masquerade party.

"Is she alive?" she asked Henry, who handed Charlene to a paramedic and stood looking stunned.

"Yes. Thank God. Yes," said Henry, coming to his knees beside them. "You saved her, Jones."

Jones shook his head in protest. "No. I got lucky."

In the ambulance, Maggie sat beside her husband, holding his hand. He had an oxygen mask on his face; the front of his shirt was soaked with blood. Every breath seemed hard-won. Over and over, she heard her own voice saying, "It's okay. It's okay. It's okay." She kept a comforting smile frozen on her face. She didn't want Jones to look at her and see what she was feeling—stone-cold fear.

Out of the back of the ambulance, she watched as the police took Marshall away, his hands cuffed behind him.

"He's still out here," she heard Chuck say. "We'll need more men to find him on this property. We've got acres and acres to cover."

"Did they get Crosby?" Jones asked under the mask.

"Travis? No," said Maggie.

"The old man is dead," said Jones.

"We'll talk about it later. Chuck can handle it for now."

She braced herself to push Jones back onto the gurney. But he never tried to get up as she'd anticipated, he just nodded and closed his eyes.

"I love you, Jones," she said. But he didn't seem to hear her.

By the time they arrived at the hospital, it was already a carnival of news vans and parked police vehicles with lights silently flashing. Maggie watched from the back window of the ambulance as Charlene was lifted out of another vehicle and rushed inside. A comet's tail of reporters and flashing cameras trailed behind her. She looked impossibly small on the gurney, like the child she really was. Charlene's eyes swept past Maggie, seeing nothing. The sight filled Maggie with horror for Charlene, for everything she'd been through, for everything ahead of her—not the least of which was the media circus bound to follow one of the most terrible and sensational things to have happened in The Hollows. Maggie watched as Melody ran in from somewhere out of view and took Charlene's hand. She was surprised to see that Melody was not hysterical, not making a drama in front of the cameras. She was stone-faced and strong. Police officers held back reporters at the doors to the emergency room. And the next thing Maggie knew, she and Jones were in the center of the storm—Jones being pushed into the hospital, she rushing behind, trying to ignore the shouting and the cameras.

What happened? Can you tell us what happened to Charlene Murray? Is she going to be okay? Who are you? What is your relationship to the victim?

Maggie wanted to cover her ears; instead she just kept her eyes on her husband, felt weak with relief when they passed the police line that had formed, and all the chaos and noise faded behind the closed doors.

How did they find out about all of this so fast? she wondered. It was as if they were waiting on the periphery, monitoring police frequencies. *Of course. Of course that's what they were doing.*

"You have to wait here. You can't go any farther." A young girl—how could anyone that *young* work in a hospital?—stood in front of her, placed a strong hand on Maggie's arm.

"That's my husband," Maggie said.

"You have to wait here, ma'am. I'm sorry. Someone will come and talk to you."

And then they were wheeling Jones away, taking him down a long white hallway until he disappeared behind another set of doors. Maggie felt like her knees were going to buckle beneath her. Was this really happening? It *couldn't* be happening.

"Mom? What's going on? Was that—was that *Dad*?"

Maggie turned to see her son, looking pale and afraid. She didn't even think to ask how he came to be there, she just grabbed him and held on tight. She wanted to tell him that everyone was okay now, that everything was going to be all right. But she didn't know that, she didn't know that at all.

25

Maggie gathered her mother's things from the dresser. Three night-gowns, several pairs of panties, and some bras—all newish things for which Maggie had recently taken her shopping. She took five of the knit shirts her mother favored, each with its own little wisecrack—IF IT'S NOT ONE THING, IT'S YOUR MOTHER; IF YOU CAN READ THIS, YOU'RE STANDING TOO CLOSE TO ME; NO DRAMA MAMA—and packed them into the waiting suitcase. The day Elizabeth had sworn would never come was finally here; she was moving in, at least for a while, with her daughter, son-in-law, and tattooed grandson.

Maggie knew she should be dreading having two patients in the house, neither of them easy even when well, but all she could muster was gratitude. She was sure a few days of playing nursemaid would put an end to that. But at the moment, still shaken by the idea that she could have lost two of the most important people in her life in one night, she was glad everyone would be under one roof for a while.

The lightest scratching of a tree branch against her mother's bed-room window sent Maggie jumping out of her skin. She understood fi-nally, in a small way, the concept of shell shock, of being so inundated by noise and chaos and stress that the brain shut down, refusing to process any additional stimuli. She felt like a twitching mess. Hollows General Hospital was a hive of reporters from all over the country, camping out in the parking lot. Law enforcement from the state and federal levels swarmed the cafeteria. There was a manhunt for Travis Crosby, who was still missing. And Maggie, like most everyone, still couldn't quite believe what had happened.

She could hear Ricky downstairs; he was gathering Elizabeth's books, her knitting, and a few of her photo albums—all things her mother had requested. Maggie had asked him to clean out the refrigerator, too. And he, also unnaturally quiet, altered in a way by everything that had happened, complied without complaint. They hadn't talked much about his feelings or how he was dealing with the knowledge of what had happened to Charlene. He'd tried to see her, but Melody hadn't allowed it, said Charlene wasn't ready to face her friends. Maggie's questions about how he was handling things were met with slow shrugs and monosyllables.

Maggie picked up her mother's watch from the silver tray on her dresser. Elizabeth had worn that watch, a wedding gift from Maggie's father, every day for as long as Maggie could remember. A thin strand of diamonds and gold, a small mother-of-pearl face with roman numerals, it looked fragile, felt light in her hand. As a child, she had coveted it, wanted to wear it when she played dress up. And even though her mother cherished it, she'd always let Maggie wear it for a little while.

"Someday it will be yours anyway," she'd say.

"When?" Maggie remembered asking. She'd felt a tingle of excitement, laced with dread, though she couldn't have said why. She was far too young to know what her mother meant.

"Someday."

But not today. Elizabeth, laid up at Hollows General Hospital with a fractured hip—likely broken days before her fall from the ladder—was out of sorts and embarrassed, making herself impossible to everyone trying to minister to her. Yet somehow she remained popular with the nurses and especially the doctor, who had once been a star pupil at Hollows High. Elizabeth wanted her watch. Maggie put it on her own wrist to carry it safely to her mother but shivered when she closed the clasp. She took it off and put it in the pocket of her pants.

Jones was equally unhappy, recovering from a flesh wound. The bullet delivered by Travis Crosby had lodged in the flesh of his abdomen and was removed in surgery.

"It's a good thing you're so fat, Jones," his doctor said in recovery. It was a bit insensitive, Maggie thought.

"I thought the same thing," Jones said to him. "If I'd dropped that twenty-five you've been bitching about, I'd be dead right now. Some doctor."

But she could see his fear in cheeks that had no color, in eyes that lacked their shine. Jones told her that he had been certain he was having the heart attack he'd been dreading for a decade. *I thought I was going to die out there, Mags.* But his heart and arteries were strong and healthy. The chest pains, the shortness of breath? Panic attacks, his doctor told him, could be as painful and frightening as any cardiac episode.

Looking at herself in the mirror, Maggie felt the urge she'd been quashing swell to the point of bursting. Her hair was wild; there was still blood on her jacket. The skin on her face looked pasty and soft. A heaving sob sat in her center, waiting—waiting for Elizabeth and Jones to be okay, waiting for Rick to be strong enough to deal with what had happened to Charlene. It would wait until she was alone. The sounds from downstairs reminded her that she couldn't afford to break down now. Rick was stoic, but the depths were volcanic; she feared the eruption wasn't far off.

"I demand that you go home and get some rest right now," Elizabeth had said. "You look like a woman on the verge. You've been up all night. You need to take care of yourself, too, Maggie. You never did learn that."

Maggie had left, more out of annoyance with her mother than anything else. But Elizabeth was right about her. Jones, too. They both saw something in her that frightened them. And they were right to be afraid. She didn't know how to, didn't always want to, stop at the edge when others were going over. She'd keep just enough weight on solid ground to pull herself back before it was too late. One day, she might misjudge and tumble over; that's what Jones and Elizabeth feared. Looking into Marshall's eyes last night, that unsettling green, she thought someone could drown there, in that pit of need and despair. She understood why Marshall's aunt Leila had pulled back from him and taken her family with her. And why she had to do the same.

"How do you know if you're a good person or a bad person?"

Marshall was stuck on this point, had been since she and Henry

found him in the woods surrounding the Crosby house. Was still stuck
when she stopped by to see him before she left the hospital. She couldn't
get him to move on from the mental loop. It was not a straightforward
question under the circumstances. There were so many different ways to
answer.

Charlene was going home to her mother today, after being in the
hospital overnight for a battery of tests, for evidence collection, and to
replenish her fluids. She was badly dehydrated, which was the most
dangerous of her physical conditions. She had a concussion, lacerations,
and bruises. She'd been repeatedly raped, not by Marshall, according to
reports, but by Travis Crosby. The physical injuries would heal. What
concerned Maggie were the less obvious injuries. Charlene's most sig-
nificant wounds were psychic. In a few weeks, she'd been physically well.
But the trauma to her spirit, to her psyche, would take much, much
longer to heal. According to what Maggie had heard, Charlene claimed
not to remember what had happened at home to precipitate her running
away. She remembered only that she'd contacted Marshall for a ride to
New York, that he'd brought her to the Crosby boathouse and kept her
there against her will. Melody wouldn't let anyone near her, and the details Maggie was picking up about Charlene's captivity through reports
given to Jones were grim.

On her way out of the hospital, Maggie found Melody in the smoking lounge. The stink of the room was almost unbearable to Maggie, but
she pushed inside.

"Melody?"

"Maggie," she said, startled from her thoughts.

"How is she?"

Melody shook her head. "Broken. Maggie, she's broken." The other
woman started to weep then, and Maggie came to sit beside her, took
the cigarette from her hand and extinguished it. Melody leaned against
her, and Maggie rocked her slowly.

"What he did to her—he's a monster. God, he *always* has been. I
wish Henry Ivy had killed him that day. I really do. You have no idea
how much better the world would be without a Travis Crosby in it."

"I'm so sorry."

"You don't know, Maggie. You don't know the things he's done."

She held on tight to Melody.

"I want you to bring Charlene to me, as soon as she's ready. No charge, of course. I want to help her, Melody. I want to help her get through this, if I can. Talking is so important for her now."

"She won't talk to me, Maggie. Not really. She won't tell me what happened."

"It's so hard to talk to our parents sometimes. You remember, don't you? The relationship is so complicated and loaded; that's why she needs to talk to someone who can be impartial. Please. Bring her tomorrow, Melody."

"It's my fault. In so many different ways, this is my fault. Do you know how much it hurts to know that your best was not even nearly enough? I wasn't half of what I needed to be as her mother."

"We all do what we can, Melody. None of us is perfect, and we all make mistakes. You didn't do this to Charlene. Whatever mistakes you made, you didn't do *this*."

She sat with Melody like that for a long time.

The sound of the doorbell downstairs made her realize that she'd been standing in front of the mirror, zoning out, for too long. She *did* need to try to get some rest before she saw Charlene later that afternoon. She'd have to be strong and alert.

"Mom," Ricky called from downstairs. Maggie descended the staircase to find a tall, blond, youngish man in a pair of gray coveralls standing in the foyer. The embroidered patch on his chest read, AAA ANIMAL TRAPPERS, CHARLIE. It took her a second to remember the noises that had had Elizabeth climbing into the attic in the middle of the night.

"Ah," said Maggie, offering her hand. "You must be the one helping my mother with her rodent problem."

"Charlie," he said. His grip was firm and confident. "We'll get it taken care of. Your son said that Mrs. Monroe fell. Is she all right?" Something about his gentle tone made that urge to weep almost overtake her again.

"She will be," Maggie said. She stepped aside to let him pass into the house. "Do you know the way upstairs?"

"I do."

They were almost done with everything by the time Charlie came back downstairs. Elizabeth's suitcase was by the door. The contents of the refrigerator had been emptied and brought out to the garbage.

In one hand, he held a covered trap, in the other a yellow bucket. The covered trap bucked and pitched in his hand, whatever was inside growling and hissing. Charlie lifted it a bit.

"Raccoon," he said. "A big one." He lifted the bucket. "And family."

Maggie walked to him and leaned over the bucket. Inside, three squeaking baby raccoons huddled together, looking up at her wide-eyed and frightened.

"Oh, poor little guys," said Maggie, feeling Ricky come up behind her.

"They really burrowed themselves way back. I had to move a lot of stuff around to place the traps and then to find the little guys. Sorry for the mess up there."

"No problem." Maggie couldn't remember the last time she'd been up in the attic. But she remembered it always being a terrible mess.

"What will you do with them?" Ricky asked. The tone of his voice made her think of the baby squirrel he'd tried to save.

"Relocate them together," said Charlie. "There's a place I go, just outside of town. It's a state park. Maybe you know it. Technically, I should go farther, but I've never had anything come back from there. And it's a nice place for animals."

Maggie knew the place he was talking about; Jones used to go there a lot when he was younger. But neither of them had been there for years.

"One of the little guys didn't make it. That's what I smelled the other day. I have to get back up there and clean him out."

"Oh," said Maggie. She was silly to feel bad about it. But she did.

"Let me put these guys in the truck and I'll be right back to clean up."

When he was done, they stood in the foyer and, leaning on the small table under the mirror, Maggie wrote him a check. Ricky was already waiting in the car. She'd follow Charlie out and lock the door.

"I heard they found that girl—your son's friend."

"Yes," she said, looking up at him. "How did you—?"

"I'm the one who saw her get into the car and later called about the transmission fluid. Detective Ferrigno said that's how they found her."

"Oh," said Maggie. She looked out and saw Ricky in the car, leaning forward, obviously seeking an acceptable radio station. "Wow."

He told her about the conversation with Elizabeth and the television news report and how those things had jogged his memory.

"You did a good thing," she said. He seemed like a nice man, a kind person. She found herself smiling.

"I just wish I'd heard about it sooner. I hope she's okay."

"I think it's going to take time." She handed him the check and pulled out a ten-dollar bill she happened to have in her back pocket.

"Thanks," he said. He attached the check to a clipboard and handed her the service receipt, folded the ten, and put it in his pocket.

"Anyway, I'm glad they found her. A girl I knew ran away once. They never found her. It's the worst thing imaginable, to not know, I think. To always wonder."

Maybe it was the worst thing, to not know. Maybe it was worse than grief. The mind, the psyche, adjusted better to catastrophe than to uncertainty. She hoped she'd never have to find out either way.

"Oh," he said. He turned around as he was about to leave. "The attic access door was stuck. I couldn't get it closed."

"Okay," she said. "I'll check it. Sometimes when the weather is crazy like this, it gets tricky to close it."

After she'd shut the door behind him, she went back upstairs and wrestled with the ladder for a few minutes, trying to remember how her mother had shown her to maneuver it up. She considered going out to get Ricky but then wound up, on a whim, climbing the ladder. She hadn't been up there in so long. She wondered if her father's paintings would be easily had. She'd been thinking she wanted to get some of them framed, hoping they would inspire her to do some painting of her own.

She sneezed immediately in the dust and the mold, which had no doubt been kicked up by Charlie's search for the raccoons. She reached up and pulled at the string that turned on the light. Out the window in the back, she could see all of The Hollows stretched before her—the church steeple, the town square, the high school off in the distance. In her current state of gratitude, she felt a wash of affection for the town where she'd grown up and returned to marry Jones and raise their son together. This morning Ricky had told her, out of nowhere—maybe he'd sensed that she needed some good news—that he planned to accept his early admission to Georgetown. *DC has a fairly lively music scene,* he'd said. *That's great,* she'd said. *I'm really proud of you. Your dad will be, too.* And then, mingled with the pride and joy for her boy, had come an unexpected aching sadness. Motherhood was a widening circle of good-byes.

She ran her eyes over the field of clutter, and toward the back of the attic she saw what looked like a pile of canvases. Maggie made her way past the old sewing machine (Elizabeth never sewed a thing in her life; even her knitting had never amounted to anything but the world's longest scarf), her old bicycle with flat wheels, a stack of record albums, an old trunk (who even knew what was inside?); even some of Ricky's baby things (how in the world had those ever made the trip from their house to hers?) sat dusty in a canvas bag. Just before she got to the canvases, she saw a gray plastic bag. This was obviously where the raccoons had made their nest; a little spot covered with hair and dander had been hollowed out. She should clean it; it smelled. Better yet, she'd just empty the bag of its contents, throw it in the trash, and do a better cleaning job when things had settled. But for some reason, as she did this, she felt a tingle on her skin, a trickle of dread down her spine. She knelt and pulled open the zipper.

Inside was a violin case and an old book bag. Maggie had never played the violin and had never owned a backpack like that one, simple navy with no flourish whatsoever. She felt a dryness in her mouth as she opened the lid on the violin case and looked at the instrument inside. The wood gleamed as if it had been recently polished. She plucked the strings; they were badly out of tune. A little pocket at the tip of the case contained a few rectangles of bow rosin. In the red velvet that lined the case, there was a name embroidered with black thread. She willed herself not to look at it, blurred her eyes so that she couldn't read it. Her hands wanted to slam down the lid of the case, shove everything back into that gray bag and forget that she ever saw it. But, of course, she couldn't do that. She made herself read the name Sarah.

"Mom, what's wrong? You look sick."

Maggie had rushed from his grandmother's house and into the car as if she were trying not to get wet in the rain—except it wasn't raining. In the driver's seat, she looked pale, shaky.

"What happened? Did you see another raccoon?"

"I'm just tired," she said. Her voice sounded hoarse. "It's catching up with me."

Everyone always talks about how well mothers know their children. No one ever seems to notice how well children know their mothers. He always knew when she was lying. She didn't do it very often, and she wasn't very good at it. He decided not to press her; they were both under stress. But this was the first quiet moment they'd had together, and Rick had something on his mind.

"Grandma said a lot of crazy things when I found her," he said. His mother had started the car and was backing out of the drive.

"Like what?" Maggie was absent, her mind elsewhere.

"Weird stuff. Like, 'She was already dead when he found her.'" His mother stopped the car and turned to look at him. Her always fair skin was a ghostly white, her blue eyes looked stormy gray, like they always did when she was sad or angry.

"I thought she was talking about Charlene," he said. "But that wasn't it. I asked her about it today when you went to get the car. She said she doesn't remember."

His mother still hadn't said anything, was staring at him but clearly not seeing him. She had a glazed and distant look in her eyes.

"I didn't believe her—that she didn't remember," he said. "She wouldn't look at me. Told me to forget the 'deranged ramblings of an old woman.'" He did his best Elizabeth impersonation on the last words, but Maggie didn't crack a smile, just continued looking at him with that blank expression. He went on, even though he was starting to feel uncomfortable. "She said she was embarrassed by how I'd found her and not to make it worse."

Maggie put the car into park and rested her head on the wheel.

"Mom?"

He put his hand on her shoulder; it scared him to feel her shoulders start to shake. He'd rarely seen her cry—once or twice after a fight with his father, maybe. Once when a patient of hers had died. The other night, when they were fighting about the tattoo, he'd seen tears spring to her eyes. But he'd never seen her break down.

"Mom? What is it? Why are you crying?"

Listening to her cry, he felt like crying now, too. Everything—his grandmother, his father, and Charlene, all of them broken and hurt—the stress and pain of it was an expanding pressure behind his eyes, a ratcheting ache in his neck and shoulders. He felt like opening the car door and running and running until he was too exhausted to feel anything at all. But he didn't; he stayed in his seat, stayed with his mom.

"I'm sorry. I'm okay," she said, lifting her head suddenly and looking at him. She wiped the tears from her eyes and then reached out and put her hand on his face. Her palm felt damp and warm. "I'm so sorry."

"Mom," he said, leaning in to hug her. "I'm not three. You're allowed to cry."

She held his eyes for a second, then gave a quick nod and started digging into her purse. She pulled out a little rectangular package of tissues, blew her nose and wiped her eyes. She handed him a clean one, and he took it even though he didn't need it.

"Mom. What do you think she meant?"

"You know what, kiddo? I really have no idea. I'll talk to her."

She put the car in reverse and started backing out of the driveway. He felt a release, then. He'd told his mother; he'd felt an urgency to do that. And now that he had, some of the tension he'd been holding left him.

"When you see Charlene, will you tell her I want to see her? Just as a friend. Will you tell her that? That I just want to be her friend."

"Is that true?" she asked. She turned onto the main road that would lead them home. "That you just want to be her friend?"

His mother seemed more solid but still not herself. Her voice was distant and strained.

"I don't know," he said, blowing out a breath. "I don't know what I want."

The sound of the blinker seemed unusually loud, and he realized that he'd turned the radio off. He leaned forward and turned it on; he'd been looking for music his mother would like on the XM radio. He'd picked the eighties station. He didn't recognize the song that was playing.

"You're right, you know?" she said. "You're not three anymore. You're old enough to understand that Charlene has been through something awful, something that will take time, a lot of time, to move past. Are you prepared to be her friend through that, to be what she needs when she needs it and put your own desires aside?"

"Yeah," he said. "I guess." He hated the way his own voice sounded—boyish and petulant.

"Good," she said. "That's good."

She started driving again. They didn't exchange another word until they got home.

"Are you hungry?" his mother asked.

"Maybe I'll order some Chinese?" he said. He *was* hungry, ravenously hungry.

"That sounds good," Maggie said. She reached into her bag and handed him her wallet. "I just want some soup."

She went up to her bedroom and closed the door. He stood at the bottom of the stairs and watched after her, feeling like he should apologize or comfort her—or something. But instead he just grabbed the cordless phone and ordered enough food with his mother's credit card to feed the neighborhood; then he turned on the television and zoned out for a while.

Worse than the violin were the contents of the book bag—textbooks Maggie remembered well, notebooks filled with scribbles and doodles, Sarah's name and address written neatly on the inside covers. A red one for math, a blue one for English, a green one for science. A biology quiz on which she'd earned a B plus. There was a note obviously passed back and forth between her and Melody for days: "Don't you think Jones Cooper is the cutest boy in school? No doubt! Let's watch MTV after school today."

She hated that she'd seen those things, hated that she'd touched them. She could barely stand to ask herself how they'd gotten in her mother's attic. Who had put them there?

In the master bath, she ran the shower, stripped off her clothes, and got beneath the scalding hot stream. She let it soak her hair and beat on her shoulders. She took the shower gel on the ledge, squeezed it onto a loofah, and started scrubbing her body, hard, hard enough to hurt. She wanted to clean it all off her, to shed the skin she was in. She couldn't name everything she felt—anger, fear, the siren song of denial luring her from instinctive dread. It *could* be some bizarre coincidence that had led those missing pieces of evidence to come to rest in her mother's attic—Elizabeth and Jones both ignorant of their presence. Couldn't it?

Does Jones ever talk about it? Melody had asked. It was such a strange question, staying with her, tugging at her pant leg for attention. And then there were Elizabeth's words to Ricky: *She was already dead when he found her.* God, what did that mean?

But worse than even those things was the image she had of Jones last night—his frantic search of their son's room, the things he'd said. *Anyone is capable of anything, given the right circumstances, the right motivations.*

The water couldn't be hot enough; she was light-headed in the steam, her skin was red and raw. But in the solitude, she could weep.

She'd barely held herself together in the car, but now she let it all out, knowing she couldn't be heard.

She found herself remembering what it was like to be in love with Jones. Not the kind of love they shared now. But the kind of breathless, helpless, anxious, ravenous in love with him she'd been after her father's funeral. Her passion was a burning city, a five-alarmer that raged out of control beside the cavern of her grief for her father. It was a distraction that kept her psyche busy, that kept her from wallowing in the sorrow of loss.

She knew by their second date—he came into the city and took her to dinner at Joe Allen and they saw *Cats,* even though she'd already seen it—that she was going to marry him. He seemed uncomfortable, the way out-of-towners always do in the city—looking around at people who seem more glamorous than they can ever hope to be, overwhelmed by the sound, the lights, the masses of people. She liked that about him, that he was humble, that he was willing to be out of his element to be with her. She was so used to the arrogance of the men she met here; they all seemed imbued with a sense of self-importance just because they were New Yorkers. She already loved the earthy smell, the salty taste of him, the thickness of his powerful body. It was more than lust; it was hunger.

"Why didn't you leave The Hollows?" she said.

It was loud in the restaurant. A big party of tourists beside them was celebrating something—lots of raucous laughter and clinking glasses.

He shook his head, took a sip of the red wine he was drinking. Even then, he knew a lot about wines. He'd chosen a bottle of Chianti Riserva from Montepulciano. And she knew to be impressed, even as she wondered how much it cost.

"I couldn't really," he said. A chorus of laughter erupted beside them.

"Your mother. She was ill."

"Yeah." He looked down at his glass. "That was part of it."

That's when she saw it, the shadow. It flashed over his face and was gone in a heartbeat. But she saw it, how he went dark at the mention of his mother. She knew a little bit about Abigail from things Elizabeth had told her, how she'd kick up a fuss every time Jones needed to be in an away game, how she'd keep him home when she was feeling low and then write him a sick note, how she'd harass his teachers if she thought he was being treated unfairly. *That woman is a piece of work,* Elizabeth would complain.

"But it was more that I just couldn't imagine myself living outside The Hollows."

"You feel like you belong there."

"More like I don't belong anyplace else."

After the play, they stood on the sidewalk as throngs of people pushed around them and started hunting for taxis. There was an awkward moment, when he looked up at the buildings and she stared at the folded *Playbill* in her hand.

"I parked in a lot a few blocks from here," he said. He turned to point uptown. During the performance, they'd held hands. And then he'd started doing this lovely thing after intermission. He'd reached over with his other hand and stroked her arm, in soft, slow circles. Something about it built a heat inside her; there were moments when she could barely focus on anything else. "Do you want to get a drink?"

"Take me home, Jones."

Did they take a cab, a subway? Did they go to his car? Now she couldn't remember. All she remembered was taking him back to her tiny one-bedroom apartment. She remembered him kissing her neck as she unlocked the door. Once inside, her bag and their coats were shed to the floor. An ambulance wailed past her window, filling the apartment with light and sound.

"I haven't felt this way about anyone," he said. "Not like this . . . in so long. Maybe never, Maggie."

She'd imagined him with a parade of women—the prom queens of the world, all throwing themselves at him, as they always did in high school. But those girls with so much apparent promise were just housewives and mothers now, married to other men who commuted to the city to work at banks and firms. She'd seen them all at her father's funeral. There was nothing wrong with them; they all seemed lovely, normal, satisfied in their lives. But that luminosity that had been afforded by their youthful prettiness, their palpable *coolness*, was gone. It surprised her to discover that Jones was lonely. It surprised her more to discover that she was lonely, too. She realized that her passion was always spent on her studies and her work.

"I haven't, either," she said.

She didn't remember the details of their lovemaking, but what she did remember about that night was an overwhelming feeling of happiness and relief, a soul-deep sense of satisfaction, of homecoming.

It seemed like so long ago. It was. And the years, the lifetime, between then and now were a patchwork of good and bad days, failures and successes, joys and disappointments—like every life that isn't derailed by catastrophe or tragedy, however gigantic or mundane. Somehow the things she'd found in the attic—even though she didn't know how they'd come to be there or who had put them there—made her feel as if it all lay upon a rotting foundation. She felt as if she might be about to step through the floorboards of her life.

As she turned off the water, she thought about something Jones had said on their wedding night. It was something that came back to her often, filling her with a sense of deep warmth for her husband. She remembered it when she was angry at him, during times when she felt like they couldn't be further apart, and it never failed to fill her with the same pleasure, the same thrill it had given her the first time he uttered it.

He said, "Maggie. You saved me."

Only now, nearly two decades later, did she wonder what he'd meant.

26

He mostly talked. He talked about his mother, about his father, about how he'd always felt like a loser, an outcast.

Without the usual mask of black makeup, Charlene looked about twelve. She sat curled up on Maggie's couch, wearing sweatpants and an old black T-shirt, clutching a pillow against her center. Her hair was freshly washed, pulled back with a barrette in a girlish way. Maggie had the urge to hold her.

"Once he asked me to sing while he masturbated."

She looked up at Maggie with a flat stare, as if daring her to be shocked.

"And how did that make you feel?"

She blew a breath out of her nose. Charlene was going for jaded, unaffected, but Maggie could see her hands shaking.

"It made me sick." She spat the last word. "But you know what's weird? Part of me was, like, flattered. Does that make me a freak? I mean, I was tied up in a boat. *Tied up,* you know, singing, while this asshole spanks the monkey, and I was thinking, *Wow, he really likes my songs.*"

Maggie nodded her head, holding back a smile. Charlene was tough; she had a strong inner spirit. And this was a good thing for someone who'd endured what she had.

She told the girl as much. "You're not a freak, Charlene."

"I got in touch with him because I didn't know who else to ask. I cared about Rick too much to ask him to help me." She cast Maggie a sheepish look. "I know I hurt him. I'm sorry."

"It's not about that right now, Charlene," Maggie said. She gave the girl a smile. "Right now, it's about helping you sort out what happened to you, so you can deal with it and move on in a healthy way. Your relationship with Rick is your business. Okay?"

Charlene sighed, as if releasing some tension she'd been holding. "Okay. Thanks."

She sat for a second, looked down at her nails. Then she went on.

"I fell asleep in the car. I was so tired. I'd already been sick to my stomach by the side of the road. When I woke up, it was so dark. And we weren't on the highway anymore. I didn't know where we were."

She took a deep, shuddering breath and looked out the window. "Is Rick here?"

"No. He's at the hospital with his grandmother."

Charlene leaned forward and picked up a crystal lotus flower that sat on the end table. She held it to the light and watched the rainbow flecks that hit the far wall. She turned it back and forth so that they danced over the shelves of books, the wall of family pictures and Ricky's crayon drawings, the wood door that led to the waiting area.

"He said he wanted to show me something," she said, still turning the piece in her hand. "I was really afraid all of a sudden. No one knew where I was, and I realized that I didn't really know that much about Marshall. But I decided to pretend like I was curious, to play it off. I figured I'd wait and watch for an opportunity to run if things got weird."

Maggie noticed that the delicate features of her face looked strained and pale, her eyes shining. She gave the girl the respect of silence.

"It's fuzzy." Charlene put the lotus flower down, rubbed the back of her head. "He hit me from behind, I think. The doctor said I have a concussion, that my memory might be murky for a while, maybe always about this. But I think he hit me from behind with something. The next thing I remember was being on the filthy, smelly boat. I woke up in the dark, tied and gagged."

Maggie went to get a box of tissues from her desk and handed it to Charlene, who had abandoned her tough façade and started to cry.

"Sometimes he would just sit there, staring at me."

More silence. Maggie heard her computer ping, announcing the arrival of an e-mail.

"He never touched me," Charlene said. She paused to wipe her eyes and nose. "I mean, after he hit me and tied me up. He just wanted to talk about the stuff I told you, and whether he was a good person or a bad person, and how did we know those kinds of things. But he didn't want me to answer him. He only took the tape off once to give me some water, and that time he wanted me to sing.

"Then he'd leave me down there for long stretches. He never brought me food."

She put her head in her hands, and her shoulders started to shake.

Maggie abandoned her professionalism and joined Charlene on the couch, took her thin form into her arms and held her while she sobbed.

"I felt so scared." The words came out in a kind of wail into Maggie's shoulder. Charlene was healthier than Maggie would have imagined. She had a good handle on her emotions, was not afraid to let them out. "I never knew if he'd come back or I'd just die down there."

"I know, kiddo. You're going to be okay," Maggie said. She found herself rocking a little. When Charlene pulled away after a bit and her sobbing subsided, Maggie patted her on the leg and returned to her chair.

"Then his father found us," she said. She let go of a grim little laugh. "I thought I was saved."

"What happened?"

"He raped me," she said. She said it flatly, matter-of-fact. "Twice. And you know what was weird? He hardly said anything. He came one night, right after Marshall left me. He must have followed Marshall out to the lake and been waiting, listening."

"I'm so sorry," Maggie said. She knew she was dangerously close to crossing the line between personal and professional. She realized that she should have referred Charlene to a colleague, that she cared too much to be her doctor.

"The only thing he said was, 'I fucked your mother, too. But you're a sweeter piece of ass.'" Charlene began to sob in earnest.

Maggie felt a wave of anger and sadness so intense she might have

channeled it directly from Charlene. But she tried to keep her compo-
sure and gave a careful nod. "Do you want to talk about how you felt
while this was happening?"

Charlene looked at her; there was something injured and confused
on her face.

"I don't know. Grossed out, I guess. He was so frightening, so cold.
I was freaked out that he had this connection to my mother I didn't
know about. I don't know. It was like it was happening somewhere else,
to someone else. I felt so disconnected from it. It hurt. But it hurt *someone else.*"

Charlene shifted on the couch, folded her legs beneath her.

"There were rats down there. They were everywhere, scurrying on
the dock, on the boat. I was afraid they would crawl on me, bite me. But
they stayed away."

The mention of rats got Maggie thinking about the attic at her
mother's house. She tamped back another sick swell of fear and anger.
She'd deal with all that later. She could help Charlene. She couldn't help
Sarah.

"The second time he raped me, Marshall was there."

Maggie thought about Marshall's phone call, tried to figure out the
timing. He'd already had Charlene. Where had he been calling from?
She didn't suppose it mattered now.

"Marshall was there when his father walked in. I remember hearing
something just before. A loud bang. But I was so out of it by then, just
numb. Starving, so thirsty, in pain—but in this really distant way."

She was starting to get a glassy look. Maggie got up and took a
small plastic bottle of water from the little fridge she had by the
coffeemaker. She opened the lid, and Charlene took the bottle from her,
drank nearly half of it in one gulp, as though she were still dying of
thirst.

"He said something like, 'Let me show you what they're good for,
Son.' But then Marshall had a gun. I saw it, but his father didn't. He was
already . . . at me. I didn't even have the strength to fight.

"Then Marshall started firing. God, I never knew how loud gunfire
was. It was awful. I don't know how he didn't hit something, but his fa-

ther ran past him. Marshall turned to fire at him again, but the old man was there instead. Marshall shot his grandfather. Got him right in the chest. I remember that Marshall started wailing and wailing. And then he just walked off."

She shook her head at the memory, as if she were trying to knock the pieces into place. "It's like it all happened on a show I saw, a bad picture."

"Just take your time with it. The mind distances itself from horror. It's a survival mechanism."

Charlene took another long sip of water.

"The next thing I remember is Mr. Cooper. He was hurt, too. But he saved me. I always thought he hated me."

Maggie smiled. "He never hated you. He's—he's a difficult man to understand sometimes."

"Well," she said. "Tell him thanks for me."

"I will. Or you can tell him yourself."

Then, "What's going to happen to Marshall?"

Maggie shook her head. "I'm not sure."

She knew he'd face charges: kidnapping, manslaughter, illegal firearms possession—these were all on the table. He needed a lawyer, that much was certain. She didn't know if he'd be charged as an adult or a minor. Maggie was certain that her evaluation of his condition would have some impact.

"It's weird, but even after everything that happened," Charlene said, "I feel bad for him. He seemed so sad. So lost. I think he really needs help."

"There are people who care about him." Even as Maggie said it, she wondered if it was true. "There's a system in place."

"That's good," Charlene said. She sounded young and uncertain.

"Let's talk about why you left in the first place."

Charlene leaned back on the couch. "I had a fight with my mom. About the phone."

"The phone Graham got for you."

"Right. It was stupid. Everyone has a phone. Even Graham knew that."

"Your friends—Britney and Rick, in particular—said you were afraid of him. That he was inappropriate with you. Is that true?"

Charlene shrugged. Maggie noticed that her eyes started moving around the room, looking everywhere but at Maggie. "I don't know. He's all right, I guess. Stupid. He and my mom have a really bad relationship. They bring out the worst in each other."

Maggie wondered what she was holding back. "Your mother told Jones that she hit Graham with a baseball bat."

Charlene looked up, surprise lifting her eyebrows. "She told him that?"

"They found blood in the kitchen."

She nodded, looked back down.

"That's when I left. Last time they fought, I got in the middle and wound up with a black eye. I promised myself it wasn't going to happen again."

"How was he when you left?"

"He was on the floor, moaning and cursing at my mom. She was screaming at him. I don't even think they noticed me pack and leave. I don't know what happened then. There was blood. He didn't look good."

Charlene shook her head. "Mom said he left and said he wasn't coming back. I don't really blame him."

She was quiet a minute. Then, "I didn't know my real father. He died. I think she really loved him. She talks about him all the time, even now. She thinks things would have been different if he was still here."

Maggie had a vague memory of the man Melody had married, someone she'd met at college. She found she couldn't remember his name. Brian, maybe? Or Ryan? He'd died in a car wreck, killed on his way home from work by a drunk driver. Strange. Maggie hadn't thought about it in years. Melody had experienced a lot of loss.

"It doesn't do us much good to think that way, how things might be if this or that hadn't happened. We have to deal with circumstances as they are and adjust."

Charlene didn't answer right away, picked at a thread on the hem of her pants.

"But you almost can't help it, right, when things are bad, to wish they could be better?" she said finally. "It's natural."

"It *is* natural. But it's more productive to look ahead than to look back. We can make that choice even when it seems to go against the natural tendencies."

"That's why I wanted to leave, go to New York."

"To be with your boyfriend?"

Charlene looked down at her feet again. She put her thumb to her mouth and started chewing on the nail. Maggie remembered that Melody did the same thing.

"He wasn't—isn't—my boyfriend." She gave a little laugh. "He was just some guy I met who said I could crash at his place. They all say that." She looked at Maggie and rolled her eyes, offered a self-deprecating smile.

"He had a band that plays at a couple of bars in the East Village. He said he was about to be signed." She took her thumb from her mouth and released a sigh. "But I think that was bullshit. Anyway, he never even returned my calls. I thought I loved him. I always think I'm in love at first. It feels all fiery, so life-changing. Then it's just gone. That's not love, right?"

Maggie couldn't help but smile. She remembered being Charlene's age, remembered when every feeling was so powerful that you couldn't believe anyone had ever felt the same.

"Probably not," Maggie said. "Love is not just initial intense feelings, not just about that early rush. There has to be more to it."

"Like friendship."

"That's right."

Charlene gazed out the window again. "I'm so tired," she said. "I feel like I'm going to be tired and sad forever."

"You won't be," Maggie said. "But you have a lot of healing to do. I'm going to recommend counseling for a while to help you process everything."

Charlene glanced back from the window; she wore a worried frown. "Can't you be my shrink?"

Maggie hesitated. "Let's have a few sessions and see how it goes. I'm a little worried that we might be too close for me to be an effective therapist for you."

Charlene uncrossed her legs and slipped into the shoes she'd worn there, a beat-up pair of Chinese slippers with embroidered roses.

"Okay," she said.

"Don't worry," Maggie told her, keeping her voice light. "We're going to get you through this."

Another silent nod. But Charlene kept her eyes down.

"I was a virgin—before this." She spoke the words softly; Maggie had to lean forward to hear her. "I just wanted you to know that I wasn't some slut. I was always afraid you thought that about me, that I was sleeping with Rick."

Maggie struggled to keep the surprise off her face. But it wouldn't have mattered anyway; the girl didn't look up to see the reaction her words had caused. She just folded over and started to cry again. Maggie came to sit beside her, put an arm around her back. Charlene shifted to lay her head on Maggie's lap, and Maggie let her cry it out, rubbed her back while she did.

"I'm so sorry you had to go through this, Charlene," she said. "I'm so sorry."

Maggie felt like she was saying that a lot these days, apologizing for how ugly the world was, how bad things could get, how unfair. She thought about her mother and Jones, about the terrible things she had discovered in the attic and what they meant for all of them. Out the window, the light was growing dim, and she felt a sudden urgency to face the things she was hiding from in this room, in the space where she helped others but often ran away from herself.

Everything looked different. She wouldn't have been able to say how. But as she stepped out of Dr. Cooper's office and into a misty rain, everything—the trees, the sky, the grass on the lawn, the wet driveway, even her mother's car—seemed altered. She'd felt this way since she was first aware of herself again in the hospital. When she woke up in the semidark to see her mother sleeping in a chair by her bed, lights washing in from the half-open door, the edges of everything seemed indistinct, the colors not quite right, like in one of those old movies. There was an

empty bed beside her, and her first thought was to wonder why her
mother hadn't stretched out there. She looked so uncomfortable in the
hard chair. It was a strange thing to think under the circumstances, but
that's what she wondered first.

Then she'd been aware of how much she hurt. How her body
ached—her wrists, her back, her neck. Even *down there* she felt pain, inside and out, a bruised tenderness. Then she'd been aware of a scratchy
dryness in her throat, a dull pressure behind her eyes. Everything hurt,
but just a little, like after she and her mother were in that fender-bender
a couple of years back. She felt as if her whole body had been shaken
once, really hard. She knew she would get up and walk out of there. And
it seemed wrong, because what she felt inside was so black and cold and
ugly that she wished she was in traction, wrapped in a full-body cast, on
life support. Because that's how she felt inside, damaged beyond repair.
It wasn't fair that people couldn't see that.

Charlene paused in the doorway, dreading the walk from the safety
of Dr. Cooper's office to the overwarm, smoky interior of her mother's
car. Somehow, now, the world seemed too big, too menacing. There
were too many wide-open spaces where bad things could happen. And
she felt so small. But she drew in a breath and moved quickly toward the
car. She didn't run, though she wanted to. Charlene didn't realize she
was holding that last draw of air in her lungs until she'd closed the door
behind her and locked it. As she put on her seat belt, her heart was
pounding as if she'd sprinted a mile.

"How was it?"

Her mother was staring at her in this new way she had, as if Charlene were some kind of alien, someone whom she didn't recognize and
didn't quite know what to do with. But it wasn't mean. It was tender,
somehow, careful.

"It was—I don't know. Good, I guess, to talk about it. You know,
with a doctor or whatever."

Melody gave a slow nod. On impulse, Charlene reached out for her
mother and took her hand. Melody's eyes widened a bit in surprise, then
she almost smiled. But it dropped from her face quickly, as though it had
no business being there.

"Did you tell her everything, Charlene?"

Her mother seemed so sad, all the power drained from her some-how. The lines around her eyes had deepened. And she hadn't bothered with any makeup for a couple of days, leaving herself to look washed out and plain.

"You mean about Graham? No," Charlene said. "Of course not, Mom."

"It's my fault. All of this. I know that."

"No, Mom. It's mine."

Charlene felt that quaking within her again. She had the strong urge to put her head in her mother's lap like she used to, even though a few days ago she'd have rather set her own hair on fire than cuddle up to her mom. Now she didn't like Melody to even be out of her sight for too long. She didn't want to be alone.

Melody put her hands on Charlene's shoulders, gave her a gentle shake.

"No, Charlene. None of this is your fault. There are things that were set in motion before you were ever born."

Charlene shook her head and fought back another rush of tears. It was exhausting to be crying all the time.

"Charlene," Melody said. She looked down at the seat between them. "God, there's so much you don't understand."

But it wasn't true; she understood everything. She'd been there.

When Charlene came down the stairs, she'd found her mother on the kitchen floor weeping. At first Charlene thought something had been broken, spilling a dark, red, viscous fluid across the floor. Then she saw the bat beside her mother. And for the next few moments, she thought her mother was hurt—the way she was folded onto herself, as though doubling over in terrible pain.

And then she saw Graham, pale and moaning on the floor, a hand to his head.

"You goddamn crazy bitch," he was saying, soft and low, over and over like a mantra.

"What happened?" asked Charlene. She kept her distance, standing by the doorway. This was new, Graham down and bleeding, looking like he was hurt bad. She remembered the price she paid for getting between them the last time. So she kept her distance.

Melody looked up at her quickly, surprised, as if she didn't realize Charlene was in the house. And maybe she hadn't. They might not have known she was upstairs painting her nails. Her mom's purse was on the counter, a pile of mail next to it. It looked like they'd just gotten home from work. Charlene saw it then; the bill for her phone on top of the pile. She had forgotten to intercept the mail when she came home from school. She felt her stomach bottom out. Melody saw her looking at it.

"Where's that phone, Charlene?" Her voice was surprisingly soft, almost sweet. "Bring it to me right now."

"Mom. No."

She wouldn't give up her phone; it was hers. God knows she'd earned it by putting up with Graham. "It's not a big deal. Everyone has a phone. I don't use it in school."

Charlene looked over at Graham. He looked really bad. *Was all that blood coming from his head?*

"Charlene," he said. "Call 911. I'm hurt bad."

But her mother started shrieking to bring the fucking phone. And the sound of it, like an alarm, and the sight of all the blood shook Charlene to her core. She ran upstairs and fished it out of her purse. Why didn't she dial 911 right then? She should have. She'd had a lot of time to think about how if she'd done that, nothing that happened later would have happened at all. But she didn't do that one thing, the right thing. She never could do that.

She brought the phone downstairs. She still didn't want to walk into that kitchen, so she slid it across the floor to her mother. Her mother stood up, pitching and wobbling like a drunk, though Charlene knew she was sober. Melody lifted the bat high over her head and Charlene started to scream, *No, Mommy, don't!* Because she thought Melody was going after Graham. But then Melody proceeded to pound the phone to bits, yelling, *You think I don't know what you've been doing to her? You think I don't see? It stops here, you stupid shit. How much further did you think I was going to let this go?*

Charlene fell silent, drowned out anyway by her mother's rant, and looked on, fixated, sick to the core with guilt and fear as her mother kept shouting, pounding on that phone, barely hitting it at all because it was so small and in so many pieces, until she seemed to just run out of gas and sank back down, weeping.

"I never touched her," Graham said. He struggled to push himself up. Half his face was smeared with blood. "Tell her, Charlene."

She shook her head, opened her mouth to speak, but wound up issuing a sob instead. Finally, "He didn't. Mom, he didn't."

Melody looked up first at Charlene and then back at Graham.

"I know that," she said. She had pulled her face into a nasty grimace, her voice more like a growl. "If you *had* touched her, you'd be dead."

"Mel, please, get me to the hospital. I'm hurt."

He fell back then against the floor, his eyes looking blank and glassy. The moan he was issuing almost didn't sound human; it was otherworldly.

"Mom," Charlene said. "We have to help him."

Still, Charlene couldn't bring herself to cross the threshold into the kitchen. Melody just looked at her, and Charlene was sure she was going to start raging about what a slut she was, about how she'd ruined all their lives.

But instead, Melody said, "I'm sorry, Char. I've failed you in all sorts of ways." And Charlene didn't know what to say to that; they both cried.

"I'm going to call 911," Charlene said.

"No, Charlene." Melody stood and wiped her eyes. She sounded calmer, stronger. "Just help me. Pull the truck into the garage and help me get him in. I'll drive him."

"I think it's better—"

"Just do it, Charlene!"

And she'd done it, pulled the car into the garage even though her mother hadn't even let her get her learner's permit yet, and shut the door. Charlene had helped her heave Graham into the car, both of them straining under the effort, while he continued to groan. The side of his face looked purple and swollen, but the bleeding from his head and his nose had slowed.

"Charlene," Melody said from the driver's side window, "Graham and I will work out what we say about what happened. You weren't even here."

"But—," started Charlene.

Her mother lifted a hand. "Please, Charlene, don't say a word about this to anyone. You *can't*. Do you understand? Just pretend you weren't here. Things are going to be different for us from now on."

She didn't like the frightened, desperate expression on her mother's face; she looked unhinged. Charlene nodded her agreement.

"Mom," she said. But then the garage door was opening, and Melody was backing down the driveway. And then they were gone down the street.

Charlene went inside. Looking back, she didn't remember feeling anything then. She was just hyperfocused on the task of cleaning all that blood. She went to the computer and looked up how to do it. Then she got some of the cleaning supplies from the laundry room and managed to do a fairly decent job of it, though she thought she could still see the shadow of the stain in the linoleum. After a certain amount of scrubbing with bleach, she felt light-headed and sick. She threw everything— gloves, rags, and scrub brush—in the trash outside.

When she was done, she looked at the clock. It was after seven; she knew Rick was waiting for her at Pop's. She could call him there, have him come get her right then. But no. She wouldn't do that. Charlene knew somehow that she'd passed through a doorway with her mother. Rick couldn't follow her through, and Charlene could never go back with him. Thinking about that, about Rick waiting for her, about how she couldn't just go and have pizza with him, fool around in the back of his car, laugh and complain about The Hollows and their stupid parents—fear and sadness left her. Anger filled her back up.

She went to her room and threw some things into a backpack. She had almost a thousand dollars in her drawer, rolled up in a plastic Hello

Kitty bank saved over years from allowance, birthday, and Christmas money. She stuffed that deep in the bottom of her bag. This was it, the end of her life in The Hollows.

She wrote Rick a note and posted an update on Facebook. She tried to call Steve, the guy she was crushing on in the city, but he didn't answer. It seemed like a bad omen. But she left a message, convinced herself he'd be waiting when she got there.

She remembered Marshall Crosby had promised her a ride anytime she needed it. She saw the way he looked at her, with a kind of desperate hunger. She knew he'd come and drive her where she needed to go. So she wrote him a message and didn't wait for a reply. She didn't want him to come to her house—she needed to be gone before her mother got back. And she needed to walk, to think. So she picked a random point between their houses and figured it would take her a while to walk there.

Then she left her room without a second glance. She remembered thinking that she had to get away from these people, this ugly life, before it killed her. And then she'd walked out into the cold night, alone.

"I did an awful thing, Charlene."

They hadn't really talked about that night. When Charlene had asked about Graham, Melody told her that they'd fought again in the car. He'd kicked her out and she'd walked home. He'd said he was going to go hunting and to think about the future of their relationship. He'd gone off and not yet come back, couldn't be reached on his phone—and good riddance.

But Charlene knew, as daughters do, that this was a lie. Graham was in no condition to get up and fight again after they got him into the cab of his truck. And he was certainly in no shape to kick Melody out and start to drive. But Charlene didn't call her on it. Besides, she wanted it to be true. She really did.

"What happened to him, Mom?"

Melody blinked at Charlene, as though she wasn't quite sure what her daughter meant.

Then, "I'm not talking about Graham."

Charlene felt confused. "Then what? What did you do?"

Melody put the car in reverse and backed out of the Coopers' drive. Charlene looked up at Rick's window and saw that it was dark. She wasn't ready to see him yet, but she found she missed him more than she would have imagined. Maybe love, real love, wasn't what she thought it was at all. Maybe it wasn't a brushfire, a shift of tectonic plates. Maybe it was a held hand, a strong shoulder, a soft voice in your ear. Maybe it didn't change the world; maybe it just made two lives a little better, a little softer, not so horribly lonely.

"I don't want there to be any more secrets, Charlene. Can I tell you something that I've never told anyone?" Her mother wasn't looking at her but at the road ahead of them.

Charlene was tired, feeling like the load she was carrying was too heavy already. But her mother looked so sad, so alone.

"Of course you can, Mom."

She reached out for her mother's hand. And, as she drove them home, Melody told Charlene all about another girl she'd failed, a lifetime ago.

Years earlier, Maggie had watched a documentary about psychics who solved crimes. It was a cable show, low-budget, lots of melodramatic music and bad camera angles. But Maggie watched it because it featured the solving of the Sarah Meyer case, with shots of The Hollows and interviews with people she knew.

It was the psychic, a woman named Eloise Montgomery, who'd led the police to Tommy Delano, who'd claimed to have a vision of Sarah's murder. She had a connection to Sarah's family, occasionally cleaned for them and other families in town.

His name begins with T, she told them. A crackling recording of her statement made her voice sound otherworldly and strange. *He knows her well. He's been watching her, wanting her. I see woods, a flight of terror. Oh, God. He's so angry. She's so terribly afraid. He's sick. He wants to be close to women, to girls. But he hates them, too. He hates himself for wanting them.*

Eloise claimed to have had visions on the night Sarah disappeared, only to learn the next morning that Sarah was missing. It took a few days for her to convince the police to listen to her, and it was only desperation that caused them to do so.

But there's more to the story. It's unclear. It may always be unclear. But I'm sorry. She's gone. She's not with us anymore. She's at peace. The dead see us with loving detachment. There's no pain for her now. Just music.

Once she said that the killer's name began with the letter *T,* suspicion turned immediately to Tommy Delano. He'd been spotted on a road near where the body was found. When they went to question him, he'd already fled.

No one was sure why or how he knew suspicion had turned to him. They found his room full of clippings about Sarah, photographs of her and other girls at the school, her underpants in the trunk of his car. He'd disappeared on foot into the hills behind his house. It was a strange thing to do, when he had a car at his disposal.

He's scared and tired. He wants to go home. He knows you're looking for him. He just wants it all to be over. You're going to find him. Very soon.

And they did. His confession came some hours later.

Eloise Montgomery still made her living as a psychic detective, traveling the world to help police with cold cases and cases that couldn't be solved. For some reason, her gift was limited to women and young girls—the missing, the murdered, the abducted. Her website made this clear: Please don't contact me about any other type of case. My talents are very specific. A few years later, after another high-profile case, Eloise had teamed with the retired detective who'd worked Sarah Meyer's case at the Hollow's PD, Ray Muldune. Maggie recognized him vaguely from his photograph.

But there's more to the story. It's unclear. It may always be unclear. Those were the words Maggie had in her mind as she drove in the twilight out of town. And then there was the odd feeling that lingered from the call she'd made. She'd found Eloise Montgomery's number on her website and dialed on a whim, expecting to get voice mail. But instead, an older woman answered. Maggie could hear a television in the background, a dog barking somewhere distantly.

"Is this Eloise Montgomery?" Maggie asked.

"It is." She had the tone of someone who was used to waiting patiently while people figured out what they wanted to say.

"This may sound strange," she said. "But I have some questions about an old case."

"What can I do for you?" Maybe that was her shtick, to sound as though she'd been waiting for your call, to sound as though she already knew what you wanted.

"It's about Sarah Meyer. About her murder."

"Ah," Eloise said. "Yes."

Eloise sounded as though she could go on. But she didn't, and Maggie felt tongue-tied all of a sudden, didn't know how to continue the conversation. She wasn't going to tell this stranger what she'd found in her mother's attic. Why had she done this? Why had she made this ridiculous call?

"You have new information about the case," the other woman said. "You're concerned about people close to you."

Her voice was soft, almost coaxing. But Maggie still couldn't get any words out. Her heart was a bird in a cage, flapping, panicked. She had the irrational urge to slam the phone down.

"I'm free now," Eloise said into the silence. "Do you know where I live?"

Maggie was staring at Eloise Montgomery's address on the website. "I do."

"Can you come?"

"I can be there in an hour."

"Okay," she said. "See you then."

And Eloise ended the call. Maggie stood, gathered her things, and left her office before she could change her mind. The urge to go to this woman, to hear what she had to say about the case, was magnetic, a draw powerful enough to lead Maggie away from her family in an acute crisis. The part of her that was always tending, managing, fixing, controlling was quiet for once.

·   ·   ·

On the drive, she had time to rationalize the things Eloise had said. Probably most of the people who called out of the blue about old cases thought they had new information. A large majority of those people were likely motivated by concern for someone they loved. Maggie had heard that this was the technique of many so-called psychics, to play the odds, to use verbal and visual clues to make educated guesses about people. It wasn't so different from being a psychologist. People were unique, each with an impossibly complicated inner life, a mosaic of personality, history, and perceptions. Their inner lives were vast, nebulous symbioses of memory and the present moment, no incident or experience standing alone from the incidents or experiences that formed them. But the problems people faced were often the same. And things like appearance, tone, body language, facial expression spoke volumes to the trained observer, to someone with empathy. Maggie's fear and hesitance to speak must have told Eloise Montgomery everything she needed to know about why Maggie was making that call.

By the time she pulled into the short drive in front of a small white house, Maggie felt more solid, more in control of herself and her intentions. The house was off a narrow rural road about twenty miles from The Hollows. It sat prim and proper on a small rise; everything—white clapboards, black shutters, a red door—looked freshly painted. A few piles of raked leaves lay beneath the towering oaks on the property.

Even as Maggie made her way up the stone path to the porch, golden and orange leaves were fluttering around her. The sun had already dipped below the horizon. But the air had gone balmy again, the frigid cold from yesterday forgotten.

As she rang the bell and waited, Maggie noticed that three large pumpkins and a collection of gourds sat by the door and thought how she hadn't bothered to put out their fall decorations. And something about that thought brought tears to her eyes. She was wiping them away as Eloise opened the door and led her inside.

.   .   .

"I'll start by telling you that there is no confidentiality here. So anything you don't want me to know, you should keep to yourself. I'm not a lawyer or a priest."

Eloise ran thin fingers over her short, salt-and-pepper hair as she sat across from Maggie. Maggie remembered her as bigger, more powerful. She had the look now of someone who didn't think much of food, with lean limbs and thin lips. Her collarbone pulled her skin taut. But there were three pies cooling on the counter in the kitchen where Eloise had led her, filling the air with the scent of warm pastry. Eloise had offered coffee, and Maggie had declined. But Eloise had placed a cup in front of her anyway, prepared with milk and one spoonful of sugar. Maggie sipped it to be polite and found that it was just what she needed.

"I was a junior in high school when Sarah was murdered. My mother, Elizabeth Monroe, was the principal of Hollows High."

"I remember her. She's a good woman."

"Yes, she is," Maggie said. "Thank you. Recently, she hurt herself. My son found her and she was delirious. She told him some things, things that have me worried. Things that have me remembering Sarah."

Eloise nodded slowly, looked down at her fingernails. Maggie noticed they were ragged and bloody, bitten to the quick.

"She told my son, 'She was already dead when he found her.' She claims now that she doesn't remember saying it. But it resonated with me."

Eloise looked at her with dark eyes, as though she knew something more powerful had led Maggie here. Maggie looked away, cast her eyes about the kitchen. A ceramic hen, a chalkboard covered with scrawled notes, a countertop peeling at the corners—she looked everywhere but back into those dark pools.

"Once, a long time ago, your mother sat where you're sitting now. She didn't believe Tommy Delano killed Sarah Meyer."

Maggie issued a surprised little laugh. "No," she said. "I'm sorry. No offense, but I just can't see my mother visiting a psychic."

Eloise smiled. "She came here to ask me why I'd said what I did. She accused me of being a fraud."

"Are you? Are you a fraud?"

Maggie was surprised at herself for asking the question. It was disrespectful, crass, and unlike her. It was more like Elizabeth.

But Eloise just shook her head slowly. "I wish I were. I wish this were all just a scam I came up with to make money. I wish I didn't spend half my life seeing things no one would ever want to see."

There was no anger or bitterness in her tone, just the level of sadness of someone resigned to her condition. Maggie noticed a battalion of prescription bottles by the sink, all lined up.

"What did you tell my mother?" The refrigerator started to hum, and Maggie heard some cubes drop from the ice maker in the freezer.

"I pick up frequencies, images. The best way I can describe it is to say that there's something inside me like a scanner. I see things with varying degrees of lucidity. Some things make sense; some things don't. Sometimes I'm connected, like I was to Sarah's family. Sometimes the things I see are a world away. There's no pattern."

Eloise caressed the edge of the table with her fingertips, seemed to have finished what she was saying.

"Did Tommy Delano kill Sarah?" Maggie asked.

"I used to think so, though I knew there was much more to the story than I could see. I knew he had a terrible rage inside him, something that had lived in him since he was a small boy. It didn't belong to him; his spirit was cursed with it. It was something inherited, that he couldn't exorcise, didn't know how. I knew that he had a hunger for her, that he'd been watching her, following her for a long time. He kept that demon caged for so long, but it was thrashing inside him. I saw him touching her, cutting her."

Eloise's eyes had taken on a shine; she was staring beyond Maggie as though she was no longer there. But her voice was as steady and unemotional as if she were talking about something she'd seen on television.

"And that's all I told them. Because that's what I saw. He later confessed."

"And now what do you think?"

Eloise lifted a finger, got up, and left the room. When she returned a moment later, she held an envelope in her hand.

"A few days after Tommy Delano died in prison, I received this in the mail. He hanged himself, maybe you remember. *It* hanged him. That terrible anger."

Maggie felt a cold shiver, an urge to get up and run. But she stayed rooted in her seat. Outside, the sun had set and it was dark. She felt like they were the only two people in the world.

"This is his suicide note. He sent it to me."

"Why? Why would he send it to you?"

"He wanted someone to know the truth, to know who he was, what he'd done. He claimed he could feel me inside his head. I don't know if that was true or not. I doubt it, but I've learned not to judge. There are too many things we don't understand."

Eloise handed Maggie the letter. As Maggie reached to take it from her, Eloise held on to her hand. Her grip was gentle but firm. Maggie looked up to meet the older woman's eyes and saw only kindness there.

"I knew you'd come here and want answers one day," Eloise said. "I knew it the day your mother came to see me."

Something about her words or her tone brought tears to Maggie's eyes again. "How could you know that?"

Eloise sat back down and wrapped her arms around herself. "Because I told your mother to stop looking for answers. I told her to accept things the way they were, and let Sarah and Tommy Delano go. I told her that if she didn't, she'd lose you. I didn't know the specifics, how or why. I just knew that it was not her place to keep looking, and if she did, she'd pay an awful price."

The information landed hard and dead center. Maggie remembered what her mother had said to her in the car when she'd asked Elizabeth if Tommy Delano hadn't killed Sarah, then who had. She'd said, *Now, the answer to that might just be what kept me from asking the question in the first place.*

But Elizabeth was not a superstitious woman, not one to bow to the prophecy of a psychic. Maggie said as much to Eloise, who offered a deferential nod of her head. Maggie realized that Eloise was a woman accustomed to being disbelieved. It didn't faze her in the least. The longer Maggie spent with Eloise, the more credible she seemed. Maybe Elizabeth had come to feel the same way.

Maggie held the letter in her hand for a moment, then slipped the page from its envelope. Tommy's message was written in a looping, childish hand.

Dear Miss Montgomery,

I believe you're the only person alive who knows me. I can feel your eyes on me and I know you can see who I am, but you don't judge me. There are things I need to say, things I need you to understand. You see a lot, but you don't see everything.

I will tell you that I did not kill Sarah Meyer that night. But I'd killed her a hundred times already in as many different ways. I want to tell you that I loved her and that I thought about her all of the time. A lot of times, like you told the police, I followed her. I was nearby when she died. It was an accident. She was with some boys, I won't say who, and there was a fight. She ran from one of them. And then she fell, hit her head on a rock. They left her there, alone in the dark. So I took her. She belonged to me. I wanted her warm and screaming. But I took her as I found her, so cold and so quiet.

You know what I did to her. You were there. I felt you even though I didn't understand it at the time. I won't write those things here. They are nightmares. I hate who I am. I always, always have.

There was pressure to confess. They were at me for hours and hours. But that's not why I said I killed her. I said I did it because I would have one day. And if not her, then someone else. I couldn't keep the animal in his cage much longer, especially not after he'd tasted blood. It's better that I'm here, caged with the other animals. Don't feel bad that you got it wrong. You were right in all the ways that count.

This is the last anyone will hear from me. And I know no one

will miss me. Everyone thinks I'm a monster. I am. I hope my mom
is waiting for me. But I doubt it. I remember how she looked before
I pushed her down the stairs. I know she loved me. But when she
looked at me she was so sad.

Sincerely,

Tommy Delano

Sorrow seemed to leak from the page into her fingers. Maggie
found herself thinking of Marshall, another damaged boy turning into a
dangerous, unstable man. She thought of Sarah's violin in her mother's
attic, Charlene weeping on her couch, her mother and husband lying in
their hospital beds. She thought of Ricky going off to college, and she
was glad that he was going to be far, far away from this place, even
though she knew the loss of him was going to lay her low. There was
something about The Hollows that held on tight, kept you here though
you'd intended to leave, or brought you back when you weren't paying
attention. It made promises that it didn't keep—safety, peace of mind,
tranquillity—until one day you were too tired to even want to find another place to live.

"Did my mother know about this letter? She must have."

Eloise nodded. "I shared it with her after some time had passed.
Even now, I'm not sure why. It only caused her more pain. But I tend to
follow my compulsions; I've found that there's usually a reason, even if I
never understand it myself."

Maggie thought of her mother, her will so powerful, her sense of
right and wrong so clear. How could she have lived with this?

"Eloise," Maggie said. "Do you know who killed Sarah?"

Eloise looked out the window over the metal kitchen sink, then
back at Maggie.

"No, I don't. I'm sorry."

Maggie believed her.

Henry Ivy rarely locked his doors. When he was a kid, the doors were always open. And even though The Hollows had changed a lot since then, he rarely thought to do it, couldn't remember the last time he'd used his key to get in. But standing on his porch, he noticed the door was ajar. He wouldn't have left it that way. It was an old door that stuck, especially on a night like tonight, when yesterday it had been cool and today it was humid. He had to pull the door closed and push it open hard.

He briefly considered leaving, turning around and getting back in his car, using his cell phone to call the police. But then if there was no one in there, he'd look foolish. And while everyone in The Hollows liked and respected him, thought he did his job well, no one thought of Henry Ivy as a tough guy. He wasn't the guy you called when you needed a hero. In The Hollows, that guy was Jones Cooper. If he called the cops and there was no one in his house, everyone would be very polite about it, but there'd be lots of laughing at the bar after the shift had ended. The story would circulate to wives and girlfriends. Two days later Margie, the receptionist, would be looking at him with a sympathetic smile he didn't understand.

He pushed the door open and walked into the foyer, stood listening. The air felt different. There was an odd scent, something unpleasant. He walked into the living room to the right of the foyer and saw Travis Crosby sitting in the wing chair by the fireplace.

The room was exactly as Henry's mother had decorated it decades ago. When his parents had sold him the house and moved to Florida, they'd wanted all new things down there. Henry always thought he'd sell the furniture he'd been lying around on since childhood, gut the house and redo everything. But he never had. Not for any reason other than a kind of inertia that had settled over his life. Everything was fine. It had always been fine. That was what he told himself.

"What are you doing here, Crosby?"

He didn't feel particularly alarmed to see this wanted man in his living room. In a way, Henry felt as though he'd been waiting for Travis, like they had some unfinished business they'd never gotten around to settling.

"I used to go to AA meetings. On the job, they like you to do that. Promise they'll treat your addiction like a disease, give you your shield back when you're cured. But that's not the way it works. They'll put you back on the payroll but not on the street. You run the desk or the equipment room, maybe the evidence locker if you're lucky."

Henry noticed a half-empty bottle of Jack Daniel's and a bag of chips by Travis's feet. He'd obviously been there awhile, helped himself to things in Henry's kitchen and liquor cabinet.

"I didn't become a cop to file paperwork."

"No," Henry said. "You became a cop so that you could continue to bully people *and* get paid for it."

Travis issued an annoyed little laugh, rubbed nervously at the sweat on his brow. "You never did know when to keep your mouth shut, Ivy."

Henry noticed the gun in Travis's hand then, a flat, black menace. Still, Henry didn't feel any fear, just a kind of tingling awareness. He felt that same thing rear up in him that had caused him to beat Travis at homecoming. It was something ugly and raw, but not unwelcome.

"What do you want, Crosby?"

"I still think about that day, you know? When you beat me in front of the whole school?"

"So do I."

"I feel like everything went bad for me starting there. That nothing good ever happened again after that."

Travis stared at Henry with watery eyes, his face flushed, leg pumping. He looked bloated and filthy, with some kind of dark stain on his shirt and pants. Henry still remembered the lean, terrifying boy he'd been. He'd been all the more menacing for his beauty and charm. The man before him was a ruin.

"You're kidding, right? You tortured me for years. I finally stood up to you. And now you're going to blame me for ruining your life. That's classic."

Logic dictated that Henry should be talking Travis down, mindful of the gun in his hand. But Henry was tired of being quiet, of doing the right thing, the logical thing. That was what he'd been doing all his life. What had it gotten him, actually? What did he have to show for all that right action? If he thought about it, beating the crap out of Travis Crosby was the only honest thing he'd ever done.

"In rehab, they tell you that you have to make amends, to say you're sorry to all the people you hurt with your addiction. But I kept thinking, What about all the people who hurt me, who fucked me over? My father, you, my ex-wife. When do *they* start to make amends?"

"Seems like you might have missed the point, Crosby."

"I don't think so."

Travis got to his feet quickly, and Henry took an unconscious step back. He saw a predator's satisfied smile turn up the corners of Travis's mouth.

"And what really gets me?" Travis said. "What really *kills* me? My son talks about you all the time, like you're some kind of oracle. *Mr. Ivy says. Mr. Ivy says.*" His voice turned into a nasty mimic. "You! The faggot I wiped the floor with for years. He looks up to you."

Henry saw it then, that all the sadness, fear, and self-loathing that lived in Marshall had lived in Travis first. It had probably lived in the chief before that. And for the first time in his life, Henry felt compassion for Travis.

"He loves you, Travis," Henry said. "He loves you so much, more than you know."

But Travis didn't seem to be listening. He was lost in whatever hurricane was raging inside him.

"Sometimes I think if it hadn't been for that homecoming game, I wouldn't have gotten so angry. I wouldn't have chased her. She wouldn't have fallen."

"I don't know what you're talking about."

"It doesn't matter now. It's too late for her. It's too late for me."

Henry drew in a deep breath, keeping his eyes anywhere but on the gun in Travis's hand. It was just surreal to see him in his parents' living room, so broken and defeated, still intending Henry harm, even though a lifetime had passed. Henry found himself wondering why people held on to anger and sadness, gripped it tight, let it dictate the course of their lives, but found it so hard to find and keep love. He noticed that Travis was shaking.

"Look, Travis," he said. "I'm sorry I hurt you that day."

He wasn't just trying to placate an angry man holding a gun. He truly was sorry. He was sorry he had let Travis bring him so low. He'd never forgotten how much it hurt to hurt someone else, no matter how much he deserved it.

Henry saw Travis soften a bit; his shoulders dropped from the tense hunch they were in.

"Christ, Ivy, even now, you're such a fucking faggot."

Henry felt nothing but pity as Travis raised the gun and put it to his own head. Henry backed away and closed his eyes as Travis pulled the trigger. But there was no concussive boom. Just a soft click—then silence.

Henry opened his eyes to see the look of shocked disappointment on Crosby's face. It might have been comical if it weren't so hideous. Travis collapsed in the chair, howling in pain, tears streaming down his cheeks.

Henry bent down and easily took the gun from the other man's hand. He checked the barrel. It had fired on an empty chamber, but the gun still had three bullets. For an elastic moment, he thought about how easy it would be to shoot Travis. He could easily claim self-defense. Given the circumstances, their individual reputations, no one would doubt him for a moment.

But it was just a fantasy. He thought about Marshall, who'd lost so

much. And he thought about himself, how he knew the folly of retalia-
tion, what a hollow victory it was. But most of all, he thought about
Travis Crosby, about how his life as it was and would be was a more ex-
quisite justice than anything he could hope to dispense.

Henry turned from the weeping man and called the police.

Maggie stood in the doorway of the darkened hospital room and
watched her husband. He didn't look big and powerful, as he always
had. He looked fragile, deflated. It was long past visiting hours, but the
nurses all knew her and no one moved to stop her as she walked past
their station.

When she got to his room, though, she didn't know how to step inside. What was she going to say? How was she going to ask the questions she had? What would he tell her? And who would they be after all
was said and done?

No one but Jones could have put those things in her mother's attic.
She knew that. Elizabeth hadn't been up there in years, couldn't even
make it up the ladder when she'd wanted to. And beyond that, Elizabeth
might have been guilty of not asking the hard questions, might have
bowed for whatever reason to the fearful predictions of Eloise Montgomery, but she would never have concealed evidence that proved someone else's involvement in the murder of a young girl. She could never
have lived knowing those things were in her attic.

"Mags? Where have you been? We were really worried. Your cell
went straight to voice mail."

She came into the room, pulled up a chair to sit beside her husband.
In the low light, he looked like his younger self, The Hollows's heartthrob, the boy she had loved from a distance. She wondered how he had
carried this load for so long, never even hinting at how painful, how
heavy, it must have been.

"Jones," she said. She put a hand on his arm.

"What is it, Maggie? Ricky okay?"

"He's fine."

"Because I've been thinking about him. I've made a lot of mistakes with that kid. I can do better." He released a heavy sigh. "It's not too late, is it?"

Something about this, in spite of everything that lay before them, washed her with relief. Because it mattered how well they loved one another, how well they treated one another as a family—that was the root, that was the trunk of life. All the rest was just leaves that grew and fell, were raked away and grew again.

"It's never too late, Jones."

And that's when she told him about what she'd found in her mother's attic and where she had been while he was looking for her. And when he started to cry, she climbed into the bed beside him and held him until he stopped. Then they talked in a way they hadn't since they first fell in love, with the intensity of discovery. He told her everything about the night Sarah died, and everything that followed. And Maggie knew that, for the first time in their marriage, he was revealing all of himself to her.

Sometimes Chuck Ferrigno didn't like his job. His parents had tried to talk him out of it. They'd wanted him to be an accountant, use the talent he had for math in some way. But numbers bored him. He didn't see the poetry or the music in math equations that some did. To him it was all so dry, so predictable. Not like life. Life was messy and imprecise, decided by the variables of humanity rather than by the constants. That's what intrigued him, motivated him. Besides, when he was a younger man, all he wanted to do was run and chase. He wanted to deliver justice and help people in need. He wanted to race into burning buildings and rescue children. He wanted to carry a gun.

But that wasn't the job most of the time, of course. Every once in a while, there was a moment that lived up to the dream. But generally the job was more like it was now, standing in a rest stop parking lot, looking at a rotting corpse in a pickup truck, wondering about the implications, dreading the mountain of paperwork.

Graham Olstead, husband of Melody Murray, had been dead for a while by the looks of him. In the cab, his hunting rifle hung on its mount, and there was a box of provisions that would have lasted him a few days; beside him was a knapsack of clothes.

Melody Murray had said he was going hunting, and it looked like he'd planned to do just that. But, for whatever reason, he'd pulled over into this rest stop and died here. Chuck had a feeling he knew why. He'd seen it before.

"Subdural hematoma." Katie sounded like she was talking to herself. He hadn't seen her flinch at the body, or even shrink from the smell. She turned to him, and when he looked at her, he saw the same creamy skin, unblemished, unlined, that he saw on the faces of his own children. She was too young to be doing this job. He understood now why his parents hadn't wanted him to be a cop. Maybe later he'd try to talk this sweet, small-town girl into being a kindergarten teacher or something.

The wind was picking up, and on the highway beyond the stand of trees, the sound of an air horn was mournful and heavy in the night air. The moon was hidden behind cloud cover, the sky an eerie silver-black.

"If he took a blow to the head with the baseball bat, there might have been a period of lucidity, as Melody Murray claimed, when he could walk and talk." Katie pointed to the items in the cab. "He'd be able to get ready for the trip, drive off. But if the blood from the broken vessels didn't clot properly? And maybe if he took a Motrin for the pain, it wouldn't have. Then, a few hours later . . ." She let the sentence trail, lifting a slender palm toward the corpse. She moved in closer, and Chuck followed.

Katie pointed to a purple, flowering bruise by Graham's temple, an ugly contrast to the grayish white of the skin beneath it.

"We won't know until the autopsy," she said. "It's just a theory. Coroner's on the way."

When he still didn't say anything, she said, "I'll get my camera."

Chuck didn't like to arrest women, but he was going to have to get a warrant and bring Melody Murray in. He wished Jones were around to do it. He had the feeling Jones wouldn't mind at all. He wondered, not for the first time, what their history was; he knew there was one. Everyone in this town seemed connected to everyone else somehow.

Coming from New York City, Chuck found this strange. He was used to distance, to the anonymity of the crowd. But his wife loved The Hollows. Loved that she went to the store for milk and saw three people she knew, that she'd get a call from a neighbor up the way to say the kids were playing off the cul-de-sac where they were supposed to stay with their bikes. But he found it oppressive, the way people knew your business, stopped by with baked goods, commented on your kid's performance at a soccer game you hadn't been able to attend. He wondered what it would be like to grow up in one place and stay there all your life, to forever be defined by your childhood relationships, to never know if you got to be the person you wanted to be, to always be the person you were when you were young.

When he looked over at Katie, she was staring at the body. For the first time since she'd arrived, she looked unsettled, brow furrowed, her professional veneer slipping.

"I think my mother used to date him," she said. "A long time ago, in high school."

"That doesn't surprise me," he said. "It's a small town."

"She said he drank too much. That he was kind of a jerk."

Chuck looked back at the dead man, a stranger to him, someone he'd never met in life. He wondered if it was true, what Katie said. If just saying something made it true, in a way. There was a story Chuck's father used to tell about the boy who spread a rumor against a good doctor in the town where he lived. When the boy went to make amends, the doctor asked him to cut open a feather pillow and let the wind take the feathers away, then to come back the next day. When the boy returned, the doctor asked him to collect all the feathers and put them back in the pillowcase. Of course, it could never be done. Those feathers had been carried far, alighted in places where they couldn't be seen or found but stayed there just the same.

"But you didn't know him?"

"I just saw him around The Hollows. Like everyone."

Something about the way she said it made him look at her.

"Didn't you go to John Jay?" he asked.

"I did."

"Why did you come back home?"

She shook her head, still staring at the body. "I don't know. I missed my sister and her kids. The world out there, the city, it seemed so big. And I always felt small."

The wind picked up again, making the trees bend farther and whisper louder. The air smelled like rain suddenly, and Chuck felt a sinus headache coming on. This place was hell on his allergies.

Katie walked away and starting taking pictures as two more prowlers pulled into the lot, lights flashing but sirens quiet. He'd called some bodies in to help him secure the scene. He watched as they blocked off the entrance and exit to the rest stop.

Chuck pulled the phone from his pocket to call in an arrest warrant.

He looked at Katie, but she was immersed in her task, their conversation forgotten. The busy night ahead loomed large.

Leila hated her father's house. She'd gone there as little as her sense of duty and obligation would allow while he was alive. And even now, with her father dead, she couldn't muster any affection for the place. As she walked the rooms, which were exactly as her mother had arranged them all those years ago, she felt nothing but a tingling numbness, a persistent disbelief that it had all come to this. She waited for grief, anger, sorrow, all the things she should have been feeling at the violent passing of her father. But all she felt was the low rumble of nausea, a deep inner quiet.

She sank onto the stiff couch and found herself staring at the empty crystal candy dish that sat atop a dusty lace doily on the old mahogany coffee table. It had borne witness to every misery her father and brother could offer within the walls of this house. It had sat there, looking pretty, doing nothing. Just like her mother. Leila loved her mother, missed her every day. But God help her, the woman was weak, stood by and observed every abuse from the petty to the criminal. And still she got up before dawn to cook the old man's breakfast and see him off to work with a kiss and a smile.

Above and around her, Leila could hear the heavy footfalls of her husband and her sons. The old clock on top of the television set—a wooden monster standing on four legs that hadn't worked in years—read almost nine. She'd lost her energy to clean and organize, to find her father's important papers, some indication of his final wishes, and to make the arrangements she needed to make. It was getting late, too late to make any more calls; she couldn't stand to look in any more old boxes, to see any more old photos. More than anything else she hated those photographs, which her mother had painstakingly arranged in albums, labeled in her looping hand with little captions. Leila hated to see them, some combination of the four of them stiff and fake, smiling for whoever was holding the camera. Every time she looked at one of those pictures, all she could remember was what happened before or after. She and Travis in matching pajamas on Christmas morning, smiling, surrounded by gifts and a drift of torn wrapping paper—what were they? Maybe six and eight? Her mother's caption: "Our angels on Christmas morning!" Leila remembered her father sulking because he felt that her mother had spent too much on gifts. Then later, her father beat Travis because he'd broken a dish while helping to clear the table. She remembered her brother screaming, trying to run up the stairs away from her father, her father chasing and yelling. *You stupid little shit.*

Chief, please. It's Christmas, her mother said. Even she called him Chief. At some point, it had become his name. There were pictures of him young—in uniform, at their wedding. He was handsome once, strong and virile with broad shoulders and narrow hips. He had a wide forehead and a wide, long nose that somehow looked right on his face. But those eyes. Those ice water eyes, they were always small and narrowed, as though he saw through your skin and flesh to every bad and rotten thing that even you didn't know was there. She didn't know what it was like to be loved by her father, to be held and comforted, to be adored like they say little girls should be. He'd never once told her he loved her, never hugged or kissed her except in the most awkward way. She'd given up wanting or hoping for that long ago. But the knowledge that his life had passed the way it had, leaving her with only an empty space inside where he should have been, slumped her thin shoulders, drained her of energy. Still no tears, no sadness at all.

"You grieved years ago," her husband had said. "He's been dead all your life, honey." Mark was right. He was always right.

She saw her warped reflection in the picture tube, ran a hand through her dark hair, which had pulled away in strands from her ponytail. There was a smudge of dust under her right eye. She wiped it away.

"Mom?" It was Ryan. "You okay?"

He sat down heavily beside her, threw his feet onto the coffee table, making the candy dish rattle. She was about to scold him. But why? He could jump up and down on that table, reduce it to scrap, shatter that dish beneath his boots and what did she care? What did anyone care? It was all garbage. She wouldn't keep a thing.

She looked at her son. She remembered when he was a tiny bundle in her arms. Now when she reprimanded him, she had to look up at him. Sometimes when she needed to get tough, she tried to do it from halfway up the staircase, to give herself more height. *Ryan and Tim, clean up those rooms! You're a half hour past curfew! You're grounded!*

But they were good boys. They listened to her. She'd managed to keep them away from Travis and her father, kept them closer to Mark's family, where men treated their loved ones with affection and respect, not distance or violence. In marrying Mark, she'd broken the chain of misery and violence for her family. She was proud of that.

"Look what I found in the closet upstairs," said Ryan. He still had sun on his skin from his summer job as a swim teacher and lifeguard at a local sleepaway camp. On his lap was a varsity jacket, HOLLOWS HIGH LACROSSE.

"Your uncle's, I guess."

Ryan shook his head and flipped it over. The embroidered name on the front was JONES COOPER. It looked new, the white leather arms still shiny, the navy blue wool body still stiff and pristine.

"Hmm," she said. "That's strange. How did that get here?"

Ryan offered a shrug, his communication of choice. "I bet he wants it."

"I'll bet he does. Put it in the car. I'll bring it over to their house to-morrow."

As Ryan crashed off—what was it with those boys, why did their very existence create so much noise?—she thought guiltily of her last conversation with Maggie Cooper. Leila had hung up on a good doctor who was trying to help her nephew. She wondered if Maggie under-stood why she'd had to do that. She'd taken a big risk by reaching out to Marshall, by exposing the boys to a disaster Travis had created. She only did it because she knew they were all strong enough to help Marshall—as long as Travis was out of the picture.

Was she in some way responsible for what had happened—the ab-ducted girl, the murder of her father? Now her brother was missing, proba-bly still on the property somewhere. She walked onto the porch and heard the rotting wood groan; one of them could step right through some of those old boards if they weren't careful. She leaned against the railing and looked out into the thick stand of trees. The sky above was clear and riven with stars, the moon waning. It was a pretty watercolor night in a place where she'd never found beauty or love or comfort. And the sight of the black trees left her cold and angry. She'd have this place on the market as fast as she possibly could. They'd make a fortune on the land alone. And she'd use some of that money to help her nephew. She wouldn't leave him to the system. Lord knew Marshall's mother, Angie, wasn't going to be of much help.

Leila heard the calling of a barred owl, eight sad notes on the air. *Who mourns for you? Who mourns for you?* She thought about yelling Travis's name into the night. But she knew, even if he could hear her, he wouldn't come. There was no connection there, their sibling relationship strained and confused by their father's abuse, their mother's failures. They didn't know how to be family for each other; they'd never been taught. Angie, for all her many shortcomings, had called it years ago. *You two aren't even speaking the same language. The old man never hit you, never humiliated you. You might be brother and sister, but you didn't grow up with the pressure of being the chief's only son.*

In her pocket, Leila's cell phone started to vibrate, startling her. She pulled it from her jeans and looked at the screen: Hollows General Hospital. She answered quickly.

"Aunt Leila?" A young voice on the line, sounding faint and afraid.

"Marshall."

She was surprised by the wave of relief she felt at the sound of his voice. His voice always sounded sweet to her ears. Even now, with the knowledge of all that he had done and all that he had become as Travis's child, she could still remember when he was born. She could remember when they were all born—Marshall, Ryan, and Tim—how it was in their wide eyes and round cheeks that sweet innocence resided. Sometimes, especially when they slept, she could still see the light of childhood on Ryan's and Tim's resting faces. Her boys had been sheltered, adored, blessed with good looks and charming personalities. Because of this, they were younger than their years. They slept on their backs, arms slung wide open, faces slack and peaceful. Marshall slept curled up in a ball, a frown on his face, blankets wrapped around him like a protective cover.

"I'm so sorry," he said. He sounded dull, was probably heavily medicated. "I didn't mean any of it. I hurt my mom, Charlene. Even though I loved them, I still hurt them. It feels like a curse."

It is *a curse*, she thought. *Violence is a curse; it curdles the blood, damages the DNA. From father to son, to son, to son, stretching backward and forward until someone says, No more.*

"I know, Marshall. I understand." She was gripping the phone with both hands.

"He was *raping* her," he said. His voice cracked with emotion. He started a frantic ramble that Leila struggled to follow. "My *father*, even though he knew I loved her. I just started shooting. I couldn't believe how loud it was. And I was so angry, so afraid. I never would have hurt her. I just wanted someone to talk to. I thought she'd understand. She's a poet. And then I was firing that gun that I got from my mother's house."

He paused and took a shuddering breath. "I wanted to kill my father, Aunt Leila. I thought if he was gone, I'd stop hearing his voice in my head. But instead I killed Grandpa. I didn't mean it."

"Oh, God, Marshall." Finally then, the tears came. A great river of them that flowed from a time before she was even born. And the tears washed in a red tide of anger and grief so powerful it almost took her away.

"I know I've done bad things, Aunt Leila. But I don't think I'm a bad person. I mean, I think I can do better. Dr. Cooper says that we're more than what we do. That there's more to us than our mistakes. Do you believe that?"

She took in a sharp inhale. She wasn't sure she'd ever heard him say so much. He was a reticent boy, seemed to struggle to put words together so that it was almost painful to talk with him. You wanted to help him finish his sentences.

"I do believe that, Marshall. I do."

"I know I don't have a right to ask you. But can you help me, Aunt Leila?"

Part of her didn't want to. Part of her wanted to end the call and shut him out—him, her brother, her father, all these damaged men who left so much wreckage in their paths. This part of her knew that the best thing was to get as far away, as fast as possible. Just hearing him now, she understood for the first time how sick, how unstable, he was. She didn't know if the damage could be undone, or even managed. But another part of her, the mother in her, the part of her that wanted to believe that with enough love anyone and anything could change, held on tight.

"I will, Marshall. I will help you. I'll do anything I can."

Once upon a time, he'd loved his mother. He *remembered* loving her, thinking she was the prettiest woman in the world. He loved the smell of her perfume, the sound of her voice, the feel of her hand on his forehead when he was sick. And that love had never died, exactly. It had just been buried, smothered under layers of resentment and anger, shame and emotional exhaustion. But when he thought of Abigail now, all he could feel was a flat, stubborn apathy. Even the negative feelings he'd had for Abigail had long ago burned themselves out. In life, she had been a black hole of need; she'd sucked so much of him into her void that when she died, huge parts of who he might have been went with her—the part of him that knew how to love a child well, the part of him that could bear the peaceful day-to-day of a life lived outside the hurricane of Abigail's ceaseless health crises and emotional dramas, the part of him that could stand the intimacy of a real relationship.

He watched Matty Bauer being lifted onto the gurney from the collapsed hole in the ground. It was only about twenty feet down, but the light above looked far, far away. He shouldn't even be down here. The other men had protested his decision; he was barely well enough to be back to work. But he had to go. If that hole was going to cave in on anyone, it was going to cave in on him. Buried alive. He was that already.

With Travis and Melody in jail, and Maggie and Elizabeth finally knowing the full truth of what happened to Sarah that night, Jones felt as though the sky above him was filled with enormous thunderheads, waiting for the slightest drop in pressure to fill his world with light and sound and sheets of rain. But there was only silence. They all held it close, he, Melody, and Travis. They wouldn't, couldn't, release their grip on the secrets they'd carried for so long. He suspected that none of them even knew how. The ugly truth of that night had woven itself into their individual self-narratives; none of them even knew who they were without it.

"You must confront and release this, Jones," Maggie had said to him when he confessed to her. "You cannot carry it with you any longer. How you face it, what you need to do, is up to you. I support you."

"You want me to tell someone the truth. Admit to the authorities what happened that night."

She hadn't answered right away. She'd looked small and sad sitting in the chair beside his bed. Even he didn't know what the consequences would be, what he would have to answer for now, a lifetime later. It would be up to politicians and lawyers to decide who paid now for what. Sarah Meyer, Tommy Delano, Chief Crosby—even Sarah's parents— were all dead and gone. Whom did it serve to dredge up the dead? Was it right to resurrect a horror just to ease his guilty conscience through confession and whatever punishment might be doled out? He would at least have to step down from his job, wouldn't he?

He was guilty of cowardice, of inaction, of allowing an innocent man to be convicted of murder. But Tommy Delano was not an innocent man; he was innocent of murder but guilty of different things. He'd said himself in his letter to Eloise Montgomery that it was only a matter of time before he would fail to control his appetites. Maybe, in a sense, their silence had saved the lives of other girls. But, no, that was a wishful rationalization. They'd done wrong, pure and simple.

"I don't know what I think you should do," she'd said finally.

She'd pulled her knees up to her chest and hugged her legs, looked at him with wide eyes. There was something about her expression, like she was preparing herself to say good-bye.

"We're coming for you, Detective. Hang in there."

The voice above him brought him back to the moment.

"How's Matty?" he called up. His words seemed to bounce and spi-

ral. Every so often, small bits of dirt broke off from a ridge and rained
down on him.

"He's okay." Jones wasn't sure who was calling down to him. "He's
with his mama, on the way to the hospital."

"Good. That's good."

It was cold and quiet down at the bottom of the hole. Jones found
his mind clear here; he could think clearly for the first time in years.
There was no place to hide in the quiet solitude, a place he'd avoided at
all costs through the years. He always had the television or the radio on,
a newspaper or a book in his hand, a glass of wine or beer on the table
before him. He'd made a life out of avoiding himself, partaking of any
and all of the daily distractions offered in a busy-addicted world. But he
knew. He knew himself, knew what he was, knew what he was going to
do. Had there ever been any question?

He'd toyed with all the options before him. When Leila Crosby (no,
not Crosby; her married name was Leila *Lane*. Why could he never remember that?) had brought by the jacket she'd found while cleaning out
her father's place, he'd felt as though it had all come full circle. He saw
that the jacket was as clean as the day he'd received it, not bloodied and
covered with dirt, as he'd imagined all those years. The chief had lied.
But it might as well have been soaked in gore; the sight of it made him
sick, made him want to weep and scream in pain. He could barely keep
himself together in front of Leila.

"What in the world was it doing there, Jones?"

"I have no idea. Maybe Travis took it? I lost a jacket in my senior
year. Did my mom ever go ballistic, having to fork over another hundred
and fifty dollars." Lies came so easily to him; they always had.

He'd taken that jacket and shoved it in the bag still in Elizabeth's
attic, and then put the whole mess into the trunk of his car.

The rain was coming down harder, lightning strikes following one after
the other, the thunder so constant it sounded like a freight train. It was
gone, the bundle he'd been carrying around for a hundred years. It was
down in the hole, covered with dirt, buried finally. He hadn't thought

ahead. He didn't know how he'd explain to Maggie what he'd decided to do, didn't know what her reaction would be to his cowardice. He figured she'd leave him. Not right away. She'd fight the good fight, try to reconcile his actions with her love for him. They'd go to counseling, fight and cry together. But, in the end, she'd leave him. It was just as well. He didn't deserve her. He never had.

He turned to walk away from the hole and saw a slim, hooded form moving toward him. He looked around for another vehicle, but he didn't see one, not that he could see much in the rain, with the lights from his truck casting everything beyond their beams into pitch-blackness. He rested his hand on his gun as the form drew nearer. It wasn't until he was two feet away that Jones realized it was his son.

Ricky pulled back his hood. The rain had made his hair flat, washed some of the goop from it. It hung limp around his face. Jones thought Ricky looked just like he had when Jones used to lift him naked from the bath. Jones would dry his hair with a towel and kiss his face and belly and say, *I love you so much, Ricky.* And Ricky would throw his arms around Jones's neck and say, *I love you so much, too, Daddy.* It was so easy to love each other then, when he was small. Jones could so easily manage all of Ricky's needs then, help him with the simple things, like falling asleep alone and learning to pee standing up, comfort him through nightmares. He could chase his son around the house and play hide-and-seek for hours, things even Maggie didn't always have the time or patience to do. He didn't remember when that ease had left their relationship, when the stakes had suddenly seemed so high that he was afraid to appear soft, to let things slide.

"Dad, what are you doing?"

He didn't know how to answer his son, so he just shook his head.

"I know everything," Ricky said. He wiped some of the rain from his face and pulled his hood back up. A bolt of lightning lit the sky; the thunderclap that followed was weaker than the last. The rain was letting up.

"About what?" Jones couldn't believe Maggie would tell him. She wouldn't. Neither would Elizabeth. It wasn't Ricky's problem, his burden.

"Melody told Charlene about the accident," Ricky said. "She told Charlene about how that girl Sarah died, and how you all kept quiet."

Jones wanted to deny it, to push past his son and run away. But he couldn't, not anymore. There was nowhere else to go, nowhere else to run. Instead he covered his eyes. How could he look into his own child's face with such a stain on his heart?

"Dad, it wasn't your fault."

He felt his son's hand on his arm, was surprised by how big and strong it felt. He remembered when he could hold Ricky in his open palms, a tiny bundle that barely weighed ten pounds.

"It was," Jones said, looking at the boy now. He'd spent so much time trying to teach Ricky to take responsibility for himself and his actions. He had to do the same. "In so many ways it was more my fault than anyone's. I was driving. I let Travis talk her into my car." Jones had to stop for a second, his throat closing around the words. But then he went on.

"She didn't want to go with us that night. But I let him push her into it. Later, I told her what Travis had said. It made her so angry. I was the lynchpin. If I had changed anything I'd done that night, she'd still be alive."

"Dad." Ricky lifted a hand to stop him, but Jones couldn't keep the words from coming now.

"Then, after she fell, I drove us away from there. Melody and I, we left her in the park. I could have gone back for her. I *tried* to go back. But she was gone."

Ricky put both his hands on Jones's shoulders. "Dad, listen. Whatever you did, you didn't kill that girl. It was an accident."

"It's not that simple. I . . ."

"Please listen, Dad," Ricky said. "Later, after you'd gone, Charlene's mom told her that Tommy Delano took Sarah's body. He'd been following her. He was the one who did those things to her."

Jones stared at his son, who was level and calm. Jones had never discussed this with anyone except Maggie; he could barely believe that somehow Ricky knew more than he did about the night that changed his life.

"No," Jones said. "It was Travis and Chief Crosby who took her. They moved her body and they framed Tommy Delano. And still I kept quiet."

"No, Dad. Charlene's mom said that when the chief and Travis went back, they saw Tommy Delano putting her in his car. They let him take her."

The rainfall had tapered to a drizzle. But they were both soaked to the skin. Jones could hear the thunder rumbling, moving farther away. He'd never allowed himself to dwell on what happened to Sarah, on whether Travis was capable of doing those things to her. He'd never wanted to know the ugly answers to the questions he had never dared to ask. He told his son as much.

"Dad, it was an awful thing, a terrible thing, that happened. But it wasn't your fault. You didn't kill her. You didn't violate her dead body. You made mistakes. Okay. But you have to stop punishing yourself now. It's time."

Jones almost couldn't stand to hear the words. Would he be so understanding, so forgiving, with his son? He knew that he wouldn't.

"I should have said something," Jones said. His voice sounded as faint and powerless as regret itself. "At least I should have done that."

Ricky dropped his hands from Jones's shoulders, dug them deep into his pockets. "Maybe you were scared," Ricky said. "Maybe you didn't have anyone to help you be strong, Dad. You were just a kid, younger than I am now."

Jones looked at the wet ground. Was it so easy for Ricky to forgive him? He didn't have any words for the son who was already twice the man Jones had ever been.

"Do you remember when I stole that CD from Sound Design?" Ricky asked. "I was like, twelve. It fell out of my jacket when I got into the car, and you knew I didn't have any money. You made me take it back. Remember? You told me I'd never enjoy a moment of listening to it, knowing that I'd stolen it."

Jones *did* remember. He remembered the shock of seeing the CD, the wave of disappointment he felt. But most of all he remembered the fear. He was so afraid that he'd failed his son somehow, that he'd passed along some defect of character that had allowed Ricky to steal something he wanted rather than ask for it or work for it. He didn't remember the words he'd used with his son, but he knew they'd been hard, even cruel. He remembered the stricken look on Ricky's face. He'd never forgotten it.

"So I had to go in alone, give the CD back and apologize. I hated you for that then. I thought it was stupid and mean because no one would have ever known better. And, you know what? I *would* have enjoyed that CD, every last track. But I understand now that you were right. Of course you were. But maybe you didn't have anyone to help you stand up and own up. If you hadn't forced me to take back that CD, I wouldn't have. Not ever. And maybe I would have stolen again, and again, until I got caught. And maybe then I'd have paid a higher price than just a little embarrassment."

When did his kid get so smart? Jones wondered. He reached out to touch Ricky's face, felt his smooth cheek. Jones let his hand drop to Ricky's shoulder and gave it a squeeze. He wanted to pull his son into his arms and hold him close, kiss his head. Why was it so hard? With something like effort, he took the boy in a tight embrace. He held on for a second, but then he had to pull back, feeling awkward and uncomfortable.

"It's too late for me, Ricky. And I don't feel like I deserve your kindness right now."

Ricky stared at his father with wide eyes. "You saved her."

"Who?"

"Charlene. She said you came on that boat and carried her off. She said she'd never been so happy to see anyone, that when she saw you, she knew she was finally safe. You helped that kid out of the well, even though you're still hurt."

"It's my job. That's what I do."

"Yeah, but not everybody could do that job. Mom's right. She said you care about people, you help people, that's who you are."

Jones didn't know what to say to the kid, so he just stood there, studying his face. Ricky looked so much like Maggie, fine-featured with big, intelligent eyes. Maggie was right about a lot of things, like how he hadn't really looked at his son in years, could only see the things that angered him. He could see now that Ricky possessed all his mother's wisdom and kindness, her desire to fix and save.

"How did you find me?" Jones said.

"We followed you to Grandma's house, then here. We weren't sure what you were going to do. But we wanted to be with you when you did it. We tried to call you a couple of times. But you didn't answer."

Ricky turned and pointed to the SUV that had pulled up behind Jones's vehicle. Jones hadn't seen it at first through the driving rain. Maggie stepped out of the car, looked up at the clearing sky.

"Mom didn't tell me anything," Ricky said. "I came to her with the things Charlene said. We wanted you to know, thought it would help you come to terms with things. We wanted you to hear it from us."

As the rain stopped completely, Jones felt a coalescence, a melding of the facets of his life. Everything that he was—a husband and father, a deeply flawed man—and everything that he had been—a high school football star, his mother's angry son, a frightened boy without the strength to do what was right—merged there before his wife and son. And for the first time in as long as he could remember, he was not afraid.

It was only his second day as a full-time writer and Charlie was already sure he had made a mistake. Wanda had helped him fix up his apartment, clean and organize, so that the second bedroom could become his office. She'd helped him buy a desk and pick out a new computer.

"You're still young, Charlie. You have some money saved. Stop wasting your time killing rodents and give this a chance. Finish your novel and try to sell it. What have you got to lose? It's not like you're on a career fast track."

"I don't know, Wanda."

"You'll regret it if you don't. It's one thing to try and fail. It's another thing to never try at all. That's the stuff that eats you alive."

What was it about that woman? Everything she said sounded like gospel to him. But now that he was alone with the blank page, the glowingly empty screen of his brand-new computer, the silence of his apartment, he felt desperate, inadequate in the extreme. He wasn't a writer. It was just a fantasy he had about himself. On reading the novel he'd been writing for the better part of ten years, he couldn't believe how terrible it was. How could he have ever thought he was any good? He called his mother.

"So how's the writing life?" she asked.

"Miserable."

She gave an indulgent chuckle. "Oh, my tortured artist."

"Maybe they'll give me my job back."

"Day two and already you're hanging it up?" She made a tsking sound with her tongue.

"Mom?"

"What is it, honey?"

"What do you remember about her?"

There was a pause on the line, and then he heard her release a breath.

"Lily? It was a long time ago. I guess I remember that she always looked so sad. She was a tiny thing, so delicate, with such a soft voice. But that sadness inside her, it was angry, powerful."

He had forgotten what she looked like, in a strange way. Her essence was still with him—he could smell the scent of her skin, remember the way she said his name. But in the few pictures he had of her, she didn't look like he remembered her. In the pictures, she looked like any suburban girl with a cheap haircut and a knit sweater, just a kid. In his mind, she was a luminous beauty who stopped his heart with only a certain kind of look she had.

"Did you ever doubt me? Did you ever think I could have hurt her?"

"Never. Not for a minute. I know my boy. Your love is good and sweet, Charlie. You don't have an unkind bone in your body."

"Thanks, Mom."

"Is that what you're writing about?"

He flopped down on his bed and laid his head on top of one of the new pillows Wanda had picked out. It was a silvery gray with thin embroidered stripes, an accent to the navy comforter and matching drapes. She'd made him take all his old books from their boxes and stack them on shelves and in artful piles around the apartment. *A writer's home should be full of books. For inspiration.*

"In a way, I am. But all that stuff that happened here, that girl who was abducted, the one I saw on the street? That has kind of captured my imagination, too."

"Another missing girl. I see a theme."

He told her about the rest of the story, how Charlene's mother, and the father of the boy who'd abducted Charlene as well as a Hollows detective, had confessed to events that had led to the accidental death of a girl back in the late eighties. How another man had been convicted of her murder and then committed suicide in prison.

"What led them to confess, so many years later? That poor girl's parents. How awful to have it resurrected like that."

"I think everyone associated with the victim is dead."

"That's terrible."

In the background, Charlie could hear the sound of the television. He could visualize his mother in the kitchen, still living in the house where he grew up. There would be a paperback novel spine up on the kitchen table, a half-finished cup of coffee beside that. Everything would be neat, in its place, the kitchen sink wiped clean, pot holders clean and hanging on little plastic hooks by the stove. In her retirement, his mother was a much better housekeeper than she'd once been.

"Where's Dad?" As if he had to ask.

"Playing golf with Frank." He wondered how she stood it. If Charlie's father had ever paid half as much attention to them as he had that stupid game . . . Well, Charlie didn't know what. He hadn't. And that was that.

"Did you tell him that I quit my job to finish my novel?" He hated the way he felt a kind of inner cowering, a dread at his father's disapproval, even though when it came to the old man he knew little else.

"No, Charlie. Of course not. Anyway, it wouldn't kill you to call when you knew he was here. You *could* make an effort."

"What would we talk about? I don't play golf."

She let a moment pass; he heard her filing her nails. "You know, once upon a time your father used to write. Poetry. Short stories. He was pretty good. Over the years, he just sort of stopped."

Now, that was new information. "Really? Wow."

"You should ask him about it sometime."

"Maybe I will." Then, "I better get back to the writing."

"I love you."

"Me, too."

He hung up the phone but didn't rise from the bed. The sun was streaming in through the opening between the drapes, and he heard the voices and intermittent hammer bursts of the workers remodeling the old house across the street. Outside his window, he knew the air had grown cold and the branches of the trees were a line drawing against the sky. While he was lying there, he thought about Lily and how childish was the love he had for her, compared with what he was just starting to feel for Wanda. He thought about Charlene Murray, and wished for the hundredth time that he'd just called out to her that night; he might have saved her from a world of pain—or maybe not. He thought about the story he'd been following on the local news—another lost girl, killed years ago, the truth of her death finally revealed, far too late to do anyone any good. There was something there—a story. He could sense how all those individual souls were connected by the gossamer strands of love and history, secrets and regrets. He could sense the mingling of the past and the present, how one couldn't exist without the other. He wanted to find his way there, to a place where he could understand it all, make sense of those connections that were too fragile to be easily defined. He knew of only one way. He got up from his bed, sat down at his computer, and started to write.

31

There were no news vans when Jones pulled into the driveway. It was the first time in days that there hadn't been at least one reporter hoping for a statement, an ugly candid, maybe flinging insults to get a rise. It didn't bother him as much as he would have predicted. He'd ignored them mostly, offering not even a glance in their general direction. As he put Maggie's SUV in park and killed the engine, he thought that they'd missed out on a good day to be there, with the contents of his office in three boxes in the backseat. He hadn't been fired from his job; he'd offered his resignation, which had been reluctantly accepted by the Hollows PD chief, Marion Butler, a woman he'd come up with from the academy.

"I don't think this incident requires your resignation, Jones," she'd said. She'd looked down at the blotter on her desk when she said it. She had eyes that could freeze you dead, and when she'd turned them back on him, he saw her sadness.

"We both know it does," he'd said.

She'd run a thin hand through silver-gray curls. She'd been gray since the day he met her.

"The incident was an accident," she'd said. She had sat down behind her desk and picked up the letter he'd handed her. "And you were just a kid. You know it's likely that charges won't be filed."

He knew all this, and he was grateful that she still believed in him. But it didn't matter.

"I was in a position of trust. And I kept a horrible secret from this town."

She'd given a careful nod and pointed to the chair in front of her desk. He'd sat. Outside her glass-walled office, the floor had been quiet, as if everyone had frozen in their cubicles to listen to their conversation.

"You were vested in your pension last year." Her tone had taken on the practical edge he so admired in her. Marion Butler was a straight line, no artifice, no veil.

"That's a good thing. And, you know, maybe it's time for a fresh start."

"Are you sure about this? I'll fight for your job, if it comes to that. So many years of faithful service to this town counts for a lot, you know."

But, no. He *was* sure. In fact, he was sure that he should have quit years ago. He'd wanted to many times; the reasons he hadn't were myriad. Now the future lay before him, an unwritten page.

He grabbed one of the boxes from the backseat and walked inside. He found Charlene sitting at the kitchen table, drinking a cup of coffee and reading *People* in her pajamas, like she lived there. Which, annoyingly, she did—for the time being.

"Hi, Mr. Cooper," she said. She looked up from her magazine, seemed to register the expression on his face. "How did it go?"

"How do you think it went, Charlene?" he said.

"Um . . . bad?"

He poured a cup of coffee from the pot and came to sit across from her.

"How are your college applications coming?"

"Just taking a little break."

With Melody awaiting charges in the death of her husband, Charlene had needed a place to stay. When Ricky and Maggie had approached him with the request to board her until Melody was released or, in the worst case, until Charlene went to school in September, he'd surprised himself by agreeing.

They were connected, all of them, weren't they? The night that Sarah had died, and during everything that had followed, the separate passages of their lives had conjoined in ways none of them could have predicted, or even imagined. It had set even their unborn children on a collision course with each other. He felt like he owed it to all of them to take Charlene in, to right some of the things that had been wrong for so long.

Charlene had decent grades, respectable SAT scores, and a desire to get away from The Hollows for good. She'd finally figured out that an education was the way to do that. There was money left by Charlene's father and the sale of Melody's childhood home, which Melody had invested wisely in a trust for her daughter. The conditions of the trust were that the money was available to her only for school and after she had completed her degree, not to traipse around New York City trying to get a record deal. Jones felt a bit guilty for being glad that she had already decided to look at schools in New York City—Fordham, Hunter, and, in a long shot, NYU. Ricky would be going to Georgetown alone.

Ricky and Charlene both claimed that there was nothing more to their relationship now than friendship. But Jones saw the way his son still looked at Charlene. She was a pit of need into which Jones hoped fiercely that his son wouldn't fall.

"How's your mom doing?"

A little bit of the wild sadness he'd been seeing in Charlene's face since the night he lifted her off the boat was fading. But mostly when he looked at her, he just saw this lost, small thing. And in a way he felt responsible for that.

"She's okay. It *was* self-defense, you know. I saw him go for her, and she swung to defend herself." She looked down at the magazine. "She didn't mean to kill him. Her lawyer thinks the prosecution will be amenable to a deal, because, you know, of the things he did to me. Mitigating circumstances or whatever."

Jones didn't know what to say to this girl. So many awful things had happened to her, so many people had hurt and used her. He wanted to put a comforting hand on her, but he hesitated to touch her. She seemed skittish and delicate.

"I better get back to the computer," said Charlene. "I'm going to school on Monday, and I want to have everything done by then."

"Sounds like a plan, kid."

"Hey, Mr. Cooper? Thanks for asking." She didn't wait around for
him to answer.

He nodded to himself, looked out into the backyard. The pool had
been covered for the winter that had closed in on them, and the maple
trees had shed their leaves. He *really* had to get out there and clean up.
Of course, now there was plenty of time.

No sooner had he settled into a silent zone of peace, preparing to
contemplate his future, than he heard the *shuffle-shuffle-thump* that
heralded the approach of his mother-in-law, another unwanted semi-
permanent guest.

"Stripped of his badge and his gun, the retired cop has to contemplate what lies ahead," she said, putting a pot on the stove.

"Hello, Elizabeth."

They'd fought out the worst of it. But her recriminations and his
were on the table, ready to leap up at any given moment. The truth of it
was that they were both guilty of keeping quiet when they should have
been raising alarms. *The only reason you're both so angry at each other is because you're guilty of the same failure to act. Forgive yourselves and maybe
you'll be able to forgive each other.* Elizabeth didn't like to be "shrinked"
any more than he did, so when Maggie was around, they both put on
happy faces. But Maggie was in session.

"So when do you think you'll be leaving?"

"Not soon enough, Detective. Oh, that's right. It's just Jones now.
Mr. Cooper."

She came to sit across from him, *shuffle-shuffle-thump.* She looked
frail and tired; she didn't have the same vigor since her last accident. Her
weakened state did take a little of the fun out of fighting with her.

"What's it going to take to bury the hatchet, Elizabeth?"

She leaned back in her chair and looked at him. "I just can't get over
that those things were in my attic. That you hid them there."

Jones, on Maggie's insistence, was seeing a therapist a few towns
away. He drove there weekly with a brew of dread and resentment in
his belly, returning exhausted in a way he'd never experienced before.
He'd grab a big cup of coffee at a drive-through Starbucks, blast some
classic rock like Led Zeppelin or Van Morrison to try to shake off that

bone-deep fatigue. But it lived in him for at least a day after each session, lashing him to the couch. His therapist was a man about his age, a soft-spoken guy with a thick head of ink black hair, always in crisply pressed chinos and a colorful shirt. Dr. Black. They talked a lot about the items Jones had kept, why he'd kept them, what they meant, why he'd chosen Elizabeth's attic to hide them in recent years.

"I know," he said. "I'm sorry. It was a violation of our trust. It felt like a safe place to hide that part of myself."

She looked down at her hands, twisted the gold wedding band on the finger of her left hand.

"A few days after I went to see Tommy Delano in prison, I went to see the chief," she said. "He was such a weasel, that man. Not a kind or compassionate thought ever entered his tiny, little mind."

She hadn't told him this before. He took a sip of his coffee, waited for her to go on. But she didn't.

"What did he tell you?" he asked, finally. He looked out at the backyard, a view he'd gazed upon for almost twenty years. But everything out there—the covered pool, the patio furniture, the ivy-covered pergola—looked different, brighter somehow, more solid.

"He told me something I've never told anyone. It was part of the reason that psychic had such an impact on me."

"I'm listening." And he was; he felt the palms of his hands start to tingle.

"They found other pictures in his room—yearbook pictures, some snapshots—of other girls at the school. One of those girls was Maggie."

Jones let the information sink in, taking in a deep breath and letting it out slowly, trying not to imagine Tommy Delano with a picture of a young and innocent Maggie in his grease-stained hands.

"I was wrong about Tommy Delano," Elizabeth said. "And the chief? He didn't lie. What he said Tommy Delano had done, he'd done. He probably would have done worse to another girl somewhere down the line. Maybe . . ." She let the thought go unfinished.

"'I was wrong,'" he said, as if testing the words on the air. He had the urge to make light, to not focus on the horror of what she was saying. "I don't think I've ever heard you utter that statement."

She gave him a wan smile. "I've never had to."

"Hmm," he said. He offered a deferential nod.

"After I saw the chief, I was angry and unsatisfied—and frightened. Still not convinced I had the whole story from Crosby—which, of course, I didn't. So I went to see that woman, that psychic, Eloise Montgomery. I went there to blast her, to force her to tell me that she was a fraud."

They hadn't talked like this before, not really. The words they'd exchanged over the last couple of weeks had been loud and angry, designed to deflect blame and hurt each other. But sitting with her now, Jones found that Maggie was right, as usual. He wasn't mad at Elizabeth. She'd acted out of fear, just as he had.

"But there in her kitchen, she made me a cup of tea and told me what she saw. And I believed her. Something about her voice, her eyes, filled me with horror and awe. I'll never forget what she said. She told me, 'If you don't stop asking questions, if you don't let this rest, you'll lose your daughter.' I can't describe the way her words made me feel. They cut me to the bone."

He reached for her hand, and she didn't pull away. Her skin was soft and papery in his grasp. "I asked her what she meant, and she said she didn't know. But, of course, I just kept seeing Sarah lying there, stiff and unnatural, those horrible gashes filled with putty. Thinking of Maggie's pictures in his room. And the thought of losing my daughter like that was enough to bind and gag me for good."

A single tear trailed down her face, and she withdrew her hand from his to remove a tissue from her pocket and angrily dab her cheek dry.

"But now I think that maybe it was about you," Elizabeth went on. That maybe she meant you wouldn't be here to bring her back to The Hollows. It would have changed your life if the truth had been revealed about that night. Maybe for the better. Maybe you would have left this place. But I don't know."

"We *don't* know," he said. "And it doesn't matter. All that matters is how things are right now."

"My husband used to say, 'The past is history. The future is a mystery. The present is a gift.'"

"He was a wise man."

"I miss him every day."

"I know you do."

She reached out to touch his face. "You always were a good boy, Jones Cooper."

He didn't know if his mother-in-law was being sarcastic or not, but he supposed it didn't much matter.

Maggie slipped back through the door that led to her office and closed it quietly. She'd been headed to the kitchen to see if Jones was back from picking up his things, and overheard him talking to her mother. She decided to give them some space to finish their conversation.

She'd stayed out of sight and eavesdropped like a kid. She was feeling bad about it when she looked up to the top landing to see Ricky and Charlene listening, too. They all exchanged guilty glances, but none of them moved. Maggie and Ricky locked eyes as Elizabeth told Jones what she'd been keeping to herself for decades.

Now she sank into the leather chair behind her desk and looked at the flock of unopened e-mail messages on her screen—Angie Crosby checking on Marshall's progress; Henry Ivy wanting to get coffee; a referral from a friend who practiced in the next town. But she found she couldn't really focus. Her mother's conversation with Jones had triggered a flash flood of memory. And suddenly, she was remembering the thing that had been nagging at her since the night Charlene disappeared. The thing she couldn't quite remember.

A few days before Sarah disappeared, Maggie had stayed late after school to work on the yearbook. A senior girl on the project, Crystal James, someone her mother approved of, was supposed to give her a ride home. But as Maggie waited by the entrance to the building, the dusk deepened and Crystal was nowhere to be seen. Maggie walked around the back of the school to the parking lot, wondering if Crystal was waiting for her there. She came around the building to hear raised voices. Some boys had gathered around the bus yard where Tommy Delano was working.

She'd seen it too many times. It angered her, and she walked over to the group. Even now she couldn't remember who it was—maybe Dennis and Larry, possibly Greg.

"Stop it, you guys. Just cut it out." Her voice sounded weak and insubstantial, not at all strong and commanding like her mother's voice.

The boys turned, ready to fling insults in her direction by the looks on their faces. But when they saw it was her, they all went quiet. There were some benefits to being the principal's daughter.

"We're just playing around, Maggie."

"It's not funny," she said. She felt embarrassed suddenly, with so many eyes on her. "Go home."

She remembered the look on Tommy Delano's face, a kind of sheepish gratitude, and something else. After the boys had walked off, she stood awkwardly, looking into the distance for Crystal's car, a yellow Volkswagen Bug.

"Thanks," he said. "Thanks a lot. You're a really nice girl. A lot like your mom."

She bristled a little at that but knew he meant it as a compliment. "They shouldn't hassle you," she said. "It's not cool."

"I'm used to it."

She turned to look at him, and something about the expression on his face made her back away. There was something needy and strange about his energy, and she felt uncomfortable being alone with him, even though a chain-link fence stood between them.

"What are you doing here so late?" he asked, moving closer to the fence.

"I'm waiting for Crystal."

"I saw her leave a while ago," he said, lacing his fingers into the fence. "Maybe she forgot she was supposed to give you a ride?"

Maggie felt her heart start to thump, for no reason she could name.

"I could give you a lift home, Maggie. I'm just finishing up here." His tone was sweet and mild, but every nerve ending in her body started to tingle.

"I'll just call my mom."

He gave a nonchalant shrug that didn't come off. "Your mom used to drive me home all the time when I went to school."

"She did?"

Maggie relaxed a little then. If her mom liked Tommy Delano, he was probably okay. She couldn't remember ever hearing her talk about him.

"Hey, Maggie."

She looked over to see Travis Crosby in his beat-up old Dodge that was always breaking down.

"I just passed Crystal on Old Farmers Road." He had his arm out the window. "Her car is dead. She was worried sick that you were standing here in the dark. She wanted me to drive you home."

She didn't even think about it for a second, started jogging toward his car.

"Thanks anyway, Tommy," she called behind her.

She wasn't allowed to ride in cars with boys, and her mother did *not* approve of Travis Crosby. She'd get in trouble if Elizabeth found out.

"Don't worry," Travis said as she got in the car. "I won't tell your mom."

"Thanks," she said, surprised at her breathless relief to be away from Tommy.

"You shouldn't be talking to that guy. He's a weirdo, you know. He killed his mother."

"That's just a rumor," she said, looking back. Tommy was still leaning on the fence looking after her.

"No," said Travis. "It's true. My dad told me. He pushed her down the stairs and sat on the top step to watch her die."

Maggie felt a shudder move through her. Travis reached over and cranked the heat. "It's still cold," he said. "It doesn't feel like spring."

"No," she said. "It doesn't."

Then, "Thanks for the ride, Travis."

"No problem. Crystal is hot; maybe she'll like me now." He gave her a goofy smile, and she laughed. She remembered the smell of his cologne; Polo was what all the jocks wore then. She remembered the song on the radio, "Angel in Blue" by the J. Geils Band. There was a can of Pepsi wedged in between the seats; she could hear the liquid swishing around as the car moved.

"You're a dog, Travis."

"Bow, wow, wow," he said.

They chatted all the way home, and she forgot that moment with Tommy Delano. Even in the days and weeks that followed, she didn't think about that conversation with him again. It was buried deep, not available for examination until now. What would have happened to her if she had taken that ride home? Or if he hadn't been in prison a few weeks later and died there? Tommy Delano had written to Eloise that he couldn't have kept his appetites at bay much longer. How long would he have served for mutilating and violating the dead body of a girl if the whole truth of that night had been revealed? Would he have been out roaming The Hollows again while she still lived there?

As Travis pulled into her drive, the bottom of the car ground against the steep incline where the paved surface met the road. There was the unpleasant sound of metal on concrete, and then the car sputtered and died. Maggie and Travis exchanged a look.

"Shit," he said.

They both looked toward the house to see Elizabeth standing in the doorway and then stepping onto the porch. Travis tried to start the car, but there was only a sad coughing noise. Elizabeth approached, arms folded around her middle, a scowl on her face.

"You're dead," said Travis. "Sorry."

Maggie got out of the car, and Travis rolled down the window, both of them talking over each other to explain.

"Into the house, Maggie."

"But, Mom—"

"Now, please."

"Crystal's car broke down," she said. Maggie remembered that rush of angry frustration. It was something she still often felt with her mother, at Elizabeth's unwillingness to listen, at her occasional arrogance.

"You don't know how to use a phone?" Elizabeth asked. A question that didn't require an answer. "Now, go. I'll deal with you in a minute."

There was no way to explain the energy of that moment with Tommy Delano, how she would have gotten into anyone's car just to be away from him. She tried to explain to her later, but Elizabeth wasn't listening, as usual, thought Maggie was just making excuses for breaking the rules. Her punishment was no television for a week.

"I expect more from you, Maggie."

Now, as she sat in her office, all those feelings crashed over her, one wave after another, as though days, not decades, had passed. The implications were enormous, but at the same time almost too nebulous to contemplate. Maggie had always suffered through worry. Even as a kid, she'd fret about exams and projects, this or that drama at school. She'd turn problems—hers and others'—over and over in her mind. As an adult she was prone to a random dark dread, the occasional but powerful feeling of foreboding. It would wake her up at night sometimes, keep her wandering the house in the wee hours. She remembered her father's advice as clearly as Elizabeth did, how he'd sit beside her on the bed and put his hand on her forehead, gently admonishing against worry.

But she knew that it was impossible to live a life that way. It was all woven together in one great tapestry—the past, the present, the future—colors and textures mingling and entwined. It was nearly impossible to extract the present moment from what came before it, from what might lie ahead. She knew this from her patients. She knew it in her own heart.

What if Travis's car hadn't broken down that night after hitting the steep incline in her drive? Maybe then he wouldn't have needed a ride from Jones; they wouldn't have been together that night, and Jones, by his own account, would have driven by Sarah without a second glance. Sarah might have returned home unharmed. And Tommy Delano would have still been wandering free in The Hollows, struggling and probably eventually failing to keep those terrible appetites at bay. She struggled to make meaning of it all. But like all what-ifs, it had no real answer, nothing solid to hold on to. Just imaginings, fantasies that slipped through her fingers like sand.

"Mags?" Her husband's voice broke her from her thoughts. She saw, with surprise, that he was standing in the doorway. She didn't remember ever seeing him enter her office. It was strange to have him there, and oddly thrilling.

"You okay?" he asked, stepping over the threshold. "You look pale."

"Yes," she said. She stood and went to him, let him take her in his strong embrace.

"How was it?" she asked. "Your last shift?"

"You know what? It was good. I feel . . . pretty good, considering." Then, "What were you thinking about just now?"

"Jones, I overheard your conversation with my mother."

He pulled back to look at her. "I'm sorry. It's disturbing, I know."

"I just remembered something. Something from so long ago."

She moved over to the couch, and he came to sit beside her. On the coffee table, she saw the catalog she'd ordered from an art school in the city. She was thinking of taking an oil painting class once a week, maybe on Saturdays, after Ricky went off to Georgetown. She was hoping that she could convince Jones to join her, that maybe they could start spending more time in the city, doing the things she loved and had put on hold for so long. Life was short. So very short. Who knew how much time any of them had?

Then she turned back to her husband and told him about the thing that she hadn't been able to remember. As she talked, Ricky drifted in and, without asking, flopped into the chair across from them. Then Elizabeth was standing in the doorway. Jones must have left the door to her office open, something she never did. And, for some reason, her son and mother followed him into her space. It was okay to have them here; it was even good.

As she told them all about her buried memory, she felt an awe at how all their separate lives were twisted and tangled, growing over and around one another, altering, aiding, and blocking one another's paths. Not just her family but people who seemed so distant, like Travis, Marshall and Melody, Sarah and Eloise Montgomery, Tommy Delano. And how the connections between them were as terribly fragile as they were indelible.

AUTHOR'S NOTE

A lifetime ago, a girl I knew went missing. I lived in a small, quiet town in New Jersey with my family. I was fifteen years old. This missing girl was someone I knew . . . we played in the same school orchestra, said hello in the hallways. I wouldn't have said we were friends. But her disappearance and the eventual discovery of her body, the chaos that followed, the fear and sadness that lingered in the wake of her murder, have stayed with me in ways that have only recently become clear to me.

That said, this novel—one I have been trying in various ways to write for twenty years—is not about that event or about that girl. It is not my intention to exploit her memory, or to cause any more pain. In fact, I won't even mention her name here. Nothing in this book bears more than a passing resemblance to the events that occurred in the mid-eighties. I have done little or no research to improve my fuzzy recall of chronology or details. This story and the characters that populate it are wholly products of my imagination; even the town itself is fictional, not based on any place I have ever been.

As always, any inaccuracies and liberties taken for the sake of the narrative are my own.

ACKNOWLEDGMENTS

Every writer needs touchstones, places where she can go and remind herself what is real, what is solid, what has value. And as much as writers work in solitude, living inside their heads, publishing is a business of relationships. I have been blessed personally and professionally with people who keep me grounded and help me reach for the stars. I'll take this opportunity to shower them with love and gratitude.

My husband, Jeffrey, and our daughter, Ocean Rae, are the sun and the moon. Everything I am and everything I do is for them. They nourish, delight, bolster, and energize me every day, and fill my life with love. Whenever I need a reminder about what matters in this world, I look to them. I am weak with gratitude for my beautiful, funny little family.

My brilliant agent, Elaine Markson, and her wonderful assistant, Gary Johnson, control my professional universe and are the most loving and supportive friends a girl could have. This year will mark ten years working with them. At this point, I can't even begin to list everything they do for me. Let it suffice to say I'd fall to pieces without them.

I have said this many times, but it demands repeating here. A home like Crown/ Shaye Areheart Books is every writer's dream, full of intelligent, creative, passionate people who really care about books. Shaye Areheart is a magnificent editor and one of the most spirited, passionate, and loving people I have known. I am as grateful for her friendship as I am for her brilliance as an editor and publisher. Jenny Frost is a ferocious and unflinching supporter of her authors and a truly brilliant businesswoman; I have been so grateful to be under her umbrella in a stormy industry. I also offer my humble thanks to Philip Patrick, Jill

Flaxman, Whitney Cookman, David Tran, Jacqui LeBow, Andy Augusto, Kira Walton, Patty Berg, Donna Passannante, Katie Wainwright, Annsley Rosner, Sarah Breivogel, Linda Kaplan, Karin Schulze, Kate Kennedy, and Christine Kopprasch. They each bring their unique talent to the table, and comprise the most remarkable team I have encountered in my career. And, of course, I can never heap enough praise on the top-notch sales force. They are on the front lines of a very competitive business. I know that every one of my books that makes it out of the warehouse does so largely because of their tireless efforts on my behalf.

As ever, my family and friends continue to offer their love and support, cheering me on in this crazy writing life. My parents, Joe and Virginia Miscione, never tire of bragging about me, facing out books in their local bookstores, and buying lots and lots of copies. I hope they never do! This one's for you, Mom and Dad. My brother, Joe Miscione, and his wife, Tara Teaford Miscione, are endlessly spreading the word. And Tara is one of my most important early readers. Thanks, guys.

What could a girl do without her best girlfriends? I couldn't publish a thing without the eagle-eyed editing of my dear, funny, sweet, talented friend Heather Mikesell. Even though she knows I'm going to stalk her until she reads what I've sent her, she never refuses me! It seems I haven't taken a step on this journey without Marion Chartoff and Tara Popick, my two oldest friends. I'm not sure I'd find my way without them—or at least it wouldn't be nearly as fun.

As always, I owe a debt of gratitude to people who have offered their time and expertise in order to fill in my knowledge gaps. Special Agent Paul Bouffard (ret.) continues to be my source for all things legal and illegal. His tireless forbearance of my continuing barrage of questions and wonderings never fails to astound. Although I noticed he avoids working out with me at the gym, knowing that even on the treadmill he is not safe. My thanks to Wendy Bouffard for her wonderful friendship, the trip to Brantingham that so inspired, and of course her endless patience with the fact that I only refer to her husband as Special Agent Bouffard.

Dr. Richard Capiola, M.D., medical director of The Willough in Naples, was an invaluable resource in my research about the patient-therapist relationship, as well as the particular challenges therapists, psychologists, and psychiatrists face in their practice and own inner lives. I met Dr. Capiola at a conference in Naples. Little did he know that for the small amount of advice I gave him about writing, he'd be forced to answer my myriad questions in return. He is a very patient man.

Steve Collins, mechanic extraordinaire, offered his expertise about classic cars and classic car restoration, among other things. And thanks to his wonderful wife, Lee, for her ongoing support of my novels.

I am a very lucky girl.

ABOUT THE AUTHOR

Lisa Unger is an award-winning *New York Times*, *USA Today*, and international bestselling author. Her novels have been published in more than twenty-six countries around the world.

She was born in New Haven, Connecticut (1970) but grew up in the Netherlands, England, and New Jersey. A graduate of the New School for Social Research, Lisa spent many years living and working in New York City. She then left a career in publicity to pursue her dream of becoming a full-time author. She now lives in Florida with her husband and daughter. She is at work on her next novel.

READER'S GUIDE

The questions and discussion topics that follow are designed to enhance your reading of Lisa Unger's *Fragile*. We hope they will enrich your experience as you explore this tale of haunting memories and their power to redeem.

Questions for Discussion

1. Discuss the novel's title. Who are The Hollows's most fragile residents? Ultimately, who are the most resilient ones?

2. What makes Jones and Maggie a good couple? How would you have reacted to his revelations if you had been Maggie? What life lessons—for better or worse—do they impart to Rick?

3. What accounts for Travis's hatred of women? What spurred the cycles of violence in the Crosby family?

4. How did your opinion of Marshall shift throughout the novel, from his session with Maggie in chapter three to the powerful closing scenes? What does it take to defeat the emotional grip of an abuser?

5. How does Elizabeth cope with the responsibility she accumulated after shepherding students for most of her lifetime? What does she teach Maggie about motherhood?

6. In chapter nine, Lisa Unger describes the way Maggie, Melody, and Denise behaved in high school. Did they change very much over the years? Did high school predict your life accurately?

7. Is Melody a good mother? What attracted her to Graham? How did the truth compare to your theories about him?

8. Facebook plays a role in the race to rescue Charlene, but was it a healthy resource for her friends? Does it enhance or distort reality?

9. In his pivotal phone call to Maggie, Marshall asks, "How do you know if you're a good person?" How would you have answered this question?

10. How does The Hollows reflect the personalities of the people who live there? What makes it a charming place to live? How does the landscape, rugged yet scenic, make it a place where secrets can exist in plain sight? How does its proximity to New York City affect the characters' dreams?

11. Through Wanda, Charlie finally finds the courage to believe in himself. What enables him to accept Wanda's love? How does his story reflect the way the novel unfolds?

12. Who is ultimately responsible for what happened to Sarah? Could anything or anyone have prevented the circumstances that led to her death?

13. Would Tommy Delano have received better treatment in the twenty-first century?

14. Do you think of your family, or your community, as being open and candid, or do they have a lot to hide? Discuss a time when you discovered something potentially damaging about a loved one's past. How did you handle it? Has your own past ever haunted you?

15. Discuss *Fragile*'s connections to the other Unger novels you have read. How do her characters approach the line between good and evil?

an excerpt from

darkness, my old friend

by Lisa Unger

coming in August 2011

chapter one

Jones Cooper feared death. The dread of it woke him in the night, sat him bolt upright and drew all the breath from his lungs, narrowed his esophagus, had him rasping in the dark. It turned all the normal shadows of the bedroom that he shared with his wife into a legion of ghouls and intruders waiting with silent and malicious intent. When? How? Heart attack. Cancer. Freak accident. Would it come for him quickly? Would it slowly waste and dehumanize him? What, if anything, would await him?

He was not a man of faith. Nor was he a man without a stain on his conscience. He did not believe in a benevolent universe of light and love. He could not lean upon those crutches as so many did; everyone, it seemed, had some way to protect himself against the specter of his certain end. Everyone except him.

His wife, Maggie, had grown tired of the 2:00 a.m. terrors. At first she was beside him, comforting him: *Just breathe, Jones. Relax. It's okay.* But even she, ever-patient shrink that she was, had started sleeping in the guest room or on the couch, even sometimes in their son's room, empty since Ricky had left for Georgetown in September.

His wife believed it had something to do with Ricky's leaving. "A child heading off for college is a milestone. It's natural to reflect on the passing of your life," she'd said. Maggie seemed to think that the acknowledgment of one's mortality was a rite of passage, something everyone went through. "But there's a point, Jones, where reflection becomes self-indulgent, even self-destructive. Surely you see that spending your life fearing death is a death in and of itself."

But it seemed to him that people didn't reflect on death at all. Everyone appeared to be walking around oblivious to the looming end—spending hours on Facebook, talking on cell phones while driving through Starbucks, reclining on the couch for hours watching some mindless crap on television. People were *not* paying attention—not to life, not to death, not to each other.

"Lighten up, honey. Really." Those were the last words she'd sent to him this morning before she headed off to see her first patient. He *was* trying to lighten up. He really was.

Jones was raking leaves; the great oaks in his yard had started their yearly shed. There were just a few leaves now. He'd made a small pile down by the curb. For all the years they'd been in this house, he'd hired someone to do this work. But since his retirement, almost a year ago now, he'd decided to manage the tasks of homeownership himself—mowing the lawn, maintaining the landscaping, skimming the pool, washing the windows, now raking the leaves, eventually shoveling the snow from the driveway. It was amazing, really, how these tasks could fill his days. How from morning to night, he could just putter, as Maggie called it—changing lightbulbs, trimming trees, cleaning the cars.

But is it enough? You have a powerful intellect. Can you be satisfied this way? His wife overestimated him. His intellect wasn't that powerful. The neighbors had started to rely on him, enjoyed having a retired cop around while they were at work, on vacation. He was letting repair guys in, getting mail, and turning on lights when people were away, checking perimeters, keeping his guns clean and loaded. The situation annoyed Maggie initially—the neighbors calling and dropping by, asking for this and that—especially since he wouldn't accept payment, even from people he didn't really know. Then people started dropping off gifts—a bottle of scotch, a gift certificate to Grillmarks, a fancy steakhouse in town.

"You could turn this into a real business," Maggie said. She was suddenly enthusiastic one night over dinner, paid for by the Pedersens. Jones had fed their mean-spirited cat, Cheeto, for a week.

He scoffed. "Oh, yeah. Local guy hanging around with nothing to do but let the plumber in? Is that what I'd call it?"

She gave him that funny smile he'd always loved. It was more like the turning up of one corner of her mouth, something she did when she found him amusing but didn't want him to know it.

"It's a viable service that people would pay for and be happy to have," she said. "Think about it."

But he enjoyed it, didn't really want to be paid. It was nice to be needed, to look after the neighborhood: to make sure things were okay. You didn't stop being a cop when you stopped being a cop. And he wasn't exactly retired, was he? He wouldn't have left his post if he hadn't felt that it was necessary, the right thing to do under the circumstances. But that was another matter.

The late-morning temperature was a perfect sixty-eight degrees. The light was golden, the air carrying the scent of the leaves he was raking, the aroma of burning wood from somewhere. In the driveway Ricky's restored 1966 GTO preened, waiting for him to come home from school next weekend. Jones had it tuned up and detailed, so it would be cherry when the kid got back.

He missed his son. Their relationship through the boy's late adolescence had been characterized, regrettably, by conflict more than anything else. Still, he couldn't wait for Ricky to be back under his roof again, even if it was just for four days. If anyone told him how much he'd really, truly miss his kid, how he'd feel a squeeze on his heart every time he walked by that empty room, Jones wouldn't have believed it. He would have thought it was just another one of those platitudes people mouthed about parenthood.

He leaned his rake against the trunk of the oak and removed his gloves. A pair of mourning doves cooed sadly at him. They sat on the railing of his porch, rustling their tawny feathers.

"I'm sorry," he said, not for the first time. Earlier, he'd removed the beginning of their nest, a loose pile of sticks and paper that they managed somehow to place in the light cover of his garage door's opening mechanism. Mourning doves made flimsy nests, were lazy enough to even settle in the abandoned nests of other birds. So the garage must have seemed like a perfect residence for them, offering protection from predators. But he didn't want birds in the garage. They were harbingers of death. Everyone knew that. They'd been hanging around the yard, giving him attitude all morning.

"You can build your nest anywhere else," he said, sweeping his arm over the property. "Just not there."

They seemed to listen, both of them craning their necks as he spoke. Then they flapped off with an angry, singsong twitter.

"Stupid birds."

He drew his arm across his forehead. In spite of the mild temperatures, he was sweating from the raking. It reminded him that he still needed to lose those twenty-five pounds his doctor had been nagging him about for years. His doctor, an annoyingly svelte, good-looking man right around Jones's age, never failed to mention the extra weight, no matter the reason for his visit—flu, sprained wrist, whatever. *You're gonna die one of these days, too, Doc,* Jones wanted to say. *You'll probably bite it during your workout. Whaddaya clocking these days—five miles every morning, more on the weekends? That'll put you in an early grave.* Instead Jones just kept reminding him that the extra weight around his middle had saved his life last year.

"I'm not sure that's a compelling argument," said Dr. Gauze. "What are the odds of your taking another bullet to the gut, especially now that you're out to pasture?"

Out to pasture? He was only forty-seven. He was thinking about this idea of being out to pasture as a beige Toyota Camry pulled up in front of the house and came to a stop. He watched for a second, couldn't see the person in the driver's seat. When the door opened and a slight woman stepped out, he recognized her without being able to place her. She was too thin, had the look of someone robbed of her appetite by anxiety. She moved with convalescent slowness up his drive, clutching a leather purse to her side. She didn't seem to notice him standing there in the middle of his yard. In fact, she walked right past him.

"Can I help you?" he said finally. She turned to look at him, startled.

"Jones Cooper?" she said. She ran a nervous hand through her hair, a mottle of steel gray and black, cut in an unflatteringly blunt bob.

"That's me."

"Do you know me?" she asked.

He moved closer to her, came to stand in front of her on the paved drive that needed painting. She was familiar, yes. But no, he didn't know her name.

"I'm sorry," he said. "Have we met?"

"I'm Eloise Montgomery."

It took a moment. Then he felt the heat rise to his cheeks, a tension creep into his shoulders. *Christ,* he thought.

"What can I do for you, Ms. Montgomery?"

She looked nervously around, and Jones followed her eyes, to the falling leaves, the clear blue sky.

"Is there someplace we can talk?" Her drifting gaze landed on the house.

"Can't we talk here?" He crossed his arms around his middle and squared his stance. Maggie would be appalled by his rudeness. But he didn't care. There was no way he was inviting this woman into his home.

"This is private," she said. "And I'm cold."

She started walking toward the house, stopped at the bottom of the three steps that led up to the painted gray porch, and turned around to look at him. He didn't like the look of her so near the house, any more than he did those doves. She was small-boned and skittish, but with a curious mettle. As she climbed the steps without invitation and stood at the door, he thought about how, with enough time and patience, a blade of grass could push its way through concrete. He expected her to pull open the screen and walk inside, but she waited. And he followed reluctantly, dropping his gardening gloves beside the rake.

The next thing he knew, she was sitting at the dining-room table and he was brewing coffee. He could see her from where he stood at the counter. She sat primly with her hands folded. She hadn't taken off her pilled houndstooth coat, was still clutching her bag. Those eyes never stopped moving.

"You don't want me here," she said. She cast a quick glance in his direction, then looked at her hands. "You wish I would go."

He put down the mugs he was taking from the cabinet, banging them without meaning to.

"Wow," he said. "I'm impressed. You really *are* psychic."

He didn't bother to look at her again, let his eyes rest on the calendar tucked behind the phone. He had an appointment with his shrink in a few hours, something he dreaded. When he finally gazed back over at her, she was regarding him with a wan smile.

"A skeptic," she said. "Your wife and mother-in-law offer more respect."

"Respect is earned." He poured the coffee. "How do you take it?" he asked. He thought she'd say black.

"Light and sweet, please," she said. Then, "And what should I do to earn your respect?"

He walked over with the coffee cups and sat across from her.

"What can I do for you, Ms. Montgomery?"

It was nearly noon. Maggie's last morning session would end in fifteen minutes, and then she'd come out for lunch. He didn't want Eloise sitting here when she did. The woman could only bring back bad memories for Maggie, everything they'd suffered through in the last year and long before. He didn't need it, and neither did his wife.

"Do you know about my work?" Eloise asked.

Work. Really? Is that what they were calling it? He would have thought she'd say something like gift, or sight. Or maybe abilities. Of course, she probably did consider it work, since that was how she earned her living.

"I do," he said. He tried to keep his tone flat, not inquiring or encouraging. But she seemed to feel the need to explain anyway.

"I'm like a radio. I pick up signals—from all over, scattered, disjointed. I have no control over what I see, when I see it, the degree of lucidity, the power of it. I could see something happening a world away, but not something right next door."

He struggled not to roll his eyes. Did she really expect him to believe this? Really?

"Okay," he said. He took a sip of his coffee. He didn't like the edgy, anxious feeling he had. He felt physically uncomfortable in the chair, had a nervous desire to get up and pace the room. "What does this have to do with me?"

"You're getting a reputation around town, you know. That you're available to help with things—checking houses while people are away, getting mail."

He shrugged. "Just in the neighborhood here." He leaned back in his chair, showed his palms. "What? Are you going on vacation? Want me to feed your cat?"

She released a sigh and looked down at the table between them.

"People are going to start coming to you for more, from farther away," she said. "It might lead you to places you don't expect."

Jones didn't like how that sounded. But he wouldn't give her the satisfaction of reacting.

"Okay," he said, drawing out the word.

"I wanted you to be prepared. I've seen something."

When she looked back up at him, her eyes were shining in a way that unsettled him. Her gaze made him think for some reason of his mother when he found her on the bathroom floor after she'd suffered a stroke. He slid his chair back from the table and stood.

"Why are you telling me this?" He leaned against the doorway that led to the kitchen.

"Because you need to know," she said. She still sat stiff and uncomfortable, hadn't touched the coffee before her.

Okay, great. Thanks for stopping by. Don't call me, I'll call you. Let me show you out. Instead, because curiosity always did get the better of him, he asked, "So what did you see?"

She ran a hand through her hair. "It's hard to explain. Like describing a dream. The essence can be lost in translation."

If this was some kind of show, it was a good one. She seemed sincere, not put on or self-dramatizing. If she were a witness, he would believe her story. But she wasn't a witness, she was a crackpot.

"Try," he said. "That's why you came, right?"

Another long slow breath in and out. Then, "I saw you on the bank of a river . . . or it could have been an ocean. Some churning body of water. I saw you running, chasing a lifeless form in the water. I don't know what or who it was. I can only assume it's a woman or a girl, because that's all I see. Then you jumped in—or possibly you fell. I think you were trying to save whoever it was. But you were overcome. You weren't strong enough. The water pulled you under."

Her tone was level, unemotional. She could have been talking mildly about the weather. And the image, for some reason, failed to jolt or disturb him. In that moment she seemed frail and silly, a carnival act that neither entertained nor intrigued.

The ticking of the large grandfather clock in the foyer seemed especially loud. He *had* to get rid of that thing, a housewarming present from his mother-in-law. Did he really need to hear the passing of the minutes of his life?

"You know, Ms. Montgomery," he said, "I don't think you're well."

"I'm not, Mr. Cooper. I'm not well at all." She got up from the table, to his great relief, and started moving toward the door.

"Well, should I find myself on the banks of a river, chasing a body, I'll be sure to stay on solid ground," he said, allowing her to pass and following her to the door. "Thanks for the warning."

"Would you? Would you stay on solid ground? I doubt it." She rested her hand on the knob of the front door but neither pulled it open nor turned around.

"I guess it depended on the circumstances," he said. "Whether I thought I could help or not. Whether I thought I could manage the risk. And, finally, who was in the water."

Why was he even bothering to have this conversation? The woman was obviously mentally ill; she belonged in a hospital, not walking around free. She could hurt herself or someone else. She still didn't turn to look at him, just bowed her head.

"I don't think you *can* manage the risk," she said. "There are forces more powerful than your will. I think that's what you need to know."

For someone as obsessed with death as Jones knew himself to be, he should have been clutching his heart with terror. But, honestly, he just found the whole situation preposterous. It was almost a relief to talk to someone who had less of a grip on life than he did.

"Okay," he said. "Good to know."

He gently nudged her aside with a hand on her shoulder and opened the door.

"So when do you imagine this might go down? There's only one body of water in The Hollows." The Black River was usually a gentle, gurgling river at the base of a glacial ravine. It could, in heavy rains, become quite powerful, but it hadn't overflowed its banks in years. And the season had been dry.

She gave him a patient smile. "I don't *imagine,* Mr. Cooper. I see, and I tell the people I need to tell to make things right. And if not right precisely, then as they should be. That's all I do. I used to torture myself, trying to figure out where and when and if things might happen. I used to think I could save and help and fix, drive myself to distraction when I couldn't. Now I just speak the truth of my visions. I am unattached to outcomes, to whether people treat me with respect or hostility, to whether they listen or don't."

"So they're literal, these visions," he asked. He didn't bother to keep the skepticism out of his voice. "You see something and it happens exactly that way. It's immutable."

"They're not always literal, no," she said.

"But sometimes they are?"

"Sometimes." She gave a careful nod. "And nothing in life is immutable, Mr. Cooper."

"Except death."

"Well . . ." she said. But she didn't go on. Was there an attitude about it? As if she were a teacher who wouldn't bother with a lesson that her student could never understand.

She moved through the door and let the screen close behind her. He didn't know what to say, so he said nothing, just watched as she stiffly descended the steps. She turned around once to look at him, appeared to have something else to say. But then she just kept walking down the drive. Her pace seemed brisker, as if she'd lightened her load. She didn't seem as frail or unwell as she had when he'd first seen her. Then she got into her car and slowly drove away.

New from Lisa Unger

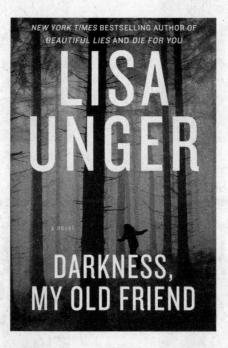

NEW YORK TIMES BESTSELLING AUTHOR OF
BEAUTIFUL LIES AND *DIE FOR YOU*

LISA UNGER

a novel

DARKNESS, MY OLD FRIEND

Darkness, My Old Friend
A Novel
$24.00 (Canada: $27.00)
978-0-307-46499-6

Die for You
A Novel
$14.99 (Canada: $17.99)
978-0-307-39398-2

Black Out
A Novel
$14.99 (Canada: $17.50)
978-0-307-33847-1

Sliver of Truth
A Novel
$13.95 (Canada: $15.95)
978-0-307-33849-5

Beautiful Lies
A Novel
$14.00 (Canada: $17.99)
978-0-307-33682-8

Available from Broadway Paperbacks wherever books are sold.